CRISIS

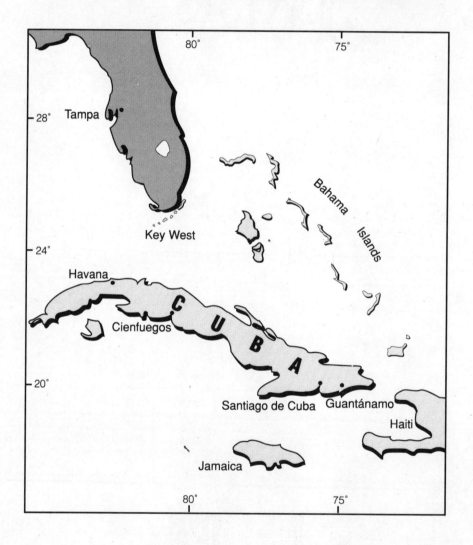

CRISIS

A Novel

Alexander M. Grace

Lyford Books
Published by Presidio Press
31 Pamaron Way, Novato CA 94949

Library of Congress Cataloging-in-Publication Data

Grace, Alexander M., 1951-
   Crisis : a novel / Alexander M. Grace.
     p.   cm.
  I. Title.
  ISBN: 0-89141-411-8
  PS3557.R1164C75   1991   90-21560
  813' .54—dc20   CIP

Typography by ProImage

Printed in the United States of America

Glossary

A-6 Intruder: A two-seat, carrier-based U.S. Navy attack aircraft. Its maximum speed is under seven hundred knots, and its normal weapons load might be twenty-eight five-hundred-pound bombs or three two-thousand-pound bombs plus two three-hundred gallon external fuel tanks. It may also carry Harpoon air-to-surface missiles or AIM-9 Sidewinder air-to-air missiles for self-defense. There exists various modifications of this aircraft, including the EA-6B electronic warfare version for radar jamming.

A-10 Warthog: A single-seat, subsonic U.S. Air Force ground-attack aircraft. It was designed primarily as a "tank buster" and is armed with a rapid-fire 30mm cannon in addition to being able to carry a variety of bomb or rocket loads.

AK-47, AKM, AKSU-74: The AK-47 is the well-known Soviet 7.62mm assault rifle, carrying a thirty-round magazine. The AKM is a slightly modified version with a folding metal stock, and the AKSU-74 is a submachine gun variant with shorter barrel and folding stock.

ARM: Antiradiation missile. An air-to-surface missile designed to home in on the radar emissions of surface-to-air missile batteries.

AV-8B Harrier: The U.S. Marine Corps variant of the British single-seat jump jet made famous in the Falklands/Malvinas conflict. While not a match for sophisticated air superiority fighters, the Harrier has the advantage of being able to take off and land vertically (V/STOL, or Vertical/Short Take-Off and Landing), enabling it to operate from ad hoc airfields or strips of roadway close to the front.

AWACS: Airborne Warning and Command System. Generally a large converted aircraft, either a commercial passenger design such as the Boeing 707 or a bomber such as the Soviet Mainstay, equipped with a massive radome and other electronic gear for obtaining information on enemy air activities, jamming radar, and signals intelligence.

BMP: A Soviet-made armored personnel carrier, reputed to be the best in the world. It carries a crew of three, with eight passengers. It also carries a 73mm gun in a small turret along with a coaxial 7.62mm machine gun. It can also be fitted with an AT-3 Sagger antitank missile.

CH-53 Super Stallion: The U.S. Navy/Marine Corps heavy-duty transport helicopter. In its various configurations the CH-53 can carry up to fifty-five troops or some thirty-two tons of cargo at up to one hundred-seventy knots over some eleven hundred miles (one-way, without refueling).

DGI/DGCI: The Cuban General Directorate of Intelligence or of Counterintelligence. Combined, these two organizations perform the same function as the Soviet KGB, responsible both for foreign intelligence collection and defensive counterintelligence and political security functions.

DGPNR: The Cuban General Directorate of National Revolutionary Police. The uniformed police force, comparable to a state police force in the U.S.

Dong Feng-4:   "East Wind," also known as CSS-3. A two-stage, solid-fuel Chinese intercontinental ballistic missile. It is some twenty-seven meters long and has a range of approximately seven thousand kilometers.

F-4 Phantom: The venerable American two-seat fighter-bomber of the Vietnam War era. The F-4 is still used in its updated versions by Air National Guard units and by several Allied countries.

F-7M: The Chinese version of the MiG-21 single-seat fighter.

F-14 Tomcat: The two-seat U.S. Navy carrier-based fighter. The F-14 is a swing-wing design capable of Mach 2.34. It carries four Sparrow and four Phoenix air-to-air missiles in addition to its 20mm cannon. The F-14's powerful radar suite enabled the Iranians, who possessed a few of them, to use the F-14 as a sort of mini-AWACS during the Iran-Iraq War, vectoring other fighters in to their targets.

F-15 Eagle: The single-seat U.S. Air Force air superiority fighter. It can carry up to eight Sparrow and Sidewinder air-to-air missiles in addition to Maverick air-to-ground missiles and its 20mm cannon. The F-15E two-seat version can also carry a wide range of precision-guided munitions in a strike role. The maximum speed of the fighter version is over Mach 2.5.

F-16 Fighting Falcon: The U.S. Air Force single-seat fighter. This versatile aircraft also has a fighter-bomber version and has been adopted by a large number of foreign countries, including Israel, Venezuela, the Netherlands, Belgium, and Norway. Its high power-to-weight ratio permits the aircraft to execute unique combat maneuvers, such as accelerating while climbing vertically. It can carry six air-to-air missiles in addition to its 20mm cannon. As a fighter-bomber it can also be equipped with a variety of precision-guided air-to-ground munitions. Its maximum speed is over Mach 2.

F-18 Hornet: The U.S. Navy and Marine Corps replacement for the F-4. It is a single-seat, low-cost, multimission fighter-bomber that has also been adopted by a number of foreign countries, including Canada, Australia, and Spain. It carries two Sidewinder air-to-air missiles on its outboard wing stations plus a variety of other air-to-air or air-to-surface weapons and a six-barrelled 20mm gun. Its maximum speed is over Mach 1.8.

GAZ: The Soviet-manufactured equivalent of the American jeep.

GRU: Soviet Military Intelligence.

JCTF: Joint Caribbean Task Force. Created by President Carter at Key West upon the "discovery" of the Soviet mechanized brigade that was stationed in Cuba. The general purpose of the JCTF is to coordinate any armed action ever taken against or in response to Cuba.

KGB: The Soviet intelligence and security organization. The KGB is responsible for internal security, including a large armed force of border guards, counterintelligence and suppression of political dissension, and foreign intelligence collection. In American terms the KGB combines the functions of the CIA, FBI, Coast Guard, Border Patrol, Secret Service, and then some.

Koni-class frigate: A Soviet-made ship, of which there are three in the Cuban inventory. It carries a twin SA-N-4 surface-to-air missile launcher, two twin 76mm guns, two twin 30mm guns, and two rocket launchers with twelve tubes each. Its top speed is 27 knots.

Makarov: A 9mm Soviet-made semiautomatic pistol. It is standard issue with the Soviet Armed Forces.

MCM: Mine Countermeasures. More commonly referred to as mine sweepers, these craft are usually wooden-hulled, to limit the danger from magnetic mines. In the U.S. Navy nearly all of these are operated by the Naval Reserves, as evidenced by the fact that several such mine sweepers had to be obtained from the Reserves for duty in the Persian Gulf during the Iran-Iraq War, although they were manned by active duty navy crews.

MI-8 Hip: The workhorse Soviet utility helicopter, capable of carrying up to twenty-eight troops or four tons of cargo. Its maximum cruising speed is 135 knots, and it has a range of 270 nautical miles.

MiG-21 Fishbed: The typical Soviet single-seat fighter of the 1960s and 1970s, still in service in many Third World nations, including Cuba,

Vietnam, and Iraq. It is a contemporary of the American F-4. It would typically carry four air-to-air missiles in addition to its 23mm gun. Unlike the more versatile F-4, the MiG-21 has only a limited ground-attack capability. Its maximum speed is approximately Mach 1.

MiG-23 Flogger: A more recent generation of Soviet single-seat fighter, also in wide use throughout Eastern Europe and the Third World.

MiG-29 Fulcrum: A very recent (since 1985) single-seat fighter, designed to counter the American F-15. It has also been exported to a number of East European and Third World countries including Cuba, India, and Poland. It has a maximum speed of Mach 2.3 and carries six air-to-air missiles and a 30mm gun. Its powerful Doppler look-down, shoot-down radar closed an important technological gap between the Soviet and American fighters.

Osa guided-missile boat: A high-speed coastal defense craft of Soviet manufacture. It is armed with four Styx surface-to-surface missiles, one SA-N-5 surface-to-air missile, and two twin 30mm guns. It was one of these boats, in Egyptian service, that sank the Israeli destroyer Eilat, ushering in the age of naval missile weapons.

PKM: A Soviet light machine gun.

RPG-7:   A Soviet rocket-propelled grenade launcher. Related to the World War II bazooka or *panzerfaust,* this weapon is generally effective at under two hundred meters range and only against lightly armored targets or bunkers.

SA-2 Guideline: An antiaircraft missile still in wide use after more than twenty years. It is operated from a permanent site and is radar-guided.

SA-7 Grail: The equivalent of the American Redeye antiaircraft missile. It is similar to a man-portable rocket launcher in shape and fires a heat-seeking missile effective against low-flying aircraft.

SA-8 Gecko: A mobile antiaircraft missile, fired from a lightly armored vehicle. Radar guided.

SIGINT: Signals Intelligence. The information gleaned from the capturing and deciphering of radio, telephone, and telemetry signals, which is the territory of the NSA in the United States. This is differentiated from HUMINT, i.e., human intelligence sources, or spies.

SU-25 Frogfoot: A Soviet single-seat attack aircraft, generally similar to the American A-10. Like the A-10 it is relatively slow (147 knots), but it can be armed with a wide variety of precision-guided munitions for close ground support. It saw extensive service in Afghanistan and has been modified for use on the new *Tblisi* carrier.

Su-27 Flanker: A Soviet single-seat fighter equivalent to the F-15. It carries up to ten air-to-air missiles and a 30mm gun and can reach speeds in excess of Mach 2.3. It also possesses a powerful look-down, shoot-down radar system. It has been modified for use on the *Tblisi* as well.

T-54:   An aging Soviet main battle tank. The T-54 carries a 100mm cannon, coaxial 7.62mm machine gun, and a 12.7mm machine gun mounted on top of the turret. It weighs thirty-six tons loaded and has a crew of four. It is widely distributed among Third World countries.

T-72:   A more recent version of the Soviet main battle tank. It carries a 125mm smooth-bore gun, a coaxial machine gun, and another mounted on top of the turret. It has a crew of only three, due to the use of an automatic loader. It weighs forty-one tons.

TE: Cuban Special Troops. Roughly equivalent to the American Special Forces, they number approximately three thousand men and are highly trained in parachuting, demolitions, small arms, and guerilla tactics. They are frequently used as advisors in foreign countries, but they are also an elite corps whose members have been particularly pampered by Castro to ensure their political loyalty.

UH-60 Blackhawk: The replacement for the ubiquitous Huey helicopter of the Vietnam War. It can carry eleven fully equipped troops or about 3 1/2 tons of cargo. It has a range of 880 nautical miles if equipped with external fuel tanks and a maximum speed of 158 knots.

VN-22 Osprey: This twin-engine, tilt-rotor aircraft has been under development for the use of the Marine Corps for some time, but its future has been put in doubt due to defense budget cuts. At this writing, two twelve-plane squadrons have been created for study. The Osprey carries some 28 passengers or nine tons of cargo at 300 knots over 1,200 nautical miles, which is twice the cargo, at twice the speed, and with over 50 percent more range than the Blackhawk, while still maintaining the ability to land and take off vertically like a helicopter.

YAK-36 Forger: The Soviet version of the Harrier, a V/STOL fighter for use on the older Soviet carriers that cannot launch conventional aircraft. Like the Harrier, it is not a match for most high-performance fighters.

ZSU-23/2:   A twin-barrelled Soviet-made 23mm antiaircraft gun. Its high rate of fire makes it an effective weapon against ground targets in the direct fire mode. The ZSU-23/4 is an antiaircraft tank, with a four-barrelled version of the gun mounted on a tank chassis and lightly armored. It also possesses its own tracking radar.

Introduction

This book grew out of a dinner meeting I had with James F. Dunnigan, editor of *Strategy & Tactics Magazine*, and several other war game designers in late October 1989. Among other things, we discussed how the recent changes taking place in Eastern Europe and the Soviet Union might affect the nature of international conflict in the rest of this century and the beginning of the next.

One of the staple themes for war games (the details of which I will spare the reader), in addition to historical subjects such as Napoleon's campaigns or World War II, has been a potential NATO–Warsaw Pact conflict in Europe. As the Soviet empire in Eastern Europe seems to be crumbling as I write and the military establishment that supported it is scaled back for economic reasons, this kind of stand-up fight appears less and less likely. Perhaps it never was likely, as it never did occur despite a number of close calls over the years.

We threw around ideas for other potential areas of world conflict, such as Rumania vs. Hungary, Poland vs. a united Germany, a resurgence of pan-German tendencies and a Western European effort to prevent a new *Anschluss*, a civil war between nationalities within the USSR, and so on. While the specific subject of this book was not mentioned, as it would not have made a particularly feasible war game, the unspoken premise of our ramblings was that no one at that table believed that we were about to enter upon a new age of peace and brotherly love.

A good deal has already been written, in one form or another, about the approaching "end of history." While I could be wrong, this strikes me as particularly superficial thinking, geared mainly toward having something profound to say in time for this week's Sunday supplement that is different from last week's. Martin Schama, in the opening of his superb book on the French Revolution, cites the anecdote of Chou En Lai being asked what he thought the impact of the French Revolution was on history. Chou's answer was, "It is too soon to say." While events, especially in Eastern Europe, are occurring at a rate and in a direction that literally no one foresaw even five years ago, to extrapolate this into a millenial transformation of the entire world is at best premature.

While there are strong and welcome forces for peace and stability abroad in the world today there are also forces of intransigence and potential conflict. The rise of Muslim fundamentalism in its more violent forms is one. So are separatism and revanchism, which have hardly disappeared.

The essence of this book is another of these forces, that is, that not everyone sees these changes as welcome or beneficial and that some powers opposed to change have the means at hand to do something about it. If there is a moral in this story, which in the final analysis is primarily meant to entertain, it is that the favorable changes in our world will be more lasting and deeper if we do not take them as faits accomplis and recognize that things can always go wrong.

Chapter One

William Featherstone was already sitting upright in bed by the time he came fully awake. There was someone in the house! With a mind still clouded with sleep he tried to think quickly to figure out what had happened and what to do. The shades in the bedroom were drawn, but the first bluish light of dawn was beginning to show around the edges of the windows. He quietly reached for his glasses and focused on the digital clock on the nightstand. It was nearly five A.M. and his wife, Anne, was still sleeping soundly next to him.

Featherstone could hear the sound of movement coming from the living room down the hall. In previous diplomatic postings in Latin America crime had been a real cause for concern, not only pickpockets or car theft on the street but gangs of armed thugs who would break into the best-protected homes, occupied or not, to loot them and kill any potential witnesses. However, during his nearly two years as DCM (deputy chief of mission) at the U.S. Interests Section in Havana burglary had never been a major worry. Considering the constant surveillance to which all foreign diplomats, especially Americans, were subjected by the government, few criminals would have had the nerve to attempt to get past the armed secret policemen prowling the diplomatic enclave of Havana.

1

On the other hand, Featherstone had never heard of a forced entry by the Cuban G2 (formally DGI, General Directorate of Intelligence, or DGCI, General Directorate of Counterintelligence), which kept watch on all foreigners, into a residence when the occupants were home. Certainly the G2 had entered his home before, to service or replace the microphones installed everywhere, to look for "interesting documents," simply to find out more about his and his wife's personal lives for blackmail, or to seek any signs of disgruntlement that might prove useful. The G2 men were usually pretty slick, but they sometimes left obvious signs of their presence to put Featherstone and his colleagues under increased psychological pressure, such as an ashtray full of foul-smelling Russian cigarettes or a toilet that had been used and not flushed. This, however, was definitely something different. He had never heard of such a thing, even during the uproar caused by the airing of the six-hour Cuban documentary about U.S. spying in Cuba, which included embarrassing footage of American officials allegedly servicing dead drops and taped interviews with Cubans who had supposedly been recruited by the CIA and then either turned by the DGCI, or who had been dangled from the beginning.

Featherstone had decided to get the shotgun he kept in the closet and had climbed out of bed and made it halfway across the floor when the door burst open and he was blinded by powerful flashlights.

"Stay where you are, Sr. Featherstone," a deep voice boomed out in Spanish. "I am Captain Estigarribia of the Ministry of Interior, and I have orders to transport you to an urgent meeting."

Featherstone meant to say something to the effect of "What's the meaning of all this?" but all that came out were splutterings accompanied by the shrill gasps of Anne, who was now awake and terrified. Estigarribia, in any case, was obviously not there to communicate.

"You can save your protests for the appropriate authorities. You can dress yourself quickly or you can accompany me in your underwear. It makes no difference to me."

Featherstone's eyes had now focussed, and he could see that

Estigarribia was braced in the doorway, shining a large flashlight in his face. A second man was next to him, playing another flashlight around the room, stopping on the form of his wife, who was now crouched on the pillows with the sheets clutched just beneath her red-rimmed eyes. Both men held pistols in their free hands. A third man was kneeling just inside the room with an AKM assault rifle pointed directly at Featherstone's chest.

Featherstone could see that any argument would be pointless and reached for his shirt from yesterday, which was draped over a nearby chair. If one was going to be summoned to a meeting in this manner there was no use in trying to dress to impress.

"I can only hope that you have sufficient authority for this abomination to prevent your execution," Featherstone said, trying hard to convince the intruders that this sort of thing was all part and parcel of his official function. With the absence of the chief of mission (there was no official ambassador to Cuba) for the last three weeks, Featherstone was the ranking U.S. government official in the country, and he knew that it would not be proper for him to show the very real fear tearing through his stomach.

"I would be more concerned about my own future if I were you," Estigarribia snapped.

"I expect that I will be permitted to telephone one of my colleagues to advise him of what is happening," Featherstone stated as he carefully put his diplomatic carnet in his pocket.

"Unfortunately," Estigarribia coolly replied, "the telephone services for Havana are temporarily out of order."

"We have learned to expect that in the worker's paradise," Featherstone jibed. "We have radio communications. Naturally, you are welcome to listen to everything I say, as it will undoubtedly be on the front pages of most of the world's newspapers by lunchtime in any case." Featherstone did not add that he was aware that the Cubans monitored the mission's radio frequencies as well as its telephone calls.

Estigarribia's smile grew broader. "I'm afraid you will find that radio communication is also impossible."

Featherstone knew that his face had betrayed his concern. Telephone lines can always break down, but not radio links. They can only be jammed. This was definitely something new.

"Your wife will remain here," Estigarribia added. "Unauthorized travel within Havana by foreigners has been temporarily prohibited."

Featherstone's brow knitted further at this. Why had Estigarribia, who was obviously not a man given to ad libs, said "foreigners" and not just "Americans"? Curiouser and curiouser, Featherstone thought as he gave Anne a wink, hoping to convey an amusement with the situation that he certainly did not feel.

Featherstone pulled on his shoes, sans socks, and walked over to his wife's side. She grasped his hand and whispered to him through clenched teeth, "I don't like this, Bill. Not one bit."

He kissed her on the forehead and smiled. "I suppose this is just a new brand of harassment. Don't forget, just two months to go," he said, gesturing to their "short-timers' calendar" hanging on the bedpost, with each day of their tour crossed out in red. "If you hear from Alan or anyone else, let them know where I am." Featherstone intentionally did not mention the name of his "political advisor," Carl Popper, but after her long years as a Foreign Service wife, Anne knew to whom she could talk and what to say.

"Excuse me," Anne said, raising her eyebrows, "but I won't know where you are, will I?" Anne had been an American citizen for over twenty years and hadn't lived in her native England for nearly thirty, but centuries of British genes came through in times of stress with a show of excessive politeness.

"Quite so," he conceded. "Captain Estigarribia, I don't suppose you could give us any more information."

"You know what you need to know already," he stated. "I can only add that I do not expect you to come to any harm."

"That's most comforting," Featherstone chuckled. It really was beginning to get a little silly. Just another harassment tactic, and they really had me going for a minute. He began to suspect that the bit about radio communications being out was probably a bluff, but he concluded that he might as well ride this one out with as much dignity as possible. One had to give the Cubans credit. Every time he thought he had them completely figured out they came up with some new ploy. They might not be able to produce enough chickens to feed everyone, but one couldn't fault them on a lack of malignant ingenuity.

He kissed Anne again, harder this time, and squeezed her shoulders. "I'll be back as soon as I can. Maybe you can talk to Stan and Mary when you hear signs of life over there." It would be hard for the Cubans to keep Anne from talking with their next-door neighbors through their facing bathroom windows. Stan Martin was the mission administrative officer and, as such, the post security officer as well. As bad as relations between the two governments had been over the past year or so Stan still had regular contacts with the local police, who might provide some additional information on the situation. Featherstone felt sorry for Anne as he headed for the door. Whatever happened, he would know just what was going on and whether he was all right. Anne could only sit at home and imagine the worst, and unfortunately she had a vivid imagination. I think this will be my last tour out, he thought as he walked out the door, sandwiched between Estigarribia and his men.

The sun was starting to come up now, as Featherstone was loaded into the backseat of a Lada next to Estigarribia. He could see two Special Troops (TE) jeeps parked in his driveway, which quickly backed out to let them leave, one of them following the Lada down the street and the other taking up a post blocking the driveway again.

Featherstone found it increasingly odd that TE troops would be used for this sort of activity. Usually regular police would be expected. The TE were the Cuban equivalent of the American Special Forces, all crossed-trained as guerrillas and parachutists, many as demolition experts and scuba divers. They were also a kind of praetorian guard for Castro personally, under the Ministry of Interior, not the Ministry of Defense, which was his brother, Raul's, personal fiefdom. They received higher levels of pay and benefits than regular army troops, and Castro frequently displayed his favoritism to them in public pronouncements. While most of the members of the TE had combat experience from Angola or Central America, Castro tended to keep them close to him physically, possibly to forestall any coup attempt such as the one that was rumored to have been in the works when General Ochoa and a number of other senior military officers were executed in early 1989, allegedly for drug smuggling and corruption. Castro might be a Communist, but the difference between him and a Trujillo or a Somoza was largely academic.

As they drove through the city Featherstone abandoned his thoughts for a moment and began to notice the streets around him. Something was different about them too. By this time in the morning, even though it was still before sunrise, the corners should have been crowded with workers standing in line for the hopelessly inadequate number of buses so that they could get to work on time and avoid the punishment of extra hours of unpaid overtime. Today the streets were virtually empty. On several street corners he could see armored personnel carriers, and in one large cleared area he could see a crew of soldiers setting up a twin-barrelled antiaircraft gun.

This was unusual, but perhaps Castro was launching another "Yankee invasion" scare to explain why there was no rice on the market shelves again this month. Still, this seemed a little more involved than Featherstone was used to.

They finally pulled into the courtyard of what had once been a rather lavish home in eastern Havana. TE soldiers were guarding the gateway of the property and more were posted inside, not lounging around but dead serious about something. He thought he recognized the Soviet ambassador's car in the courtyard. Just perfect, he thought, the Soviets have changed mightily since Gorbachev came to power, even more since late 1989 when their Eastern European empire came apart, but Russian diplomats can still get a kick out of Yankee-baiting.

Featherstone was escorted through large double doors into the foyer of the main house and shown into a small reception office. Andrei Osman, the Soviet ambassador, was standing against one wall staring, unseeing, at a horrible example of Cuban socialist-realist art on the wall. When he turned to see Featherstone enter Osman did not have the smug look of anticipated pleasure that Featherstone had expected. His clothes were rumpled, he was unshaven, and he had apparently not washed since he slept last. Uh–oh! was all that Featherstone thought.

Chapter Two

Lance Cpl. Tyrell Johnson walked slowly along the pier at the U.S. Naval Base at Guantánamo Bay. He was wearing tropical-weight camouflage fatigues of the U.S. Marine Corps, but with the added load of his web gear and his "Fritz" combat helmet and rifle he felt heavy and was sweating like mad. Even though it was mid-January, this place never seemed really to cool off, even at night. Coming from Buffalo, New York, Johnson just couldn't get used to the tropics.

Johnson hated pulling guard duty at night almost as much as he hated this posting. He'd been to quite a few unpopular posts. He'd even done the "Root" just before the marine headquarters there was bombed, but this place was the worst. It was like being in prison, except that here he was on guard to keep people out.

Johnson was looking forward to a transfer around summertime back to Quantico. Now that was good duty. A regular nine-to-five schedule most of the time and then carpooling with two or three other young EMs up to the shopping malls at Springfield or Potomac Mills, not so much to shop as to "hunt." Actually, on the hunting expeditions of that kind he'd been on little had ever been accom-

7

plished, as most of the girls there had no desire to tie up with three or four bald-headed marines with only one car among them and hardly enough money to impress anyone. Still, the flirting was fun, the girl-watching was great, and lack of action never had been a handicap in spinning yarns about their conquests back at the base.

But this place was hell. There was no contact whatsoever with any of the millions of other people on this island, and Johnson could only assume that some of them were women. The only Cubans the marines or sailors at the base ever saw were the hard-eyed border guards dug in around the perimeter, and lately they had seen precious little of them. Even in Beirut you could cruise the beaches during the calm times and see the girls in string bikinis. There were several hundred women stationed at Guantánamo but most of them were long since spoken for, and those who weren't tended to look like Ernest Borgnine.

Johnson smiled as he looked out over the calm, dark water of the bay. There was little reason to be on special alert here. The only excitement there ever was was when some poor slob tried to climb the wire or swim into the base to claim political asylum. Johnson had been here nearly a year and had seen or heard about a dozen attempts. None of them made it, but one or two had apparently still been alive when the border guards dragged them off to the trucks, beating them all the way. One whom he had seen himself had actually been a border guard. He had obviously been planning it for some time and had been making good progress across the minefield and through the razor stripping and tripwires. The Cuban had been black too, and Johnson remembered thinking that the guy would have made a great tight end. But then the other border guards had opened up with their AKs and machine guns and literally tore the guy to shreds. That was what Johnson could never quite understand. The men firing the weapons weren't policemen or officers. They were the messmates of the man they killed, and half of them probably had had the same idea at one time or another themselves. Johnson had needed every ounce of discipline that had been pounded into him back at Parris Island not to give covering fire.

Like virtually every marine on the base, and certainly every one of them under thirty-five, he had never seen any real combat. He hadn't been in on Grenada and he hadn't seen any fighting in Beirut. There were a number of NCOs and a lot of officers who had been to Vietnam, but that seemed like ancient history now. Johnson had little reason to believe that this would ever change.

He looked out over the water and thought he saw something dark moving along the seawall opposite him, but it must have been a shadow. He turned to look for Private First Class Pacheco, his partner on this sector of the perimeter, but he couldn't see him. For no good reason Johnson stepped back into the shadows of a storage shed and walked quietly along the wall in the direction Pacheco must be. Then he saw it.

A boot was lying on the asphalt, just sticking out from behind several oil barrels. As he watched, the boot was dragged out of sight. It didn't move! It was dragged! Just then the figure of a man appeared off to Johnson's left, and he heard the distinct metallic click of a weapon bolt sliding home. Johnson didn't turn to look. He didn't stop to take his own weapon off his shoulder or go through the motions of taking it off safe and chambering a round. He dove head first over a low concrete-block wall just as a swarm of bullets chewed up the ground where he had been standing and the face of the wall behind him.

"Shit!" Johnson said automatically. "They're shooting at me." His first reaction was to scream insults at the stupid jarhead who had loaded live ammo for a training exercise. Then he realized that he hadn't heard any shots. "Holy shit!"

Johnson had rolled back against the storage shed and now had his weapon loaded and ready, pointing in the direction of the firing. A man suddenly came walking around the corner of the shed behind him, very noisily. It was a marine, lighting a cigarette as he walked. Johnson had only turned his head to look when the marine's chest exploded and he pitched over backwards. Johnson squeezed his own trigger even before turning his head back, and he heard a scream as a dark figure dropped back behind the wall, letting a long object fall at

Johnson's side. Johnson stared at it for a moment before getting up to run toward the trees to his rear. It was a Soviet-made assault rifle with a folding stock and a dark cylinder about the size of a large salami on the barrel. It was a silencer, of the kind Cuban commandos use.

Johnson was yelling now, firing random shots into the air to raise the alarm, but that was no longer necessary. Loud explosions were coming from all over the base. Some of them he recognized from Beirut as incoming artillery. Others appeared to be secondary explosions from the storage sheds near the water, either from artillery hits on ammunition or fuel dumps or from demolition charges set by the commandos. Jets were flying low over the base too now, and he could see streams of tracer rounds pouring from under their noses into what he knew was the barracks area. He dove behind some shrubs and lay gasping for air. He'd just seen a marine killed and may have killed his first man and he still didn't know what the hell was going on. Had the Cubans gone crazy? Or the Russians?

SANTIAGO DE LAS VEGAS, CUBA

Col. Alexandr Ogarkov, commander of a motorized rifle battalion that formed part of the much-publicized Soviet mechanized brigade located at Santiago de las Vegas, just east of Havana, knew that someone had certainly gone crazy and that it wasn't the Russians. He stood in his undershirt, along with half a dozen of his staff officers, facing a Cuban TE lieutenant and two troopers armed with automatic weapons. These men had rousted Ogarkov and his officers from their quarters before dawn with no explanation. Major Zhdanov was gingerly holding a purple welt on his jaw, the mark of a Cuban rifle butt applied when Zhdanov had protested too loudly.

Ogarkov assumed that a coup was in progress, and he seriously doubted whether his superiors in Moscow would want his men to support the old Fidel anymore. Many changes had occurred in the Soviet Union and Eastern Europe in the past couple of years and Ogarkov thought they were long past due, although he would never say that to anyone, just in case the pendulum began swinging back again. The only thing that had prevented even broader changes in the Soviet Union was the fact that the reformers had proven no more capable than the communists of solving the country's serious economic problems. In Poland, the switch to a largely free-market economy had put thousands out of work and raised consumer prices through the roof, a fact that *Pravda* was only too happy to reveal.

Castro, however, had seen no reason to change even an inch. There were reports from the KGB in Cuba that a sizeable dock-workers' strike in Cienfuegos had left hundreds dead and over a thousand on their way to concentration camps.

Relations had cooled substantially over the past year between the Soviet Union and Cuba. This was due primarily to the Soviets' announcement that the ten million dollars a day they had been pumping into the Cuban economy could not be counted on indefinitely. Of course the Soviets had been hinting at this for some time to both Cuba and Nicaragua in the hope that both countries would do something to make their economies more rational, but in mid-1990 the Soviets had put a one-year limit on the aid, and this had only some six months left to run. The Soviets had even demanded cash payment for further arms shipments and there had been rumors that, for budgetary reasons of course, Ogarkov's brigade might soon be withdrawn. Castro had responded with more attacks on the Soviet Union in his speeches lately than on the United States, accusing the Soviets of selling out their revolution for a truckload of blue jeans and a Nintendo game.

Ogarkov plunked himself down in a folding chair with a studied gesture of acceptance and reached for a pack of cigarettes. He waved them at the Cuban lieutenant, raising his eyebrows, asking permission. The lieutenant nodded stiffly. Ogarkov took out a cigarette, lit it, and reached for the real object of his attention, a heavy glass ashtray on the card table near him. As he did so he looked at his officers, meeting their furious eyes with his own steady gaze, and received two or three nods of comprehension. His grip tightened on the ashtray. With luck, if he could hurl it into the face of the Cuban soldier farthest from him he might take out that automatic weapon long enough for his men to rush the others. Some would die, of course, but that was what they had signed up for.

Ogarkov raised the ashtray imperceptibly from the table but then quickly replaced it as the door to the room was thrown open and several more Russian officers were shoved into the room, some of them wounded and bleeding, escorted by half a dozen Cuban TE troopers. Two of the Cubans joined their guards, one of them standing halfway out of the door with his rifle trained inward. So much for that plan.

Ogarkov and his men made room for the newcomers, laying the more seriously wounded ones on some wooden benches. Lieutenant Colonel Yezhov, executive officer of the brigade's tank battalion, had a bad bullet wound in the leg, and Ogarkov cradled his head in his arms while another officer used paper napkins from a dispenser next to the room's hot plate to try to staunch the flow of blood.

"What can you tell me, Yezhov?" Ogarkov asked, talking as softly as possible.

Yezhov winced with the pain but realized the importance of getting the information out. "I think they rounded up the whole brigade, Comrade Colonel. I was out near the gate on the Havana road when they came through, about a battalion of tanks from the 101st Armored plus mechanized infantry. No warning. No artillery. They just drove up the road at sixty kilometers an hour with every gun blazing. They went through the perimeter guards like nothing. I think there was another attack from the east, but those were just diversions. It looks as though most of the work was done by TE troops who infiltrated from the coast and through the fences."

"Yes," Ogarkov admitted. "I suppose that we assumed that we had nothing to fear here and let our guard down."

Yezhov gritted his teeth for a moment and continued. "The Cuban liaison officers had planted bombs near some of the barracks and set booby traps near the armories to catch anyone trying to draw ammunition. The TE troops set up ambushes around the vehicle parks and cut the men down when they tried to mount up. The radio jamming was pretty effective, but we got one message from Lieutenant Ivanov that he had a couple of T-72s and BMPs laagered near the north wire with about fifty infantry and was holding out, waiting for orders."

"Excellent!" whispered Ogarkov. Ivanov was a communications officer of his battalion, and Ogarkov congratulated himself on recognizing the stuff of a great soldier in the young man. "At least someone is saving the honor of the brigade."

"But he can't last long, Colonel," Yezhov gasped. "The general is dead, and I'm sure over a thousand of our men are either dead, wounded, or captured. The tank battalion and the artillery simply don't exist anymore, and I think they took a lot of men prisoner in their barracks."

"Was there any indication of what this is all about?" asked Ogarkov desperately. "Things haven't been good with the Cubans lately, but neither the KGB nor our own GRU ever gave us any hint of anything like this. Is there some kind of horrible mistake?"

Yezhov laughed a pained laugh. "You know, Comrade Colonel, that my great-uncle ran the KGB, or NKVD as they called it then, during Stalin's time, during the purges. They say that everyone the Chekists brought in, all of them already condemned to death or the camps, all of them insisted that it was some kind of horrible mistake. I think we would be well advised to assume that these Cuban bastards know exactly what they're doing."

Just then a gunshot broke the quiet and the Cuban lieutenant who fired it screamed at them in Spanish to shut up and stand against the walls. Ogarkov suspected the man did not speak Russian and assumed that anything said was part of a plot, but there was nothing to do but to comply and wait. But wait for what?

Chapter Three

Featherstone stood facing Osman for a long time. Each of the men probably assumed that the other had some hand in his inelegant summons at this early hour. Osman had less reason to believe so than Featherstone, and the latter had serious doubts about Osman's complicity, given his bedraggled appearance.

Featherstone did not particularly like Osman. He was one of the new breed of Soviet diplomats who had begun to appear in the past decade, especially in Latin America. Instead of the old Party hacks who had been given juicy diplomatic postings as rewards for service—"old snipers" as the Soviets themselves referred to ignorant World War II veterans—who left the running of the embassy to staffers, these new Soviet diplomats had long years of experience in studying the politics, economics, and culture of their areas of service. They invariably spoke the local language at near native level and often English as well, and they were tough competitors in any impromptu debate on the diplomatic cocktail circuit. As such, they were frequently responsible for uncomfortable moments for American diplomats who were not fast on their rhetorical feet.

Osman was definitely one of these. He was young for an ambassador, about fifty, and his close-cropped silver hair and relatively

14

trim figure did not bespeak a man who indulged in too many luxuries. Featherstone looked disapprovingly at his own decidedly growing midriff and noted that it made him look older than Osman, even though he was several years younger. Osman never hid behind ideological dogma to make a point and he always had at hand an inconvenient statistic or quote from the Western press or Western literature to support his case. Featherstone wondered whether Osman had changed his style since perestroika and glasnost became fashionable, but he now seemed the ideal representative of the newly liberal but still highly competitive Soviet Union.

Featherstone had just made up his mind to break the ice and greet Osman with some witty remark his brain had yet to provide him, when the doors at the far end of the reception area opened and another Cuban officer in combat fatigues curtly gestured for them to enter. The two soldiers at the door behind them moved forward briskly, their rifles at port arms, as an indication that this was not a topic for discussion.

The two diplomats entered a rather dark room, lighted in fact only by a green-shaded lamp on the large desk to their right, behind which sat Fidel Castro, dressed in his habitual fatigues and smoking his habitual cigar. Behind Castro stood several armed TE officers, and Featherstone noted that the two soldiers from the reception area had followed them into the room and closed the doors behind them. Castro definitely did not rise to greet them.

Featherstone squared his shoulders and prepared to deliver the stinging speech he had been rehearsing mentally since he left his bedroom less than an hour before, but another voice broke the silence.

"As ambassador of the Union of Soviet Socialist Republics I demand to know what justification there could be for the forced entry of my official residence by armed Cuban soldiers and my virtual arrest at gunpoint, in gross violation of diplomatic immunity!" Osman was fairly trembling with rage, a rather carefully practiced rage, Featherstone suspected, but effective nonetheless. Give him hell, Andrei, Featherstone thought.

"Needless to say," Featherstone added, raising a finger lest he be forgotten in the battle between the two socialist allies, "I echo the feelings of my distinguished colleague and insist on my immediate release and the liberty of communication with my superiors in Washington to advise them of this unfortunate occurrence and of the Cuban government's explanation for it."

Castro stared at them, and through them, for what seemed a very long time, puffing occasionally on his cigar. He then put down his cigar, balancing it on the edge of the desk, put on his reading glasses, and picked up a sheaf of papers from the desk. He looked over his glasses at the two nervous diplomats and began:

"You will both remain silent and listen to the following message I have for your governments. You will be given copies of the message translated into your own languages as well as in the original Spanish, to avoid mistakes, and then you will be transported back to your respective missions, from which you will be permitted to communicate with your governments on any topic you care to discuss. A similar message will be transmitted later today over Radio Granma."

Castro paused briefly, probably more for emphasis than to offer the opportunity for response, and Featherstone calculated that the TE officers behind him would have liked nothing better than to hog-tie both of them, gag them, and let them listen to the rest of the speech while hanging from the rafters by their balls. He opted for discreet silence. Castro took another puff on his cigar and continued, reading this time from the page before him.

"It has become increasingly apparent over the past several years that the United States has not learned the lesson of Vietnam and that the imperialist warmongers in Washington still plan to dominate the world, if not through direct military conquest, then through economic subversion. It has also become evident that the Soviet Union, the nation to which Cuba and other progressive nations have freely opened our hearts and our borders as the only defender of the downtrodden against the venal international bourgeoisie, has decided to abandon the role of vanguard of the working class in exchange for a few pieces of Yankee silver. The insidious plot of the two so-called superpowers to rule the world jointly through their combined military and economic might is now exposed to the freedom-loving peoples of the world, and it will not go unanswered. In fact it has already failed. The Cuban government recognizes that a state of war exists between the hegemonist powers and the nations of the Third World.

"This morning, shortly before dawn, heroic units of the armed forces of Cuba took into custody all members of the military machines of the hegemonist powers present illegally on Cuban soil. In keeping with their gangster upbringing, some of these foreign invaders opened armed hostilities in a totally indiscriminate manner and inflicted heavy casualties on the Cuban civilian population in clear violation of the Geneva Convention. Those responsible for these acts will be held as war criminals and tried and punished accordingly. Since the hegemonist powers have a long history of abusing the rights of civilian individuals to provide cover for paramilitary and espionage activities, the Cuban government has also taken into custody all civilian citizens of the hegemonist nations on Cuban soil. These individuals, estimated at some seven thousand Americans and twelve thousand Soviets, except those found guilty of war crimes, will be released to representatives of a neutral nation when the following conditions have been met:

"One: Each hegemonist nation must make a formal declaration of the national sovereignty of Cuba and withdraw all military personnel and bases from Cuban soil immediately.

"Two: The foreign debt, both public and private, of all Third World countries to all formerly socialist nations will be paid in full by the Soviet Union, and the debt to all other nations will be paid by the United States.

"Three: In addition to the preceding, Cuba will be paid reparations by the hegemonist powers for the depredations caused by their aggressions in the amount of 100 billion U.S. dollars, in terms which will be discussed at a later date.

"Four: The hegemonist powers will agree not to interrupt the free movement of maritime or aerial commerce to and from Cuba, regardless of the source of the commerce or the merchandise contained.

"Five: The General Assembly of the United Nations will be the venue for all discussions related to these issues, and the Cuban delegation there is fully empowered to negotiate on behalf of the Cuban government."

Castro paused for another pull on his cigar. Featherstone could not help shaking his head in disbelief. Could this bearded maniac really believe that anyone would go for this? Certainly hostage-taking had never been attempted on a scale anything like this before, nearly twenty thousand people at one fell swoop, but the world reaction would be so wildly negative that the United States, perhaps in concert with the Soviets, would be forgiven any reaction, no matter how violent. Besides that, Featherstone mused, Castro might find the marines and sailors at Guantánamo, obviously the bulk of the Americans Castro was referring to, to be rather unwilling participants in this charade, to say nothing of the Soviet brigade barely an hour's drive from this very room.

There had been rumors for years that Castro was losing his balance. His record-setting speeches had always been purgatories for those unlucky souls obliged to listen to and study them, but they had originally been quite coherent and rational, if radical. Since the early 1980s, however, Castro simply rambled from one point to another, and veteran Havana-watchers took this as a sign that Castro was either sick or mentally disturbed. Featherstone stole a glance at Osman, but the Russian was staring stonily straight ahead at a spot on the wall over Castro's head. This sort of thing might not look good on a Russian ambassador's resume: presided over the complete breakdown in relations between the Soviet Union and its former most-trusted ally, Cuba.

Castro spun halfway around in his chair and talked to the Cuban flag in the corner. "Of course it should be understood, even though it is not included in the document I have just read, that any attempt by either aggressor nation to begin military activities against the Cuban people or their allies will result in the immediate execution of a large portion of the prisoners, in order to free more soldiers for the defense of the fatherland."

Castro now spun completely around in his chair and faced the wall, away from Featherstone and Osman. "You may go now and communicate with your governments. You will find additional information on the current situation will become available to you during the course of the day. We will expect a preliminary answer within twenty-four hours."

The interview was clearly at an end, and the guards near the door moved forward to escort the two visitors out, but Featherstone spoke up, "What about our families, the dependents of the diplomatic community?"

Castro twirled around suddenly and stared at Featherstone with an expression more of puzzlement than of anger. It had apparently never occurred to him that the fate of individual families would be a topic for discussion. He paused for a moment and stammered briefly, "Well, I,—you have nothing to fear for your families. You will not be permitted to leave the Havana area, but beyond that you may carry on your activities as normal—within the limits of the new state of siege."

Featherstone was about to say "Thank you," but thought better of it and walked stiffly out of the room with Osman. When they arrived in the courtyard of the house Osman turned and spoke to Featherstone for the first time.

"May I offer you a ride back to your embassy in my car, Mr. Featherstone?" Featherstone nodded, and the two climbed into Osman's black Mercedes, with Osman driving.

Not knowing where to begin, Featherstone asked, "How did you convince them to let you bring your own car?"

Osman laughed softly, "It was rather amusing. After all the melodrama of thrusting their way into my residence, when we loaded into their Ladas two of the three they had brought wouldn't start, so I had to offer them a ride back here." Osman glanced sideways at Featherstone, smiling. "Of course, those were pre-Gorbachev Ladas."

The two rode on for a moment, smiling at space, not knowing what they should or could say to each other. It certainly appeared that their two countries were in the same boat this time, but still, they were professional diplomats, trained for years, decades between them, not to have personal opinions or to make any statements not previously cleared with their superiors. The streets were still nearly deserted even though it was nearly seven o'clock in the morning. Regular army troops were in evidence at the major intersections, and groups of part-time militia were manning checkpoints and lounging by the roadside.

When they came to one intersection, Featherstone pointed off to the right. "I wonder if you could drop me at my home, over there. I'll take my own car into the mission."

Osman looked over at Featherstone again, frowning slightly. "Aha!" he said. "I thought that question about the families was merely a brilliant ploy to catch the "First Soldier of the Revolution" off guard. I see now that it wasn't. And here I was so impressed."

Featherstone laughed, embarrassed. "Well, it wasn't really a well-thought-out move, I'll admit. Diplomacy may be my job, but I can always get another job. Actually, I will be needing my own car later, and I'll want to collect my staff. . . ."

"Of course." Osman smiled. "In any case, perhaps it would be useful for you and me to get together later to discuss this most unusual situation."

"I'm sure that wiser heads than ours will be making all of the important decisions, and they may even object to our meeting, but if you ever want to talk, off the record, perhaps we two can come up with some ideas that won't occur to anyone else. We are the men on the spot—literally."

"Perfect," Osman said as the Mercedes slid to a stop on the gravel in front of Featherstone's home. "And I thought nothing interesting would ever happen here."

Chapter Four

Johnson had spent the past two hours or more moving from one hidden position to another. He cursed the Cubans for their timing. They had hit before the base was awake, for maximum surprise, but now that the sun was up there was nowhere to hide. Johnson found himself more or less in charge of a group of eight men; four marines, two sailors, and one American civilian technician, besides himself. Only three of the marines had M-16s, one of the sailors had a pistol, and they had less than a hundred rounds among them.

From the scuttlebutt he had picked up from his fellow refugees Johnson had learned that the Cubans had apparently hit the base from the landward side, along the peninsula on which the base was located, with approximately two mechanized infantry divisions in addition to the Border Guard troops normally stationed around the perimeter. This frontal attack had been greatly assisted by a heliborne assault with several companies of infantry brought in by Mi-8s and supported by Mi-24 and Mi-35 helicopter gunships. The initial wave of these troops had made it into the base before much of a reaction could be made, but a second wave was caught in a murderous fire of

Duster antiaircraft guns and Stinger antiaircraft missiles. Several commando teams had also come ashore either with scuba gear or by small boat around the peninsula, and it was one of these Johnson had first met.

There had been no preparatory artillery fire to speak of, but as soon as the leading elements of the enemy armored units hit the base wire a heavy and incredibly accurate barrage knocked out many of the base's command and communications centers. From the outset, therefore, except for a few platoons that managed to escape the worst of the opening fire, the only resistance being offered was by scattered groups of marines and sailors fighting on their own, without direction from above. The lack of friendly air cover also implied that there was no communication with American bases in Florida, within easy striking distance of Cuba. Of course, Johnson and his men had no way of knowing whether the United States was now a glowing slag heap of nuclear wreckage. Since most of the men had families back home this thought at once terrified them and gave them a grim incentive to get revenge.

A number of 122mm rockets had also been targeted on the base airfield and equipment parks. These rockets had been armed with a mix of nerve gas, smoke, and riot-control gas, all of the nonpersistent variety. The nerve gas had inflicted hundreds of casualties on the unprepared defenders, and the threat of a renewed attack forced those who could to fight in their cumbersome and hot chemical warfare gear. However, it appeared that the gas attacks were for initial shock value only and to keep the Americans from getting at some of their equipment, and that the attackers did not want their own troops' advance hampered. There had been no reports of gas for over an hour, and the Cubans Johnson's group had seen had not been wearing protective gear.

Johnson's first priority was to find an officer who knew what he was doing in order to get his men integrated into some kind of defensive plan. That was easier said than done, since the only officers the group had seen were either dead or Cuban. The group had passed near a bachelor officers' quarters (BOQ) that had apparently been hit directly with both artillery and gas. They had found no one alive.

The group had finally holed up in a small brick building normally used for classroom instruction. Johnson posted guards with weapons and took out a patrol consisting of himself and two unarmed sailors to look for help, guidance, weapons, food, water, whatever they could find. This small team ran in rushes from cover to cover around the base, occasionally coming under fire from unseen enemy forces. They found the bodies of more Cubans than Americans now, and the thought made Johnson smile grimly. At least someone was fighting back. From a large hangarlike building across the way Johnson could hear the distinctive snarl of an American M-60 machine gun, and he readied himself to make the dash across nearly two hundred yards of open ground to it.

The three men crouched like track stars and took off at full tilt, but barely fifty yards from their starting point they saw a Cuban T-54 tank wheel around a corner and come bearing down on them. Johnson skidded to a halt as his two comrades continued on, machine-gun bullets kicking up dust around them. Johnson didn't stop to think how little good his M-16 would do against a tank. He was the only armed man in the group, and he was responsible. He flipped the selector switch to full automatic and started firing from the hip. "Semper fi! Fuck you!" Maybe he could distract the tank long enough to let the others make it.

Suddenly a white flash burst on the tank's left side. The whole body of the tank was shoved about a yard to its right and the turret flipped off like the cap off a beer bottle. Johnson stared open-mouthed at the tank, then at his rifle.

"Yo, Marine!" Someone was shouting and waving to him from a window in the building he had been heading for. Now he could see the end of a TOW launcher tube protruding slightly from the opening. Oh, right, Johnson thought, feeling a little foolish. "Get your skinny black ass in here!"

Johnson came to and raced the remaining distance to the building. It was a cavernous warehouse affair with about fifty marines and sailors inside, either milling around or manning positions at the windows. The man who had yelled to Johnson came over. It was First Sergeant Glover, Johnson's own company first sergeant.

Johnson grinned. "Thanks, Sarge, but I had things pretty much under control out there."

"You're just fucking lucky I don't have my clipboard or I'd fetch you a shot upside your head. Who taught you to fire long bursts from your weapon like that? You'll melt the barrel. You can be replaced, but that fucking piece costs money." They both knew that this show of bravado when they were scared out of their skins was necessary, and it did make them feel better. Glover was only just over five feet tall but he was at least as wide, and pure muscle. His biceps were as thick as Johnson's legs, and he had pounded the Marine code into more than one reluctant recruit out behind the barracks, even in this day of a "kinder, gentler Corps."

"So what's up, Sarge?" Johnson asked after Glover had sent a man out to bring in the rest of Johnson's group.

"It doesn't look good," the older man said sadly. No more bravado now. "The battalion CO is dead, so are most of the brass. This is probably one of the larger groups left on the base in one piece. The fucking Cubans are everywhere. I heard a nasty rumor that they're already talking surrender. Shit! Nearly twenty-five years in the Corps just to surrender."

"Can't we hold out until help comes?"

"Get real, man," Glover snapped. "We'll be lucky to hold out until nightfall. They could get air in here pretty quick, assuming there's anybody left back home to send it, but it would take days to get the 2d Marine Division mounted up and shipped down here. The 82d Airborne could make it quicker, but they'd really need to sweep the sky clean before those C-130s would stand a chance. The thing is we just don't have a defensive position here. We're all scattered to hell and gone."

"How about a breakout to the hills?"

"Unless we can hold until dark, which is a long time off yet, there ain't much chance of that either. We'd have to cover miles of open country along a peninsula swarming with Cubans. You have to figure, too, that any Cuban civilian who spotted us would report it in a heartbeat. Of course if we could make it to the Sierra that would be different."

"*We?*"

"Hell, yes," Glover said. "I said *if* we make it 'til dark. Then we'd stand a chance. Why don't you make the rounds and ask who'd be interested in going?"

Just then a runner slid head first through a side door of the building as a bullet panged against the doorframe. He reported to Glover, who took him over to the ranking officer present, a navy lieutenant who was having a hand wound treated by a corpsman in the temporary aid station set up in a corner.

"Sir," the runner saluted, "I have a sitrep from Base HQ, or what's left of it."

"Let's hear the bad news," the lieutenant grunted as the corpsman finished his bandage.

"The defense is currently under the command of Captain Meese, USN. All of the other senior officers are either dead, badly wounded, or missing. We figure that we've lost about a thousand men, killed and wounded, and about twice as many as prisoners. The rest are grouped into bunches like this one, between forty and a hundred men in each, in a rough oval around the old HQ building. There seems to be enough small arms and ammunition for everyone who can fight, about fifteen hundred men in all, and a few crew-served weapons. All of the naval craft have been destroyed. There have been no communications with the States, except a couple of garbled messages, but it doesn't look like there's a general war on. It also doesn't look like any help is on the way soon. We estimate enemy strength at about two and a half of his mechanized divisions plus some supporting troops. Captain Meese has arranged a ceasefire to take effect at 1100 hours, that's about half an hour from now. It will last for four hours to permit both sides to collect their wounded and for Captain Meese to consult with Washington for permission to surrender."

"Surrender, shit!" Glover interjected.

The runner nodded to Glover. "That's what the Captain thinks too, Sergeant. He says he's going to try to stall until dark, and then he'll only agree to surrender the troops directly under his command. With the mess our commo is in, that's just about nobody, so anyone wanting to try to make it out is welcome to try. That's supposing some miracle doesn't happen and this whole nightmare doesn't end or we get rescued or something."

"Thank you, bosun," the lieutenant said. "Good work. Go get yourself something to eat while we figure out what to do."

SANTIAGO DE LAS VEGAS, CUBA

One of the wounded Russian officers had bled to death, lying on the bench in front of Ogarkov, while the Cubans coldly ignored his demands, requests, and pleas for medical aid. The others, now numbering about thirty, were crowded against one wall with the Cuban guards along the other, glaring at each other.

The door to the room opened again and in stepped a Soviet officer Ogarkov recognized as General Akamirov, one of the senior Soviet military advisors to Cuba. His arm was in a sling and there was a bandage over one of his eyes, still revealing a bluish-purple welt over much of his cheek and forehead. Akamirov held his head up as he addressed his fellow officers.

"It's over, comrades," he said in a quiet voice that still carried to every corner of the room. "The Cuban government has taken hostage all of our military and civilian personnel on the island. We will be held here at our camp until negotiations are completed to secure our release. Colonel Ogarkov, you are ordered to instruct your men still resisting to lay down their arms. Please come with me." Ogarkov could see tears of shame welling up in Akamirov's eyes.

"HOSTAGE?" screamed Ogarkov. "Whatever happened to 'prisoner of war,' or is that out of style?"

"Believe me, brother," Akamirov said. "There is nothing more we can do—*now*," he added with emphasis. "Any further loss of life at this time would be pointless."

Ogarkov walked slowly out of the room, thinking how easily he could break the windpipe of the nearest Cuban guard. They would kill him, of course, but then it would at least be all over.

Once they were outside Ogarkov walked close to Akamirov. "So who's still resisting? I haven't heard much firing for nearly an hour."

"Your Lieutenant Ivanov, up by the north fence. He's got about one weak company there with a couple of tanks. The Cubans tried an assault on the place and lost half a dozen tanks and nearly a hundred men, I understand. They've shelled him too, but he had his men dig in and they're in their protective gear, so gas won't affect them. He even commandeered a water trailer and a truckload of rations, so he could hold out for days."

"Damn fine show!" Ogarkov remarked. "Of course that kind of initiative could have gotten him shot during the Great Patriotic War, but I'm glad our young officers haven't had their balls bred out of them."

The two Russians were taken in a jeep through the camp area. There were bodies, both Cuban and Russian, scattered here and there, and the burned carcasses of several trucks, but it was apparent that most of the men had been taken before they could get resistance organized. As they neared Ivanov's position, however, the scenery changed markedly. They passed a number of charred tanks with their gun tubes pointed at crazy angles. There were many wrecked armored personnel carriers as well and lots of bodies, all Cuban, Ogarkov noted with pride. The ground had been churned by artillery, and in the near distance they could see a low berm that Ivanov's men had evidently raised with a bulldozer.

A small group of Cuban officers stood under a tree with a white flag. "This is Colonel Guerrero," Akamirov said to Ogarkov. Neither officer extended his hand. "He will accept the troops' surrender."

Ogarkov nodded and walked slowly forward with Guerrero, carrying the white flag. Ogarkov could see Ivanov sliding down the berm with an NCO, also carrying a white flag. Ivanov was limping slightly and trying to hide it, but there was pain in his face. When the two groups met Ogarkov dropped his flag and embraced Ivanov in a crushing bear hug. "You have fought a hero's fight here today, my son. Now we must leave it to others to carry on for us."

Ivanov turned to Guerrero and said, in passable Spanish, "I trust my men will be treated properly."

Guerrero sneered, "I will not dignify that remark with a reply. Call your men out, Lieutenant." He made Ivanov's rank sound rather like an insult.

Ivanov turned to his sergeant, who waved the flag in a prear-ranged signal. A number of helmeted heads appeared over the berm and watched for a moment; then the men began scrambling over.

They were unarmed, but when they had collected at the foot of the berm another NCO formed them into a column of twos and marched them forward, the wounded held up by their unwounded comrades.

Akamirov had come up now, and he and Ogarkov stiffened and saluted, Akamirov with the left hand because of his wound.

"Hands over their heads!" screamed Guerrero. "Tell them to put their hands over their heads!"

Ivanov looked with burning hatred at Guerrero and shouted the required order. Slowly, the hands went up, about halfway.

"Now give me your sidearm!" yelled Guerrero at Ivanov.

Ivanov turned slowly and flipped his Makarov pistol out of its holster, handing it to Guerrero butt first. Guerrero smiled broadly, turning the weapon over and over in his hand. He pulled the slide back to see if it was loaded. It was.

Ogarkov had been watching Ivanov's men file past and turned just in time to see the back of Ivanov's head blown off as Guerrero shot him full in the face with his own pistol.

"NO!" screamed Ogarkov as he lunged at Guerrero, but Akamirov threw his body across his legs, tackling him. But Ivanov's sergeant was closer, and his white flag was tied to the bayonet of an unloaded rifle. The sergeant thrust the bayonet, flag and all, through Guerrero's chest, and the smile was replaced by a look of shock and pain. The sergeant did not live to see this, however, as he was immediately cut down by a burst of rifle fire. Ivanov's men also turned at the sound of firing and, with a roar, started running toward their fallen leader, but they were now separated by a line of Cuban infantrymen armed with AK-47s, and a few bursts directly into their ranks stopped the survivors.

Ogarkov and Akamirov were lying on the ground, surrounded by Cuban soldiers. Ogarkov was screaming about turning this island into a sheet of glass, and Akamirov was just sobbing softly.

Chapter Five

Castro could barely remember what it was like not to be the supreme ruler of his country, and he certainly could not remember a time when he had not known that he would be the supreme ruler one day. Of course originally he had had in mind being a president in the sort of semidemocracy Cuba had enjoyed in the days of his youth, but his early exposure to Marxism had taught him that whatever the costs or benefits communism might have for society as a whole it provided a proven means of getting and keeping power. What one did with that power was one's own business.

That is, communism had been a proven system for holding power until that imbecile Gorbachev came to power in the Soviet Union. "Came to power" was not the right term. He came to give away power. With their long years of experience, didn't the Russians realize that it didn't matter whether there was toothpaste on the shelves or whether the refrigerators worked? All that mattered was the frequent demonstration that there was no alternative to the current power structure.

That was what had attracted the leaders of the emerging nations of the Third World to communism. By the time most of the countries of Africa gained their independence in the 1960s even war-ravaged

West Germany was running rings around the USSR economically, and the poorest welfare recipient in New York lived better than most of the people in Eastern Europe. No, "equitable distribution of resources" had nothing to do with it. If one had the vision one needed uninterrupted exercise of power to realize it, and communism had provided the cadres, the motivating drive, and even the propaganda machine to make it work.

Castro recognized that he could not have survived in power for over thirty years without Soviet support—financial, diplomatic, and military—but he did not owe them anything for that. They had helped him because it was in their own selfish interest to do so, and now they were about to cut him loose for the same reason. Cuba had given them a strategic base ninety miles from the U.S. astride the Americans' primary sea routes, and only the cowardice of that potato-faced Khrushchev had kept them from turning Cuba into an advanced nuclear outpost as well. The Americans never would have attacked in 1962, Castro knew it, but the Soviets had backed down. And without even consulting him! Well, that would never happen again. Castro was through with being the stalking horse for the perfidious Soviets. A new wind was blowing in the world, and it came from Havana. Wake up and smell the cigar smoke, gentlemen, Castro mused.

As he lounged in the chair from which he had spoken to the Soviet and American diplomats half an hour before Castro could hear the shouting and thumping from the reception area. He smiled as he smoked. This was perhaps the sweetest sensation of power. He could make or unmake men at his whim. The very permission to enter his presence was heady stuff for mere mortals, and denying it was like taking heroin away from an addict. It drove them wild. Having savored the sensation long enough, Castro finally gestured with a finger to the TE captain by the door, and the captain opened the door to show in his next visitor.

Raul Castro did not enter the room as much as he blew into it like a hurricane. Two TE soldiers very gradually let him push his way past them and stood, rifles at the ready, in the doorway, while two more of Fidel's bodyguards shifted slightly forward from behind the "Jefe."

"What is going on here?" Raul screamed. "There's a fucking war going on on this island. I'm minister of defense and commander of the armed forces, and I'm not informed of anything. Then I'm practically placed under arrest, incommunicado, and brought here. Now I hear from these slime-sucking TE thugs of yours that Guantánamo has been attacked and that all of the Russians in Cuba have been arrested. Are you crazy?"

A carefully placed blow from the TE captain's fist to Raul's kidneys crumpled the portly, pale-faced man to his knees.

"With all due respect, comrade," the captain said through clenched teeth, "I must insist that proper respect be shown to the Jefe at all times."

Raul spun his head around to glare at his attacker, but the total lack of fear or even respect on the captain's face was an experience that Raul Castro had forgotten. He was used to being treated with as much deference as Fidel, maybe more when it came to the Russians, but something had obviously changed.

"I'm sorry about all this, little brother," Fidel chimed in. "Momentous events have been taking place in the past few days. Not just for Cuba, but for the whole world. These events are being directed from right behind this desk, and it would have given me great pleasure to have you at my side in planning them, but I was not certain that I could count on you totally."

Raul stared at Fidel with his mouth hanging open. "Please, Fidel," Raul whined, having learned from long experience when to kowtow as well as when to attack, "what are you doing? Why don't you think you can trust me? Haven't I been with you from the beginning?"

"Of course you have, Raul," Castro soothed. "It's just that what I have begun would involve your making some very serious choices, and I could not be certain which choices you would make. Let me explain."

Fidel walked around the desk and sat on the edge, facing his still-kneeling brother. "You are as aware as I that the changes that have been occurring in the Soviet Union and Eastern Europe have altered the world's balance of power irrevocably. The Soviets have essentially let go the empire they conquered in Eastern Europe, an empire that meant far more to them strategically than Cuba ever did, and they just let it go! Without a peep! They're cutting their armed forces back. They're remodelling their political structure and their economy. Surely you can see that they've sold out to the Americans."

"No, Fidel, you're wrong," Raul complained. "They need us. They would never give us up. We owe everything to them. We must trust them."

Fidel slammed his palm on the desk and roared, stalking around the room, "This is just what I expected! You have been sucking up to the Soviets for so long that you have forgotten where you came from. The Soviets abandoned the Afghans; they make the Libyans pay cash for arms; they sell the Ethiopians down the river. How many more examples do you need? If it hadn't been for our support the Sandinistas in Nicaragua would have been overthrown and the FMLN in El Salvador would have ceased to exist. Can't you see that the Soviets have given up on world revolution and are out to put a VCR in every stinking *izbah* in Russia?"

Fidel leaned over his cowering brother, wagging his finger. "There has been a profound change in the world, and you can't see it. I knew that if I told you my plans you would have blabbed to the Russians that very minute. Then I'd be dead and you'd be sitting in that chair, and I'd be playing tag with the sharks off Cabo de San Antonio. Isn't that right?"

"No, Fidel, never," Raul whimpered. "I'd die before I'd betray you. I'm your brother, don't forget."

"Let me tell you, little brother," Fidel growled. "I don't forget anything. And I don't forgive anything. Do you wonder why Captain Fuentes isn't here?"

"F–F–Fuentes, who's Fuentes?" Raul stammered.

"Oh, you remember. You can't have forgotten your informant in my bodyguard so soon. Well, he's dead, along with about a hundred of your other lackeys. Most of them confessed before dying about your plans to replace me if I didn't stop my criticism of the Soviets. That bit of information forced me to go to great lengths to pull off my plan. I knew that the Russians would have their own informants in many military units and even in the G2, so for the last year I have concentrated on weeding them out. Ochoa was the first, along with his supporters. There were others, less well known. A traffic accident here, a plane crash there. Then I had to recruit the strike forces very carefully. The attack on the Soviet brigade could only be trusted to my own TE troops, about two thousand of them, backed up by a couple of regular battalions whose commanders were loyal to me and whose troops thought you were being held by the Soviets in their base. I could use regular troops to attack Guantánamo, but it was still difficult to keep the preparations from both you and the Soviets.

"And now it's done. I have nearly twenty thousand hostages right here in Cuba. The Arabs had the right idea, but they think too small. The Americans and Soviets are going to pay off our debts and those of the whole Third World, and they can't raise a finger against us while we have the hostages."

"But don't you think that they'll come after you when you let the hostages go, or do you plan to hold them forever?" Raul's brain was racing now. Perhaps by appearing the adoring disciple again he could deflect his brother's anger and get out of this hole. He put on his best awestruck face.

"Don't worry about that. Oh, we'll let the hostages go, but they'll never be in a position for revenge. Don't you understand, little brother, that a new world order is forming before your eyes, and we'll be right at the center of it."

Raul's face brightened as he saw a ray of hope for himself. "What can I say? It never occurred to me that there was any way out for us from our dependence on the Soviets, but now that you've come up with the perfect plan, I'm with you one hundred percent."

"I knew I could count on your support, little brother," Fidel said, patting Raul on the shoulder and helping him to his feet. "You have a very important role to play."

"Just tell me what you want me to do, Jefe!" Raul said, straightening himself and thrusting his chin out.

"Just stand right there. Captain?" Raul's eyes widened as the TE officer levelled his AKM at Raul's chest. He looked around frantically and saw that the other guards had moved off to a safe distance. Fidel sat in his chair and turned toward the wall.

"Fidel—Nooooooo!" The last scream was drowned out by the crackle of gunfire.

Chapter Six

Featherstone walked wordlessly past the guards at his house and into the living room. Anne, who had been watching from the upstairs window, came running down and threw her arms around him. They just held each other silently for some time. They had served together, as husband and wife, for just over twenty years, nearly all of it overseas. They had two children, both in college now in the States, one born in Ecuador, the other in Spain. They had undergone periods of tension in previous postings but the actual risk of harm befalling one of them had always seemed quite remote.

In Bogotá, even back in the early 1980s when they were stationed there, the crime rate was astronomical. That was before the big war with the drug lords, but embassy families were obliged to live in apartments on the third floor or higher, with armed guards at the building entrances, because of the frequency of armed assaults on detached houses. They had lived through a wave of terrorist bombings in Spain. There had been plenty of coups, but none of that had seemed to be directed against them personally. Even the anti-American demonstrations had appeared mild, were usually of short duration, and limited to a particular part of town, easily avoided. This was war, and they were right in the war zone.

They had met in Buenos Aires, where Anne had been a secretary in a British firm and Featherstone a fresh first-tour third secretary, working in the consulate. Washington was now the closest thing they had to a hometown, and they had never lived there more than two years at a time. Although they referred to it as "home," they had rented out their house in Vienna, Virginia, before their last posting and had not seen it since, the details being arranged by a realtor. They spent much of their free time now deciding whether to keep the old place or get something smaller. Neither liked Washington much, but with their son at Georgetown and their daughter just started at William and Mary they wanted to stay within striking distance of both of them.

"I really wasn't sure whether you'd be coming home," Anne sobbed into his shoulder.

"Oh, I don't think it will ever come to that," he tried to comfort her. They sat down on the couch and he explained what they had heard at Castro's office.

"What could he be thinking of?" Anne asked, shaking her head.

"The more I think about it," Featherstone sighed, "the less crazy it sounds. The only thing that is clear is that Castro's cast the die, and we'll have to ride out whatever happens. Now, I want you to go next door and stay with Stan and Mary. I expect I'll be spending a lot of time in the office for the next few days and I don't want you here alone. Take over whatever you need and keep a getaway bag by the door with a change of clothes for each of us."

"I do know the drill," she said, smiling at last. "I've been there before."

"Right." He kissed her and ran upstairs to try the radio transmitter. It worked, and he called a meeting of the country team (a committee formed of the heads of section of a diplomatic mission) in his office for half an hour later. He then ran into the bathroom to splash some water on his face and grab a quick shave.

Anne was waiting by the door with her bags when he came downstairs. He paused for a second, snatching a book from the bookcase. He had been in crises before and knew that there would likely be hours of hanging around by the communications office, waiting for something to come in. Together, arm in arm, they walked out past the guards and into Stan's garden next door.

Osman picked up his KGB *rezident*, Anatoli Kurupatin, on the way to the embassy. The rather stocky blond man was waiting by his gate for Osman to arrive and jumped into the Mercedes before it came to a full stop.

"What is all this?" Kurupatin asked, his face an even deeper shade of crimson than that caused by the tropical weather. "These bastards wouldn't let me leave my house until you came back. The phones are out and the radios only just came back on, but no one but our own embassy staff is on the net."

"Actually, I was rather hoping you could tell me, Comrade KGB Colonel," Osman sniped. Kurupatin was not a bad spy or even a bad man, for KGB, but however this affair turned out in the end, it was certainly an intelligence failure of the first magnitude, and Osman had no illusions about their respective career potentials at this point. Osman had not envisioned himself spending his retirement years sweeping snow off the steps of some tenement in Gorki.

"You know as well as I do that most of our nets were wrapped up over the past year. They were probably doubled against us even before that for all we know. All I've been able to find out is that the mechanized brigade was attacked by the Cubans and all of our military and technical advisors have been arrested." Kurupatin was breathing heavily, and Osman hoped that he wouldn't be inconsiderate enough to have a heart attack until after Osman was done with him.

Osman filled Kurupatin in on the session in Castro's office and showed him the document as the car squealed around corners, with Osman flashing his safe conduct pass at the surly checkpoint guards.

Kurupatin held his forehead with one chubby hand. "We're dead men, you know," he declared. "One look at this and the Kremlin won't bother with marines or air strikes. Oh no, there'll be a dozen ICBMs winging their merry way through the stratosphere in an hour.

You know that we haven't had much experience in the delicacy of hostage negotiation over the years, and a dead hostage is still a martyr to the Revolution."

"That's why we have to come up with a solution a little less fatal to ourselves, comrade," Osman soothed. "The only way we can save our skins is if you and I can make a contribution to the acceptable solution to this crisis. They may not give you the traditional 'nine-millimeter headache' in the basement of the Lubyanka anymore, but there are perfectly legal ways of making you wish that they had. We must make ourselves absolutely indispensable to Moscow." Osman was trying to convince himself as well as Kurupatin, and the more he talked the more possible it sounded. Kurupatin was nodding his head furiously, like a plastic dog in the back window of a capitalist sedan, as they pulled into the courtyard of the embassy.

As in most countries, the Soviet Embassy occupied a compound that included living quarters for most of the embassy staff except the ambassador and the senior KGB officers and military attachés, themselves usually GRU military intelligence officers.

The two men dashed out of their car and were joined wordlessly in the embassy lobby by Gen. Georgi Malinsky, the GRU chief, and several other senior embassy officials as they trotted to Osman's conference room. Osman noticed that there were a number of young, fit KGB men in the lobby. They were wearing casual clothes instead of their usual uncomfortable suits, and openly carrying submachine guns. Osman shouted to one of them. "I want every Soviet citizen not in custody brought to the embassy, and every weapon issued to someone who can use it." The young KGB men took off at a dead run.

Kurupatin gave Osman a quizzical look. "I know we could never hold out here if the Cubans wanted to come in, but if we have armed guards on duty that might give us a few minutes to negotiate if they do make a move, and we might be able to avoid an even worse situation." The squad of Soviet diplomats continued to trot up the broad stairs toward Osman's office.

Osman sent them into the conference room with instructions to

Kurupatin to brief the group fully and to obtain any new information anyone had been able to come by. He continued on alone to the communications room, next to his own office. He passed through the KGB receptionist's area as the young man there worked the action on his submachine gun, springing to his feet as the ambassador passed. The two communications officers were always armed, and Osman noted that perestroika had not involved taking down sinister posters in the commo room of a bloody Uncle Sam lurking in the shadows for anyone unwise enough to break with security procedures.

Osman threw himself into a stiff metal chair at a small desk and began scrawling on a notepad. After about five minutes' furious work he handed the sheet to the senior technician along with the Russian version of Castro's declaration. "Get this on the air immediately. I will expect confirmation of reception within fifteen minutes. Then send it again to be sure."

"Yes, comrade." The former military man involuntarily snapped a salute and set to work at a keyboard.

When Osman returned to the conference room he found the embassy officers clustered around a large figure seated uncomfortably in a straight-backed chair nursing his arm, which was in a sling. General Akamirov advised the group of all that had happened to the mechanized brigade and his military advisors and technicians.

"Well," Osman began when the general had finished, "by my rough calculation that gives them nearly the twelve thousand Russian prisoners—hostages—" he corrected himself, "that Castro claimed to us, although he appears to have underestimated the number of our men who would be killed in the assault. General Malinsky, you'd better get a summary of all of this new information on the air to Moscow immediately. Is there any word of escapees or about the Americans?"

Kurupatin spoke up. "We do still have some reporting sources with good communications. One of our military people, Cuban that is, in Santiago got a message through to us just now reporting very heavy fighting at Guantánamo. Lots of artillery and air strikes. Lots of Cuban casualties being delivered to the local hospitals. From the sound of it the Americans haven't surrendered yet officially, but the bulk of the base is in Cuban hands."

"Gentlemen," Osman began, "I think it's only fair for us to be totally frank with each other. There does not appear to be much chance of a rescue mission being launched by the Soviet Union. General Akamirov, do you agree?"

Akamirov leaned back and began to reel off statistics as if he were giving one of his canned briefings for visiting Soviet delegations, as he had done so many times in the past. "The Cubans have about ten active divisions, one armored and the rest mechanized, scattered around the island. Their divisions are smaller than ours, about five thousand men each. They also have about a dozen reserve divisions and some independent tank and infantry brigades that can be brought up to strength in a matter of a day or two and over a million militia members who have had rudimentary military training, but these could be mobilized only by bringing the economy and services of the country to a complete halt. There are also special Ministry of Interior troops and police with light weapons, a regiment of marines, and between two and three thousand TE troops, but I suspect these last took heavy casualties spearheading the attack on our brigade and the Americans. Unfortunately their army, even the militia, probably has a higher percentage of combat veterans, from Ethiopia and Angola, than any in the world, and that's not a factor to be taken lightly. Basically, I think that we would only have to worry about the active and reserve forces on a practical level.

"They've got virtually no navy, just a couple of frigates and some coastal patrol craft, although these are armed with missiles and could get lucky. They also have a couple of attack submarines that any rescue force would have to watch for.

"You would also have to figure on their air force, which, thanks to us, is equipped with MiG-21s, MiG-23s, and even some MiG-29s. Their pilots also have considerable combat experience, but not against high-performance aircraft. It's not world class in size, but it would be more than a match for anything we could support at this distance from Russia.

"The big problem would be *where* the hostages might be. We've got few sources of information with functioning communications. On the one hand, when you're talking about perhaps twenty thousand people the situation is a little easier than if it were just one person who could be shoved in some closet. That many people take up space and would be far easier to locate by one means or another. On the other hand, if the Cubans are smart, and we had damn well better assume that they are at this point, they'll keep the hostages scattered in penny packets all over the place so that you would have to take the whole island simultaneously to secure them. I'm reminded of a story I heard about the '62 missile crisis: When the American politicians were talking easily of invading Cuba some American general just put up a slide of the eastern United States with Cuba superimposed on it, on the same scale. The island stretched from the Mississippi to the Atlantic. This is a big damn place. I would have to agree that a military solution is not realistic."

"Comrade Kurupatin," Osman said, turning to the KGB *rezident*, "can you add anything?"

"We still have some sources around the island that the Cubans haven't wrapped up or doubled—as far as we know. I've had my men send out instructions for them to place themselves in the best possible positions to provide further information, but we will have to be patient. They will all be under close scrutiny and they will not have many chances to communicate with us securely, even with the sophisticated commo equipment we have issued them. You'll forgive me if I don't go into more detail. Even here in the secure conference room we cannot be too careful.

"I would have to agree that a negotiated solution is virtually the only way out for the present. The actual cost of this fiasco does not appear to be as great for us as for the Americans. After all, we have made it a policy over the years to dump our secondhand military hardware on our Third World allies and charge them good prices for it. The financial loss from our cancelling our debts would be hard, especially regarding oil supplies and such, from which we obtain significant foreign exchange, but it would be tolerable. The secondary effects might actually prove greater, in that if the Western financial community is badly shaken by this severe shock to the American economy we can expect foreign economic aid and investment, which we need to get our own economy modernized, to dry up rather quickly.

"Of course the big question is what Castro has up his sleeve to prevent us or the Americans from seeking revenge on him personally once the hostages are released."

"My guess," said General Malinsky, who had just reentered the room, "is that he has no intention of releasing the hostages, at least not all of them. That would be the only solution for him. There is no way that world public opinion would even bat an eye at an American invasion after this, and once the U.S. gets its forces mobilized that is the only thing that might stand in their way."

"There would be precedent enough for that," agreed Osman. "Didn't Stalin hold onto German and Japanese prisoners of war for years? And our Vietnamese brothers-in-arms allegedly still have Americans there.

"I suggest that we all adjourn to our respective offices to supervise our subordinates' activities. There is little we can do now until we get some reply from Moscow. I also suggest that you take time to shower and shave and eat if you have the stomach for it. This could be a long couple of days."

As the men filed out of the room Osman took Kurupatin aside. "I want you to delegate your best man to look to the defense of the compound, someone with combat experience. I want an inventory of functional weapons and a list of people trained to use them. I'm not sure what we're going to do, but that seems like a step that will at least help morale."

"That would be Gregorevich. He was Spetsnaz before we recruited him into the KGB, and he won a chestful of medals in Afghanistan."

"Good, brother," Osman said, in a low voice. "Maybe I'm being overly optimistic, but I have a feeling that there may be a way for you and me to get out of this with our skins. Oh, also," he added, "I want your sources to concentrate on how much backing Castro has for this gamble. Are there opposing factions? And where is that lickspittle Raul?"

*   *   *

Featherstone glanced around the conference table at his country team. It was comprised of Popper, the political advisor, Martin, the post administrative and security officer, the consul, John Everly, Alice Van der Bourg, the head of USIS (the United States Information Service), Jaime Epstein, the head of the political section, and Maj. Emilio Rodriguez, the army attaché. Like its Soviet counterpart, this conference room was supposedly proof against "audio penetration," i.e., bugging, but at this point the Americans knew little that the Cubans did not already know in any case.

Featherstone had sent off his message to Washington and had just rejoined the meeting already in progress.

"I was just saying," Popper said, "that we just got a land-line call from Guantánamo. The Cubans opened a line, and they are apparently not the least concerned that we could do them any harm by hearing the whole story. Of course our people there weren't about to divulge anything over an open line, but we still know better what's going on.

"They did hit Guantánamo this morning, hard." Popper had served three tours in Vietnam, two in the Special Forces and one as a Department of Defense civilian employee. He had seen his share of combat, but his eyes had an exceptionally hard look and his jaw was set as he spoke. "The estimate we were given was over two thousand prisoners taken and about a thousand other casualties, many of them from nerve gas. They guessed at about five hundred Cubans killed and even more wounded. They've even taken about two dozen prisoners themselves. There is still an organized defense of sorts, and the Cubans seem to have gotten a bloody enough nose to prefer to try negotiating a surrender rather than risk another direct assault. I suppose," he added sadly, "that the sons of bitches would rather have live hostages than dead ones. If the base commander does surrender I would expect that would put about four thousand Americans in Castro's hands, maybe more."

"I wonder where Castro came up with his figure of seven thousand," Featherstone mused.

"I've been giving that some thought," said Everly, the consul, who had been jotting figures on a yellow pad. "If you figure an optimistic estimate on his part of how many he would take at Guantánamo, plus the hundred or so of us and our dependents—" every head snapped up at this, and all eyes drilled into Everly. He had dared to say what they all knew was true but had not wanted to admit out loud. "Sorry," he said nervously, "well, we still come up way short, unless you take a rough guess at the number of American civilians on the island."

"This isn't exactly a major tourist attraction," Epstein remarked.

"The Cubans have been pushing family reunion-type visits for Cuban exiles lately," Everly countered. "We thought it was to raise hard currency, but maybe this was all part of a well-laid plan. There are also always several hundred Venceremos Brigade types or general American leftists, basking in the glory of the Isle of Youth and the People's Revolution." All at the table were aware that during the heyday of radical chic in the 1960s and early 1970s hundreds of middle-class American youths, eager to experience the Cuban Revolution for themselves, had travelled to Cuba to take part in weeks or months of sugarcane cutting, political indoctrination classes, and, for some of them, even paramilitary training. However, the novelty of this endeavor had waned during the early 1980s due to Cuba's military involvement in Africa as a Soviet surrogate. There had been a brief upsurge during the late 1980s, growing out of displeasure with American policy in Central America, but Cuba's rejection of the democratization process that occurred in Eastern Europe in 1989 had driven away all but the most diehard friends of Castro.

Featherstone turned to Popper. "Carl, have your people got anything at all on this?"

"I'm sorry to say that we have no contact with any of our sources, but, given the fact that none of them even gave us a clue of what was afoot, I think we can assume that they are either not in any position to know anything of value or they're working for the other side. Maybe some Cuban source overseas will pick something up, but we're not in any position to go out and make meetings here anyway, even less than usual. Just as a piece of personal speculation, though, I suspect that if Castro kept this from the Russians as well as us, and the Russians have had thirty years of asshole buddy contact to make all sorts of penetrations, this thing must have been more closely held than the crown jewels. No one's sources knew because only one man knew the whole story and he wasn't talking. That may sound like a cop-out, but that's the only way I can explain to myself how the Russians got taken in too."

"There's no doubt about that," Featherstone agreed. "I'd give my eyeteeth to know just how close to the edge old Fidel is playing this. Anyway, there isn't much else for us to do now except to wait for Washington. Meanwhile, I have a date with a Soviet down the street."

Popper raised his eyebrows but said nothing.

Featherstone walked out of the Interests Section building. It ostensibly belonged to the Swiss Embassy, under whose protection the American diplomatic presence in Cuba operated, just as the Cubans worked under Czech sponsorship in Washington. He was not too surprised that the guards paid him little attention. There would be surveillance, of course, and so far as he was concerned it was like leaving a jail cell to walk in the exercise yard, not much of a change. After walking about two blocks through the largely deserted streets he met Ambassador Osman at the corner and time they had arranged on the phone earlier.

The two professionals exchanged the pertinent information in their possession in a matter of minutes, naturally withholding anything that they considered at all sensitive for their own side. After all, they had not had any formal instructions yet from their respective governments, and each was taking something of a risk in discussing the issue with the representative of a still officially hostile government.

At last Osman turned to Featherstone and asked, "How many Americans are there in your mission all told? Do you have any kind of physical security against forced entry?"

Featherstone thought for a moment. Osman could probably get this information back at his office in any case. "About eighty, actually at post and counting families. Thank God there are no children here now. As far as security goes we have six marine security guards and a few privately owned weapons. If the Cubans want in, we're in about as good shape as the embassy in Tehran was, maybe worse. Why do you ask?"

"I've just been thinking. It hasn't come to it yet, but it might occur that providing security for our people for even an hour or two might be important at some point. We're not in much better shape than you are, but we are about four hundred at last count in the compound. That includes, unfortunately, a large number of dependents of technicians and advisors who are in custody. I would estimate, though, that we could field about forty armed men in a pinch. It probably won't matter, but I wanted you to know that I am taking it on my own authority to offer your people the protection of our compound, as much as it is in our power to give, if you ever decide you want it."

Featherstone stared at Osman for a long minute, frowning. "A lifetime of enmity is hard to put aside over a stroll in the park, but my immediate reaction is to thank you sincerely, and I think it best to go with that. I only hope we never have to impose on you."

"I'll keep a bottle of Stolichnaya on ice, just in case."

Chapter Seven

Jacob Wiznezhsky unbuttoned his overcoat as he trotted from his car to the west entrance of the White House. It was a brisk day but still unseasonably warm for Washington. Wiznezhsky had been national security advisor to President Bush for only about four weeks, and this was his first real crisis. There had been coup rumors in Thailand, the assassination of an Italian legislator by the Red Brigades, and constant turmoil and bloodshed in the Middle East in general, but those were not matters on which the fate of the world might turn.

Wiznezhsky had studied international relations and had even specialized in crisis management during his more than two decades at Duke and Yale, as both graduate student and professor, and had written reams on the subject both for academia and as a government consultant to the Reagan administration, but this one, for the first time, was *his*.

It was funny, he thought. He had always imagined crises taking place around midnight, the strange comings and goings at odd hours, the slamming of car doors, government officials showing up for cabinet meetings in their overcoats and pajamas. But here he was in the late afternoon. His beeper had gone off just as he was ordering coffee after a very nice lunch at "1789" in Georgetown with the

47

British ambassador. He had made a point of grabbing the waiter and paying the check as he ran off after hurried apologies. Washington was a place where rumors about a Jewish official intentionally having himself called away just as the check came could get started more easily than a fire in a match factory.

He had stopped at his own office to pick up the latest traffic and had almost lost his steak au poivre vert at the message from Havana. He knew that no one at the National Security Council meeting would be asking for the reason for the summons.

When he rushed into the conference room, after passing through the mandatory security checks by the Secret Service, he found everyone but the president already present, at least everyone he expected to see. Secretary of Defense Cheney was talking quietly with Maj. Gen. Albert Weems, recently appointed as chairman of the Joint Chiefs of Staff. Adam Leach, the relatively new secretary of the treasury, fiddled nervously with his fountain pen and did not look up when Wiznezhsky entered. "Judge" Webster of the CIA was poring over papers on a clipboard in his lap, and Secretary of State Baker was talking on a secure telephone.

Just then the president blew into the room, accompanied by his press secretary, Larry Donka, his usual warm smile replaced by a rather pale, nervous look. His customary handshake and brief personal word with each person present were obviously going to be dispensed with today. Baker hurriedly hung up the phone and all conversation ceased.

"Gentlemen," said the president as he pulled up his chair and all eyes turned toward him, "you all know why we're here. Let's save time and go to General Weems first and then Judge Webster for any updated information they might have since Havana 2358 and 2359 came in." He was referring to Featherstone's original telegram and the follow-up from the consul on the possible number of Americans being held hostage.

General Weems cleared his throat and picked up a sheaf of papers from the conference table. "What little radio traffic we've been able to get from Guantánamo basically confirms the mission's reporting thus far. As of half an hour ago some of our forces were still holding out. A local ceasefire is in effect and has been for several hours. The acting base commander, Navy Captain Meese, has requested discretion in surrendering if immediate help cannot be promised him.

"We have placed all air force units in the southeast on full alert, along with the 2d Marine Division, 82d Airborne, and the 7th and 9th Light Infantry Divisions. Task Force 65, which includes the aircraft carrier *Nimitz*, has been directed to proceed from off Bermuda toward Guantánamo at full speed and Task Force 61, including the battleship *New Jersey*, has been ordered to put to sea from New Orleans and head toward the north coast of Cuba. I suggest we call up the Air National Guard for the Gulf states as an additional security measure and place the 101st Airmobile, the 29th Mechanized, and 1st Cavalry Divisions on alert as well.

"Meanwhile, we have aerial reconnaissance birds en route from southern Florida to try to confirm the Russian portion of the story, but radio intercepts seem to confirm that as well."

"Thank you, General," the president said, scribbling notes on a yellow pad. "Judge Webster?"

"I would be less than candid if I did not say up front that this incident has caught us completely by surprise." He stared over his reading glasses at the assembled officials and went on, "even now, with a couple of hours' hindsight to work from, neither DDI, DDO, NPIC,* DIA, nor NSA can point to any crumb of information from any source that would have indicated anything like this occurring. Needless to say, NSA is now directing its full attention to Cuba and anything worldwide related to Cuba, and we have a real-time imagery satellite moving into geosynchronous orbit over Cuba right now. It should be in place within the hour. The DDO is scouring its human sources on five continents for information, but I suspect that the only people who know what's really happening and what's going to happen

---

*DDO, Deputy Directorate of Operations; DDI, Deputy Directorate of Intelligence; NPIC, National Photographic Interpretation Center (satellite photos).

are all in Havana, within about fifty yards of Fidel Castro. Naturally, I have tasked our Special Operations people with working on a scenario for a rescue attempt, but that does not look like a viable option to me at this point.

"The one remotely positive angle of this is that NSA and our humint sources agree conclusively that the Soviets have been taken as much by surprise by all this as we have. I suppose it could be a hoax of a monumental scale, but my judgement is that the Russians have been victimized just like us. Consequently, instead of having to compete with the Soviets' impressive capabilities, we might actually hope for some level of cooperation. On the other hand this will also imply that we will need to coordinate actions with them, both out of deference to their own involvement and to prevent their taking some unilateral action that might jeopardize our position."

"Thank you, Judge," the president said, taking off his glasses and rubbing his eyes with thumb and forefinger. "Jim, what's new on your front?"

Baker adjusted his seat and leaned forward for emphasis, "The UN General Assembly is scheduled to meet in emergency session tomorrow at 10 A.M. Our game plan is to go for a strongly worded resolution condemning Cuba and calling for the immediate release of the hostages. The text of Castro's message has only just become public, and it will be difficult for a lot of the delegations to get specific guidance from home in time for a vote. This will actually work in our favor, as we have all night for our people to buttonhole delegates and try to get their votes. This would obviously be a good time for the Agency to call in any debts outstanding to people at the UN." He paused and glanced at Webster, who nodded his assent.

"Certainly we can expect the support of the Soviets on this one, as well as from the NATO allies and Israel. The Soviets don't have the pull they used to have with the Eastern Europeans since the disbanding of the Warsaw Pact, but they should be able to swing enough votes for us to get us a comfortable majority, especially with the high abstention rate I expect from the Third World. Once we have this resolution in hand we'll be in a strong position to whittle down the Cubans' demands, probably obtain gradual release of the hostages, and possibly, and this is my own speculation, deprive Castro of the quick kill he is probably counting on to keep his own people in line."

Judge Webster raised a finger. "I'd like to second that. The great unknown here is how much backing Castro has internally. Here he is literally putting his country's life on the line, and the very secrecy of the move implies that he didn't consult with very many people beforehand. There's no question that Cuba has one of the most efficient and repressive security networks in the world, but there will always be those around Castro with an eye out for a weakness to exploit. If this thing drags on and starts to cost Cuba dearly, and it's already cost them quite a number of lives, any opposing factions will have plenty of ammunition to use against Castro. Naturally, anything we can do to keep him from seeming to score an immediate victory would work to this end."

"Very well," said the president. "Let's go around the table and get some suggestions. Please say what you think. This is just a discussion session, and I don't think we can rule anything out at this point. No one's staking out a position here. I just need some options to toss around in my head, and we can refine them as more information comes in."

Cheney motioned for General Weems to start. "About all I can suggest for now is to enact the alerts I have mentioned so that we'll be in a position to do something when the time comes. The lead time between the start-up order and when our forces could be in action is our biggest enemy, and whatever we can do to cut that time down will stand us in good stead. I would also suggest a military demonstration, something that would not put any hostages at risk. One option that you might consider would be an air strike to take out every Cuban naval unit we can find. That would both show the Cubans that we are pissed and tend to show the Cuban military that this adventure is going to cost them some of their toys. We would need strong air cover, but I would stay away from preemptive strikes on their airfields until we get a better fix on where the hostages are.

"I am also sorry to conclude that any kind of effort to support the few men still holding out at Guantánamo would be counterproductive. From our information, the Cubans can overrun them in a matter of minutes whenever they decide they are willing to pay the price. An air strike from the mainland would have to fight its way across the width of Cuba, and the Cubans are obviously ready for them. The losses would just be too high. I suggest granting Captain Meese the discretion to surrender that he has requested."

"I endorse General Weems's thoughts," said Webster, "but I would put off any military action at all until after the UNGA vote tomorrow to show that we have a clear mandate for action. We might want to look into a way to get the Soviets involved directly if that's physically possible. Another point is that we should make a public announcement as soon as possible, both summing up the nature of the incident and describing our military mobilization. When we were dealing with the Soviets we didn't have to tell them we were putting units on alert. Their SIGINT capability told them immediately. Now that we're dealing with a second-rate technology, we'd better make sure they get the signals we're trying to send."

Baker leaned forward again. "I would agree with all of that with the stipulation that we make negotiation the centerpiece of our overall plan. I'm convinced that Castro won't be able to stand the universal opprobrium he'll be receiving over this for long. I'm also convinced that most of his demands can be trimmed down substantially. For example, his dollar figure for reparations is certainly blue sky, and I suspect that his definition of which nations are Third World and which aren't is open to some maneuvering. I don't suppose he gives a damn about El Salvador's debt, or South Africa's. When he's under the gun, I'll bet he just looks out for Number One, which means that we won't be out much at all in terms of money."

Secretary of the Treasury Leach came next. "Foreign affairs is hardly my bailiwick, much less military operations. I can only say that if we take Castro at his word and have to forgive the debts of even most of the Third World, we're in for the worst economic ride since 1929. You'll remember that he wants us to pay off all the outstanding debts of Third World nations to non-communist creditors, which would run into the hundreds of billions of dollars, but even if we lost only the outstanding loans of American banks to those governments we'd have businesses falling like a house of cards. Now

I'm assuming like Secretary Baker that the $100 billion in reparations is mainly a bargaining chip, but I can only warn you that we have to avoid this debt thing. I can envision a fat and happy Europe and Japan watching us founder and then coming in to pick up the pieces."

Wiznezhsky listened to each speaker in turn, fascinated by the juxtaposition of his academic studies and real life. He had often read and written about the inner workings of committees and similar groups operating under pressure, everything from studying the transcripts of governmental meetings like this to experiments conducted with teams of university students acting out roles. One of the phenomena he had noted was what is called "groupthink," a process in which members of a committee unilaterally soften their positions, trying to shoot for a reasonable-sounding middle ground so as not to appear too radical. The goal is to guess at what one's colleagues want and compromise beforehand, regardless of what one really thinks. The great peril to avoid is being left alone, standing against the majority. While the fear of losing one's job has something to do with this, it is more a subconscious process of acting out what a person thinks people are supposed to do when working in a group. Wiznezhsky was not certain whether his opinion was affected by his conscious desire to avoid this pattern or whether he really did disagree.

"I realize that I'm new to the team and quail before the combined global experience in this room," he began with typical academic self-effacement, "but I have some serious doubts about our general direction here. My main concern is that there are several key elements of the problem that we are not considering. First, we have to admit that this entire operation was executed with singular brilliance, whatever Castro's ultimate motives, and we should not assume that he has made many mistakes. There is the very big question of how he expects to avoid our revenge once the hostages are released. He has something up his sleeve. Maybe he just plans to hang onto a few hostages indefinitely, but that seems too simple for the rest of the scenario.

"Second, I think we had better not take for granted our support in the UNGA. I agree that the vote there tomorrow is vital to our position, but the Cubans seem to have left us and the Russians pretty much on our own. Castro isn't stepping on anyone else's toes and is offering the Third World a pretty big carrot. There's not much we can do about that, but we had better not assume anything right now.

"Lastly, regarding military action, I think that we should make a decision fairly soon as to whether we intend to invade and conquer all of Cuba and accept the deaths of most of the hostages, or forget the whole thing. This isn't Entebbe. This isn't even Iran. You don't have a handful of hostages guarded by a handful of terrorists or a handful of hostages guarded by a whole army. You have an army of hostages guarded by another army. By now they could have the hostages spread out over the entire country. Also, in regard to the demonstration attack, it seems that we are forgetting Castro's threat to kill hostages in the event of any kind of attack. There is nothing we can do to protect the hostages, so we had better make the decision right now whether this demonstration is worth the lives of a hundred or a thousand or however many hostages Castro decides to off. We can't say he didn't warn us."

Wiznezhsky had given his speech staring at the desk in front of him. This wasn't like lecturing a group of freshmen. When he looked up everyone in the room was carefully staring off into space, expressions set, except for Webster, who regarded him benignly, and the president, who looked at him over his reading glasses with what appeared to be real concern.

"Thank you, Jacob," the president said quietly. "Well, here are your marching orders for now. General, Dick, let's go ahead with the alerts and get the fleet units in position. I think we can also put a lot of planes in the air around Cuba without violating their airspace, just to let them know we're there, and I want those boys to have orders to shoot down anything with the Cuban flag on it they find outside the twelve-mile limit, whether they're fired on first or not. The same goes for the navy and any Cuban surface ships found in international waters." He paused for a moment, looking at Wiznezhsky. "Let's put off the attack on Cuban naval forces for now. We just don't have enough information to go on yet. But it still remains an option," he added, turning to General Weems, who did not appear to be appeased. "And you may communicate to Captain Meese that he is to use his own judgement regarding surrender. Tell him he and his men have done all that could be asked of them, and that we will now do everything in our power to get them home safely."

"Jim," he said, pointing at Baker, "pull out all the stops on the UNGA vote. There is no tomorrow on this one. Let everyone know that we'll evaluate their relationship with the U.S. based on this vote for a long time to come. And Judge, I want a report on my desk tomorrow morning by 0800 hours with a country-by-country breakdown of where every nation stands on this from all sources, technical or human, proven or rumor. Also, Jim, get the Soviet ambassador over here ASAP. We'll see if we can set up a conference call with Gorbachev for later. Adam, do some number crunching for me and let me know how bad the figures look, best case, worst case, and as many variations in between as you, State, and the Agency can imagine."

Lastly he turned to his press secretary. "Larry, let's clear my schedule completely for the next couple of days, except for the meeting tonight with the president of Zaire. I may as well earn my keep and do a little lobbying on the UNGA vote myself," he laughed a little in a self-conscious way and, of course, got the immediate round of chuckles expected of professional bureaucrats. "I want a televised press conference set up soon, and I'll hit all the points we talked about. Let's get to work!"

Everyone rose with the president, who strode out of the room with Donka in tow. The others gathered their papers and moved purposefully out the other door without speaking. Wiznezhsky took his time gathering his things, staring at the floor. When he looked up Judge Webster was leaning against the door frame, smiling at him.

"It's clear that you have a lot to learn about the real workings of bureaucracy," he said in a jovial tone. "Usually what we do is mumble something acceptable here in front of the president and then sort out the dumber things among ourselves later. The important thing is to be a team player."

"I've got a sneaking suspicion that this might be my first and last crisis," Wiznezhsky laughed as he pulled on his coat. "So this is how Disraeli got his start?"

"Let me walk you out to the car," Webster said. "Hmmm, honesty in government, quite a concept. Maybe it will even catch on." The two men looked at each other as Webster put a comradely arm around the younger man's shoulders, and they both said simultaneously, "Naaah!" and walked out laughing, much to the confusion of the Secret Service guard in the hall, who had thought that tensions were supposed to be high.

WASHINGTON, D.C.: 1900 HOURS, 25 JANUARY

A smaller group met again in the Oval Office that evening at seven o'clock. The president sat behind his desk facing Wiznezhsky, Baker, and General Weems. With them now were also the Soviet ambassador, Nicolai Bogdanov, his chief military attaché, Gen. Vladimir Dolgoruki, and the president's Russian-language translator. All were seated in a rough semicircle around the speakerphone on the president's desk. A small red light came on over the speaker, and a delicate rush of static could be heard.

"Hello, Mr. President?" a slightly squeaky voice came through.

"Yes, I'm here. Mr. Secretary General, how good to hear from you."

"I wish we could he speaking under more pleasant circumstances." There was a pause between each exchange as the translating was being done at the Russian end. "I am here with your ambassador and military attaché, as well as my foreign minister and several members of the Soviet High Command. We have been discussing the strategy for tomorrow's UN vote and, as I am sure Ambassador Bogdanov has already informed you, we are working hard to get the resolution passed."

"Yes, Mr. Secretary," the president said, leaning forward toward the speaker instinctively but unnecessarily. "We have been concentrating on the relatively secure votes and moving toward more neutral ground just to see how far we have to go, but things look promising thus far."

"Well done. I have some updated figures that you and the ambassador might wish to note. We were fortunate that the holidays caused a number of our people in Cuba to be out of the country. We had a total in our mechanized brigade of 2,547 men, of whom 432 were killed and 750 wounded; we had 2,465 military advisors of whom 67 were killed and 115 wounded; there were some 1,840 signals intelligence personnel," a shuffling and grumbling noise could be heard in the background over the speaker, and General Dolgoruki winced a bit as well, "of whom 23 were killed and 87 wounded. We have some 513 people in our embassy, none of whom were harmed, including 107 dependents, women and children, and there are a total of 3,987 other Soviet citizens on the island, mostly agronomists, technicians, and a few tourists of whom some 1,230 are women and children. After subtracting the over 500 killed, that leaves some 10,800 Soviets in Cuban hands."

"I am very sorry, Mr. Secretary, for your many dead and wounded."

"Yes," came the voice over the speaker. Then a pause. "We Russians have learned to live with heavy losses, but, contrary to popular misconception, we do not forget them. Every Soviet in this room has either lost a friend on that island or has one there whose life is in extreme danger. Sr. Castro has much to answer for." Another pause. "I have one personal message as well. I regret to inform General Dolgoruki that his son-in-law, Lt. Petr Gregorievich Ivanov, was among those killed fighting against the Cubans. I know it is small compensation, but based on General Akamirov's report, Lieutenant Ivanov has been named a Hero of the Soviet Union."

Wiznezhsky turned toward the general to express his condolences, but the general just stared stonily ahead, without a glimmer of reaction. Wiznezhsky felt a cold chill down his spine, and he thanked God that he had not been the one to provoke that look in the general's eyes.

After a long moment, the president spoke again. "We also have some new figures from our embassy. As you are probably aware, our forces at Guantánamo Bay surrendered an hour ago after resisting for thirteen hours. Of the original 3,615 servicemen on the base, mostly marines and U.S. Navy personnel, 580 are reported killed in action with another 916 seriously wounded. There were also 652 civilian contractors and dependents on the base of whom 62 were killed and 138 wounded. We have 83 people currently in our Interests Section of whom 17 are non-staff women and children. We, too, were lucky that the holidays kept the numbers down. In addition, there were an estimated 2,000 other Americans on the island, about 600 of them Cuban exiles gone home to visit their families for the holidays, and perhaps as many as 1,500 private American citizens in Cuba without official permission or sanction. We understand that all of these have been taken into custody. We therefore estimate a maximum of 6,500 American hostages."

"I share your grief for your fallen as well, Mr. President," the speaker crackled. "Truly, we face a challenge of unprecedented proportions. We have both had to deal with hostage situations of one kind or another in the past, but never on this scale. The political/economic demands made by the Castro government also add an unusual complication, the extent of which I do not believe we can yet appreciate. A great deal of formerly sensitive information has already been exchanged between our two governments at a working level, and I hereby propose that we work jointly in attempting to reach a solution to this problem. I have studied your military precautionary measures, and I find them prudent and timely. My only request is that we be consulted before any further military action is taken."

"Of course, Mr. Secretary," the president affirmed. "We are quite aware that there are nearly twice as many Soviet hostages at risk as Americans. We must work together."

"Quite. In that vein, I wish to inform you that we are sending a naval task force to the Caribbean for possible future use. The new aircraft carrier *Tblisi* had been undergoing its shakedown cruise in the Mediterranean and is currently en route, along with its escorts, including a battalion of naval infantry. A second force is forming even as we speak, composed of the carrier *Kiev*, the cruiser *Frunze*, and an amphibious force that includes a naval infantry regiment from our Red Banner North Sea Fleet. I have no idea whether these forces will be used, but we need to have them in position. I would also request that our respective military advisors work on the possibility of the movement of a Soviet Desant (Airborne) Division and some Air Force squadrons to the southern United States. I know that this is an unusual request," the voice on the speaker added hastily, "and, if your government finds it unacceptable, we will understand, but you will appreciate that this would be the only way that our forces could participate at any appreciable level should military action become necessary."

"I cannot promise anything, Mr. Secretary," the president said, looking around to his nonplussed advisors and seeing nothing but raised eyebrows and shrugging shoulders. "In fact, I never thought I'd live to see the day, and I suspect you never did either, when such a request would sound at all reasonable. I have a meeting with the congressional leaders of both parties right after this conference, and this is one of the matters I promise we will discuss."

"Thank you, Mr. President."

"Thank *you*, Mr. Secretary, and we'll be in touch tomorrow after the UNGA vote."

Baker and the Soviets rose to leave. "The ambassador and I will be flying up together to New York now to work the halls at the UN personally," Baker said.

"Get on it, Jim," the president said, giving a half-hearted thumbs-up sign.

After the Soviets had left, General Weems put his head in his hands and said, "Soviet paratroopers in Florida? I must be dreaming."

"I know what you mean, General," the president soothed, "but we have to keep one thing in view. We've been dealt a pretty poor hand on this one, and we're going to have to play it out. However, whatever the outcome of this emergency, some good might actually come out of it if, by the way we handle ourselves, we can forge ties to the Soviets and put behind us nearly a century of bad feelings. The more superficial editorialists make it a habit of talking about all the wonderful "opportunities" we have for improving relations, easing tensions. I notice it's always the United States that has the opportunities that usually involve caving in on something, but this really is an opportunity to make some good out of a bad situation."

"I don't suppose it's occurred to anyone that this might be the whole point of this operation," the general opined, gazing at the ceiling. "I mean a large Soviet fleet, with marines, right off our coast, and goddamn paratroopers on the ground. What if the Cubans and Soviets are still in bed together and this whole thing is a hoax just to get their foot in the door?"

"Really, General!" Wiznezhsky moaned. "Do you think that five thousand paratroopers and half as many Soviet marines can conquer America? They've just evacuated Eastern Europe, cut their ground, air, naval, and nuclear forces, to say nothing of making some real progress toward pluralist democracy at home, and NOW they think it's the moment to storm New York? Don't forget that, while this is the biggest armada the Soviets have ever put together for long-distance operations, they're going to be right in the middle of the bulk of our navy too and sitting in the lap of the air force. That would be the worst possible move they could make, if war were on their minds."

The president could see that Wiznezhsky was just getting wound up, so he cut in. "Thank you, Jacob," he said, silencing his national security advisor. "I tend to think that it's unlikely that this is a cooked-up job, but it is a question that needed to be asked. Naturally, if, and I say IF, we let some Soviet units base in the United States, we'd want to take the appropriate precautions. We'd just want to be sure that it was done discreetly. I think the Russians would understand, but the press would have a field day. But that is definitely a bridge we don't have to cross yet. Now, I have a state dinner to attend, and I suspect you gentlemen have enough to keep you occupied for awhile as well."

Chapter Eight

Osman had certainly seen his share of mass demonstrations. They were a standard part of Soviet life and he had seen copies, more or less good, in China, Ethiopia, East Germany, and of course here in Cuba. They were never spontaneous, but a studied eye could gauge the level of enthusiasm in the crowd and among the marchers. Sometimes there really was fury or joy or sorrow, or whatever emotion the organizers wanted expressed, but that was an exception. If the weather was fine most people took the occasion of a few hours or a whole day off work to stroll or lounge with friends, chat, eat and drink the wares of the street vendors, and generally make a holiday out of it. If the weather was bad one usually saw a sullen throng rapidly going through the evolutions required in order to get home as quickly as possible.

The demonstration heading toward the Soviet Embassy did not impress him. There were the regulation number of banners, but they were all made at the same place and bore only two or three different messages, attacking the Soviets and their American "masters," with no sign of anything remotely original. There were organizers along the edges of the crowd like sheepdogs with their flock, shouting out the chants, which you could never understand anyway, but the answer from the crowd was decidedly subdued. All in all a pretty mediocre show, he thought, as he sipped his coffee on the roof terrace of the embassy.

Castro had made the public announcement last night on television and radio, repeated hourly since, that the military action of the previous day had resulted from the murder of his brother, Raul, minister of defense, at the hands of a drunken Soviet Army lieutenant who had then taken refuge in the base of the Soviet mechanized brigade. When the Cuban authorities had demanded that the culprit be turned over for trial they were met, the story went, with a hail of gunfire that killed an additional six unarmed Cuban policemen. Consequently the Cuban Armed Forces, under the personal direction of the First Soldier of the Revolution himself, had stormed the base, although the original criminal was killed in the assault.

Castro admitted that he and the rest of the Politburo had become somewhat carried away with the emotion of the moment, but they had decided "as one man"—Osman chuckled to himself with nostalgia at the Stalinist phraseology—to eliminate the foreign military domination and humiliation of Cuba once and for all, and had ordered the attack on the American base at Guantánamo and the arrest of all Russians and Americans on the island. Faced with the need to defend themselves against the unjust wrath of two nuclear superpowers, Castro was forced to hold the prisoners hostage until some kind of guarantee of Cuba's sovereignty could be arranged. The demand for elimination of Third World debt was something of an afterthought, but the Politburo had cheered the idea as long overdue.

Osman smiled again. As bad as things might look, some chinks were appearing in Castro's armor. Of course he had to concoct some kind of story for the people, but the total surprise of the move implied that a number of very powerful people had also been kept in the dark, particularly most of the military, who had largely been loyal to Raul. The chronology of the story did not hold together well, as the soldiers would know, in that the attack on Guantánamo was simultaneous with that on the Soviets, not subsequent to it as Castro claimed. If they noticed this discrepancy the whole story of Raul's death would start to smell, and then their reaction might be quite interesting. In any event, Kurupatin's remaining agents would begin spreading this theme around in a discreet fashion.

The snakelike column that now approached the embassy was Raul's funeral cortege. In the center of the throng Osman could just make out the guard of honor surrounding an armored personnel carrier with Raul's coffin on top. The crowd had been kept back about fifty yards from the coffin, and Castro followed on foot, alone and bareheaded. What a showman, Osman thought.

As Osman watched, the rhythm of the chanting of the crowd was broken by a dull roar. He put his binoculars to his eyes and saw another large group coming out of a side street. At first he thought it was just another workers' contingent, but this group was different. It numbered only about two or three hundred so far as Osman could tell, as opposed to the two hundred thousand or so in the main group, but the men in it were running, not trudging as were the others, and they carried homemade signs and red flags, not manufactured banners; Osman could not make out their legends, however. They also carried baseball bats and broom handles.

The smaller group charged into the main column just ahead of Raul's coffin. The official marchers scattered like rabbits and the few policemen posted along the march route were brushed aside. Then the intruders ran headlong into the double ranks of soldiers that formed a hollow rectangle around the coffin.

The soldiers fought back with rifle butts and bayonets at first, but soon shots began to ring out, and then automatic weapons fire. Most of the main column of marchers had moved off about a hundred yards and many of them now took off—for home, probably. Prudent, Osman thought. Some of the rioters were calling to members of the march and some of the marchers were joining them.

Suddenly, several official-looking cars roared through the mob on the far side of the column. The soldiers managed to get out of the way in time, but Osman saw at least one woman, or perhaps a young girl, run over by each car in turn. The cars screeched to a halt next to Castro and the circle of bodyguards that had materialized around him. He could see Castro, one foot inside the largest car, gesturing furiously in the direction of the rioters before he disappeared inside, followed by two stocky bodyguards dressed in white guayabera shirts and brandishing submachine guns.

Osman saw one rioter smash a soldier full in the face with a baseball bat. The soldier toppled over backwards, his face spouting blood. The rioter then picked up the soldier's AK-47 and let rip on full automatic into the packed mass of troops around the armored personnel carrier. Several more soldiers fell before the rioter was himself killed, but now truckloads of fresh troops were arriving. Not bothering with crowd control methods, these troops opened fire directly into the crowd, without sparing the overly curious marchers who had not been wise enough to vacate the area.

The actual rioters, now numbering less than two hundred, a number of whom had obtained rifles, were gradually retreating up the avenue in the direction of the embassy. Osman could tell from their movements that there were combat veterans in that group, as they used cover and controlled their firing.

"My God, did you see that?" shouted Kurupatin as he came puffing across the roof to where Osman was sheltering behind the wall at the edge of the building.

One of the armed KGB men posted at a corner of the roof let out a whoop and yelled, "Kill the bastards!" in Russian.

"Keep that weapon out of sight," Osman snapped. "They're going to blame us for this anyway. No point in giving them film footage of the 'snipers' on the roof of the Soviet Embassy.

"By the way, Comrade Colonel," Osman said, turning to Kurupatin, "*did* we do this?"

"As much as I would like to take credit for it, no," admitted the red-faced KGB *rezident*. "One of the signs I could read said 'Death to Castro, Murderer.' I can only suspect that they are very pro-Russian or very anti-Castro people who put something together on their own. Perhaps it's actually a prodemocracy group, as in Eastern Europe, that is just using this as a pretext for a showdown."

"Well," Osman observed coolly, "they should have brought a few more cowboys with them. It's just about over."

A tank and several armored cars had now joined the government troops and were hosing down the street with machine-gun fire. The few rioters who had not fled or who were not already dead now made a break for the embassy gate.

"Oh, no!" moaned Osman. "Don't open the gate!" he yelled to the guards below. "Everyone back inside the building! Run!"

The KGB guards looked about confusedly for a moment and then broke for the main entrance, where other guards were rolling down the metal shutters. Some of the rioters reached the gates and tried to climb over, but the soldiers had caught up with them and bayonetted them off the bars. From the screaming Osman could tell that others had been caught in front of the ten-foot wall around the compound as well. A moment later the firing stopped, and Osman could hear the wail of ambulance sirens approaching.

Osman slumped down with his back propped up against the wall. "Now that was *interesting*."

"That's not the adjective that jumped into my mind right off," Kurupatin said as he sat down next to Osman.

"Well, let's put some of the pieces together, shall we?" Osman said. "From your own reporting, it seems that while the attack on Guantánamo was run essentially by the regular army the attack on our brigade was done almost exclusively by the TE, Castro's pampered pets. The arrests of our advisors were conducted by the G2, not the military or police. That implies limited military involvement in the plot.

"Now, we know that Raul wasn't killed by a Russian. Of course Castro had to come up with a good story for popular consumption, but Raul is evidently very really dead. So that further implies that this whole thing is strictly Castro's one-man show.

"Lastly, we see this rather mediocre demonstration, not much public enthusiasm, capped off by a wild display of opposition, for whatever motive. And *we* didn't organize it. That implies that our friend, Fidel, is skating on very thin ice in terms of support for a very big gamble. My grand conclusion to all of this is that he'll really need to show a spectacular victory to keep his own head. He pulled off the gloves first, probably blew away his own brother into the bargain, and there are some other Cuban sharks out there eager for a chance at power. An 'acceptable' solution just won't do for him anymore. It's really going to have to be monumental."

"You're reaching a little," Kurupatin said, then paused, "but not much. Yes, I think there's something to work with here."

"Let's write it up and send it off to Moscow. They could use some good news."

Chapter Nine

Secretary of State James Baker sat at a desk behind the American ambassador to the United Nations as the General Assembly convened. He had showered and shaved and downed several cups of coffee to disguise the fact that he had not slept the night before, and he sat upright with a look of intense interest to disguise the fact that he felt drained and beaten. The opening formalities had just begun, but Baker knew that the joint American-Soviet resolution was already defeated.

Through hours of intense lobbying the night before, he had learned that out of over a hundred votes to be cast, the resolution condemning Cuba and calling for an immediate release of the hostages would garner barely two dozen. There would be a number of abstentions from the wafflers, including a number of the NATO allies, but the negative votes would outnumber the affirmative ones by nearly three to one. The CIA report provided both to the president and to himself earlier that morning had only confirmed what he, the UN delegation staff, and the Soviets had learned by bitter experience. Simply put, the attraction of a cancellation of the debt of the Third World, however achieved, was too strong a narcotic for most countries to forego. Only Britain, Israel, and the Netherlands had actively supported the resolution, and the Soviets had been able to hold the Eastern Europeans in line with the argument that they would lose any hope of financial help from the West if these kinds of resources were suddenly diverted to the Third World, but that was about it. A few other votes had been swung into line, including Zaire's, thanks to the president, but not nearly enough.

The American ambassador was reading the resolution now, but Baker had been over it so many times in the past twelve hours that he could have mouthed the words from memory. It deplored the needless loss of life, accused the Cubans of unprovoked aggression, demanded the immediate return of all hostages, and called for the creation of a UN commission to study the issue of Third World debt, as if this hadn't been done before. It agreed to the withdrawal of all Soviet personnel, including diplomats, from Cuba, proposed the closing of both Cuban and American Interests Sections in their respective countries, and even recognized the loss of Guantánamo as a fait accompli. The Joint Chiefs had balked at that one, but the president wanted to remove all possible roadblocks to getting the hostages out, or more precisely, to make clear that the hostages were being held for ransom, not out of any sense of offended nationalism. The resolution even promised that no military action against Cuba would be undertaken if the other elements of the resolution were adopted promptly. Lastly, it called for three-way talks between the United States, the USSR, and Cuba to resolve the issue, in order to get the problem out of this circus at the UNGA.

As planned, the Soviet ambassador to the UN had spoken next, adding his arguments to the Americans'. He noted that the Soviet troops and advisors had been in Cuba at that government's request and that no suggestion had ever been received that they were no longer welcome.

Baker expected the Cuban ambassador to give his counterarguments, but the Mexican ambassador stood instead. Baker adjusted his earpiece to listen to the instantaneous translation and was appalled to hear the Mexican introduce a counterresolution. He made an impassioned speech declaring that, while any loss of life is deplorable, thousands of men, women, and children were dying daily in the

Third World as the result of the economic and military aggression of the industrialized countries. He stated that the world must take into consideration the circumstances that caused the outbreak of violence in Cuba, repeating verbatim Castro's story of Raul's death and its aftermath, and adding that even this incident probably would not have resulted in significant violence had it not been for the pent-up tensions brought on by centuries of exploitation of the South by the North.

The Mexican ambassador then outlined his own resolution as the American and Soviet delegations took frantic notes. Another surprise, thought Baker.

The Mexican resolution recognized the right of any nation to defend its territory against foreign military forces. It recognized the existence of economic aggression as a crime against world peace equal in importance and horror to armed aggression. It recognized the right of weaker nations to use whatever means were at hand to eliminate injustices perpetrated on their soil by more powerful states and to protect themselves from violent reaction. Getting more specific, it called for an end to violence in Cuba but placed the blame for the violence squarely with the industrialized powers, which had intentionally ignored the just pleas of the lesser-developed nations for a redress of the gross imbalance in the consumption of the world's resources, thereby forcing the poorer nations to resort to more intense methods to get their case heard. It found the Cuban proposals moderate, even generous, and suggested that further negotiations be begun under UN auspices.

While the reading of the American resolution had been met with the scraping of chairs and assorted murmurs around the Assembly Hall, the Mexican resolution was followed by thunderous applause, culminating in a standing ovation.

Several other nations took the floor to support the Mexican proposal: Nigeria, Indonesia, India, Libya, and Brazil. Baker began to tune them out. Oh well, he thought, they've been passing anti-Israeli resolutions in the General Assembly for ages, but American and Soviet vetoes in the Security Council always keep them from having any teeth. Still, there went the game plan as far as "seizing the moral high ground." Baker was about to leave the hall so as not to be present during the certain humiliation of the votes when the loud humming that filled the hall was suddenly hushed.

The Chinese ambassador had taken the floor and was reading from a prepared text. After a brief statement of support for the Mexican resolution, he announced that the taking of hostages (he was the first speaker to use the term) was certainly a measure unbecoming a law-abiding nation, but that his government understood from its own experience that weakness in the face of overwhelming military power can force a country to take desperate steps in a just cause. For this reason his government had decided, in consultation with the government of Cuba, to emplace several medium-range ballistic missiles equipped with nuclear warheads on Cuban soil.

The roar that went up from the delegates in the hall was deafening, but Baker could hear the continuing translation of the ambassador's speech in his headphones. The missiles, he went on, would remain under Chinese control and would be guarded by two divisions of the Peoples' Liberation Army. He added that the missiles and troops were already en route to Cuba and he called upon the member nations of the UN to ensure the free use of international waters to effect this measure.

In conclusion, he stated that once these missiles were in place they would secure Cuba from external aggression, just as the emplacement of Soviet missiles in 1962 was to have done. He then launched into a diatribe, accusing the Soviet Union of hatching a vicious plot in combination with the United States to ensure their hegemony over the entire world, but added that a new power was being born in the world. This power included all of the true followers of the communist path and their allies who had so recently been abandoned by the USSR and the Eastern Europeans. He announced that a military, economic, and political alliance had been created among China, Cuba, North Korea, Vietnam, Laos, Cambodia, Iran, Libya, Ethiopia, Yemen, and Syria, called the Peoples' Revolutionary Bloc (PRB). He said that the PRB welcomed friendly relations with all nations, regardless of ideology. He then bowed stiffly and returned to his seat.

Baker heard the results of the UNGA votes as he flew back to Washington. The mention of missiles and of the formation of the PRB had actually shaken a few fence-sitters onto the American side in both votes, but the American resolution went down to defeat twenty-four to seventy-three and the Mexican proposal passed seventy-two to twenty-five. Baker noted that a number of major Western European nations had abstained from both votes, probably thinking of their future share of the PRB market, he thought, and Spain, Portugal, and Greece had voted against the U.S. both times. He did not look forward to getting home.

Chapter Ten

Captain Estigarribia had never seen Castro so furious. Certainly the Jefe was given to outbursts of temper, but here he stood before some twenty of the most senior military, police, intelligence officers, and government officials in the country, screaming like a madman. He had literally picked up General Jose Ibarra, chief of the DGCI, Cuba's internal security organization, by the collar and was screaming into his face.

"And where were your shit-eating spies today, comrade?" he shrilled, his face growing redder by the minute. "Here I have just pulled off the greatest strategic coup since Pearl Harbor, and you and your fat, stupid policemen are too busy chasing whores to tell me that *hundreds*, do you hear me, HUNDREDS of people are going to attack my brother's funeral! I can tell you what Washington and Moscow are going to do every day for the next month, and you don't even know what's going on around the fucking corner!"

He shoved the general back into his seat, leaving him pale and shaking. Castro strode around the conference table at which all of the officers were seated in nervous silence. "How many of my soldiers killed? Twenty? Forty? Do you think killing a fucking couple hundred rioters will pay for that?" He thrust a finger again at Ibarra. "I want every person who ever met one of those stinking rioters in prison, and I want them each skinned alive, men, women, and children, until I know who organized that abortion. Look at *this*!" he screamed, leaning low over the table and giving each officer a view of a small scratch near his scalp line where a rock or bottle thrown from the crowd had grazed him. "Just look at this. And you fat asses are paid to protect this government!"

"You're right, of course, Jefe," said Albaro Icaza, head of the PCC/AD, the America Department of the Cuban Communist Party, normally responsible for contacts with and secret funding for pro-communist parties throughout the hemisphere, and also a leading Party ideologue. "However, you have to keep in mind that, in order to pull off your coup, most of us had to be kept in the dark. Quite justifiably, of course," he added hastily.

"You're damn right! If I had told one more of you about my plans, some lickspittle would have scuttled over to his Russian mama to spill his guts."

"Exactly, Jefe," Icaza went on soothingly, "but the price for that secrecy was that none of our offices could work to full potential, not knowing what to go after or what to guard against. Now that we know, we can all put our heads together and tie up the loose ends."

"Loose ends? And who the fuck are you to tell me I have loose ends in my plan?" shouted Castro, giving Icaza the cold, hard look that was the last thing more than one man had seen in this world.

"Oh, it's not your plan that's at fault, Jefe. It's the people," said Icaza, gracefully sidestepping. "You've said yourself many times that the youth of Cuba, the youth you pampered and in which you had such great hope, have gone soft." Always quote the great man to himself. He loves it, thought Icaza. "You saw the lack of enthusiasm at the march, even before the riot. We're asking a lot of the people now. We here at this table know how well thought-out this plan is, but they see only the fringes of it. We need something to get their juices going if we are to expect them to stand tough against both the Yankees and the Russians."

"What do you suggest?" Castro asked, looking suspiciously at Icaza but having calmed down markedly in the past minute.

"What about a victory parade?" Icaza asked.

"What, with troops and tanks and things? They see that too often as it is. They just use it as an excuse to skip work and then don't even show up, half of them."

"No, I thought something more emotional. How about letting the people do the watching instead of the marching. I was thinking of gathering all of the prisoners in their uniforms, with officers in the front, and having them march right through Havana as evidence of our victory. Maybe with their hands behind their necks or something."

"I thought the plan was to keep the hostages—I mean prisoners—separated all over the island, for security," piped up an air force general.

Castro spun to face this new speaker. "That's the trouble with you stiff-necked soldiers. That's why we guerrilleros will always defeat you. You have no flexibility, no imagination. Take the fucking hill! That's all you ever think about. War is ninety percent politics and ten percent fighting. I like your plan, Albarito," Castro said, taking great relief from this suggestion. "I want you to work up a detailed program for my approval.

"There is one additional element of the plan that I have not discussed with the entire group, although Comrade Icaza has been working on it since yesterday," Castro added. "Perhaps you should spell it out for everyone."

"Certainly, Jefe," Icaza began. "As most of you are aware, we have decisively gained the initiative before world public opinion with our inclusion of Third World debt relief as one of our demands. That worked well enough at the level of the UN and with the press of the Third World itself. What we would like to do now is further undermine public opinion in the United States and Western Europe. The Europeans are already wavering, since this entire scheme isn't costing them anything and because they all secretly would welcome seeing both of the superpowers humbled. There isn't much we can do about opinion in the Soviet Union, and despite the 'liberalization' process, it still doesn't count for much anyway. Where we can really hit them hard is in the United States media and the Congress.

"To do this we have come up with the following proposal." Icaza knew, as did everyone else present, that a "proposal" from Castro was rather more than an ordinary proposal, but he wanted to make every effort to keep from ruffling the feathers of the military further. "As you know, among the American prisoners are nearly two thousand civilians. About two-thirds of these are American leftists, true friends of Cuba, and the rest are gusanos who were here visiting relatives. We propose letting them go. We have treated both groups very well since their arrest, and none of them has seen any of the violence involved in the initial assaults on the Soviets or at Guantánamo. I think we can count on the leftists to preach our line to the press back home, as they always have done, and we can make some less-than-subtle hints to the gusanos that any unfavorable comments on their part might affect their family members here. In any case they can't testify to any excesses. This will give us an image of reasonableness and generosity which the media and left-leaning commentators will use to pressure the U.S. government to match.

"We also propose releasing the seriously wounded and the women and children among the official prisoners."

"Wait a minute," said an army general. "These people have seen a lot of what happened, the use of gas, the lack of warning—well, everything." He stopped himself before he raised the question of Castro's story of Raul's death, which most of the military leaders already knew was false. "What's to stop them from talking?"

"I'm glad you asked. Who are they going to tell?" Icaza smiled knowingly and winked at Castro, who was sitting now with a satisfied grin on his face as well. "The deal would be that these prisoners would be released into the custody of a neutral nation on the agreement that they be kept completely incommunicado. We've already had positive indications from the Indians on this. Our message to the Indians would be that if they are not kept totally isolated we will cease to consider them as part of the Third World, which means their debt doesn't get cancelled. If the Americans or Soviets balk, the question for them is whether they prefer to have the prisoners incommunicado here or in India. Certainly no government in the U.S. could defend a refusal in that case. This would make us look even more generous and eliminate the risk of more of the wounded prisoners dying on our hands, which several have already done. It also cuts down the number of useless mouths we have to feed by over five thousand, not an inconsiderable issue given our economy, without seriously decreasing the magnitude of the hostage factor itself."

"Comrades," said Castro smiling warmly, "I think we have them like this!" He held his hand palm-up and made a slow, firm squeezing motion with his fingers. "Now, General Lopez, give us an update on the missile question," he said, rubbing his hands together gleefully.

Gen. Guillermo Lopez, commander of the air force, put on a pair of glasses and read from his notes. "The Chinese transports with the security troops and the initial shipment of missiles, launcher and erector vehicles, and equipment should arrive by February 4. Work is proceeding according to schedule on the base sites, and now that the basing of the missiles has been made public we can add additional personnel and move things forward even more quickly. We estimate that from the time the first missiles are unloaded in Cienfuegos at least one missile will be operational within five days, and within a month all eight will be operational from the temporary launch positions. Construction of the silos is only just beginning, but with the SA-2 and SA-9 batteries we're placing around the launch positions they should be secure enough until the silos are completed."

"But will the Yankees sit still for us putting the missiles in?" asked the navy commander, who, because of the lack of involvement of his service had been the least informed of the commanders to date. "They didn't in '62."

"Last time we didn't have thousands of Yankee hostages, did we?" Castro retorted happily. "More importantly, things have changed since 1962. No one in the U.S. has talked of 'massive retaliation' for years; they aren't about to start a nuclear war with the Chinese to stop us, and we and the Chinese know it."

"But won't that put us in the uncomfortable position of actually having to kill some hostages when their navy tries to stop the transports from arriving?" the navy commander persisted.

"Aha!" Castro gloated. "I think you'll find many things have changed since 1962. We're not dealing with the pussy Russians any more. Cuba was always a sideshow for them, just a convenient way of pulling the Americans' chain. Our allies now see our victory as their victory, and they see it as a question of life and death, of their governments if not of their countries. But please, let me reserve this one surprise for the moment, and just trust me that the missiles will arrive. Excellent, gentlemen," Castro said, totally restored to good humor. "You all have your assignments. Get to work."

Castro rose to leave first by his private entrance; the other members of the group remained standing until he had left and then began to file out by the other exit. Captain Estigarribia stood near the door with another TE officer, and the two followed Gen. Federico Murguia, commander of the western army, out the door. Estigarribia was talking rather loudly with the other TE officer, saying, "Did you see the wound on the Jefe's head? Another inch or two and he could have lost an eye!"

"Yes, scandalous," agreed the TE officer, rather uninterestedly.

General Murguia turned slightly and said, "Yes, a very serious wound. He should have it seen to."

Estigarribia smiled inwardly as he watched the black cloud pass over Murguia's face. Murguia had lost his eldest son in Angola. The son was buried there, somewhere, following Castro's orders not to permit the repatriation of bodies so as not to affect popular morale. The general had arranged at least three trips to Angola to Estigarribia's knowledge, ostensibly to review troops or training, but primarily to visit his son's grave, a typical Latin reaction. But the Cuban withdrawal from Angola had deprived him of even this slim consolation. One step at a time, thought Estigarribia.

Chapter Eleven

Wiznezhsky stared around the conference table at the same group of men that had met the previous day. All were more haggard, more irritable than the day before, as things seemed to go from bad to worse.

The president was still reading the latest intercept traffic on Cuba, but Baker began the discussion. "I, for one, would like to know how it is possible that Chinese missiles could possibly be en route to Cuba, to say nothing of twenty thousand troops, without even a hint from any intelligence source." Baker looked directly at the president, but the question was obviously meant for Judge Webster.

"I won't make any excuses," the Judge began, "for what is certainly another intelligence failure. I can only explain what we know and why we didn't know it sooner." He rearranged some sheets of paper before him, stood up, and walked to a small easel set up against the wall. He removed the cover sheet, which was labelled "Top Secret" and revealed two aerial photographs of what appeared to be freighters.

"This first photograph shows two Chinese freighters in port at Shanghai approximately three weeks ago. You can see that their

78

decks are covered with a canvas awning and that they are docked next to a large covered warehouse. It was deduced, correctly I might point out, that this involved some kind of missile delivery, and it was duly reported as such to the entire intelligence community, including the Pentagon and State." He paused, glancing at Baker, who was carefully studying the photographs. "This second photograph shows one of the freighters at sea, eight days ago, headed southeast across the Pacific. We had originally suspected that the missiles involved were either Silkworms or SCUD rockets for Iran. When the ships did not head toward the Gulf or any other hot spot of the time, the presumption was that missiles were not involved after all. There was no analyst worth his salt who would have been willing to speculate that these were ICBMs headed for Cuba, and none of us in this room would have believed it if he had.

"The story is pretty much the same for the Chinese troops. Two mechanized divisions were reported out of their garrisons about three weeks ago, and again, this was duly reported. However, the assumption was that the divisions had been moved closer to Beijing in preparation for expected demonstrations protesting the 1989 Tienanmen Square massacre. The divisions, of course, never showed up there, and NPIC and NSA were busy looking for them in training areas, border regions, anywhere else they might have been transferred. Since the Chinese had never moved more than a few hundred troops by sea in their history, the ports were not high on our list of places to look, and again, if they had been spotted in a port, there was certainly nothing to connect their presence there with an incident in Cuba that had not occurred yet. In fact, unusual troop activity was reported at two Chinese ports during this period, but it was suggested that this might have to do with reinforcing the Chinese garrisons in the Spratly Islands, which are under dispute with Vietnam.

"What we have here is a classic case of bits of valid information that, in hindsight, appear significant, but that at the time could not be distinguished from the ever-present background noise the intelligence world generates. There are literally hundreds of reports of troop movements, ship loadings, proposals for alliances or the breaking of alliances, etc., etc., each day, but most of them come to nothing. Unless you have the strategic-level information to put the pieces into perspective or such a weight of small pieces that they form a pattern, you have nothing. The former situation implies a penetration, in this case of either the Cuban or Chinese Politburo, which I readily admit we do not have. The latter situation implies a very sloppy foe, which did not apply in this case either. The Chinese side of the equation was handled very carefully, obviously with night work and camouflage, probably timed to avoid our satellite passes, and probably with only a handful of people fully informed of the purpose. In Cuba, I doubt that ten people on the island knew the whole story, and none of them was talking. If the Soviets didn't pick up on it, our chances were virtually nil."

He paused to take a drink of water. "Now, that's what we didn't know. Here is what we know now." He turned the page on the easel again, revealing a diagram of a Chinese missile, side-by-side with an American one for comparison of size, and an aerial photograph of a piece of what appeared to be jungle terrain.

"From the dimensions of the canvas covers on the Chinese freighters and some other indicators, we surmise that the missiles involved are Dong Feng-4s. Those are two-stage, single-warhead missiles with a range of seven thousand kilometers. From our knowledge of Chinese inventories, the location of some of the missiles, and the number of freighters and their capacities, we estimate that no more than eight to twelve missiles are involved."

"What does that mean, from a strategic point of view?" the president asked.

General Weems spoke up. "That would give them coverage basically of everything east of the Mississippi, depending on where they were based."

"Exactly," continued Webster, "and from this second photograph we have an idea of where that will be. The Cubans have apparently been working on two sites. Now that we know what to look for they're obvious, but prior to that the work looked like any large-scale construction project, with the telltale elements being carefully concealed or camouflaged. It looks like they're going for a quick fix, an aboveground setup, and would start building silos at some later date.

One site is in the southeast, near the port of Manzanillo, the other in the center, near Cienfuegos. It's only been since the day before yesterday that work has begun on additional antiaircraft defenses in these areas, since that would have prompted our NPIC people to look for what these defenses were protecting. The fact that two Chinese divisions are coming also implies two sites. I suspect that the Russian lesson has not been lost on the Chinese, and they don't plan to trust the Cubans any farther than they can throw them. With an entire division defending each site there should not be much concern that the Cubans could seize the missiles by a coup de main."

"So," said the president wearily, "where are these missiles now?"

"The departures were staggered, but we have the Chinese troop ships rounding Cape Horn about now, say a week to ten days out of Cuba. One missile carrier is with them and the rest are strung out across the Pacific. There is no indication that any further missile loading is underway, but we did pick up one Chinese freighter that is loaded with F-7M fighter crates, also in mid-Pacific. That is the Chinese version of the MiG-21. These would not add perceptibly to the Cuban air capability, and we suspect that they would be manned by Chinese pilots to add to the security of the missile sites. This would mean that at least some of the missiles would be operational, say, within a month at the outside, perhaps less.

"After all of this bad news, it's only right that we look at the good news that has come out of this, as slim as it is. First, one of the big questions has been answered. We were speculating on how Castro hoped to avoid our vengeance after the return of the hostages. Well, the missiles are his guarantee, so we don't have to worry about him not releasing the hostages.

"The second thing is that we know that there was already some discontent in the military since the execution of General Ochoa and other senior military officers in early 1989 for alleged drug smuggling and corruption. There's always the chance that a rift may develop between Castro, who's taking a tremendous risk for his country on his own authority, and the military, and we may be able to exploit such a rift."

"That's all very well and good, from an academic standpoint," said Secretary of Defense Cheney, "but what are we going to do *now*? The hostages are there *now*, and the missiles will be emplaced before we know what hit us, and then it will be too late to do anything."

"What worked once should work again," chimed in General Weems. "This is an identical situation to 1962 with the Soviet missiles. Our blockade of Cuba worked then, and I don't see why it shouldn't work even better now, since China is even less of a power than Russia was back then. The Russians threatened to overrun West Berlin or all of Western Europe and they could have done it, but they backed down. The Chinese can't do beans to us. I say we set up a naval cordon just outside the two-hundred-mile limit and politely turn the Chinese ships back when they arrive—and sink them if they argue about it. Hell, we could even ask the Russkies to join in, in the spirit of international solidarity. If we can make the Chinese blink, maybe that will be the setback the Cuban military is looking for to unseat Fidel."

"You're overlooking some rather significant differences between 1962 and the world nearly thirty years later," interjected Wiznezhsky. He was trying hard not to sound like a college professor correcting a mediocre term paper, but these men were dealing with the fate of the world here, and they were definitely off on the wrong track.

"First of all," Wiznezhsky said, gesturing with his hands, "the installation of medium-range missiles in Cuba in 1962 really would have altered the nuclear balance of power. The Soviets didn't have more than a handful of missiles that could reach the U.S. from Russia then, and placing them in Cuba effectively bypassed our early warning system along the Arctic Circle. Today, with submarine-launched ballistic missiles as well as air- and submarine-launched cruise missiles, we're open to a nuclear attack from any direction and have been for years. Placing missiles in Cuba won't change that. The only real question in that regard is whether the Cubans are to have control over them. The Chinese have stated that they won't, and the Chinese, for all their bad press over the years, have been scrupulously honest in complying with their international commitments.

From the size of the security force they're sending, it certainly sounds as though they intend to keep control of the missiles and would be able to resist any Cuban attempt to seize them.

"Then there's the question of international support. There was widespread sympathy in 1962, at least in the Western world, for the blockade. From State Department reporting from around the world, it would appear that the exact opposite situation applies today.

"Lastly, there's SDI." Wiznezhsky paused for a moment. He could see that he was not convincing General Weems, but he was too realistic to expect that. If he could convince the president and the others the battle would be won.

"Star Wars is a dead issue for all practical purposes," opined Larry Donka, breaking his usual code of silence at NSC meetings.

"Not really," interjected Cheney. "A lot of the funding has been cut since first proposed, and the Phase One deployment has been indefinitely delayed, but research and development has continued, and we are virtually at production stage on a number of the kinetic kill systems."

"That's just it," continued Wiznezhsky. "SDI probably never would have been the 'astrodome' that President Reagan originally envisioned, and congressional budget cuts made sure of it in any case. The critics of the system always said that in a mass attack enough missiles would always leak through to cause unacceptable damage, thus making the whole system worthless. However, when we're talking about only a handful of missiles, the chance of any leakers getting through is reduced almost to nothing. This means that the danger to us from some screwball nation getting its hands on a missile or two is very much reduced. Now, if we put this argument to Congress, I think the chances of getting a limited defensive system approved are very much better, especially if we can keep it within the bounds of the 1972 Anti-Ballistic Missile Treaty, although I suspect that the Russians would be the last to complain if we didn't. With what we've got on the drawing board and already tested, I suspect we could have a workable system in place, maybe focussing on the air-craft-launched missiles, which have tested well, within a year or two.

This would make our window of vulnerability very small, during which time the missiles in Cuba would be highly vulnerable themselves.

"I guess what I'm getting at is that the risk to our strategic position by letting the missiles into Cuba would be far less costly than the risk to the lives of the hostages by trying to intercept them. The bottom line is, we have some twenty thousand people whom Castro has sworn to kill if we get in his way on this, and I tend to believe him, on the one hand. On the other hand we have some missiles that may not be used in the next couple of years, and I remind you that none has ever been used yet and that the people who own these missiles could launch on us now, if they wanted, and that after that time those missiles won't be a threat to us anyway."

General Weems could feel himself being outflanked. Cheney was obviously thinking about getting a major defense project refunded. Weems, like most professional military men, tended to look upon purely technical strategic programs as stealing funds and attention from the real purpose of the armed forces, which was conventional warfare. Of course, such men recognized the need for nuclear deterrence and fought endless bureaucratic battles to see that their respective services got their share of the nuclear fund pie, but the air force would always insist on its manned bombers, the navy would always look upon ballistic-missile submarines as a burden to the rest of the service, and Weems, as an army officer, always looked askance at the whole thing, since the army had the smallest nuclear role and usually took the deepest budget cuts to pay for the program.

But this was more than just a bureaucratic budget battle for Weems. He sincerely believed that U.S. prestige, credibility, and security were all being seriously challenged and, as yet, the U.S. had done nothing to respond. Like most people, Weems also felt more comfortable with a familiar situation; for him the parallels with the Cuban Missile Crisis of 1962 were inescapable, and the methods that proved so successful then should work again.

"That was wonderfully informative, Dr. Wiznezhsky," Weems said, when Wiznezhsky finally sat back in his chair. "However, I can only see the United States being held for ransom by a penny-ante dictator and this great nation rolling over for it. Here we have a clear opportunity to stop this thing cold, and we're busy arguing about whether they might or might not use the weapons we put into their hands. My suggestion, based on my twenty-five years of military experience at all levels of command," Wiznezhsky took the thinly veiled reference to his own background "reading the papers," "is that we stop the missile carriers on the high seas. If Castro is enough of a barbarian to actually begin massacring the hostages, we should have a plan afoot to launch an immediate rescue mission to save as many of the hostages as possible, and accept the losses.

"What I want to avoid, and this is a possibility that the good doctor has failed to mention, is that the missiles will be installed, the hostages retained, and then Castro starts adding to his list of demands. Evacuation of the Panama Canal bases, cutoff of military aid to El Salvador, et cetera, et cetera. Given the events of the past couple of days, I really don't think that this is beyond comprehension. Then he's got the hostages, *and* we can't even try to save them militarily because we're staring at this limited window of vulnerability. A year or two can be a long goddamn time if you're sitting on a hot stove." Weems sat up, his back ramrod straight, glaring at Wiznezhsky.

"Well, gentlemen," said the president, hoping to avoid open warfare across the conference table, "we appear to have two very strong arguments before us. This isn't the decoration committee for the prom, so I won't ask for your votes. I'm the one who has to decide, and I thank both Dr. Wiznezhsky and General Weems for their very well thought-out presentations. It is clear that there is no school solution to this one, and whatever course I choose will have some very high costs involved." Wiznezhsky and Weems were staring at each other now, both apparently thinking thank you very much, but get on with it.

"My view is that this is more of a political decision than a purely strategic one. There is no doubt that the strategic threat to the U.S. from these missiles is not on a par with that of the 1962 crisis, but I must agree with General Weems that our national prestige is very much in question. I am also concerned about the possibility of expanded demands from Castro if we do not call his bluff now. We learned that total appeasement does not work from our experience with Hitler before World War II.

"The element that I believe is missing from this scenario which was very much in the forefront in 1962 is the threat of total nuclear war. The Chinese have not threatened a nuclear strike if we stop their ships. The only threat hanging over us is that of the hostages, and the threat is not going to lessen by giving in here.

"My decision is this. The navy will declare a two-hundred-mile exclusion zone and will set up a blockade to enforce it. The Chinese ships, which fortunately are neither armed nor escorted, will be stopped and searched at this line and turned back if they are carrying missiles or related equipment. If they refuse they will be *disabled*, not sunk, preferably without loss of life, but I am willing to risk casualties on our side to increase the likelihood of none occurring on the Chinese side. This should decrease even further the chance of a rash Chinese response.

"If Castro's rhetoric suggests that hostages will be put to death, or if our sources inform us that such an action has begun, we must have a plan in hand and troops in position to intervene immediately to secure as many of the hostages as possible while doing the maximum to prevent Cuban civilian casualties from resulting. This operation would also not, I repeat, not have the goal of overthrowing the Cuban government or occupying the island militarily, just the rescue of the hostages. I will discuss this plan with the Soviets first, and offer them the opportunity to participate in both the blockade and in any rescue attempt, to include basing several squadrons of Soviet combat aircraft and a Soviet airborne division at Hamilton Army Airfield, which is just being closed down in southern Texas. I will also ask Secretary Baker to discuss this at an emergency session of the Organization of American States which has been scheduled for to-morrow evening, to attempt to secure its support if not actual par-ticipation."

Wiznezhsky was still looking at Weems and could read in his face the same thought that was burning in his mind: a fucking compromise.

"Well," said the president, trying to break through the heavy atmosphere by changing the subject, "we still have the problem of the debt demand. Adam, what have you come up with?"

"As you know," Leach began, "the Cubans have published their list of Third World countries and, as expected, it excludes most of the countries with decidedly pro-U.S. backgrounds, such as El Salvador, South Korea, Taiwan, etc. It looks like there was some discussion among the members of the new PRB on this one. India figures prominently, but so does Pakistan, probably at the urging of the Arab element, who are interested in an Islamic bomb and are willing to overlook Pakistan's pro-U.S. stance. Mongolia and Afghanistan are not on the list, as they still pretty much take their guidance from Moscow. Syria is on, so is Egypt, but Morocco is not. King Hassan is apparently too pro-U.S. for even the Arabs to stomach.

"That leaves us the question of what to do about it. I propose we make our own offer, separate from the Soviets and insisting that it is also independent of the hostage issue in Cuba. We can offer a complete abandonment of all public-sector debt owed by all Third World nations to the United States, period. As a part of that package we would cancel all government aid programs to nations accepting this offer for the next decade, including funds approved but not disbursed as of a given date. That would limit the amount to a monumental figure but stop short of the ludicrous.

"Now that would be our public offer. We would make no mention of the other provisions of the Cuban demand, i.e., private debt or debts owed to other nations, or of the specific countries on Cuba's Christmas list. In private consultations with each recipient we would make clear that we cannot take responsibility for other nations' finances, nor can we control the private sector to this extent. I will leave this to you professional diplomats to arrange but, as I have discussed already with Secretary Baker, a strong message should be given to each country that this is our gift, not the Cubans'. Their demanding any more will put them, in our eyes, into the same boat as the hostage-takers. We should point out that full compliance with the

Cuban demand is simply a financial impossibility and that if the lives of the hostages were to depend on this, we would be forced to take our chances on a hostage rescue operation, after which, whether successful or not, we would then review aid and loan negotiations with those nations that had proven intransigent.

"Of course you'll need to get congressional approval for something like this, but I really think we can pull it off."

Baker raised a finger. "I agree with Adam. We've already sounded out a couple of the larger pro-Western debtor nations, and they seem more than ready to take this very large bird in the hand, even without the veiled threats. It's an incredible freebie for them, and the more rational ones recognize that the full plate of Cuban demands is not realistic. They also probably fear that the Cubans might eventually cut their own deal with us and drop them altogether if the need for diplomatic support fades."

For once, Wiznezhsky looked around the table and found all heads nodding in rhythm.

"How much, exactly, is this going to cost?" the president asked cautiously.

"A lot," Leach replied quickly. "I'll have exact figures for you when we go to Congress. We could save a few bucks by not including those nations not on Cuba's list, but Jim and I agree that the less we make this look like kowtowing to the Cubans the better. Also, how would it look if we punished our friends for their loyalty and rewarded our enemies? Fortunately the really hard cases, like Yemen, for instance, do their business with the Soviets anyway. We could also think about excluding a country or two with which we have another axe to grind, like South Africa maybe, but I'll give you all the numbers to play with."

"Sounds good to me," said the president. "I'll meet with the congressional leaders tomorrow morning and see if they'll go for it. It appears that it would undercut a good deal of the support the Cubans have gotten worldwide and save us some face into the bargain. I'll also have a press conference tomorrow announcing the blockade, right after the OAS meeting, assuming no major hangups there. We'll also need to talk with Gorbachev tonight if possible on the blockade and basing proposal. I expect he'll go for it. General, I want some very detailed plans for a rescue attempt ASAP!"

"Yes, sir!" snapped the general.

As the Security Council members filed quickly out of the room, the president called Judge Webster and Wiznezhsky aside and asked them to stay on. The three then slipped into the Oval Office, where coffee was waiting on the sideboard.

"I'll be honest with you, Mr. President," Webster said, as they sat down in chairs near the fireplace with their coffee cups balanced in their hands. "I don't feel good about the blockade at all. Our reporting from Latin America in particular tells us that support will be almost nonexistent and we will probably face a good deal of hostility."

"I expect you're right, Judge," the president admitted, "but I don't think we have a viable choice. Doing nothing hasn't gotten us very far to date."

"I suppose you wanted to talk about our other alternate plan." Wiznezhsky's ears suddenly perked up, since he had been totally unaware of the existence of another "alternate" plan.

"I don't really find the idea any more appetizing than you do," said the president, "but your own ops people have suggested both the plan and the man, and it may be our last resort."

"The reporting on the riot in Havana certainly does seem to suggest that Castro is the only man holding this thing together," Webster admitted.

"Yes, and if he can be eliminated, cleanly, it could save hundreds or even thousands of lives."

"*Eliminated*?" Wiznezhsky almost shouted. "I thought that stuff went out with the Keystone Cops."

The president turned to his national security advisor and said in a soothing tone of voice, "I know what you're thinking, Jacob, but this is an option we cannot entirely rule out."

Webster continued, "The Agency tried and failed to kill Castro various times in various ways back in the 1960s, and I'm not going to insult your intelligence by suggesting that *those* attempts weren't sloppy, but *this* one is absolutely perfect. It's a long shot. There's no denying it, but if it does succeed it will solve a lot of our problems at one time."

"Isn't there a law against murdering other heads of state?" Wiznezhsky asked.

"As unenthusiastic as I am about the project," Webster said, "this is a rather unique situation, war in fact. Castro actually declared war on the United States, so the gloves are off. We've already talked to the House and Senate Select Committees on Intelligence and to other congressional leaders. No politician is going to dare counsel moderation or oversight at this time. Even the War Powers Act is a dead issue. They've promised to procure the funds if we don't go for a declaration of war and would undoubtedly vote to declare war if we asked. What we want to avoid is declaring a war and then finding out that we really can't do anything. That would make us all look bad."

"Still, I can't believe you're serious about this," Wiznezhsky said.

"As I said," Webster answered, "I'm not wild about the idea either, but you have essentially a single madman who has declared open season on the rest of the civilized world. He makes Khomeini look like a choirboy.

"In any event, the plan has the virtue of simplicity. In brief, there is a Cuban exile, defector really, who was at one time trained and prepared for this exact mission. Just go in, take a shot, and run for it. The plan was dropped before he was ever sent in. He was very young then, that would have been in the 1960s. He became a citizen, went into the army, served in Vietnam doing pretty much what we had wanted him to do in Cuba, which was being a sniper. He earned a ton of medals and then came with us after 1973. He's worked for us as a paramilitary trainer ever since."

"You mean you've dug up some fifty-year-old warhorse and are going to just reactivate him?" Wiznezhsky was not convinced.

"He's forty-five to be precise, can run a mile in under six minutes, gave up the amateur karate tournament circuit only last year, and can fire every weapon known to man, very well too. He's single, never married, has no family outside of Cuba, and the ones inside assume that he died decades ago. He also has absolutely native Spanish with a Cuban accent and knows Havana inside and out. We had been keeping him in reserve as a support asset in case we ever had to exfiltrate someone 'black' from on-island, and he's been back three times on one kind of mission or another—no violence, just operations. This mission doesn't call for an Olympic athlete. It calls for brains rather than muscle, getting to the right place at the right time. Can you think of a better hypothetical candidate?"

"Well, no," Wiznezhsky stammered. "I mean this isn't really the sort of policy alternative I'm familiar with."

The president leaned back in his chair and put his empty cup on a table. "I think this is the difference in perspective between study and policy-making, Jacob. In the academic world, if you make a mistake, who remembers? Where are all the pundits who favored the nuclear freeze as the only reasonable step in the nuclear arms race? Did they all lose their jobs when the INF Treaty was signed and eliminated a whole class of nuclear weapons, not just American ones but Soviet as well? Of course not. What happened to the revisionist historians and political scientists who said the Soviets were really peacelovers, that they didn't commit the Katyn massacre in Poland in World War II, that the Krasnoyarsk radar didn't violate the ABM Treaty, when the Soviets themselves came out and denounced their own imperialism, admitted Katyn, admitted intentional violation of the treaty? They're still right where they were before, just with ten years' more seniority and several more book titles to their credit.

"On the other hand, Mussolini and Ceaucescu made policy decision mistakes, and you know what happened to them. Of course, it usually isn't that drastic, but it frequently means loss of elections or, worse yet, permanent damage to your nation's interests or damage that costs billions of dollars, thousands of lives, and/or decades to set right. In policy decision-making it's not enough to state a position articulately; you have to make it work. You can't just sit back and take pot shots at the decision-makers, unless you're in Congress."— he and Webster chuckled good-naturedly—"You've got to make your suggestions and then *show* that they were right.

"You're an important member of the team here, especially now, just because you do ask the right questions, but the one thing you need to learn is that if you shoot down one plan, you'd better have a workable one to suggest in its place."

"So the decision is taken, then?" Webster asked.

"Yes," said the president, somewhat sadly. "How long before he can be in position?"

"Just getting him there will probably take two to three days at least. Then, of course, he'll have to look for the right setting and trust to luck."

"And what about exfiltration?" asked Wiznezhsky, now caught up in the energy of the other two men.

"Well," said Webster, "if he's successful there'll be such a commotion that he shouldn't have much trouble at all holing up until he can either make it to one of our prearranged pick-up points or until, as in Eastern Europe, the whole damn wall comes tumbling down and he can just walk up and book passage on the nine o'clock ferry to Key West."

Webster paused long enough for Wiznezhsky to ask the obvious next question. "And if he isn't?"

"If he tries and fails? I know this man. At least I know enough of him from men who have served with him that I would expect he will keep trying until they bag him. I doubt very much that he would allow himself to be taken alive. Of course if he never really gets a chance there'll be much less pressure, and he can get out when he gets an opening.

"The tricky part will be getting him ashore. I take it things are tighter now in Cuba than they have ever been, what with watching for a rescue attempt or an attack on the missile sites. We plan to let him pick his own spot, route, and all. In fact, we're not even going to ask him how or when he plans to do any of it."

"Is that standard procedure?" asked Wiznezhsky.

"Far from it. Ordinarily we micromanage these things to death. In this case, however, it's my decision that, since there's nothing we can do to help him from the time he crosses the beach, there's no point in running even a small risk of a leak. Just among the three of us, the possibility that someone, whether they be the Soviets, Chinese,

Cubans, Israelis, or whoever, has a deep penetration at a high level of the Agency is something that always nags at the back of my brain. I believe in the efficiency of our security and counterintelligence people, but *perfection* is a dangerous thing for someone in my position to count on."

"Thank you, gentlemen," the president concluded. He didn't rise to see them out and neither man felt offended. He called as they reached the door, "I don't suppose I need to tell you to keep me posted."

Chapter Twelve

SANTIAGO DE LAS VEGAS, CUBA: 1300 HOURS,
27 JANUARY

Ogarkov and his officers grumbled as the Cuban soldiers shouted at them to hurry along, as they dragged the few personal possessions they were allowed out of their quarters and onto a waiting bus. Ogarkov could see similar scenes of disorder taking place on about half of the base as they drove to another officers' billet about a mile away.

"What is all this?" Ogarkov asked a reasonably amiable-looking Cuban soldier standing by the door of the bus when they arrived at their destination.

"I don't know exactly, Colonel," the soldier replied with a deference that rather surprised Ogarkov. Old habits die hard, he thought. "I heard, though, that they're going to bring the American prisoners here as well, so they want all of the Russians to double up and make room. That's the rumor, at least."

"Thank you, trooper," he nodded to the soldier as he and Major Zhdanov carried their small bags into the obviously overcrowded billet. "That's odd," said Ogarkov. "Not only are they keeping all of the Russians together, combat troops, advisors, technicians, everyone, but now they're going to concentrate the Americans here as well. That defies the rules of hostage management—if there are such things."

"Maybe they think it will be easier to guard us all together," mused Zhdanov, not noted as the deepest thinker in the brigade.

"No, that doesn't make sense. They're not worried about our escaping. Where would we escape to? They should be more concerned about a rescue attempt. In that case having us split up, with ten men in each stinking village on the island, would be their best bet. They should also separate the officers from the men. Now that *is* standard procedure for handling prisoners according to some field manual or other. They must have something particular in mind.

"Anyway," Ogarkov continued casually, "it will be interesting to meet with some Americans for a change. I suppose contact is freer now, but I've been here since before Gorbachev's time, and things haven't changed much here, obviously."

As they walked into the building Ogarkov stole a glance at a metal grate set in the ground near the foundation of the structure. It did not look as though it had been disturbed. Although the Cubans had emptied all of the armories of the brigade, moved out all of the fighting vehicles, and conducted fairly competent searches of the troops' living quarters, seizing any weapon that they found, they had apparently not considered that the Soviets would have had the foresight to cache small stocks of weapons around the base. Ogarkov doubted that anyone in the Soviet High Command had ever considered a turn of events such as had occurred in the past few days, but he thanked the gods for the traditional Soviet paranoia that had called for this provision.

Only a few officers and NCOs knew of each cache, and they didn't contain very much. All over the base there were perhaps between one and two hundred AKM assault rifles with folding stocks, a couple dozen pistols, a few submachine guns, one or two PK light machine guns, some cases of grenades, and a handful of RPG-7 rocket launchers and ammunition for each. That wouldn't permit his men to hold off the Cuban Army for fifteen minutes, with their armor and artillery, but it was comforting to know that in a pinch at least some of his men could defend themselves, and even a few minutes' time could be important.

SOUTH CENTRAL CUBA

Johnson was fighting to keep his breakfast down as he stood, swaying, in the back of an open truck along with forty or fifty other marines. He reckoned they were headed toward the town of Guantánamo, although he had never been farther inland than the first line of barbed wire on the base. He had casually studied maps of Cuba in the preceding months, and now he wished he had done so more thoroughly.

It appeared to Johnson that the Cubans had commandeered everything in the region with wheels, and all of the Americans from the base were loaded up and moved out with little warning. He noted with some relief that he had seen that the civilians and dependents, mostly women and children, had been loaded into more or less respectable-looking buses for the trip and that the wounded had been loaded into regular ambulances, either captured American ones or Cuban Army vehicles. At least they weren't being too barbaric about it.

Sergeant Glover worked his way back to Johnson from the front of the truck. "Here's the latest poop, son," the sergeant said happily. "A guy up front there was talking to some officers, and the word is that we're going to bunk in with the Soviets at their base near Havana."

"Is that good or bad?" asked Johnson.

"Can't tell," admitted the sergeant, "but Havana is several hundred miles closer to the States, so that can't be worse at least."

"Any word on an escape attempt?" Johnson asked.

"The officers say, and I tend to agree, that we should wait until we get to wherever we're going. More importantly, I think they're hoping to get some word, maybe through the Interests Section in Havana, from the outside about any rescue plans, so that whatever we do can be coordinated with that. It wouldn't do for us to be running one way when the 2d Marines is coming in from somewhere else."

The convoy was passing through a small town now. Johnson had feared that the people would be so stirred up, by the deaths of so many of their own soldiers in the fighting if nothing else, that the prisoners would be showered with stones, garbage, and abuse. But the people they saw looked more worried than jubilant or angry. They just stopped what they were doing as the trucks rolled by and stared, expressionless.

Chapter Thirteen

"Is there any reason to hope," asked the president in an exasperated tone of voice, "that we have seen the last surprise, or at least the last unpleasant one, in connection with this affair?"

The president languidly waved the front section of the *Washington Post* at the assembled members of his National Security Council. The banner headline announced the arrival in Miami of the first Cubana de Aviación airliners with the released American civilian hostages. Crowding it for room were other screaming headlines advising of the refusal of the OAS to support any kind of blockade of Cuba and of the Cuban offer to transfer all wounded prisoners and dependents to isolated refuge in India.

"Which one of these interesting topics shall we take first?" the president said, challenging someone to break the silence.

Oddly enough the first to speak was his press secretary, Larry Donka. "The Cubans are beating the living daylights out of us in the press. Tune in to just about any news/commentary program you wish and there are these liberal journalists, analysts for those innocuously named think tanks, or regular academicians, all saying how it's really the developed world that has forced the Third World to the extreme of taking huge numbers of hostages to make their just claims heard.

They're saying that it is time for a significant reallocation of resources between North and South, meaning that the developed
countries are rich only because they stole it from the underdeveloped
ones, and now it's time to give it back. The odd conservative
economist, like Milton Friedman, who, after all, has only *one* Nobel
Prize to his name, is just drowned out when he points out that the
vast majority of industrial countries' trade is with other industrial
countries and that this trade accounts for most of the profits.

"Then you've got live minicam coverage of the arrival of these
Venceremos Brigade people, waving little Cuban flags, saying how
great they were treated and suggesting that, *if* there was any shooting,
the Russians and Americans probably started it. One guy said he
lived in Guantánamo City and that the only casualties he was aware
of seemed to have been caused by a furious artillery barrage by
American guns directly into the residential neighborhoods of
Guantánamo City itself. You get a decidedly different flavor with the
returning Cuban exiles, but not a word against the Cuban government.
'Oh, no! We were very politely treated. They just suggested we
should return home for the present.' Bullshit! Those people were
scared out of their wits. You could see it in their faces, but you
couldn't prove it in court."

"Of course," Judge Webster cut in, "we've been getting an entirely different story from them in private interviews. Lots of threats
against family members still on the island being the primary moti-
vator, but they absolutely refuse to go on the record."

"And then there's this isolation of the wounded and dependents
in India," Donka continued. "It's brilliant! Here they pick up all sorts
of brownie points for their humanity and generosity with the people
who want us to cave in anyway, and they don't have to worry about
unseemly stories of shooting prisoners, unprovoked attacks, and such
hitting the airways. And the beauty of it is that there's no way in hell
we can reject the offer."

"Then there's the question of the OAS slapping us in the face on
the blockade," Baker joined in. "As the CIA reported just prior to the
OAS meeting, feelings were running high in Latin America, partly
due to the typical 'sovereignty' sentiment, which is opposed to any

kind of intervention on our part no matter what the justification, partly due to the debt business, which they rightly see as Cuba's gift to the world. They're still afraid we can back out of the debt relief we've already offered if we can get the upper hand on the Cubans. Consequently, far from supporting us on the blockade, they denounced the very idea."

"It's worse than that," added General Weems. "According to our latest satellite imagery the Argentine aircraft carrier *25 de Mayo* and escorting frigates have rendezvoused with the leading Chinese troop ships and missile carrier and are escorting them. A Peruvian frigate and an Ecuadorean corvette have picked up another missile carrier in the Pacific and are accompanying it south, and Brazilian ships and fighter aircraft are also being readied to join the convoy.

"This puts the situation in a whole different light. While there's no question that we could brush aside these forces, given the balls the Argentines proved that they had in the Falklands, we will have to assume that bluff alone won't work with any of these navies. We could also probably disable the missile carriers with submarine attacks with minimal loss of life to the Chinese and none at all to the Latin Americans, but that would just likely force the Latins into even more open support of Cuba than is already the case." Wiznezhsky was impressed. The general, for all his bluster, was able to incorporate new information and change his views when the situation called for it. He also seemed to have a pretty good grasp of the Latin character, probably from his time as USCINCSO in Panama. "We are now faced with the situation that we cannot expect to turn back or even search the missile transports without some loss of life, possibly among other Latin American nationals. In this case, I can see no alternative to letting the ships through. That would not eliminate the possibility of destroying them as they're unloaded or installed, but it involves a whole different level of commitment, to say nothing of the hostage situation."

"I agree, General," the president said. "We're going to have to go back to the drawing board on that one. I want the blockade to continue to keep the Cuban Navy and Air Force within the twelve-mile limit, but the ships should be pulled back so at least we don't have the humiliation of being forced to back down publicly."

"Well, there is a semibright side to the day's news," chimed in the treasury secretary. "Just about every Third World country, at least all of the ones we care about, has lapped up our version of the debt package like men dying of thirst offered a chilled Perrier. While I don't think anybody's fooled into thinking that we would have spontaneously made the offer had it not been for the hostage crisis, I think acceptance of the package is being viewed as taking our side against the Cubans on that particular issue."

"I'll second that," added Baker. "I think it's taken away a good deal of the grudging public support Cuba was getting for this desperate action. Since we worded the declaration in such a way that they get their debt relief regardless of the outcome of the hostage crisis, most countries, particularly the basically pro-Western democracies, find it far more comfortable to distance themselves from this kind of business, take their money, and go home. So now it appears that it's the Cubans who are prolonging the crisis by unreasonable demands."

"There's another relatively positive development," General Weems added. "While we may be taking a beating in the public relations field with this prisoner release business, we should probably be used to that by now anyway. The good side is that it's cut down the number of hostages to worry about by more than five thousand, including all of the children and most of the women, except for female staff officers in the two diplomatic missions and with our forces at Guantánamo. That leaves some three thousand Americans and less than eight thousand Soviets, still an awful lot, but a considerably more manageable number if we ever decide to do anything aggressive in terms of rescue. There's also another development along these lines, but I'll let Judge Webster fill in the details on that."

The Judge went to his easel again and displayed a large map of western Cuba. "We got the first indications from Soviet reporting, but our own sources, both in the Interests Section and through technical means, have confirmed it. The Cubans have decided to concentrate all of the remaining hostages in the old Soviet mechanized brigade base of Santiago de las Vegas, just east of Havana." He indicated the spot on the map. "The Soviets have been bunched into one sector of the base and the Americans are currently being trucked up from Guantánamo. The Cubans are announcing a major victory parade to take place on February first at noon. Details are thin, but from the lack of assignments to worker contingents to participate and from the concentration of the prisoners, we surmise that they plan to march all of the prisoners through the middle of Havana to try to stir up public feeling for this move. Satellite photography shows that a large reviewing stand is being constructed directly across from the Soviet Embassy, and it looks like the people really being held up for humiliation will be the Soviets. I'm not sure yet what kind of chance this would give us to try a rescue operation, but it's certainly better than it might be, with hostages cached all over the island."

"General," the president asked, seeming to take renewed life from this news, "what exactly is our military posture?"

"It's rather ironic, but the operation is being coordinated by the Joint Caribbean Task Force at Key West, which, as you may recall, was originally created by President Carter following the revelation of the existence of the Soviet mechanized brigade in Cuba. Now it's being used to plan a possible joint American–Soviet intervention to save the members of that brigade." General Weems shook his head ruefully. "The JCTF is under the command of Lt. Gen. Andrew Freeman.

"We have two carrier and one battleship battle groups in position northwest of Cuba. We have two squadrons of F-15s, three of F-16s, two of A-10s, and a marine air wing all based in southern Florida, with more on the way, and constant satellite and AWACS coverage of the entire region. The 82d Airborne Division is also in southern Florida, ready to move on an hour's notice or less, along with a brigade of the 101st Airmobile. There is a reinforced marine amphibious brigade of the 2d Marine Division at sea with the fleet, with enough helicopter and amphibious transport to get them ashore quickly. The rest of the 2d Marines is loading or already at sea, and both the 7th and 9th Light Divisions are in the process of being transported to southern Florida as well. We have also assembled an impressive number of MCM (Mine Countermeasures) craft, to clear the way if we have to go in over the beaches with amphibious forces.

"That's *our* forces. Now the Soviets are also making good time. Their combined fleet, including the *Tblisi*, should reach the area of operations in less than two more days. Since the *Tblisi* is equipped with a squadron each of SU-27 Flanker B fighters and SU-25 Frogfoot attack aircraft, we agreed with the Soviets that their air force contingent should be composed of these types as well, to help us with identification, and three squadrons of the former and two of the latter have begun to arrive in Texas. That way the only MiG-21s, 23s, and 29s will be Cuban. The 76th Guards Airborne Division already has its advance elements at Fort Hamilton, and they'll keep enough Antonov-124 transports on hand to paradrop a full regiment. Their fleet is also carrying the equivalent of a reinforced naval infantry regiment with amphibious transport.

"In the event that we do decide to go in, now that it looks like the hostages will all be in the Havana area, that will be our only principal target. If we decide to go after the missile sites, which are all on the southern side of the island, we'll do that with airpower alone, and we've got a squadron of F-111s with the necessary fighter cover and electronic warfare craft assigned to each site. The navy will also take out the port facilities at Manzanillo and Cienfuegos if the Chinese ships haven't actually arrived by that time.

"We envision a vertical assault by the 82d Airborne to try to seal off the area the hostages are located in and to protect them until more help can arrive. One regiment of the 76th Guards will also be moved to southern Florida to participate in the first wave if we have enough advance warning. We also have some navy SEALs, Special Forces, and Soviet Spetsnaz units, which can be put ashore both ahead of the first wave and also elsewhere on the island to cause general trouble and keep some of their troops tied down. While the paratroopers are establishing their airhead the marines will move onshore with both helicopters and amphibious craft, to set up a secure beachhead. The

7th and 9th Light and the 101st Airmobile will move through them to link up with the paras and bring them and the hostages out over the beach.

"The key to the entire operation will be establishing total air superiority over the area where the hostages are located, the nearest beach, and the route in between. We're going to entrust the combat air patrol over the allied fleets to the YAK-36 Forgers off the Soviet light aircraft carrier *Kiev* and to two squadrons of Air National Guard F-4 Phantoms based in Florida. That will free the main fleet air elements to participate in the operation. The SU-27s and F-14s from the fleet and F-15s from shore will deal with any aircraft they get off the ground, while the SU-25s and F-16s and the navy A-6s and F-18s from the fleet go after the nearest enemy airfields to keep their heads down and also to hit the enemy antiaircraft installations to open the way for the airdrop. We're counting on the A-10s and the Harriers and F-18s of the marine air wing to provide the close support, along with the choppers we plan to move into the beachhead as soon as possible, with the aircraft laying down a curtain of 30mm cannon fire and bombs around the hostage area to keep the Cubans off them until we can get to them. Naval gunfire will perform this same function if the target area is within range, which it probably will be.

"As our ace in the hole we also have a squadron of F-117 Stealth fighters on call to hit antiaircraft missile batteries in advance of the main strike. The stealth technology might already be eroding somewhat in relation to the Soviets, but it should cut quite a swath with the Cubans.

"We also have an additional carrier task force coming in from the Second Fleet, which will have the role of conducting a diversionary attack on the Guantánamo Bay area, as if we were trying to seize the base back. One battalion of the 2d Marines will be assigned to this task, with the navy ships and planes generally shooting the place up and the marines making very visible preparations for a landing, hopefully thereby keeping a good portion of the Cuban Army tied to that end of the island waiting for them."

"I think you're aware, General Weems," the president commented, "that the main thing I want to avoid is the sort of lack of interservice cooperation that crippled the Iran hostage rescue attempt and that could have turned the Grenada intervention into a disaster. What's the military term for that?"

"I believe the term you are looking for is 'cluster fuck,' Mr. President," General Weems answered.

"Yes, exactly," the president laughed.

"We're not going to have that trouble this time. My only supposition is that in both of those other cases, you had a rather underemployed military trying to milk the maximum benefit out of a rather small situation. Each service was in there, defending its turf tooth and nail and even trying to inject itself where it was not wanted. That's why you had marine pilots on the helicopters in Iran, when the marines were unused to long overland hauls and their machines were not up to it. It was because, 'Well, the marines *had* to have some part in the thing.' We're running this operation like a real military operation with a clear chain of command and responsibility. As it happens, this is an operation where each service will have a role to play, but it's also a much larger operation too, so there's less room for petty turf battles. If I have any problem with a member of any service balking at orders of his superior in our chain of command because that officer is from another service, I will either have that balker cashiered on the spot, or you will have my resignation on your desk within the hour!"

"Thank you, General," the president said. "You can rest assured that you will have my full backing on this. If we do have to go in we will go in to win, win quickly, and with the minimum possible casualties on all sides, and I will not hesitate to replace any officer of any service who stands in the way, as well as any member of his service who defends him.

"Now, on another topic, I think it would be well if, starting in about forty-eight hours, we had the paratroopers, including the Russians, ready to go on even less than an hour's notice, even to the point of having an air attack force airborne at all times, and having part of the paratroopers literally sitting in their transports with the motors running. I know that this can take the edge off of troops quickly, but things may start to unravel rather quickly in Cuba and we may have to move at the drop of a hat to secure the hostages."

The general nodded his assent with something of a confused expression on his face, but Wiznezhsky knew that the president was hoping against hope that the CIA man would get lucky. It would probably take him at least forty-eight hours to get into position. From then on it would be a question of waiting for a clear line of fire.

"All things considered," the president continued, "I'm rather pleased with our situation right now. The feeling I get is that world opinion recognizes that we and the Soviets have complied with as much of the Cuban demands as we reasonably can and without humiliating ourselves unnecessarily in doing so. I've talked with Gorbachev, and they have taken pretty much the same tack on the debt issue as we have, selecting the recipients themselves and largely ignoring the Cuban list. It was easier for them because, in most cases, they really didn't expect to see any of the debt money again in any case, most of which was for the purchase of arms which the Soviets had provided as a political tool, not so much as a foreign-exchange earner, although it had that function when dealing with some of the oil countries like Libya.

"For better or worse, we do have several thousand hostages out of Cuba now and that's good, regardless of the public relations ramifications. While we are apparently going to have to let the missile ships into Cuba, because of the escort being provided by the other Latin American nations, an act I think they'll regret someday and not because of any action on our part, all other aspects of the blockade of Cuba remain in effect, and interestingly enough, Castro has been rather quiet on that subject. More and more he's appearing like a common criminal with his hostages, waiting for the satchel full of money and a plane ride out. In fact, he's been rather quiet about his demands in general since the first declarations. Any thoughts on that, Bill?"

Judge Webster cocked his head to one side. "The only thing we've learned decisively in the past few years about the Cubans, and this applies to most any country when you think about it, is that you are most likely to make major mistakes in analysis when you impose your own set of priorities on others. We might have assumed that Castro's primary goals were to rid the island of American and Soviet troops, to get the missiles safely installed, and to hammer both the American and Soviet economies while making a few bucks on the side. It rather looked like his appeal to the Third World on the debt issue was just a ploy to get the other developing countries to run interference for him, something that worked very well in fact.

"Now, however, it's starting to look very different to our analysts. Maybe Castro's got his sights set on something bigger. He's alluded to it a couple of times in his statements, something about a new world order in the formation of this Peoples' Revolutionary Bloc. Maybe he sees for himself the role of organizer of a new superpower based on the Third World. It's not such a crazy idea. With the man-power of China and some of the larger Middle Eastern nations, the military might of China, Cuba, Vietnam, North Korea, Iran, Syria, et cetera, they're a force to be reckoned with. They've got control of significant amounts of vital natural resources. They've got strategic positions around the world. The only thing they don't have is high technology, and with Japan, a possible united Europe, and some of the emerging new generation of industrial nations, like Brazil, all competing for their business and possibly their protection, there wouldn't be much that they couldn't buy. So maybe Castro sees it as unbecoming of such a world-class leader to haggle over the repara-tions issue and the details of the debt arrangements. His great stroke was setting the whole thing up. He's counted coup on both of the old superpowers and gotten away with it. He's shown the Third World he can deliver on the issue closest to their hearts, debt relief, and when the missiles arrive he won't have to worry about our getting even. Of course that's the way it looks to us here and now. He might still have other items on his hidden agenda that we can't even guess at."

"That makes some sense," the president concluded. "Another question now comes to mind. The Cubans have left our Interests Section and the Soviet Embassy largely alone. After the first couple of hours of rousting about and, of course, much heavier guards on the missions and diplomats' residences, they've been left pretty much on their own. Why?"

"The obvious reason would be that they don't want us to cramp the style of their mission at the UN. As the FBI has informed us, they've essentially closed down their Interests Section in Washington and moved the personnel up to their mission at the UN. They might also be goosey about stirring up public sentiment on seizing diplomatic hostages after the precedent of Iran. The last thing the Cubans want to do is to galvanize American public opinion. Hitting a hostile military base on your own soil, well, that can be rationalized, but taking a diplomatic mission is something else. Mainly, however, I think it's a question of the missions being a convenient channel of communication if they want it handy, and after all, even if the diplomats are still in their old offices and living in their old housing, they *are* hostages just the same as the military prisoners. With the massive Cuban jamming directed right at the missions we essentially have no secure communications with them anyway."

"Well, let's just hope it doesn't occur to them to get any tougher," the president sighed. The president hadn't said so, but he was also pleased that General Weems had apparently come around to the idea of close military cooperation with the Soviets. He suspected that Gorbachev's gesture of placing all Soviet units assigned to the Cuban mission under American operational command had something to do with it. It was a largely honorary designation, since the Soviet units obviously would not do anything that their instructions from Moscow forbade, but it was certainly a first. Not even during the alliance of the Second World War had such close cooperation existed between the two armed forces, and the president had real cause for hope that however this crisis turned out, they were laying the groundwork for an era of reduced tensions and even pooling of resources on a lot of problems that would long outlast the current situation.

The president smiled to himself as he watched the general lumber out the door. He noticed that the general tended to forget his West Point posture when something was on his mind, and he stooped a bit. He knew that another reason that the general had knuckled under to letting Soviet units base themselves in the U.S. also had to do with the two squadrons of F-4 Phantom jets from the Air National Guard that the air force happened to have assigned to "combat readiness training" about fifteen minutes' flying time from Hamilton Army Airfield, where the Soviets were located, and the fact that the 1st Cavalry Division at Fort Hood was not earmarked to participate in any Cuban intervention immediately but was on full alert, watching the Russians' backs. The president doubted that these precautions were necessary, but he certainly would not want to be proven wrong on that score.

Chapter Fourteen

Osman, Kurupatin, and Akamirov rose to greet the Americans as they entered the secure conference room in the Soviet Embassy. Featherstone had been in the large reception room downstairs several times and in the ambassador's office once or twice, but since no American had ever been inside a Soviet secure conference room anywhere, anytime, to the best of his knowledge, he was duly impressed by the experience. Actually, the room looked like those in the American embassies where he had been stationed, basically a large, clear plastic box located inside a normal-looking room, with the conference table and chairs inside the box. The clear plastic box supposedly would prevent the installation of microphones, while some kind of electronic "stuff" in the walls of the room, which Featherstone did not pretend to understand, allegedly would louse up the signals transmitted by any listening device that might be carried into the room, such as the famous radio transmitter the Poles or Romanians or someone had put into the American ambassador's shoe heel years ago.

Featherstone was accompanied by Carl Popper and Capt. Eric Meese, who had been brought up by helicopter from Guantánamo by the Cubans so that the full story of the Cuban 'victory' could be passed on to Washington by the Interests Section. This was another first, as far as Featherstone knew. While the CIA station chief and the KGB *rezident* in a country usually knew each other by reputation and occasionally met at a diplomatic function, it was certainly unusual for them to meet in their official capacities.

Akamirov was still sporting a sling for his injured arm. Captain Meese was wearing a uniform borrowed from another navy officer, since the only one he had that had survived the burning of his quarters in the assault had seen several days of hard use. The replacement was a clean summer-weight dress uniform with the appropriate insignia, and the sleeves were a bit short and the pants a bit baggy on Meese's trim frame, but this did not detract from his quiet dignity. There were smiles all around as trays of sandwiches, coffee, and vodka were placed on the table, but the rings under everyone's eyes testified to the fact that this was not a social call.

Osman got quickly to the point after the initial pleasantries had been exchanged. "I've invited you gentlemen here because I have a very important, very sensitive, and very strange proposition to put before you."

"Nothing could seem overly strange to us after the events of the last few days," Featherstone joked, his decades of diplomatic repartee training taking over like instinct despite the gravity of the situation. "We are all in the same boat, and we greatly appreciate the information you've provided us on the local situation since, well, since the other day. You can rest assured that you've got a receptive audience if you've got a solution that might help us all out of this."

"How would you like to fight your way out of Cuba?" Osman asked in a casual tone of voice.

The Americans just stared blankly, first at Osman, then at each other, then back at Osman. After a moment, Featherstone said, "I assume you're not just conducting a poll. You do have something in mind that would permit us to do this, don't you?"

"I'm glad you asked," said Osman, smiling more broadly than ever. "Here are a number of somewhat disjointed facts about our situation that I'd like to run through first, some of which you're aware of, some not. Then I'll put them together in my own fashion and we'll see if you agree that it makes some sense.

"First, we are currently sitting in the Soviet Embassy compound, which is two city blocks square, surrounded by high cinderblock walls and with buildings made of solid steel and concrete.

"Next, on February first Castro plans to hold his big victory parade through Havana, passing the reviewing stands you all saw under construction directly across from the embassy gates, as a little lesson in humility for us all, I think. Since all of the wounded, civilians, and dependents have been evacuated safely the parade will consist of your and our captured soldiers and our technicians, many of whom are also military. And, with your mission staff and mine, these are all of the hostages on the island—at present."

"What do you mean, 'at present'?" asked Featherstone, fearful that the Soviets had learned of some horrendous new Cuban plot to seize more.

"I'm getting to that. Now, here's something you didn't know. We have some weapons cached at our Santiago de las Vegas base, where all of the Russian prisoners are being held, and to which point the Americans are being transported at this moment." Osman smiled again as he saw Meese's eyebrows rise halfway up his forehead. "We don't have a great deal of weaponry," he added hastily, raising his hand, "but it's mostly small arms, easily concealable, and enough to arm several hundred men after a fashion. We also have some weapons here in the embassy, mostly for the security guard detachment, some additional weapons we just happened to store here, and the personal hunting and household security weapons of some of our staff, enough to arm about one hundred and fifty to two hundred more men. I suspect that you are in a similar situation in your mission, on a proportionate scale."

Featherstone nodded uncertainly.

"Now, here's my suggestion." Osman paused dramatically, looking from face to questioning face on the American side of the table. Featherstone saw from the Soviets' faces that they had already been briefed on the plan and apparently had approved it, which gave him some hope, but not much. "Suppose you move your mission staff here, into the embassy compound in the next day or two. We could fabricate a minor altercation with a Cuban guard to justify it, and we would, of course, obtain Cuban permission for the move."

"All right, I'm following you," Featherstone answered, "wherever the hell you're going."

"Then suppose that when the column of prisoners, which I estimate will extend for over a kilometer from head to tail, reaches the level of our embassy and the reviewing stand, the men suddenly attack their guards, with the weapons they smuggle out of our base and with support from us here, and make a break for the embassy. There would be losses, certainly, but I suspect that the surprise will be so great that the casualties would be very small, at least in comparison to those we have suffered already."

"That's an interesting theory, Ambassador," Captain Meese interrupted, "but I seriously doubt that the Cubans are going to be deterred by the inviolability of diplomatic property. In half an hour this whole compound would be reduced to gravel with artillery and air strikes and armored vehicles attacking, against which we couldn't do squat."

"I don't think so," Osman answered. Featherstone thought that there was a serious danger of the ambassador's head splitting in two if his smile grew any more. "You'll forgive my melodrama, but I left out one important step in my account. Do you know who will be on the reviewing stand for the parade?"

"Castro!" said all of the Americans at once, and their mouths stayed open after pronouncing the final *o*.

"Exactly!" shouted Osman. "Castro, and probably the entire Cuban General Staff and Party Politburo, all within fifty yards of nearly eleven thousand very irritated Soviet and American soldiers and sailors."

"And guarded by a small army of security men," Meese added.

"Of course," Osman admitted. "We anticipate, from our sources, that the march route will be lined with armed troops, about one every ten meters on each side of the avenue. Castro will have his usual security detachment, but those are trained and equipped to deal with snipers or a handful of terrorists, not a human wave assault by armed soldiers. If our men can seize Castro and his staff, or even a goodly number of senior officials, and bring them into the embassy compound, there won't be any bombardment."

"Aha!" said Featherstone aloud. "Those were the 'other' hostages you alluded to."

"Precisely. Now, the Cubans would know that we'd never kill the hostages, and we'll tell them as much at the time. That would be simple suicide. But they then couldn't do anything themselves to put their lives at risk unduly either. They could assault the compound, but they'd have to do it man-to-man, and very gingerly at that. And *that* means we can buy time for our forces to smash through and rescue the lot of us."

"Jesus H. Christ!" exhaled Meese. Then he sat for a long minute, just thinking, drumming his fingers furiously on the table. "But even so, we could never hold out for very long. I don't know how much ammunition you have stashed away, but I'll bet it doesn't fill a small warehouse."

"That's the rub," Osman continued. "Neither you nor I have any kind of secure communications off the island. We will have to find a way to make sure that your government, in particular, is watching, recognizes its chance, and has the forces ready to take advantage of it."

"The Cubans have permitted me an open-line telephone link with Washington for tomorrow afternoon," Featherstone offered. "I don't think it would be too difficult to make sure that they're at least monitoring things here, real-time, but as to their brain functions and whether they've got troops ready, we'd risk blowing the whole thing if we try to get too specific."

Meese rubbed his close-cropped head with both hands. "I'm still not convinced that our men won't just be massacred out in the street, and I'm even less convinced that we can snag Fidel."

"I'll leave the tactical details to you military men, but I'm convinced that we stand a far better chance with this plan than just sitting here and trusting to the mercy of this madman," Osman countered. He didn't add: and watching my career going up in smoke. "In any case, nothing will be set in stone until the troops set out for the parade, with their hidden weapons. If we get wind that security precautions will be significantly tighter, and we should from our sources, we can always cancel the whole thing and be no worse off than we were before. Even if we don't get Castro or enough senior officials to make it worthwhile we can surrender again. We will have taken some losses, of course, and blown our one chance, but I feel that it's both a risk and a sacrifice worth making."

"If it comes to that," Akamirov spoke up, "we are ready to do this on our own. We could position your men so that they would be relatively protected in the center of the column or at the end, where they could surrender immediately and bow out of the fight."

"No," said Meese. "If anyone's going to do something, we had all better go in together. I doubt that the Cubans will make fine distinctions between active participants and passive observers. Also, we're talking about some ten to eleven thousand men or so in the column. Where will you put them all?"

Osman answered. "We have our four-story embassy building, with a very strong basement, plus several separate buildings in the compound, each also with a basement. I think that that should be sufficient to provide some protection for everyone. The other buildings are all concrete construction, typical socialist style, and we saw in Beirut how well modern buildings stand up to modern warfare, especially when it's mostly small arms fire."

"General Akamirov and I will have to sit down and discuss just who is going to do what, how the weapons are going to be concealed, what the signals will be, who will be informed and when, everything. It would help if we could get a detailed map of the area to work from."

"That's easily done," said Osman, confident now that the plan was afoot and that he had recruited Meese, the professional military man, who was now engrossed in the minutiae of tactical planning. "Why don't you and General Akamirov stay on here and talk business while the rest of us leave you and talk nonsense in the reception hall."

Osman put his hand on Featherstone's shoulder as he rose from the table. "Will you bring your people in, pending the military review of our plan?"

"Yes," he answered, "it certainly can't hurt anything, and it might help our security overall in any case. We'll have to do something to justify it, though. As you spoke, it occurred to me that a mild shoving match between one of our marines and a guard would do. I could then tell the Cubans that it would be best for all of us if our eager young men were separated by your compound wall."

"Wonderful," gushed Osman. "I'll leave that up to you. There's plenty of room here, right now anyway. We won't start making preparations for your arrival until it's official, but I'm sure you'll be quite comfortable."

"Comfort isn't our main worry, but thank you anyway."

Featherstone felt a great sense of freedom, if no happiness. Earlier in his career, when he had small children as well as his wife, in posts where there existed some element of physical danger he had always worked under a great weight of responsibility. What if he were killed by the local terrorist group while en route to some silly official function? Didn't he owe it to his job to go? Didn't he owe it to his children not to? Now, in Cuba, although his children had gone off to college, where they would be exposed to a whole different range of dangers, he had felt guilty for submitting his wife, Anne, to the constant daily pressure of surveillance and hostility of the local officials. When the crisis began there appeared the very real possibility that, to follow him in his career, she had placed herself in a position that could cost her life. Now that she was in the States, having been included in the last group of dependents to leave, he felt a tremendous sense of relief. Since she had been in Havana the whole time, she was not a witness to anything and so had not been sent off to "exile" in India.

As they strolled through the embassy toward the reception hall he kept up casual conversation with the Russians, always avoiding the sensitive purpose of their visit by sheer reflex, and he continued to analyze this emotion. He felt free. He felt young. Perhaps it was that for most of his adult life his and his family's fate had been in the hands of powers beyond their control. Whether it was a matter as mundane as the personnel officer's power to arrange the next assignment in a nice post or a hellhole, or something as terrifying as this current threat of imminent death, their own desires and efforts seemed to count for so little. Now he was alone and, just as important, virtually cut off from Washington.

He felt like those nineteen-year-old marines in the security details of the embassies. He felt immortal. It was not that Anne would not miss him or that he was not looking forward to growing old with her, waiting for grandchildren to come along for him to spoil. He was in a situation not of his own making, and whether he got out of it or not would depend more upon himself and his actions than at any time that he could remember. More importantly, now he didn't have to *worry* about anyone else. Whatever action there was would be taking place right before his eyes and he would know the results immediately, for better or worse. He was making an effort to remain cool, calculating, and above all conservative, as the representative of his government in a situation of global proportions, but the excitement was overwhelming.

Chapter Fifteen

CAIBARIÉN, CUBA: 0530 HOURS, 29 JANUARY

Paco Lechin slouched on the bench at the bus stop on the outskirts of Caibarién on the north central coast of Cuba. The sun would be up soon and then he could read the day-old newspaper he had picked up from the bench. The bus would be along an hour or so later to start the long drive to Havana. He was wearing a typical worker's guayabera and a pair of pants that might once have been part of a two-piece suit but were now much patched and spotted with paint, and an uncomfortable pair of Russian-made sneakers with no socks. He was a typical working man. His identification papers showed him to be Norberto Rodriguez, native of Caibarién, a construction worker en route to a three-month job painting a building in central Havana. Nothing about him—his pocket litter, haircut, aftershave, toothpaste—nothing would suggest that he had ever set foot off the island.

This was the first night he had spent on the island in over a decade, however. When the man he knew only as Leo, despite having worked with him off and on for nearly twenty years, had shown up at his back door several days before to advise him that the time had come for the mission, Paco had just turned off his electrical appliances, locked the door, and gone. He had been reading about the events in Cuba, and he knew that if he had been president of the

118

United States he would have sent someone like himself on this mission long ago.

There had been over twenty-four hours of intensive briefing on the situation in Cuba, how Havana might have changed since his last visit, and contact instructions for "after." Paco had paid little attention to that, since he seriously doubted that there would be an "after" for him. This mission was what he had prepared himself for for most of his adult life, but he had been kept from it by the indecisiveness of politicians. Once it was over he would not know what to do with himself. Everything he had done for a quarter of a century had either been to prepare himself for this mission or to fill time until it was initiated.

Paco was glad that they had insisted on little specific training or planning of the mission. After less than ten minutes on the firing range they had been satisfied that his weapons skills needed no honing, and the hand-to-hand combat session had lasted less than a minute. He sincerely hoped that he had not done any permanent damage to the young Korean black-belt instructor. They had told him that he could expect no support once he was "inserted," and that was the way he wanted it. If no one knew, no one could tell. If any mistakes were to be made they would be his, and Paco was confident enough, having worked his way through this mission step by step hundreds of times, that there would be no mistakes. There was only the question of luck, and Paco was a great believer in making one's own luck.

Paco had not slept in over twenty-four hours, but he was too excited to sleep now. Besides, there would be long hours to sleep on the bus on the way to Havana.

When the final word to go had gone out yesterday morning Paco had been sitting with Leo in a coffee shop at Miami International Airport. Leo's beeper had gone off, and he had made a very short telephone call. Leo returned to the table, pulled from his pocket a round-trip ticket to Port au Prince, Haiti, on the next available flight, for which Paco could see that he had several alternates, and had walked Paco to the departure gate.

The two old warriors had sat together again in the departure lounge, hardly talking now. When they had first been reunited they had regaled each other with their latest crop of jokes, most of them dirty, but now the jokes had run out, and small talk seemed out of place. When the flight was called, Leo gave Paco a firm *abrazo* (hug), told him to watch himself, and then stood in the window of the lounge until the plane taxied out of sight, probably to be able to report back his confirmed departure, Paco had thought.

In Port au Prince Paco purchased another round-trip ticket for a domestic flight to Cap Haitien on the north coast. There he proceeded to a safe house, actually just a small apartment maintained for this purpose in town. The apartment had its own entrance, which was difficult to observe from the rest of the building, and Paco found the radio playing when he entered, turned on by a timer to give the appearance of occupancy. Paco left his unused return tickets in a prearranged desk drawer along with the false American ID he had used to come thus far, and he changed into the Cuban-purchased clothing stored there. His American things would be picked up later and probably destroyed, Paco assumed.

At 1835 hours, just after dark, a local taxi drove slowly down the alley behind the building and paused at a doorway about fifty yards from the safe house long enough for Paco, who had positioned himself there, to climb in. The taxi, driven by his only local contact, drove him in silence to a small clearing about an hour out of town and left him. He watched the taxi's taillights disappear in the darkness, and he sat down on his haunches to wait as he had learned to do in Vietnam.

After about half an hour Paco could hear a dull purring in the air, and suddenly a small, single-engine aircraft popped over the nearest treeline, slowed almost to a stop, and then settled down on the grass of the clearing. Paco rushed from his hiding place and clambered into the small passenger door of the airplane. It then turned, revved its quiet engine, started to roll, and took off in less than one hundred yards.

This was a commercially made STOL (Short Take-Off and Landing) aircraft, originally designed in Switzerland for landing on and taking off from isolated glaciers in the mountains. The engine, which seemed to occupy about two-thirds of the plane's short length, had been specially modified by the Agency to limit its noise signature, but other than that it was nothing that any hard-working drug trafficker wouldn't use. In fact, behind Paco and above the auxiliary fuel tank installed where the rear seats would have been were jammed large plastic garbage bags filled with a passable grade of marijuana. That would be their cover if they were discovered in the air or on the ground in Cuba, just another drug flight. Paco knew that the plan called for the pilot to dump the grass into the Caribbean after delivering him to Cuba and to continue on to Miami International normally, but he wondered if the pilot had not found a way to augment his income by inadvertently dumping the load where a friend could recover it. Paco didn't know or care. He had other worries on his mind.

The pilot had been wearing night vision goggles for the landing, again something he could have purchased on the black market in Panama or elsewhere, nothing too fancy. When he took them off Paco thought he recognized the face from his Vietnam days, a sort of weather-beaten Nordic-looking face, but he could have been wrong. Neither man spoke during the flight. First they headed north toward Florida, then, dropping close to the water and off the radar screens, instead of continuing northward, where the U.S. Coast Guard would probably be searching for them, they headed westward along the north coast of Cuba.

This was the trickiest part of the trip. With the American, Soviet, and Cuban military all scouring the sky for each other with the latest look-down, shoot-down radars, both men sat stock-still and hardly breathed as the pilot zipped in between the chain of islands along the coast, so close to the water that sea spray clouded the windshield. They had picked a spot as far as possible from the primary points of interest of the past few days—Havana, Cienfuegos, Guantánamo, and Manzanillo—and still within reasonable travelling time from Havana. Just before reaching the coast they flew low over a small fishing boat. The pilot swore, but Paco suspected that the boat probably did not have a radio, even if the occupants had been awake and had cared, and would thus require some time to report their presence. That was what he hoped, in any case.

Less than a mile inland and several miles west of Caibarién the pilot donned his goggles again, looking like some kind of insect, and slowed the plane's forward progress to a crawl. He then dropped the plane down almost vertically into a grassy patch about a mile through the woods from where Paco had seen vehicle headlights marking the road to Camajuaní. Even before the landing gear touched the ground Paco had the door open, and he quickly hopped out. As he turned to shut the door he saw the silent pilot staring at him, expressionless, and then the pilot's right thumb deliberately rose in the universal thumbs-up signal, which Paco returned, smiling. Then Paco ducked and dashed for the woods, where he crouched in the shadows.

The plane had no running lights on and it was painted a greenish gray, which looked ordinary enough when parked at a commercial airfield, but which permitted the craft to disappear into the wisps of fog as it rose and turned toward the coast again.

Paco knelt silently for long minutes after the muffled sound of the plane's motor had faded. He had long ago decided that if he were to be caught the two most dangerous points in the mission would be now and the time between his picking up his weapon and his establishing himself in a secure firing position. Paco didn't count the risk of trying to get away *after* firing at Castro. That was secondary. When he had satisfied himself that there was nothing present in the area that should not be, he picked his way through the sparse woods toward the road. He placed each foot carefully, using all of the jungle skills he had learned in Vietnam. He made some noise, as he could not see to avoid twigs underfoot, but he was quieter than most animals in the woods that night. He then paralleled the road, still out of sight of the occasional passing truck or car, into Caibarién and the bus stop.

The sun was coming up now, and Paco picked up the copy of the newspaper from the bench. The front page and most of the others were filled with eulogies of Raul Castro and eyewitness accounts of valorous battle against the foreign invaders. The one story that caught Paco's eye was a front-page call for "everyone" to come to Havana for the victory parade three days hence. There were schedules for special buses to the city from all over Cuba, names of hostels where visitors who wanted to spend more than the day of the parade could stay, and, most importantly, a street map of part of Havana with the route of the parade marked out, along with the location of the viewing stand where Castro would be standing. When he finished reading he folded the whole paper up and stuck it into the cloth shoulder bag in which he had a couple of items of extra clothing. It wouldn't be long now. The bus rolled up, jammed with people and the odd chicken, with loads of baggage on top. It was already quite full, but he wedged himself into the rear seat anyway and settled down to snooze.

Chapter Sixteen

If Captain Estigarribia had never seen Castro more furious than at the last general meeting of the Cuban military and Party hierarchy, he had never seen Castro more jubilant than today. Official word had just come from the Chinese Embassy that the Argentine aircraft carrier *25 de Mayo* had taken station astern of the small group of Chinese transports loaded with troops and the first installment of CSS-3 Dong Feng-4 missiles for Cuba. Two Argentine frigates were also present, as were two more from Brazil. There was no doubt that the U.S. Navy could pierce this thin screen, either with attack submarines or surface-to-surface missiles, but it was apparent from Washington's public statements that there would be no armed challenge to the missile delivery as long as the navies of Latin America interposed themselves.

Castro was laughing and joking with Albaro Icaza, and Estigarribia noted that he was bearing up well, very well, since the death of his dear brother. Castro was taking pains to repeat each statement of doubt or concern, voiced mostly by his military general staff, about the risks of his gamble and then crowing about how he had been proven absolutely right and the "professional soldiers" wrong. He attributed this, time and again, to his background as a guerrilla fighter, having to think on his feet to overcome the enemy, as opposed to regular soldiers who rely on more firepower and technological tricks. Estigarribia made a point of standing behind General Murguia, and he enjoyed the general's comment that there was more combat on a lively weekend in Miami than there had been in Cuba during the whole of the Revolution. Estigarribia liked General Murguia and, more importantly, he was certain that he would be useful.

Icaza, who was in charge of preparations for the victory parade, commented favorably on the cooperation he was receiving from both the Soviet and American commanders, who had apparently thrown themselves into organizing the parade with typical military love for anything martial, regardless of the source. Icaza had a large-scale map of Havana and was briefing the group with a pointer.

"The prisoners will be trucked from Santiago de las Vegas to the assembly point here." He indicated a red block on the map. "The entire parade route runs for about five miles. We've picked avenues with wider sidewalks and no center divider to make the thing look neater. It should take the entire column, which will stretch out for over a kilometer, about an hour to reach the reviewing stand here, in front of the Soviet Embassy. At this point, we've decided to have the column form up as tightly as possible in front of the stand, and the Jefe will deliver a short speech."

"Not more than four or five hours," Castro joked, waving his hand nonchalantly in the air. This brought the obligatory round of chuckles from the assembled group, but Estigarribia could see in their eyes that there was no mirth there. Four or five hours *was* a short talk for Castro, and he and all of the men present had had to sit or stand, hour after mind-numbing hour, through many of these speeches over the years. It was not something to look forward to.

Icaza continued. "Even packing the prisoners in fairly tightly, not all will be within actual earshot, but then again, many of them don't even speak Spanish. The main audience for the speech will be our people in the bleachers going up here, here, and here, and the television audience, of course.

"The column will be formed ten men abreast in alternating

blocks of one hundred Russians followed by fifty Americans. The Soviet and American officers requested, and we agreed, that they could better move the men smartly through the necessary maneuvers if we let them scatter their officers and NCOs throughout the column. We don't want a mob out there. Also, we've given permission where possible for the officers and men to be issued fresh uniforms from the stocks we seized at both bases. We feel that this will give an even greater impression of our victory in a visual sense. Lastly, during the last half mile before arriving at the reviewing stand, the prisoners will march with their hands clasped behind their necks, officers included. That will really put the cap on it."

"What about security during the parade?" asked General Murguia. "We don't want another abortion like at Raul's funeral."

Estigarribia saw a dark cloud pass over Castro's face as the memory came back to him.

"Oh, no. That could never happen again," insisted General Ibarra, who was in charge of security. "There will be fully armed soldiers posted every ten meters on each side of the parade route, and of course there will be a reinforced security detachment at the reviewing stand. We feel that we've gutted the group that launched the attack of the other day. They were political dissidents who thought that they could do here what was done in East Germany or Poland. What they didn't realize was that while the communist regimes in Eastern Europe were essentially imposed on an unwilling people by foreign invaders, our regime is the product of a popular revolution and therefore has the full support of the masses. We've arrested close to two thousand people, and it appears that the ringleaders were mostly among the three hundred or so killed in the street. That gives you some idea of the shallowness of the movement. You didn't see Lenin or Trotsky actually leading the attack on the Winter Palace, did you? No, a true revolutionary leader, with any kind of a following, would have been behind the scenes, planning and guiding."

Estigarribia saw the smirk on Murguia's face and could easily read his mind. Or Castro leading the troops in Angola or Grenada, he was thinking.

"Since the only credible threat, short of an all-out imperialist invasion, against which the armed forces are already guarding, is from some remnant of this group or a similar one not detected before, we have decided to post company-sized units throughout the city. In the immediate vicinity of the march we'll have riot police squads at each major intersection, backed up with armored cars and water cannon, and we'll have an even larger contingent of police within a few hundred yards behind the reviewing stand, equipped with shields, batons, and riot guns. No, there won't be any chance of any group forming up within miles of the march, and if they try they'll be rounded up or dispersed immediately."

General Murguia rubbed his chin thoughtfully. "As a field soldier, as opposed to a policeman," he said, making the last word sound rather like an insult, "I'm not comfortable with dispersing our forces so much. With the troops on the line of march and the groups spread all over town, you've used up more than a division of regular troops with no viable reserve force."

General Ibarra continued. "We have the appropriate troop concentrations, planned by the High Command, for meeting any full-scale assault from off the island, as you yourself are aware. And as you yourself said, this is more of a police matter. In these cases the job is to be everywhere at once to prevent a sizeable threat from forming, not to be prepared to meet a concentrated enemy at a key point." He added with rather arrogant finality, "Besides, we have had these dispositions approved by the Jefe himself."

"In that case I'm satisfied," Murguia surrendered quickly.

"Thank you, General," intoned Castro. "I think we've learned that it's never out of place to make doubly sure of security arrangements. Now, if you'll excuse me," he said, rising, "I have a meeting of the ambassadors of the new PRB nations to attend."

Chapter Seventeen

SANTIAGO DE LAS VEGAS, CUBA: 1700 HOURS, 29 JANUARY

Captain Meese, General Akamirov, and Colonel Ogarkov stood side-by-side, watching the last of the trucks carrying the Americans from Guantánamo roll into the base. After they had saluted the last one into camp they strolled off toward a soccer field where they could talk safely.

"I'm very pleased with the preparations that I have seen you two making for the first," Akamirov said. "I understand you now have a final plan to present to me."

"Yes, sir," said Ogarkov as the American nodded for him to make the presentation. All three men were fluent in Spanish, but the Russians' English was good enough that they had chosen to make this their language of communication.

"The trickiest part will be getting the weapons from here to the reviewing stand undetected. The Cubans don't bother us much inside the camp, being satisfied with perimeter guards and occasional patrols through the grounds and buildings, but I'm sure we can make our preparations securely, using lookouts to warn of trouble. We're going to have to forego the machine guns and the few mortars. They're just too large to risk, even dismantled. Our main weapons for the assault will be the submachine guns, AKMs with folding stocks, pistols, and grenades. The AK-47s and a couple of PK light machine guns will be completely dismantled into their component parts and reassembled after we're inside the embassy compound, to support the defense.

"The pistols and grenades, and also as many bayonets as we can find, are easy enough to conceal under slightly baggy shirts. With the AKMs, which will be our primary source of firepower, we plan to tape one to the back of every other man in the third file in from each edge of the column and, especially, of every man in the third row from the front of the group as we will be formed up in front of the reviewing stand. On our signal the man behind each weapons carrier will pull the weapon out from under the shirt of the man in front. The weapons carriers will be issued jackets or extra-large shirts to help conceal this. On the second signal the outside files, or the front two rows, will drop to the ground, and the AKMs will open up. We'll scatter the pistols and grenades throughout the outside ranks, where they're more likely to have a chance to use them at close range.

"The RPG-7 rocket launchers pose a special problem. There aren't too many, unfortunately, but they are quite bulky when loaded with the rocket. Also, because of the backblast we won't be able to use them safely within the body of the column. What we've done is to designate a number of particularly long-legged men who will strap either a launcher or a rocket to the inside of one leg under oversized pants. We'll slit these pants and reseal them with Velcro strips, and place these men in the center of the column where their limping won't show so much. A man with a launcher will walk next to another with a rocket, and two unarmed men will be in front of them. On the first signal the weapons carriers will drop on their backs, the man in front of each will disengage the weapon or rocket, and the launcher will be loaded. Several men now armed with assembled weapons will move to the flanks of the column to be in a position to fire if we get armored vehicles early on. The others will retire into the embassy compound to support the defense."

"I shudder to think of the leg and body hair that's going to be ripped off in those first few minutes," Akamirov laughed.

"War is hell, General," Meese observed.

"That leaves the question of whom to tell and when," Akamirov said.

Meese continued. "Since the Cubans have been good enough to

permit us to distribute men and officers as we see fit, that problem will be minimized. Of course the technicians will not need to be told anything. At the moment of action there will be one man in the know in each section who will simply point out the direction to run, and we'll have them grouped in areas where they won't tend to get in the way of the fighting.

"The only people who will need to know as soon as possible and to begin some kind of training are the assault teams who will hit the reviewing stand. Given the limitations of arms anyway, we figure a company-sized force, about 150 men, would be optimal, with the remainder of the armed men being used to neutralize the route guards and cover the retreat of the others into the embassy compound. This force will be divided into ten-man assault teams by nationality. There's no point in language difficulties being an additional handicap. We've got troubles enough as it is."

The three men stopped and Meese began to trace in the bare dirt with a stick. "This plan has been worked out by our tactical team of officers, composed of two of my marine officers and several Soviet infantry officers, all with combat experience. The assault teams will include both armed men and former weapons carriers, in order to limit further the number of men who have to be informed of the operation ahead of time. The weapons carriers will have a first task of trying to recover arms from Cuban casualties. Two teams will charge up the stairs at either flank of the reviewing stand. Two more will provide covering fire from the front of the stand, taking aimed fire at the security people who are bound to be in the stands. This last group will be supplied with a heavy allotment of AKMs for this purpose, while the assault teams will have more pistols for close work. Three more teams will rush around either side of the stand to the back to seal off any escape and prevent reinforcement by the enemy. The remaining three teams will be held in reserve in the center under Colonel Ogarkov's command.

"The assault teams going up the right side of the stands and the covering teams on that side will be American," Meese continued. "I will lead the assault group, and I have selected a particularly efficient marine first sergeant to lead the covering force. By the way, although

I am a navy officer, I ran riverine patrols in the Mekong Delta in Vietnam and served on our SEAL teams until just recently, so I have seen my share of infantry-type combat as well."

"We've decided that professional qualifications far outweigh the privileges of rank in this case," Ogarkov interjected. "The men for each team have been selected on the basis of physical strength, quickness, weapons skills, and experience; officers, NCOs, and enlisted men all together, with the best of the lot in command."

"Quite the case," Akamirov agreed. "We can worry about hurt professional pride when we get everyone back home."

Meese went on. "Colonel Ogarkov will be in overall command, and I think you know Major Zhdanov, who will lead the assault on the left side of the stands."

"I have also selected another Afghan veteran, Capt. Boris Vlassov, to lead the covering force on that side of the stand," Ogarkov added.

Meese and Ogarkov then drew in the blocks in front of the stands that represented the formations of Americans and Soviets as they would march into the reviewing stand area. Meese commented as they drew. "As you can see, the assault force will be grouped across the front of the formation, facing the stands. Other groups of weapons teams will be scattered around the perimeter of the body to deal with the nearest guards, and a slightly stronger force will be in the rear to break open a route into the Soviet Embassy, although we will be receiving strong covering fire by that time from the embassy grounds. The central mass of the formation will be largely unarmed and will only have the job of running like hell into the compound and following instructions from guides posted inside as to where to go."

Ogarkov took up the briefing. "The training will focus on weapons familiarization for the Americans with our equipment, and recognition training for all of the assault groups on Cuban military insignia and on mug shots and names of the leading Cuban military and political figures. It wouldn't do for us to come away with twenty Cuban corporals and a street vendor as our hostages. But the big fish will be Castro himself. I think there is a serious risk of us getting blown to hell if we are relying only on senior military or Party people to provide our protection. Castro has a history of not feeling he owes much to anyone but himself. I just hope he doesn't have some fucking double taking his place on the podium."

"I doubt that," said Akamirov. "This is his ultimate moment of glory. The armed might of the two superpowers humbled before him. He's going to want to be there to gloat. The only trick will be making sure our men can cover those fifty yards or so of open ground, overcome any resistance before he can get away, and then take him alive. A dead Castro won't do us much good."

"There will also be dry runs in the basement areas, which we have kept clear for the assault teams to run through their combat drills one at a time," Ogarkov explained. "The primary purpose of this will be to give the men of each team some experience of working together. Even though we have made an effort to group the teams first by nationality and then by original combat unit, there's necessarily been a good deal of mixing. Each man has to know his precise job if this is going to work. Also, if we could get more information on the composition of the security force around the stands, it would be most welcome."

"The KGB says they have a good chance of getting us some updates before showtime," Akamirov said.

Meese added, "Most of our men, and all of those who will be taking part in the assault, have had some familiarization with Soviet weaponry, but some brush-up will be needed to ensure maximum speed in getting our few weapons into action in those crucial few seconds of surprise that we'll have at the start."

He paused for a minute. "I'd like to take the opportunity to say, speaking just for myself now, that I appreciate the chance you are giving us Americans to take a full part in this operation. I mean, most of the men are yours and virtually all of the weapons. The safe haven area is yours, and you really didn't even have to let us in on the operation at all. Well, I just wanted to say thanks."

"You're very welcome, Captain," Akamirov answered, "but it was a strictly military decision. The odds are long enough in this operation without failing to take full advantage of every ounce of military capability at our disposal. Your men did a superb job in fighting off the Cubans, despite their advantage of surprise, and we're going to need them."

Then Akamirov paused. "Speaking for myself, however, I think I would have found a way to include you even if it had not been logically justifiable. The way your men fought at Guantánamo, they have earned the right to fight their way out and not just be rescued by someone else. Whatever the differences that have arisen between our two countries in the last seventy or so years, there is a certain community of military men that survives. We talk the same language, and we live and die for the same unseen superiors." He concluded, placing his hand on the American's shoulder, "Together I think we can get out of this."

"Well, it's worth a goddamn try, General," Meese said. "So do we have permission to brief the men who will be carrying the weapons and conducting the assault?"

"Yes, Captain," Akamirov answered. "The word is 'go,' as I believe you Americans put it. There still could be a last-minute cancellation due to some new information about the negotiations that might make it appear unnecessary, or due to some change in the details of the parade arrangements that would make the attempt suicidal, but the final authorization will consist of the issuing of the weapons in the early morning of the first. Speaking of which, what are your signals to be for the assault?"

Ogarkov took the question. "Perhaps both of our armies have become too wedded to high-technology radio communications, satellite links, and such. Well, we have nothing to work with now, so we're going to go back to basics. Castro himself will essentially give the first signal. Ten minutes after he begins speaking group leaders will give hand signals to the men around them to take out the weapons from their hiding places and assemble them. For the next signal, we revert to the good old days and use simple whistles, provided by our athletic department. A series of short blasts on the whistles, begun by me, taken up by the other officers, and continued basically until all hell breaks loose, will be the signal for the outside ranks to drop down or otherwise get out of the way and for the armed men to open fire. The final signal, to be given by me, Captain Meese, or Major Zhdanov, will be a series of long blasts on the whistles to signify that our prisoners have been taken and are en route into the compound, and that the covering force can then retire."

"Which brings us to the most delicate question," Akamirov said. "What provisions have you made for taking the prisoners?"

"We anticipate that most of the security people will be on the ground around the stands and that very few of the men on the platform will actually be armed. At least that is what we hope," Ogarkov added. "That will permit us to take most of them alive. The assault teams will be supplied with short lengths of cord, and even a few pairs of handcuffs, courtesy of our military police officers, with which to secure the prisoners' hands. Each prisoner will be assigned a guard from either the assault force or the supporting-fire force, which by that time will have completed its mission, and the prisoners will be herded into the compound through the hollow box created by the covering force and the flanking forces. Then the covering force can gradually collapse that box by retiring into the compound after them."

"Your plan sounds as complete as we can make it at this time," Akamirov concluded. "As I mentioned before, we are hoping that the KGB will be able to give us some updated information on the opposition before we go in. Now I suggest you gentlemen get your teams together, and advise them of their roles and get the training underway."

The three men saluted each other, and Ogarkov and Meese strode off purposefully toward the barracks area while Akamirov remained, lazily dragging his foot over the loose soil to erase their diagram.

Chapter Eighteen

Since the assault on the Soviet and American garrisons a state of siege had existed in Cuba, with a midnight to five A.M. curfew, except for those vehicles carrying safe-conduct passes. Naturally, the Soviet and American diplomatic staffs were not provided with such benefits, but there was still time for a decent dinner at one of Havana's limited number of acceptable restaurants. To this end a Soviet Embassy sedan, a Russian-made Chaika with four embassy officers inside, departed the embassy compound in the dark of the evening. None of the passengers was a known KGB officer, but all had been carefully briefed by Kurupatin during the afternoon.

They had paused a good long while at the Cuban guard post at the gate and again waited prudently at the end of the driveway for a truck to pass, even though it was rather distant when they reached the street. Thus having allowed the DGCI surveillants ample opportunity to identify the passengers as non-KGB and therefore not worthy of the first team of veteran surveillants, they continued to drive leisurely but purposefully to a restaurant across town frequented by the Soviets. They were followed at about a block's distance by one carload of Cuban surveillants, which in turn was followed, about two blocks back, by another. A third and fourth car were on parallel streets to the left and right of the Russians' vehicle. In the event that the target car turned in either direction the following car would continue straight ahead for a block and become a flanker, while the flanking car on the side in which the target turned would fall in behind the target. Thus the target would never see another vehicle make the same turn he did. The maneuver was even easier at night, because most headlights look the same, particularly in a country where the vast majority of the cars on the road came from the same factories in the USSR.

The Russians arrived at the restaurant without mishap and backed into a parking space on an apron of concrete set back from the street. On one side was the tall wall of a house, on the other another car from the Soviet Embassy, behind a tall hedge. The surveillants of this vehicle did not know that the parking space had been vacated only seconds before by some earlier Russian diners.

When the passengers of the car had gotten out they stood for a moment by their open doors, discussing the relative merits of the restaurant across the street and the one next door. Having come to a decision, they locked the car and retired to the restaurant next door.

The Cuban surveillants watched this performance with due interest but did not notice that the trunk lid on the car had raised up slightly and then closed silently, as Yuri Kamalyan, a veteran KGB officer, rolled quickly out of the trunk. He then slid between the branches of the hedge, in a gap between the pavement and the foliage. On the other side of the hedge he quickly stood upright and walked up an alley and around a corner.

Kamalyan was an ethnic Armenian whose heritage had given him the advantage of swarthy features, dark hair and eyes, and a short stature, which permitted him to pass relatively easily for a Latin or an Arab, a factor that had greatly assisted his career in field operations around the world. His Spanish was good, though it would not pass for native, but his goal was simply to be taken by the casual observer for another Cuban pedestrian, wearing locally made T-shirt, pants, and sneakers. He would walk rather than take public transportation in order to avoid having to engage in conversation. He would make his meeting and then return to the restaurant parking lot and be waiting under the hedge for his drivers to return from dinner. If he missed that deadline he would walk to a nearby safe house apartment and wait until the following night, when a similar scenario, with different Russians, different vehicles, at a different restaurant, would permit him to slip back into the embassy, his absence never having been noted by the Cubans.

Kamalyan did not have far to go, only about three blocks. He walked casually, without appearing to loiter, as he had some forty-five minutes to kill. When he ducked under low-hanging trees along the sidewalk he would take the opportunity to check his watch, which was synchronized with that of his agent to the local telephone time service. His route actually took him much farther than the three blocks to his objective, and it included various maneuvers to discover whether he was being followed. His final maneuver—purposely walking down a long dead-end alley and then doubling back suddenly in hopes of catching an over-eager surveillant following him to identify his activities—would have definitely labelled Kamalyan as an intelligence officer looking for surveillance. It was something a field officer would not ordinarily want to do, since it would earn him the full attention of the host country's security service for the rest of his tour. However, Kamalyan's mission was important enough, and as it was probably the last one he would run in Cuba, he was willing to run that risk in order to safeguard his agent.

If he had seen signs of surveillance he would have aborted the mission and simply gone back to the restaurant, hoping to be able to get back into the embassy without being arrested. But this evening the streets were largely deserted and Kamalyan saw no evidence that his escape from the embassy compound had been noted, so he continued to his appointed meeting area, a block-long alley bordered by featureless walls.

At precisely 2123 hours Kamalyan was nearing the end of the alley when a white Lada pulled quickly around the corner in front of him. He popped the rear door open before the car had come to a halt and was lying on the backseat out of sight, with the door closed again, before anyone who might have been following the Lada would have had time to round the corner and see the act. The car continued up the alley and on a circuitous route around the city with

Kamalyan's agent, known in the embassy for security reasons only as Keeper 6, at the wheel.

"Good evening, Jose," Keeper 6 called cheerfully over his shoulder, using the alias Kamalyan used with him, although Keeper 6 was fully aware that it was not his true name. In his official position Keeper 6 could have found out his true name at any time, and probably knew it, but both were old hands at the espionage business and knew how to play the game.

"Nice night," grunted Kamalyan as he tried to twist his bent legs into a more comfortable position in the very small back seat. "How are things with you these days?"

"No security problems, if that's what you mean," he answered, "but things are very tense around the high brass. The military know that Fidel killed Raul, but since the latter's well and truly dead they're not about to put their lives on the line to avenge him. He was never really popular with the military, any more than Fidel is. The professionals think of them as being meddlesome amateurs who sometimes guess right, like Hitler. They do see the killing of Raul as a threat to themselves since he was their nominal chief."

"But is there any indication that they're going to take action against Castro in the next few days?" Kamalyan asked. Like most experienced field officers he did not use tape recorders or even take notes, the possession of which might be difficult to explain to an overly curious policeman. Instead he knew the local political situation well enough, along with the questions to which he wanted answers, that he could trust to his memory the pieces of the puzzle provided by an agent, at least until he could get back to his office to write up his reports. Only in the case of long lists of names or numbers would he have to risk written notes, and this was not one of those times.

"I doubt it," Keeper 6 answered, steering the car onto a fairly heavily travelled avenue. "They're disgruntled and even afraid, but they want to see how far Fidel's lucky streak will take him before they move. He's riding high right now. He's neutralized both military bases, with heavy casualties on our side to be sure, but without any reaction yet from either superpower. He's getting drooling support from most of the Third World for the debt relief that they rightly believe he obtained for them. And the missiles are on the way, with a multinational naval escort no less! They don't have to worry about mass popular support in a country like this if they want to launch a coup, but the generals can't be sure of the backing of their junior officers and enlisted men unless Castro makes a big, public blunder. Of course they'd be more willing to take the risk if they saw an imminent physical threat to themselves, but not now."

"Who would you pick as the leader of a coup?" Kamalyan continued.

"There are several well-liked and respected generals, not as many as before Ochoa was shot, but I would pick Murguia. He's got a chest full of medals, earned ones, he's a good public relations man within the military circles, and, more importantly, he's the commander of the 101st Armored Division, located within convenient driving distance of Havana."

"Good. We'd like to keep that option alive, literally," Kamalyan said. "We have reason to believe that Castro might try something against prominent generals on the day of the victory parade. If there is something you can do to keep Murguia separated from the other generals on that day, do it."

"That'll be difficult for me, since I'm not an army man," Keeper 6 said, shaking his head.

"I'll leave that up to you. As I said, it's only a possibility. If you can do it without burning yourself, fine, if not, Murguia will have to take his chances with the others."

"I'll do my best."

"Now, what can you tell me about security preparations for the victory day parade?"

Aha! thought Keeper 6. Risk to Murguia on victory parade day, and special interest in security arrangements. They're going to make a move! About goddamn time! Of course, Keeper 6 thought, they would naturally want to know everything about everything at a time like this, but the odds are heavy that February first would be a good day to be far away from Castro and Havana in general.

Keeper 6 had draped his arm across the back of the front seat of the car. Now, with a casual movement of two fingers he extended a tightly folded pair of thin sheets of paper to Kamalyan. "I know that you don't like me to bring out documents, but I thought you'd want the full details of the placement of all security forces in the city. The first sheet is a map of the city with the locations labelled, and the second is a legend to those labels. They're mainly worried about a repeat of the riot at Raul's funeral, so they've spread troops all over town. With the forces they have concentrated to meet a possible invasion, that doesn't leave them much in the way of an operational reserve, but your military men will see that from the map. . . . It was Fidel's idea," he added.

"Did I ever mention that when this is over, you will be able to retire to a castle in Spain or a penthouse on the Riviera at our expense?" Kamalyan laughed as he tucked the papers into his sock, not exactly an approved concealment device, but better than nothing.

"*If* I'm alive," Keeper 6 reminded him, also laughing.

"Well, yes, if you want to split hairs, but remember, if this were real easy everybody would be doing it. Well, I think we'd better head back. I want to make my rendezvous tonight if I can."

Keeper 6 had already anticipated that and had been gradually circling back toward their designated drop-off point. Again he rounded a blind corner into a dark side street, continuing to check constantly in his mirror for surveillance, since literally no one in the Cuban government was above suspicion. The back door was open and Kamalyan out and into the shadows in the blink of an eye.

Kamalyan watched Keeper 6's car drive out of sight and saw no other car pass that might have been following him. He then walked rather quickly, checking less frequently for surveillance as, if his meeting had been observed, it was all over anyway. He paced himself to arrive at the hedge just moments before the diners were due to show up at the car, and wedged himself under the hedge to wait. They were on time, and during the normal confusion of opening and shutting car doors, arguing about who got to ride "shotgun," and such, he popped the trunk again and rolled inside, shutting it quietly. When the Chaika was safely back in the embassy garage, Kurupatin was surprised to find Kamalyan curled up, sound asleep, when they opened the trunk lid.

Chapter Nineteen

Paco knelt next to a shallow hole in the dirt in the backyard of a house in the southern suburbs of Havana. He was in a small rectangle of yard wedged in between the house's small wooden garage and the tall back and side walls of the garden. Here he was invisible from both the street and the house. He was digging very quietly in the dirt with a small gardening trowel that he had carried with him in his bag.

Paco had arrived in Havana in the early afternoon and had had time to stop for a dinner of rice with a fried egg, typical Cuban fare, at least since the Revolution. Since the waiter had made it quite clear that there actually was *fish* on the menu and in the kitchen, a rare stroke of luck, the waiter had thought it odd that Paco had opted for the simpler meal, but Paco just wanted something to fill his stomach. A bad piece of fish could add a whole new set of difficulties to his task, which was already difficult enough.

He had strolled down the darkened residential street at about eleven o'clock, well before curfew but late enough for most people to be off even the busier streets. When he had reached the side wall of the house, which was on a corner lot, he had found the single spike he had driven in the wall years before as a foothold and vaulted over the eight-foot wall into the yard.

141

He had simply lain silently in the pitch black of the yard until over an hour after the last light in the house had been extinguished. Then he had carefully measured out the distances from the neighboring walls and had begun to dig, silently lifting the dirt out a small trowelful at a time, like taking sugar for his coffee.

He was now down about a foot and a half, about halfway there. He paused after every scoop, listening for approaching footsteps or vehicles. He was extremely grateful that the family in the house, whom he did not know, had not happened to buy a dog in the years since he buried the package. Of course he would have dispatched the dog if necessary, but it was one less thing to worry about now.

There was no rush. Even after unearthing the package and replacing the disturbed soil he would still have to wait until five o'clock for the curfew to end before he could go out on the street. He worked without light. He had a small East German flashlight in his bag as well, but he did not need it.

Finally his tool struck something denser than earth. It was the stiff burlap of the bag. He quickly finished uncovering it and pulled it from the hole. He cut the stitching on the end of the bag with a pocketknife and carefully felt for each item of equipment. When he was satisfied it was all there he stored the package in his carrying bag and refilled the hole, stomping the earth into place before replacing the piece of sod he had removed. It was too dark to check his handiwork, but it would have to do. At worst, someone would come along during that very day and discover that something had been buried and then dug up here. That would be all.

There were a number of separate parcels inside the sack, and he selected two of them by feel alone. He tore open the sealed plastic wrapping of the first and laid out the parts of his weapons-cleaning kit. He tore open the second and removed a small revolver, well-protected with grease, with a long cylindrical silencer that fitted over the barrel. He cleaned the gun carefully, as he had done blindfolded hundreds of times, and loaded it with rounds from a separate plastic bag that had been wrapped with the pistol. He then stored the gun, with the silencer attached, in a large side pocket of his carrying bag. With the bag slung over his right shoulder he could open the pocket, insert his right hand easily, and fire the weapon without removing it from the pocket.

When he was satisfied he braced one foot on the rain gutter of the garage and hoisted himself up to the top of the wall to check for early traffic. There was none. He checked his luminous watch. It was 0445, close enough. He placed the bag on top of the wall and hoisted himself up after it, dropping lightly onto the sidewalk on the other side and pulling the bag down to him. He scurried into some bushes across the street and sat in the shadows. In the continuing darkness he could safely wait here for fifteen minutes until curfew ended.

The bag was much heavier now than when he started. He had had several days' worth of old Cuban newspapers in it, along with a pair of old shoes, some clothes, and some simple tools, which he had discarded just before entering the yard. If he were stopped and searched now there would be no explaining the contents of the bag, so there was no point in attempting to disguise it. The bag was a rather longish cylinder, just the kind that workers often use to carry their tools, and it was carefully stained with paint, plaster, and grease.

Paco waited until just after five before he stood up and began walking in the direction of the apartment he had spotted earlier the day before. He didn't try to use a bus, as he could see that they were jammed full as usual, even at this early hour. He didn't want an accident that might spill his questionable cargo all over the floor of the bus in front of thirty or forty witnesses. He had about six miles to walk but he had walked much farther, carrying heavier loads, through jungle trails, so he settled into his habitual, ground-eating lope.

Although he was quite familiar with Havana and had had all of the analytical capabilities of the U.S. government at his disposal to plan this operation, the lack of precise intelligence on where Castro would be and when had prevented any serious preliminary work from being done. All he had basically decided was that security around Castro was too strong for him to attempt a close-in kill. That having been established, he preferred extending the range as far as possible, to place himself outside as many of the concentric rings of security that typically surround public figures. He had estimated that four hundred yards would be optimal, close enough for him to be reasonably sure of a hit and beyond all but the most peripheral security posts.

Paco couldn't help chuckling to himself. In a movie there would have been a network of support assets waiting for him in Havana. They would have dedicated their lives to waiting for the moment to hand him the keys to the perfect safe house, which would coincidentally have provided a perfect view of the target area. Of course, it would have also been equipped with his high school sweetheart, who would still look ravishingly good. In the real world, one or more of those assets would have died, or become an alcoholic, or been arrested or turned by the local security service. No, this job had to be done alone.

The announcement in the newspaper of the victory parade and of Castro's planned speech at the event had been a godsend. Of course his professional security people would know that this kind of advance notice would work in the favor of any would-be assassin and would be taking extra precautions, but he would have had to assume top performance on their part in any case.

The previous afternoon, still stiff from his long ride in the crowded bus, he had strolled past the reviewing stand area. There were several apartment blocks, each of three or four stories, within four hundred yards of the front of the stands. He had picked one that presented only a narrow flank to the reviewing stand, with a series of enclosed balconies on that side. Actually, these balconies were outside service areas, where the laundry was normally hung and washing was done, and behind which the kitchen and bathroom would likely be located. This presented several advantages for Paco. The security forces would probably be more interested in the closer buildings, which had large windows facing the stands. The narrow, louvered windows of the kitchen or bathroom could easily be opened enough for Paco's purposes, and the setback provided by the balcony and the cover of some carefully arranged laundry would make him totally invisible to observers from outside, even with powerful field glasses.

The weight of the bag dug into his shoulder slightly, but he could not shift it to his left because of the need for ready access to his handgun. He had carefully discarded in the depths of a garbage bin his garden trowel, which he would no longer need, and a night vision scope and a large silencer, to reduce the bulk and weight of the load somewhat. Since he would be working in daylight the night vision scope would be unnecessary. Since he was going for a long shot, from an apartment complex, he was relatively unconcerned about the noise of his firing, and he would need the full muzzle velocity of the round to ensure proper penetration at that distance. Paco calculated that if he barricaded himself in the apartment, by the time the neighbors figured out what was going on, called the police, and were able to break in, he could have fired off all of his ammunition anyway. Of course this would not do his chances for escape any good, but Paco was relatively unconcerned about that possibility.

He finally approached the building, a rapidly decaying four-story structure. He estimated that it was no more than ten years old, but it probably had less than ten years of life left before large chunks would begin falling off of it. There was no concierge, one of the things that had attracted him to the place at first, and he walked quickly into the courtyard and up the poorly lit staircase on the side of the building nearest the stands. He had chosen the staircase leading to the service entrances of the building. Elsewhere in Latin America he would have chosen the front entrances, as even in poor neighborhoods of poor countries everyone has a servant of some sort, and the laundry, at this time of day, would be the busiest part of the house. In Cuba, however, with no one able to afford a servant and most housewives obliged to work to help eke out the husbands' meager salaries, much of the washing would be done in the evening and on weekends, and at about nine in the morning on a weekday the laundry would be largely deserted.

As he walked, he had rummaged in his bag for a large pipe wrench, casually positioned it so that the head stuck up out of the bag, and then zipped the bag up to the wrench. His cover story, if he were discovered, would initially be that he was a plumber, come to fix a water leak reported by the apartment downstairs. Plumbers don't carry badges, so the visual proof should be enough to get him in the door.

He reached the door to the third-floor apartment. He would have preferred the fourth floor, but top floors and roofs tended to get special attention from security forces. He knocked, firmly but not too loudly. The service door of the neighboring apartment was behind him, and he did not want to have people from both apartments come to the door by mistake. Another advantage of the service entrance was that while front doors usually had peepholes the back doors did not, so they would have to open the door to see him. No answer.

He knocked again and waited. Then a third time. The building was very quiet. He could hear Latin music coming over a scratchy radio from a ground-floor apartment and a baby crying somewhere else downstairs, but there was no sound from this apartment. There was an overpowering musty smell in the stairwell, the smell of laundry, years of cooking, and a little urine, thanks to the shoddy plumbing, he thought. He knew this smell very well.

He pulled from his pocket a fat pen and popped off the end cap. In the bottom of the pen was a set of almost wire-thin locksmith's tools. He set to work on the lock and had it open in under fifteen seconds. He was thankful that there was only one lock and no chain. Although this would only have delayed him, it would have increased his risk of discovery.

He quickly entered the apartment and shut and locked the door silently behind him. He stood listening for several minutes. There was no rush now. He had only to be careful. He placed his bag on the floor in front of the door to act as a kind of alarm in case someone came home suddenly, and stalked through the kitchen with his revolver in one hand.

The apartment was definitely occupied. Clothing hung on wires on the balcony outside the kitchen, and the breakfast dishes had been washed and left in the rack to dry. He looked through the louvers in the kitchen window and saw that he had a clear view of the center of the reviewing stand, albeit at an angle. The balcony was divided from that of the neighboring apartment by a solid wall. Good, he thought.

He moved from the kitchen into what apparently served as a dining area, with a small wooden table and two chairs. No high chair, no toys; it was evidently the apartment of a working couple without children. Good. He passed through the sparsely furnished living room and into the single bedroom. There was one double bed, a small armoire against the wall, and a vanity table with mirror.

Paco figured that he had a good seven or eight hours until the couple came home, probably separately, but he would have to be ready in case one or both of them had the habit of coming home for lunch. He rummaged through the mail and other papers in the drawer of a small table in the living room. The apartment belonged to Juan Carlos and Maria Segovia, both in their mid-thirties. He worked as some kind of mechanic and she worked at a day-care center. From the addresses of their places of employment he suspected that neither could make it home on their lunch hour. Good.

He fetched his bag from the kitchen and took it into the bedroom. He took from the bag the large package from the garden and began to lay out the separately wrapped parcels within.

From one he took a small bottle of ether and placed that in his guayabera pocket, along with a stray sock he picked out of a drawer. He also took a bottle of pills and placed them on the dresser. Then he laid out the parts of his specially modified M-14 rifle with its sniper scope. The rifle had a collapsible stock and a pistol grip, and each part was carefully coated with grease. He took his cleaning kit and meticulously but efficiently cleaned each piece and assembled the weapon. When he was finished he took out the fifty rounds of exploding ammunition, divided them among the three magazines he had for the weapon, loaded one into the rifle, and chambered a round. He would have liked to have the opportunity to test-fire the rifle, but that was out of the question.

Paco could have selected a Soviet-made weapon such as the Dragunov, or some third-country product, but he had an affection for the M-14, the regular-issue version of which he had carried in Vietnam. It was not a true sniper rifle, but in his hands it performed like one. It was also handy to have in a difficult situation. He put away the remnants of his gear, stopped by the kitchen to pick up a soft drink from the refrigerator, and returned to the bedroom to wait.

Chapter Twenty

Featherstone was strolling through the grounds of the Soviet Embassy compound with Maj. Emilio Rodriguez, his army attaché, and Gunnery Sgt. Frank Michaels, head of the marine security detachment. They had just completed the move of the American diplomats, some sixty-plus individuals, to the Soviet compound, where they had been housed in adequate, if spartan, comfort. Thus far only Popper, Rodriguez, Michaels, and his five-man marine guard force had been informed of the full purpose of their move.

Not all of the group present with Featherstone were pleased with this project. Michaels, whose primary function was to protect the U.S. mission against the incursions of the sorts of people under whose protection he and the rest of the Americans now were, was as nervous as a long-tailed cat in a room full of rocking chairs. Rodriguez had more specific objections to the plan. His main concern was that their ramshackle garrison should hold out until help could arrive.

"I'll tell you, Bill," Rodriguez groaned. "This whole plan seems to depend too much on everything going just right. Suppose we don't snag anybody off the stands the Cubans just can't stand the idea of losing? Suppose those clowns in Washington are dozing when this

148

goes down or they just don't have their shit together enough to get something this big moving in a matter of hours? That's what we're talking about, you know. Even if they don't use artillery or air to just blast this whole neighborhood to smithereens, we don't have enough ammunition for more than really a few minutes of sustained combat.

"The other side of that coin is that our forces from outside aren't going to have any cakewalk either. The Cuban Army has more firepower than anything south of the Rio Grande and more combat experience than anything in this hemisphere. They've always planned their mobilization around a quick injection of reservists to bring skeleton units up to strength and form new ones, something like the Swiss except that they *start* with a full-time army about ten times the size. They've had almost a week now to get rolling, and they've put everyone into uniform they think they might need. We're not going to catch either their air force or antiair defenses off guard, and we'll face some heavy losses trying to punch through. What worries me most is that, knowing all of this, the brass in Washington is going to think long and hard before ordering anybody to come and get us. Meanwhile we die a glorious death here."

"Army ROTC some twenty-odd years ago doesn't qualify me to argue the tactical military points with you, Emilio," Featherstone sighed. "However, I've been paying enough attention to Castro over the last couple of years that I think trusting to his sense of honor and humanity is a pretty big risk itself. The Sovs have information, which I find perfectly believable, that he ordered the killing of his own brother, Raul, as part of the justification for this whole abortion, so I don't think he'd lose much sleep over our memories. I agree with you one hundred percent that our inability to communicate what we have planned securely to Washington, or the Soviets to Moscow for that matter, is a big problem. The best we can do is to try to make sure that they are watching the parade on one of those real-time surveillance satellites. Then we can hope that they will put the pieces together quickly and get us some help in time. From the information the Soviets have shared with Popper and me, it sounds as though *we*, at least, will take the Cubans completely by surprise. That might give us a few hours before they can launch a coordinated attack of any kind."

"I sure as hell hope you're right," Rodriguez conceded. "I'm a good soldier, and I'll follow this Captain Meese's orders, but I just want you to know that, as soon as I can get to a phone, I'm calling my broker and telling him to put all my money in Chinese war bonds." The three men laughed, but not very hard.

As they stood in the middle of the open compound they saw Ambassador Osman and a young, trim man dressed in blue jeans and a dark green T-shirt come striding up to them. "Our comrades in arms," grumbled Michaels.

"Good morning, gentlemen," Osman beamed. "Welcome to our little piece of Muscovy. I'm sorry I couldn't see you in personally, but I was meeting with General Akamirov out at Santiago de las Vegas earlier. I trust everything went all right on your move."

"Just as planned," Featherstone answered. "Yesterday Gunny Michaels here was kind enough to stumble into a Cuban guard at the Marine House, and harsh words were exchanged. Before Major Rodriguez and a Cuban officer could break things up several Cuban teeth had been swallowed." Michaels smiled shyly. He had briefly considered a career in professional boxing before deciding that he preferred doing his fighting with automatic weapons.

"When I made my demarche to the Cubans about the move," Featherstone continued, "suggesting that it would be easier to control everyone if they were together in an enclosed place, the Cubans jumped at the idea. I suspect that they thought, 'All the better for the imperialists to watch the spectacle of their own humiliation,' which we Americans might otherwise have missed. It also makes their keeping an eye on us easier."

"Well, it's done. One more step on our journey," said Osman. "Please let me introduce you all to Maj. Gregor Fleischmann, who will be in immediate charge of the defense of the compound, at least until the more senior officers among the military prisoners join us." Osman introduced a rather short, wiry man with short, pale blond hair and dark blue eyes, who thrust out his hand to Featherstone and the others in turn.

"Are you an army officer?" asked Rodriguez.

"No, KGB," replied Fleischmann unwaveringly. "But I used to

be in the army, Spetsnaz, you know, our special forces, until just two years ago."

Osman noted the stiffening of Rodriguez's jaw at the mention of the KGB and stepped in. "Major Fleischmann is the officer with the most combat experience present with us. He also has an excellent command of both Spanish and English, so I have selected him to lead our tiny little army. I trust you do not object, Major?"

"I suppose you speak some Farsi, too?" Rodriguez made the question sound like a statement.

"I imagine I'll lose it in time, the way you forgot your Vietnamese," Fleischmann said, sticking his already prominent jaw out even farther in Rodriguez's direction.

"Okay, fair enough," conceded Rodriguez. "Orders are orders in any event, and as Benjamin Franklin said, 'Either we all hang together or we'll all hang separately.'"

After the quiet round of chuckles subsided Osman continued. "If you gentlemen have a moment, I think it would be well for our military men to go over their preparations and coordinate their activities."

"That's what we're here for," said Rodriguez.

"Very well," said Fleischmann. "At final count, including all of the personally owned weapons among the Soviets, we have forty-five AK-47s, fifteen submachine guns, one Dragunov sniper rifle with scope and night vision device, thirty-two pistols of various types, twelve hunting rifles, and ten shotguns. This means that we can arm about one hundred men in some fashion. We also have a stock of smoke and tear gas grenades that will come in handy during the dash for the embassy. Our only problem is that we have far fewer weapons than we have men qualified to use them."

"We've just completed our own inventory," said Rodriguez, "and counting both the marines' and the personal weapons, we have one M-16, fourteen pump shotguns, three over-under sport shotguns, three hunting rifles, twenty-eight pistols, and three very illegal, privately owned submachine guns purchased by some of our people who have served in either Bogotá or San Salvador, giving us a total of about fifty weapons. We also have some smoke and tear gas grenades. We are in the opposite situation, in that of our sixty or so people only about thirty have the age and experience to make them effective fighters. So we'll be glad to donate our extra weapons to the common pool."

"That would be most welcome," Fleischmann said. As the group moved around the compound yard Fleischmann pointed to signs of apparently casual activity here and there. "You'll notice that empty oil drums or garbage cans have been placed at various points around the compound walls. There are planks at each position as well, and these will be placed over the tops of the cans to form firing steps, especially during the initial action. I do not expect that we can hold the walls for long; we will be retiring to the buildings fairly early on.

"Toward that end we have been gradually reinforcing the walls of the buildings with furniture and anything else we can find. Fortunately, one of the buildings was undergoing some renovation, so we have a certain amount of construction material available, including bags of cement, which will be used at the moment of the break to form machine-gun pits at some of the entrances. Also, the basement of one of the outbuildings was having some plumbing work done, so we have been digging through a gap in the foundation. We have opened a similar space in the basement wall of the nearest building— there," he pointed with his chin. "Hopefully, we will complete a tunnel connecting the two before the day after tomorrow. That will be convenient, but it mainly serves as a source of soil to fill sandbags without the Cubans having a view of the activity. It will also provide some additional safe shelter for all of the people we are expecting."

"Naturally, we'll contribute people to your work details," Rodriguez offered.

"Thank you, I'll introduce you to the officer in charge of that later. I suspect we'll all be very busy for the next few days."

They had reached the embassy motor pool. "We have a number of cars here that, when the surprise is revealed, we will pull into position in two long rows connecting the main embassy building with the nearest of the apartment buildings. That will offer us at least some cover for getting from one building to another. We'll use others, including a Cuban dump truck that was left here, to block off the main gate."

"It's sort of a shame you don't have the same trouble here with terrorists that we do most everywhere," Featherstone commented. "Then you'd have those huge, decorative, solid concrete flowerpots all around the place along with those roll-up steel walls that pop out of the ground in the gateway, as we do in all of our embassies."

"It will only be a delaying device in any case," said Fleischmann. "If they come with infantry alone those things won't stop them. If they come with tanks it won't stop them either."

When they had entered the garage area Fleischmann showed them into a storage room where several Soviets were busy filling bottles with a brownish liquid from a large drum.

"Aha!" exclaimed Rodriguez, "good old-fashioned Molotov cocktails."

"Yes," said Fleischmann. "We've got plenty of gasoline, and we're mixing it with a little detergent to make it stick. We'll place these bombs around the compound for close-in defense. Our major handicap right now is that we can only take steps that are not visible to the Cubans from outside the compound. Otherwise we could be digging trenches and really making a difference."

"You're doing admirably, Major Fleischmann," Featherstone commented. "I would say, 'Fidel Castro, look out!'"

Fleischmann looked at Featherstone with a smirk. "Would you like to make a bet on our chances of surviving here more than four hours?"

"Great minds work alike," laughed Rodriguez.

"Our part in the great escape will be relatively simple," Fleischmann continued. "When the troops in the open area in front of the embassy start their breakout we will open up with aimed fire at any armed Cubans we can see. Our first priority will be to help them eliminate any Cuban soldiers between the main body of troops and the embassy gate. We'll use plunging fire from the walls and rooftops to effect this, so as to avoid rounds passing through the enemy to our own men beyond.

"Several of the larger embassy vehicles will be driven quickly out the gate to form two walls, helping to protect the men at least over the last few yards to the gate. We will have a team of armed men, which should include some of your marines," he said, nodding to the gunny, "who will move out of the compound to man this barrier and to help provide covering fire for the men. Inside the wall we will have posted unarmed guides who will direct men to various entries to the buildings, which will be marked at the last minute with colored spray paint. This will help prevent overcrowding, and the men will also be directed depending on whether they have weapons or not, either to shelters or fighting positions. Again, we will need a mix of Americans and Russians to prevent language difficulties."

"That sounds like something I will be able to help with," Featherstone said, glad that he could really contribute something to the effort.

"Here's my final analysis," Fleischmann sighed. "I estimate that with the weapons our men are likely to pick up from downed Cubans we should end up with about five hundred armed men. However, we will only have ammunition enough to hold off one, maybe two, serious infantry assaults after what will be expended in the breakout itself. If what our KGB sources report is correct, it will take the Cubans a couple of hours at least to gather sufficient troops for an assault. They will probably try something ad hoc even earlier, to test our resolve, but that we should be able to beat off. Our only real hope is that our forces off-island can get in here with something that will disrupt the Cuban preparations until a rescue force can reach us. I must admit, frankly, that I am not sanguine about that possibility."

"Thank you, Major," Osman cut in. He had brought them all this far, and he did not want their morale to begin to flag at this late hour. "The air power that we know is already aloft is just minutes from here, and I have every reason to believe that our superiors are just watching for a chance like this. And we will give it to them! In any case, you can ask General Akamirov about Castro's word from his experiences at Santiago de las Vegas. This is the only chance we have, however slim it may be."

Chapter Twenty-one

Paco was standing just inside the bedroom door as the key turned in the apartment door lock. He heard the door open and close. One set of footsteps, a woman. In his right hand was his pistol with its silencer, in his left the sock soaked with ether.

He heard the woman go to the kitchen and set something down, probably a shopping bag filled with whatever she had happened to find in stock on the way home from work. Then the footsteps approached the bedroom. She walked in quickly and did not begin to turn to investigate the strange form she saw out of the corner of her eye until Paco already had the ether-soaked rag over her nose and mouth. He used his pistol hand only to pin her arms until she went limp.

He carried her over to the bed and laid her down. He took a length of cord and tied her hands together in front of her and then to the head of the bed. He then tied her feet together and to the foot of the bed. That should reassure her, he thought. She wasn't bad looking, but Paco wasn't interested. Besides, he had known a girl in college who had been raped and had later committed suicide. He hadn't known her well, but the event had impressed him a great deal. He had begun to realize that an act which as a man, and a Latin at

155

that, he had been taught to take almost for granted could be so horrible for a woman that she could not even live with the memory of it. As a last step he tied a gag in her mouth and then resumed his post by the bedroom door.

Ideally, he would not have had to occupy the apartment until the afternoon before the event, but the security precautions for such a public appearance could well begin on the thirty-first, and he could not afford to be stopped at a police checkpoint with the satchel full of goodies. This way he would be safely inside the security perimeter before it was even set up. The problem with this approach was that he now had to deal with the occupants of the apartment for over forty hours. The ether would keep them out for awhile. When they woke up from that he would assure them he meant them no harm and that he would be gone soon. He would then oblige them to take the sleeping pills he had brought, which should, with one repetition tomorrow night, keep them out until after the thing was over. He would leave both of them asleep with one of them loosely tied, if everything went well and he had a chance to escape. If he were cornered in the apartment he would stay clear of the bedroom if he had to fight and hope that the security people were discriminating enough in their fire not to hurt them. Afterward there would be the question of whether the G2 believed that they were innocent victims, but that was their society at work, not his fault. At least, that was the story he gave himself, and he was sticking to it.

Sometime later Paco, who was still awaiting the husband's arrival, sensed the woman coming around. He turned on the overhead light in the room and stood facing the woman with his pistol aimed at her head. He could see the whites showing all the way around her eyes.

"Don't make a sound unless I tell you," he said in Spanish. "I am not here to hurt you or to take anything you have, but if you do not follow my instructions I will kill you immediately. Do you understand?"

She nodded slowly. He began to undo her gag, showing her the pistol. "This gun has a silencer, so if you cry out, I will hear only a click. Your neighbors will hear nothing, and you will hear nothing ever again. Understood?"

She nodded again.

When the gag was off he said, "Where is your husband? What time will he be home?"

The woman's jaw was trembling so much that she could hardly talk. "He's in the military reserve. He was called up three days ago. I don't know when he'll be back. Please don't hurt me. You can take anything you want—"

"Shut up!" Paco snapped. "I don't want any of this garbage. Prove that your husband was called up."

"The letter is on top of the armoire."

Paco walked over to the armoire and felt around on top, keeping his gun levelled at the woman. He found a sheet of paper and glanced over it. She had not been lying.

"Good," he said. "Now, I want you to take a pill that will put you to sleep. Tomorrow night you will wake up, and I will give you another. When you wake up from that, I will be gone."

"But why are you doing this?"

"I can only say that I am a soldier on a mission. The less you know about it the better for you." He had a glass of water ready and placed the pill on her tongue. He then lifted her head and helped her drink. "Now open your mouth and move your tongue all around," he said. When he was certain that she had swallowed the pill he replaced the gag and watched her pass out.

He then walked into the kitchen and helped himself to some crackers and another soft drink. He looked out the kitchen window at the reviewing stand. The area was floodlit and workers were still hammering planks into place. He picked up his rifle from where he had propped it and sighted in on one of the workmen. It was a rather long shot, but by resting the rifle across the top of the small refrigerator he should have no trouble hitting the mark.

He could see armored cars parked facing the corners of the Soviet Embassy compound, which was also brightly lit. There was an emplacement of a ZSU-23/2 twin-barrelled 23mm antiaircraft gun in the open area off to the left of the reviewing stand. He assumed this was probably more a morale-lifting effort than a serious military measure, as the gun was only really useful against low-flying, slow aircraft, such as helicopters. He noted, however, that it was also a hellacious weapon when fired in a flat trajectory against ground targets, whether vehicles or people.

He then went back to the bedroom and stretched a thin wire across the doorway from the hinge to the leg of the vanity table, at about ankle height. With his warning device set, he reached up and unscrewed the light bulbs in the ceiling lights in the living room and bedroom and lay down on the floor on the far side of the bed, with his rifle and pistol by his side. Then he pulled a pillow off the bed and promptly went to sleep, as secure as he could be, in a hostile country with one of the best internal security machines in the world, with the mission of assassinating the head of state.

Chapter Twenty-two

Sergeant Glover was running his two ten-man squads of marines through the assault drill for the umpteenth time. They were in the gymnasium building of the Soviet base, using the folding bleachers as a mock-up of the reviewing stand. He had, besides his own twenty men, about two dozen other marines who would serve as weapons carriers and cover for the assault team.

Each of the men was carrying the weapon he would use on the morrow, but none had been issued ammunition, just in case. The men marched about, wheeling into the position they would hold just prior to the assault. The men carrying the two AKMs assigned to his unit had them taped to their backs, barrels down, under baggy shirts hanging out of their pants. On a signal from Glover the AKM men would strip the weapons from the backs of the carriers, to the accompaniment of screams and curses as skin and hair came away with the tape. Still behind the cover of the front ranks, the AKM men would load the empty clips they were carrying themselves and make the motion of chambering a round. Then they would wait.

A few moments later Glover would let loose a shrill series of whistles, using his thumb and forefinger, and the men would go into their assault. The early giggling prompted by the yells of "Bang!

159

Pow!" and other sound effects had been brought to an abrupt halt by a string of oaths from Sergeant Glover, and the men now went about their business in dead earnest. Apart from the two men with AK-47s, the rest of the men were armed with semiautomatic pistols. They charged up the steps, firing at imaginary security men, and half of them occupied the perimeter of the right half of the bleachers, while the remainder went through the motions of binding and leading away imaginary prisoners.

Johnson led a team of ten men in the exercise, the ones responsible for securing the stands. He felt decidedly underarmed with only a pistol for protection. Even the butt was too small for his broad hands, and he had decided that he would equip himself with an AK-47 from the first Cuban unlucky enough to get in his way. He had been cross-trained now on the Soviet assault rifle, and while he still would have preferred his trusty M-16, he felt at home with the rugged, heavy new weapon and would feel much more at ease when he had one. Like most of the men who had been briefed on the mission by Captain Meese the night before, Johnson did not like the odds, but like most of the men and all of the marines, he was willing to accept any odds just to get a weapon back in his hands and fight like a man.

Meese and Ogarkov watched from the doorway.

"We still need some work on getting the weapons into action without drawing any attention," Ogarkov said. "If the Cubans get an idea of what is up even five seconds too early it will be a massacre, and we won't get a single prisoner."

Meese nodded and called over to Glover. "How is the training going?" Meese asked.

"Not too bad, considering these twenty guys come from half a dozen different units," Glover answered. "We're expecting a real grab bag of guys to pull off a very sophisticated operation without ever having worked together before and with very little preparation. I won't even get into the mess of trying to get Russians and Americans to work smoothly together when most of them don't speak each other's language. I'd say our biggest risk is getting spotted when we're pulling the larger weapons. I'm going to run them through that until they either get it right or die trying."

Meese just raised an eyebrow to Ogarkov, who pulled down the corners of his mouth and nodded. "Very well, Sergeant. Carry on," Meese said.

The two officers returned Glover's salute and walked off together. "Good man," Ogarkov commented.

"That's why we picked him," Meese said. "He kept his head during the surprise attack and saved I don't know how many lives by wiping out a group of commandos single-handed. They were sneaking up on a BOQ filled with sleeping officers. Glover happened to be finishing his early morning personal PT program and saw them from behind as they approached the building. He came up on one of them, killed him with his buck knife, and took his weapon. He then opened up on the others before they knew what hit them. It permitted almost all of the officers in the building to get out alive."

"You really checked into his activities well," Ogarkov observed.

"I didn't have to," Meese smiled shyly. "I was one of those officers snoring away in his bunk while Glover was duking it out with the Cuban Army." The two men laughed. "In any case, that's why I've assigned him to train this group as well as his own. He will command the American covering force around the back of the reviewing stand. I'll actually lead the assault team, but training soldiers in combat drill is his regular job, so I thought it best to leave him in it."

"Wise decision," said Ogarkov. "I've had a look at the precise dispositions of the enemy forces provided by the KGB's source. It looks almost perfect for what we have planned. There isn't a concentration of troops larger than a company within miles of the attack position, so with the damage that I expect we'll do during the early fighting it will take them hours to gather enough force even to risk an assault on the embassy compound. The only thing that was not foreseen was the apparent presence underneath the reviewing stand of at least a squad of TE troops with automatic weapons. They'll be out of sight behind the canvas skirts hung around the stands, but they have loopholes cut in the fabric to see and fire through. I'm afraid that if we don't deal with them in the first few seconds they could cut down our assault teams before they get started."

"What about more firepower for the fire support element?" Meese asked.

"I've been thinking about that. I want to risk bringing along a disassembled PK light machine gun. It's a lot bulkier than a rifle, but if we divide it among maybe three men, with two or three others carrying the ammunition, I think we can get away with it. The trick will be getting it assembled fast enough and in secret."

"Here's an idea," Meese suggested. "How about putting the gunner well back from the front, four or five rows, letting him drop to the deck to assemble the weapon, and then having him crawl forward between the standing ranks."

"That might work," Ogarkov said.

"In any case, I suggest we talk with the NCOs about making sure that when the men come to a halt in front of the stand they are *not* in neat ranks or files. If we keep from providing straight avenues of view in either direction it will be easier for our men to work. Fortunately, the stand is only about four feet high, so the people on it won't have much of a height advantage over the men, and the bleachers on the sides are too far back to matter."

"Let's do it," Ogarkov agreed. "Let's have the men spend the rest of the afternoon going through the close-order drill to make sure everyone gets to the right place in the formation. We can do some more assault training and weapons familiarization tonight, and have another quick round tomorrow morning before we have to get the weapons concealed and mount up for the ride to the starting point."

"Yes, sir, Colonel," Meese saluted, and the two men shook hands. Meese then trotted off to rejoin Glover.

Ogarkov walked off, lost in thought. He knew that the chances of success were between slim and none, but he viewed this more as a way for a soldier to die properly than as a serious military option. There was no way that the forces outside, no matter how strong they might be potentially, could be ready enough to get to them before the Cubans could swamp the resistance in the compound. But that was not his decision. He had cheated death before, and it was simply now his time to pay up.

Chapter Twenty-three

The president sat facing his National Security Council staff, with the addition of Lt. Gen. Andrew Freeman, commander of the Joint Caribbean Task Force. Freeman, while not the first black to hold this rank in the army, since Weems' predecessor as chairman of the Joint Chiefs of Staff had also been black, was the first of his race to hold this large a combat command. He was a very dark-skinned man, born in South Carolina, and at fifty-five he could remember the days of separate washrooms, theaters, and water fountains for the races, to say nothing of schools and career tracks. However, rather than embittering him the constant hurdles he faced in succeeding in one of the world's great remaining closed societies, the military, merely hardened him. He had earned the Silver Star in Vietnam, and he considered that every moment he lived after earning his Purple Heart was pure gravy, so little things like racial slurs and having to outperform others to get the same promotions seemed like minor irritants.

"General Freeman," the president began, "I would like your best assessment of how quickly troops could be gotten into Cuba, in strength, from the moment I give the word to go. I ask this because we have reason to believe, and I cannot go into more detail to explain why, that there will be a window of opportunity, possibly as early as tomorrow, during which a rescue of the hostages might be effected. This window would not exist for long, maybe only hours, but we cannot say with any certainty when, or even actually whether, this will occur." Judge Webster and the president had just met prior to the NSC meeting, and the word from the CIA staff familiar with Paco and his mission was that Castro's presence at the victory parade would be just the kind of opportunity Paco would be looking for, if he were able to take advantage of it. Assuming he's not already dead or in some Cuban jail, the president had thought.

"Mr. President," General Freeman spoke directly to the president. While totally respectful of the man and the office, it was apparent that he was not cowed by the "celebrity quality" of being in the White House. The president liked that. "From our current dispositions we could have planes and ships hitting targets on Cuban soil within the hour. We could have advance elements of both the 82d Airborne and the regiment of the Soviet 76th Guards Airborne Division on the ground in Cuba within six hours. Per your instructions we have these men, on a rotational basis, sitting in the aircraft on the runways out at Homestead Air Base in Florida. If you have a more precise time frame when action might be likely we could beef up the air units aloft to make the first strike more decisive, and we could even get some of the paratroops airborne. That would cut the reaction time significantly. However, we could not keep that up indefinitely, and it would undercut our overall lift capability if that situation lasted more than a few hours."

"I would like you to go to that footing starting at 1000 hours tomorrow morning, General," the president announced. "If by, say, 1800 hours, nothing unusual has occurred, we will return to the current arrangement."

"Yes, sir. I'll have a battalion of the 504th Parachute Regiment in the air at 1000 hours tomorrow. We can also keep at least a full squadron of F-15s and two of F-16s up. I would keep the naval air units on their current level of alert as they have less far to go and can get into action on very short notice as it is. I will also speak to General Dolgoruki about getting some Soviet air units to go on increased alert for tomorrow."

"Very good, General." Wiznezhsky noticed that the president was increasingly nervous as the appointed time for the victory parade in Havana approached. There had been no word from the CIA operative since his insertion, although they knew that that had gone well enough. Pressure had been mounting from the families of the hostages through their congressmen for some kind of action. The press and intellectual community continued to insist that there was some sort of diplomatic gesture the United States could make to break the deadlock, but to date Congress had generally continued to support the administration in its efforts to avoid making further concessions to the Cubans.

"General Weems," the president spoke up. "Has there been any change in the overall military picture since our last meeting?"

"The first of the Chinese troop ships and missile carriers have been making steady progress and could dock as early as the morning of the second. The Soviets have moved their troops to a higher state of alert along the Sino-Soviet border, and this has been matched by the Chinese, but there have been no incidents. What's more, overhead imagery indicates that as much as a full mechanized corps of Vietnamese troops is en route by train from the Hanoi area through China, possibly toward Manchuria. That would indicate that this PRB alliance is a reality. The Chinese have also been transferring troops and air units from the Vietnamese border area northward."

Judge Webster interjected. "We should also note that there is currently a French delegation from the Mirage-Dassault aircraft firm in Beijing right now, and the Japanese have actively been negotiating economic aid and development projects with the Chinese. Nothing has actually come of these moves yet, but we're keeping an eye on them."

"Perhaps it's too early to make any judgements," Wiznezhsky suggested, "but it appears increasingly likely that what we're seeing here is a fundamental realignment of the world's power structure. For decades we have lived in a bipolar world. With the gradual breakup of the Soviet empire over the past couple of years, combined with our own relative decline in economic dominance, other power centers seem to be emerging. We've been supposing for some time that the

EEC, now reinforced by the increasing integration of various Eastern European economies, would have the economic and demographic base to stand on its own as a world power. We may see the same occur with the Japanese.

"The creation of this PRB may just be another step in this process. For years we have been judging international trends based primarily on the economic development of individual countries. However, if we take at face value the fact that the PRB exists and will survive, they have quite a power base themselves. Together, Cuba, China, Iran, Vietnam, and North Korea have tremendous military muscle, and they have significant natural resources as well. If the technological giants of Japan and Western Europe are willing to trade some of their sophistication for raw materials and, at least, freedom from intimidation by the military power of the PRB, that would go far to overcome the lack of industrial development in the PRB. We may want to start looking at this as the way the world is going to go in the future and learn to live with it."

"Our analysts are saying something very similar," Webster added. "One possible scenario is that the Japanese might have an eye on taking over leadership of the PRB, becoming the brains dominating the pure muscle of some of these Third World countries, and together becoming a superpower in their own right."

"Yes," continued Wiznezhsky, "we shouldn't let the manner in which the PRB came to our attention blind us to the nature of the change itself. The ease with which so many of the Third World countries cut longstanding ties either to us or to the Soviets implies to me a deep-seated feeling that must have been there for a long time. However this crisis is ultimately resolved, I don't think we should expend too much in resources on the dream of putting things back the way they were before. We should secure our own position as much as possible, of course, but a real sea change has come over the world, and fighting it may just bleed us dry."

"That thought has occurred to me, too," the president said, "and I think we've made a good start with our solution to the debt side of this equation, helping to keep from being isolated from the bulk of the Third World and to prevent the Cubans from getting too much benefit out of it. However, the overriding concern right now for me is the hostages. We may be looking at epochal changes in the world, but how well we do in this crisis will set the tone for everything else that comes along for years to come. So far I have been very pleased with the way the situation has been handled, but we're rapidly coming to a point at which decisive action is going to have to be taken. I am confident that General Freeman has the situation well in hand, as well as can be expected, and I have a feeling that we are coming to the climax. I want real-time coverage of Cuba by satellite fed right in here starting tonight, and I assume that General Freeman will have the same in Key West."

"It's already being done, sir," the general stated. "It may be a little passé, but I have always been a soldier of the school of marching to the sound of the guns. I should also add that I have never seen troops in a higher state of morale or eagerness to get into action. For years we have been teased and pricked by handfuls of terrorists preying on planeloads of tourists or isolated diplomats with nowhere and no one at whom we could strike back. Now we've got the enemy right here next door, and if we can find a situation where our troops can put themselves between the hostages and the enemy I don't think you'll find them wanting for élan, sir."

"I'm counting on that, General," the president said. "Now we'll let you go to get back to your post."

General Freeman stood up, saluted, and marched to the door. The president eased back in his chair. "Jim," he said to Secretary Baker, "I would like a meeting with the Soviet ambassador and General Dolgoruki here tomorrow at about 1000 hours. I would also like arrangements to be made so that we can get hold of Gorbachev on short notice tomorrow if necessary."

Most of the group rose to leave. When they had left, Wiznezhsky and Webster remained with the president.

"Do you think it was wise not telling the Soviets about our man in Havana?" Wiznezhsky asked.

"It may not have been wise, but it was necessary," the president said sadly. "Don't forget that I had the Judge's job myself for awhile. I could not in good conscience send that man in there and at the same time add to the odds against him by telling anyone else about his mission. I think it will come down to the question that, if he is successful, the Soviets will be delighted. If he fails, well, I don't see how we could be much worse off. I think that the Soviets, more than most, would understand our position." He rubbed his forehead with his right hand. "It's going to be a long twenty-four hours."

Chapter Twenty-four

Paco had slept well the night before and had spent the day restfully preparing his meals, washing, shaving, and double-checking his weapons. The woman had not disturbed him and there had been no callers at the door. The phone had rung a couple of times, probably the woman's employers, but he had let it ring, and they had likely assumed that she had taken the day off on her own authority. She would be called to task for it when she returned to work, but by then she would have an excellent excuse.

He noticed that she was beginning to stir now, and he began to loosen the bonds on her feet. She awoke with a start, apparently requiring a moment to remember where she was and what was happening. She began whining softly through the gag, and tears welled up in her eyes. He told her again that he meant her no harm and started to untie her hands with one hand while he held the pistol aimed at her with the other. Lastly, he removed the gag.

He offered her a cheese sandwich he had prepared and a glass of soda, but she just shook her head and kept on crying.

"I have to go to the bathroom," she said.

He helped her up and walked her to the bathroom, but braced himself in the doorway when she moved to close the door.

"I'm sorry," he said.

169

"Oh, my God!" she sobbed. He stared fixedly at the opposite side of the door frame, able to detect any sudden movement through his peripheral vision, but allowing her what little privacy he could.

"By this time tomorrow," he said, "I'll be gone, and you'll be safe. Nothing will happen to you, I swear it."

"I suppose that a man who breaks into someone's home with guns, ties them up, and drugs them wouldn't lie too," she sneered. "I don't know what you want here and I don't want to know. I just want you out of my house."

"I'm sorry, but I can't do that. All I can promise is that it will all be over soon."

"What will be over? What are you doing here?"

"I thought you didn't want to know," he said, starting to turn toward her, but then turning quickly away again.

"It's the president, isn't it? It's Fidel. You're here to kill him. I can see that fancy rifle you have leaning against the sink in the kitchen. It's like the one Fidel carried in the Sierra, and you're going to shoot him tomorrow at the parade." She didn't ask. It was a statement.

"Castro has killed so many people, he deserves to die, Señora," Paco said lamely.

"And who are you to decide that?" she asked. "He's taken this country from being a whorehouse for the Yankees and made it a country with a people who can stand tall in the world. You're CIA aren't you?" She pronounced it "Cee-ya". "Well, you'll fail. You clowns have tried to kill Fidel before, and you always have failed."

"Maybe that's because it wasn't me that tried before, Señora," he said in a low voice.

"I only hope I live to see you shot," she spat.

When she had finished, he turned slightly more to allow her to arrange herself and took a step out of the bathroom. She followed him without further complaint, but as she crossed the threshold her left hand grasped the neck of a tall glass vase that stood next to the sink, topped with dried flowers. As he turned toward her he saw only the vase as it smashed into his face.

He staggered backward and she ran past him toward the door. He lurched after her and caught her by the hair with one hand. She gasped but did not scream. Blinded, he grasped her by the chin with his other hand and, by reflex, twisted her head far to one side and then snapped it back with a violent jerk. She went limp in his arms.

He let her down to the floor gently and staggered into the bathroom. He ran the water and washed the blood and shards of glass out of his eyes. It was several minutes before he could see again. Blood still streamed from a deep gash in his forehead. He held a towel to it and went back into the living room where the woman lay sprawled on the floor. He knelt beside her.

"You stupid bitch!" he cried. "Why did you do that? I wasn't going to hurt you! Oh, Jesus!" This wasn't the way he had planned it at all. It had almost been done. It was almost over. He would have killed her and anyone else who had been in the apartment when he first came in if it had been necessary. But there had been no need for this. All she had had to do was take one more stupid pill, and she would have awakened after it was all over.

He picked her up carefully, letting the towel fall and the blood start to flow again from his wound. He carried her back into the bedroom and placed her on the bed. He covered her with one side of the bedspread and then took a bottle of rum out of the armoire where he had noticed it during his initial search of the apartment.

He didn't bother with a glass. He just took one pull on the bottle after another. He had killed many men in Vietnam and elsewhere over the years. He knew he had even been responsible for the deaths of women and children when calling in artillery on enemy villages, but he had never killed a defenseless person like this, with his bare hands. This wasn't how it was supposed to have worked out at all. He cried. He smashed his fist into the wall, and he continued to drink.

He had originally been recruited for this job, so many years ago, because one of his uncles, his favorite uncle, had been murdered by Fidel. The uncle had actually been a guerrillero, fighting against Batista, but he was too popular with his troops, he wasn't openly loyal to Fidel, and he wasn't a Communist. So they shot him. Paco and his family had been forced to watch the execution, and Paco had sworn then, over thirty years ago, that he would kill the man responsible for that murder. But he hadn't counted on killing this woman to do it.

Everywhere he looked in the room, throughout the apartment, he saw little touches, little things that she and her husband had done to make the place their own. They couldn't have much money and certainly had no access to the special stores exclusively for Party officials, but they had done their best: a bowl of plastic fruit, some flowers, a throw rug that the wife or some other female relative had knotted by hand. He could imagine her and her husband saving to purchase each cheap piece of furniture, shopping for it, and arranging it with care in their home. And now he had come in and destroyed it all, just because he hadn't been careful. If he had been paying attention, like the big professional he claimed to be, she never would have come close to hurting him and he never would have had to kill her.

He kept on drinking until the bottle was empty, and then he started on the bottles of beer that were in the refrigerator. At some point during the night he passed out.

Chapter Twenty-five

Captain Estigarribia thought that the meeting was more like a fraternity party. Castro was hosting an informal reception for a number of key Cuban military and Party officials as well as the ambassadors of China, North Korea, Vietnam, Iran, Libya, the PLO, Angola, Ethiopia, and a number of favorably disposed Third World countries. There was also a group of journalists from radically leftist papers in Western Europe and Latin America present, snapping photographs of Castro holding up his hand in the "V for Victory" sign with assorted other guests.

Castro was telling jokes, usually at the expense of either his international enemies or his closest advisors in the Cuban government. Castro enjoyed this. He would make it a point to tell deprecatory jokes either just within earshot of the victim or to someone he was certain would repeat the material to the subject. Right now he was making cruel fun of the lack of intestinal fortitude of his own military establishment.

Estigarribia saw that General Murguia was sipping his drink impassively, pretending not to listen to the roars of laughter from Castro, Albaro Icaza, and a cluster of fawning reporters. Estigarribia slowly moved over to Murguia and leaned close to him.

173

"General, I wonder if I could have a word with you," he asked in a soft voice, designed to become lost in the dull buzz of general conversation.

"What is it?" Murguia asked. Estigarribia could sense the hatred in his voice. The TE were not popular with the regular army. The latter saw the TE as Castro's personal gunmen, which they were, his guarantee against a coup d'état.

"Something has been bothering me since the death of Raul Castro," Estigarribia said. "I don't know whom I can tell, but I have to tell someone. I can't trust anyone else in the TE, and you're the only army officer I know who seems to be willing to stand up to Fidel."

"I'm sure that whatever it is, you can tell your immediate superior and that he will pass the information through the proper channels."

Estigarribia could see that Murguia was too well aware of the workings of Castro's inner circle to allow himself to be entrapped easily in some plot of Castro's to eliminate more of the independent-minded military officers.

"You can take this for what it's worth then, General," Estigarribia continued, "or you can forget it if you wish." He paused and leaned closer to the general's ear, pretending to reach for a sandwich from the table behind him. "The Russians didn't kill Raul, Fidel did."

"Why would you make such an accusation?" asked the general impassively.

"I was there. I saw it. He concocted the entire story and had Raul killed by another TE officer *after* the attack on the Soviet and American bases, not before."

"Captain," the general said, straightening his back and turning fully toward Estigarribia, "I believe that you have had too much to drink and that you are imagining things. If you come to my office tomorrow morning and repeat these accusations, I will insist that you bring this matter before a Peoples' Tribunal. If you do not come, I will assume that I was correct and that you are simply drunk, and I will make a comment to your superiors accordingly, without mentioning the nature of these wild charges. I strongly advise you to go home and sleep it off and to forget this entire matter."

"Very well, General," Estigarribia also straightened, "but one other thing that my hidden bottle of rum tells me. If you go to the reviewing stand tomorrow for the parade, your life will be in danger."

"Thank you, Captain," Murguia said, turning away, "but I am certain that my life could not be safer than in the company of the Jefe, and if there is to be danger there, it is my place to be at his side to face it with him."

Estigarribia smiled as Murguia walked away. He got the message, but he still fears a trap. If this conversation is being recorded, and if he doesn't show up tomorrow, that will prove that he believed it. He needs a pretext to stay away. Estigarribia had already made arrangements for that.

Castro was raising a toast to Colonel Qadafi which was loudly seconded by the Iranian ambassador. Estigarribia saw Murguia talking with his aide-de-camp in a corner of the room, near the stereo speakers. Things were going well, but he had to leave the party now if he were to finish his work for the evening.

Chapter Twenty-six

General Freeman strode into the work area occupied by his intelligence staff, trailed by the rest of his operational team.

"Where the hell are the overhead photographs of the Soviet compound in Havana?" he shouted. Men scrambled and papers flew in all directions until a large photomontage was laid on the worktable in front of the general. It included much of western Havana and its coastline. The Soviet compound had been highlighted in red, as had the announced route of march for the victory parade the next day.

"Jesus Christ!" the general bellowed. "I don't know what the hell I've been thinking of. There sure as blazes is a great deal going on that we're not being told, but here is the most important thing to come along during this whole fucking operation, and we all missed it. It's just staring us in the fucking face, and no one saw it, least of all me!"

The other members of his staff stared fixedly at the photograph, which all of them had seen many times before in the last few days, hoping the general would tell them what this great revelation was before any of them was called upon to supply it.

"Look at this!" the general shouted, jabbing at the photomontage with one long finger. "Tomorrow at noon we're going to have every blessed hostage within an area of maybe ten acres, and all within half a mile of the fucking beach! No wonder they want us to have troops in the air. Those imbeciles in Washington don't know squat about military operations though. It's not an air drop we need, not in the middle of the fucking city! We've got to do better than that."

"You mean, go in and get them out, just like that?" a rather soft-looking colonel asked.

"You'd still have a high risk of the Cubans just opening up and scragging hundreds of hostages when the first shell hits or the first chopper appears," intoned a young major. "They'll be just too close together for us to try to do anything to the Cubans."

"That's just it," said General Freeman. "They're expecting something to happen, or are hoping it will, at that goddamn parade. Whatever it is it's too secret for the likes of us to know about, so they're not talking. But something might be going to happen that will give us that margin of safety we need to get men or iron in between the hostages and the Cubans, and it won't last long. Now, gentlemen, our job is to do this right. I want an ops plan to pull off a hostage rescue mission tomorrow, right here," he said, drawing a rough rectangle around the area of the Soviet compound, the reviewing stand, and the field in front of it. "We'll go ahead and put up the paratroops because they ordered it, but I want a plan that is going to work for real.

"Have those V-22s arrived yet?" asked the general, referring to the Osprey tilt-rotor aircraft now formed into two experimental squadrons by the marines.

"Yes, sir," said a Marine Corps captain. "They arrived this afternoon and should be checked out and ready to go by morning."

"See that they are," said the general. "I want all twenty-four of them jammed with as many marines as they'll carry, it should be about a battalion's worth. I just wish to hell that the fucking Congress had seen fit to buy a few more of those babies. Next, I want three squadrons of Blackhawks fitted out with external fuel tanks to give them the range for Havana from Homestead, and I want the 2d of the 506th Airborne loaded on them. I want the fleets advised, both ours and the Soviets', and I want all of the CH-53 choppers of the marines and the Soviets' Helix-B assault choppers loaded with marines from the fleet. I want all of this done and the troops sitting in the aircraft at 1000 hours tomorrow morning. At noon I want the Ospreys and Blackhawks to take off from Homestead and move southward to a holding line one hundred miles north of Havana to await my orders. The fleet air assault units will wait on the deck for my command."

He reached over to the sideboard and poured himself a mug of coffee. "I want every available fighter and strike aircraft to be off the ground and loitering, the Americans here," he circled an area just south of the tip of Florida, on a larger-scale map "and the Soviets from Texas here," he said, circling another area about one hundred miles to the west. "I also want a full strike up from each carrier, fighters and attack aircraft.

"Now the strike from the *John F. Kennedy*, here in the south, will hit the Cuban air base at Holguín, to keep them guessing and to tie up the MiG-2ls there. The Soviets will hit the Cuban brigade of fighters at San Antonio de los Baños. Our own F-l5s and F-l4s will stay up to pick up any leakers they miss. The F-16s and navy A-6s will concentrate on the antiaircraft sites, as will the F-117s, to open a safe way for the choppers and transports, and the A-10s and marine Harriers will provide close support, protecting the hostages. Then the troop carriers will swoop in and land right on top of the fucking Soviet compound and all around it. We're not going to screw with paratroopers scattered all over hell and gone."

He took a sip from his cup of coffee and continued. "I want every MCM ship in both fleets on the twelve-mile limit opposite where the Soviet compound backs up to the beach. When I give the word they will go in full tilt and sweep channels as fast as they know how. Both our MAB and the Soviets' Naval Infantry Regiment will be standing by their landing craft and will make a rush for the beach as soon as a channel is opened. They will land from the Hotel Copacabaña Club to Calle Setenta, Americans on the east, Soviets on the west, with the center of the Soviet compound serving as the boundary marker between them. We'll do just one wave, and the landing craft will stand by on the beach to take off hostages when they break free. The navy ships will provide fire on call."

"What about the plans for Special Forces teams to land elsewhere on the island?" a Green Beret colonel asked.

"Can that," the general said unceremoniously. "If things go the way I think they're going to go, we'll all be in it hot and heavy before they could get ashore and do anything, and we'll all be back at sea before the Cubans would have heard about it. No, they're more likely to end up as new hostages than to do us any good on their own. There's going to be no time for diversions or feints in this. It's going to be a heads-up, 'slam, bam, thank-you-ma'am' brawl." The general noticed the Green Beret's crestfallen look. "What we can do is to have one CH-53 load of Special Forces and one of Spetsnaz, just for formality's sake, take station and loiter at the twelve-mile limit starting at noon. If I give the word they go in first, without waiting for the flyboys to finish with the antiaircraft missile batteries. The odds are that the Cuban gunners will be too busy fighting for their lives to look for choppers flying nap of the earth, but it's still pretty risky. Would that be gory enough for you, Colonel?" he asked, smiling.

"That's what we're paid for, General" the colonel said, smiling back, "and I think the Russkies will say the same."

"Good," Freeman said, placing his hands at the small of his back and stretching. "That's the broad brush as dictated by my strategic genius. It's now your job to make it work. Better get the Sovs over here to work out their part of the job. When we've got something put on paper I'll get General Weems on the blower and talk him into it. No point fighting that battle until we've got our ducks in a row."

Freeman walked toward the door of the room and stopped. "And I want every man here to get at least two hours' sleep tonight. I would rather cut some bureaucratic corners on the paperwork than have a bunch of zombies following me around in the middle of a fucking war. That is all!"

Chapter Twenty-seven

The leader of the commando force and his three men lay in wait along the road just outside the base perimeter, waiting for the Soviet-made GAZ jeep. A fifth man hid in the bushes a hundred meters closer to the camp, and another a hundred meters up the road in the other direction. The team leader checked the luminous dial of his watch. The officers coming off duty would be passing this way in just a few minutes en route to their quarters. He checked the positioning of the pair of his men who had set up an American M-60 machine gun, and crouched back into the bushes.

Soon a pair of headlights appeared in the distance, coming from the camp. Although the national radio and press ranted daily about the state of war that existed between Cuba and the superpowers and called upon the people to be ever vigilant, most of the soldiers did not consider the threat of attack to be serious. Only the air force and antiaircraft batteries were on full alert, along with the troops stationed directly along the coast and those guarding the hostages. The 101st Armored was held in reserve, ready to respond on short notice to any attack, but there was no need to wear the troops down with the constant pressure of full tactical standing. That was why the jeep was not using dimmed lights, and that made the commandos' job all the easier.

There was a single glimmer from a red-filtered flashlight as the jeep passed the first lookout. The team leader aimed his own Uzi submachine gun, leading the vehicle slightly, aiming for the driver, and opened fire. On this signal the M-60 and an M-16 also began to pour rounds into the jeep and its passengers.

The jeep swerved sharply to the left, away from the ambush. The driver had been hit but he was still reacting. Tracers swept up and down the vehicle, and the team leader saw the flash of a pistol being fired from behind the hood, but another burst from the leader's weapon caused the shadow of the figure behind the jeep to jerk backward, and then all was silence.

Covered by the machine gun, the team leader and one of his men ran forward. They were wearing American camouflage uniforms and boots, their faces painted to eliminate the glare of the oils in their skin. The team leader and his man rifled the pockets of the occupants of the jeep. He saw that there were four of them: one soldier, two captains, and a colonel, all regular army. On the backseat of the jeep was a flat attaché case. The team leader opened it and found it to contain deployment charts and march orders for the division. Perfect, he thought. Then he pulled a transmitter out of his shirt pocket and extended the antenna. He turned to face the camp and pressed the large red button in the middle of the transmitter. A series of explosions ripped through the night. The explosives he and his men had placed in the motor pool of the division lit up the night with the flare of burning fuel and vehicles.

From the direction of the division camp he could hear the sound of vehicle engines coughing to life, armored vehicles. Orders were being shouted, but it was already too late. The commandos were across the road and racing through the sparse woods to the north, in the direction of the sea. In the woods, hidden by carefully arranged branches, were three specially modified motorcycles. The commandos mounted up, two men per bike, and spurted off, with only the faintest hum emitted by the motorcycles' engines. They had nearly eight miles to cover to the beach. In the ten minutes it took for the men and armored vehicles from the base camp to arrive at the scene of the ambush they had already covered nearly half that distance, and they soon reached the beach without contacting any other troops. They quickly removed the palm fronds with which they had hidden their Rigid Raider assault boat. They hoisted their light bikes into the boat and five of the men grabbed hold of the boat's handles and quickly dragged it toward the water, while the sixth, with the M-60, covered them from the treeline. When the boat was in the water he too ran and leaped into the pitching craft. They pushed it out past the knee-high breakers, and the team leader started the motor.

When they had moved about two hundred yards from shore they turned parallel to the coast for several miles and then reentered a narrow inlet. There, a light utility truck was waiting near the shore, guarded by two more commandos. They hauled the boat out of the water and onto the truck. They stashed the American weapons behind the boat, quickly changed back into their proper uniforms, those of the Cuban TE, and drove off toward Havana.

General Murguia gently turned over the body of one of the men from the jeep. His chest had been ripped open by half a dozen machine-gun bullets. Murguia had seen his men die before, in Ethiopia, in Angola, but he had never gotten used to it. He blamed himself for this one. He had gone along with Castro's crazy scheme out of fear for his own career, even his life, but he had failed to take seriously that he was now involved in a war with *real* soldiers, not half-armed UNITA or Contra guerrillas, and his men had paid for his sloppiness with their lives.

"The dispatch case is missing, sir," one of the men told him.

Another man, an experienced jungle fighter, came up and said, "Americans." He held out a handful of expended cartridge cases from the M-60. "American boot prints are everywhere, jungle boots, probably Special Forces from the bases in Panama. It looks like they took off toward the beach. They probably have a boat there."

"Get the navy on the radio," Murguia snapped. "Blow them out of the water before they get out to their damn fleet."

"It's a waste of time, sir," Colonel Ruiz, the commander of his recon battalion interjected. "If we sent patrol boats out there, they'd be laying for them with destroyers or aircraft and cut them up. They know where they're going and they'll have it all set up. We'd have to search for them. We'd only get more men killed."

Ruiz knew that that would get Murguia's attention. Ruiz had been a company commander under him during the desert fighting against the Somalis in Ethiopia back in 1977. He knew Murguia would not let the fear of losses prevent him from reaching his objective, but neither would he squander men's lives without a valid reason.

"Shit!" Murguia said under his breath. He was not angry that Ruiz had questioned his order. He was angry that he had given such a stupid order to begin with. But he paused for a moment. Perhaps this would at least not all be for nothing.

"Put the division on full alert. No passes, no leave. No one leaves the base without my written order. Send a message to the president's office that I will personally be conducting the investigation into this incident and will be unable to attend the victory parade later today, and that I will advise him of the results as soon as possible. We must make certain that there are no other teams of saboteurs or assassins in our area of operations."

"Yes, sir." His communications officer saluted and trotted off.

Now Murguia would be able to stay away from the ceremony, on the off chance that that TE dog had been telling the truth, which Murguia still did not believe for a minute. Yet no one would be able to accuse him of disloyalty. Of course if they wanted to kill him they really didn't need an excuse, but there was no point in making it easier for them.

As the TE troops unloaded the boat from the truck Estigarribia congratulated each of his men on a job well done. He took his own American uniform and his Uzi out of the back of the truck and stored it with the unit's other "foreign identity" equipment. Estigarribia was glad that he was a Latin American and not some stuffy Russian or Yankee. In another army he might have been obliged to show written orders justifying an attack on members of his own country's armed forces. However, despite decades of Soviet-Communist indoctrination, the Cuban was still a Latin American at heart. These were *his* men. He was their *patrón*, and they would follow his orders alone.

Of course, he had had to tell them that he had authorization from Castro himself for this maneuver—something he certainly did not have—but that had mattered little to them. They did what he said. Whether he had authorization for it or not was of secondary importance to them, although Estigarribia wondered how long he would have lived had his men known that he had been working for the KGB for years. Now he had done everything that could possibly be expected of him. He would be interested to see what the day would bring.

Chapter Twenty-eight

The men were beginning to form up to load onto the trucks that were to take them to the starting point of the parade, near the Plaza de la Revolución in central Havana. Ogarkov and Meese watched the loading of each truck carefully. There were four Cuban guards and a driver assigned to each truck, and two of the guards stood at either side of each tailgate as the men climbed aboard, while the other two and the driver generally wandered about the area until the truck was loaded. Naturally, the real guard force for the column was provided by a full battalion of mechanized infantry and hundreds of uniformed policemen of the Ministry of Interior's National Revolutionary Police (DGPNR), who accompanied the convoy in their armored personnel carriers and their own trucks. However, it was the relative handful of reservist infantrymen who would actually ride the trucks with the prisoners that worried Ogarkov and Meese now.

If any of these men caught sight of a suspicious bulge under a prisoner's shirt, or of a protruding gun barrel, the entire operation could be scrapped. The planners of the operation had taken elaborate care to minimize this risk. Since fewer than one man in ten had any kind of weapon, and fewer than half of these had anything bulkier than a pistol, the planners had taken care that the weapons carriers would each mount a truck over the center of the tailgate, flanked by two unarmed men on either side, thus, it was hoped, blocking the view of the Cuban guards at the corners. Other soldiers would attempt to distract the guards by engaging them in conversation, on cue, when armed men were boarding the trucks. Furthermore, the weapons carriers would be seated toward the front of the truck, with a healthy buffer of unarmed men between them and the two guards, who would sit next to the tailgate. The process would be repeated when the troops unloaded at their destination, but the planners considered that phase far less dangerous, as the attention of the guards would naturally be directed toward the prisoners who had already dismounted, and to keeping them in order and in view.

From where he was standing Meese could see about half an inch of black gun barrel sticking out from below the hem of one Russian soldier's shirt. For the first time the outline of the AKM assault rifle taped to the man's back fairly screamed out to Meese. The man's clothing was intentionally bulky and he was surrounded by other men, but how could the Cubans not see it? How could they possibly load all of these armed men, unload them at the other end, and then march them several miles through central Havana, under the eyes of hundreds of armed enemy troops and hundreds of thousands of spectators, without being discovered? It was a mildly warm day, but Meese was already sweating profusely.

Ogarkov noticed Meese's nervousness. "So far, so good," he commented, patting Meese gently on the shoulder. "More than half of the men are already loaded and no problems yet. I really don't think that the Cubans imagine that *we* will be causing them any problems. They're only worried about a rescue attempt from outside. Have you seen all of the mobile SAM launchers around?"

"I really don't know if we're going to make it, Alex," Meese said. "It all sounded so good on paper and looked so easy running the drills in the gym, but it's just too damn big to keep secret." By now, Meese knew, virtually all of the men knew about the operation. While there certainly was no objection to the idea from most of them, Meese still feared that some snide remark to a guard by a feisty marine would provoke a search or a change in plans that would upset all of their calculations.

"Well, they haven't caught on yet," Ogarkov soothed. "Only about three more hours to go."

They stood silently and watched the rest of the loading before climbing into their own truck. Meese saw Sergeant Glover hang out of the back of another truck and flash him the thumbs-up signal. So far, so good.

Meese sat near the back of his truck, even though he had a 9mm Makarov pistol tucked into his waistband under his dress jacket. He was wearing the dress uniform that someone had scrounged for him for this very reason, even though it was hardly comfortable in the warm, humid weather of Cuba. The Cuban authorities had been only too happy to arrange this clothing exchange, as the fancier uniforms seemed to them to add elegance to their victory parade and grandeur to their achievement.

Meese could see the other trucks, some Soviet-made and some captured American vehicles, pulling into line, stirring up clouds of dust on the barren drill ground of the Soviet base camp. One by one they drove through the gate, occasionally leaving intervals for a platoon of Cuban armored personnel carriers to take up positions within the column, as they began their drive into the city.

As they passed an increasing number of houses, first simple country dwellings made of clapboard or bare cinderblock, more and more people flocked to the roadside to watch them pass. Occasionally there would be an organized group chanting something—Meese couldn't identify what—and waving red banners, but mostly the people just watched in silence. He had noticed this before, on the trip from Guantánamo here. There was no jubilation, no shrieks of hatred. These people were worried, he thought. They've been sacrificing for over thirty years for the Revolution and it still hasn't paid off. Now their leader has embarked them suddenly, without their approval or even knowledge, on a collision course with the two greatest military powers in the world. They have every reason to be worried. Meese looked over at Ogarkov, and the other man just winked wordlessly.

Johnson also had a Makarov hidden in the small of his back, under an overhanging shirt. He was trying to control his breathing and think through his plan of action, just as before a big basketball game in high school. He was wedged into the front of a truck, the back of which was covered with a tarp. He was glad that he couldn't see what was going on. He just wanted to get there and then tear it up. At this point he didn't really care if he survived or not, he just wanted to have this horrible waiting over with.

Sergeant Glover was sitting farther back in the same truck. He was unarmed now, but would take an AKM from a weapons carrier at the appointed moment. Apart from the attack on Guantánamo Glover had not seen real combat, and this was not how he had ever imagined going into it, unarmed and depending on a weapon someone had stuck in his underpants. What a way to run a railroad.

He had done everything he could think of that morning. He had personally checked the status of all of the weapons to be used by his group and that of Captain Meese. He had checked their concealment and had run the men through their drill several more times, screaming abuse at them even though he knew, and they knew, that they were working together like the Bolshoi Ballet. Lastly, he had given each man a little talk, less to boost morale than to satisfy himself that none of them would break under pressure. There had been a couple of doubtfuls, but he was a doubtful himself, if it came to that. Satisfied that he had done all that he could at this point, he leaned back against the tarp and closed his eyes.

General Akamirov rode in a Cuban Army staff car with two other Russian generals, two Cuban guards, and a Cuban colonel. The colonel had seemed almost apologetic about the situation, assuring them that once this negotiating business was settled they could re-establish their friendship on a level of mutual respect and trust. Akamirov thought that this officer's job must be public relations or protocol. None of the Russians had responded to him, and the Cuban had fallen into an embarrassed silence for the rest of the trip.

Neither Akamirov nor his companions was armed. There had been some argument from the senior officers, each trying to secure himself the prestige of a pistol, but Akamirov had stood firm. There

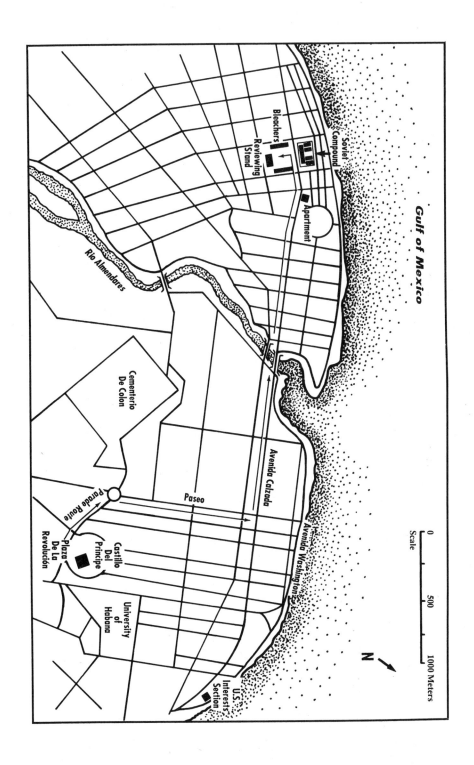

Gulf of Mexico

Soviet Compound

Bleachers

Reviewing Stand

Apartment

Río Almendares

Cementerio De Colon

Avenida Calzada

Paseo

Parade Route

Plaza De La Revolución

Castillo Del Principe

Avenida Washington

University of Habana

U.S. Interests Section

N

Scale

0   500   1000 Meters

would be no ceremonial weapons on this operation. Only assault elements would be armed. Anyone else wishing a weapon would have to take it from a dead Cuban. Interest in personal sidearms had decreased markedly after this decree.

Finally the trucks began to lurch to a halt in a large open area just east of the Plaza de la Revolución. Ordinarily the plaza would have been the terminus of the parade, as it had been for so many others during Castro's tenure, but his desire to humiliate the Soviets in particular had caused Castro to alter tradition and have the parade proceed from the plaza up toward the coast, via the Paseo, to Avenida Calzada, and thence westward, across the Almendares River to the area of the Soviet Embassy and the reviewing stands.

As the men began gingerly to dismount from the trucks Ogarkov, Meese, and the other officers were everywhere at once, making sure that each man was in his correct place and each unit in its correct order of march for the complex evolution in the reviewing stand area that would put the assault groups in their correct orientation. Ogarkov had had each group briefed on what to do if, at the last minute, either the Cubans or simple fate stepped in to destroy the layout of the assault groups. Some groups were given secondary assignments, if their location at the end of the march prevented the completion of their primary ones, but others, such as the groups trained and armed to seize the Cuban brass, would have to make their attempts regardless of the final situation. But Ogarkov knew that if these arrangements began to unravel at this late date the chances of success for the venture were virtually nil. He had to be certain that this did not happen.

Finally, by about 1030, the troops were standing in their correct formations. So far nothing had been noticed and no changes in the plan had been necessary. The column was to be headed by a wedge of Cuban armored personnel carriers sporting huge red flags and the Cuban national flag. Then came a marching band from the Cuban Navy, and then the blocks of prisoners, one hundred Soviets, ten abreast, followed by fifty Americans, ten abreast, with an interval of three or four yards.

Akamirov and the other Russian generals formed a small contingent that marched separately, sandwiched between the band and the first block of Russian prisoners. No flag-rank American officers had survived the initial Cuban assault on Guantánamo unwounded and so all had either perished or had been evacuated to India previously. Still, the Soviet officers in their dress uniforms, bedecked with medals, were show enough for the Cuban officials.

Ogarkov was in the first Soviet contingent along with Major Zhdanov and Captain Vlassov, who would lead the Soviet assault and covering forces, respectively. Meese was several American blocks back in the route of march, in order to place his group near the right-hand side of the reviewing stands, with Sergeant Glover one block back from him.

The band played revolutionary Cuban airs as the troops marched along at a leisurely pace. Johnson found it odd that the men seemed to have more difficulty in keeping crooked rows while marching, as Captain Meese had ordered, than raw recruits did in keeping them straight. Johnson supposed that you just couldn't undo hundreds of hours of drill in a few minutes, no matter how hard you tried.

The line of march was up a broad, divided avenue lined with palm trees on either side. The marchers occupied only one side of the avenue, the other being blocked off by the police and filled with curious onlookers. At each intersection Johnson could see one or two DGPNR squad cars and a small knot of soldiers. At every ten meters along both sides of the route soldiers stood with AK-47s at port arms, although Johnson noted with disdain that they slouched and looked about rather more than one should at a drill, and he noticed this tendency increasing as they marched along, meeting soldiers who had been at their posts longer and longer. These were obviously reservists, Johnson thought.

At the major intersections there was usually an armored personnel carrier, a BMP with its 76mm gun in a turret forward and probably a squad of infantry sweating to death inside. Johnson could also see, at various points through the city, mobile antiaircraft missile batteries mounted on armored vehicles, with their supporting radars sited nearby. There were also ZSU-23/4s, Soviet-made antiaircraft tanks with four nasty-looking guns and with a radar dish on top, and even some more antiquated twin antiaircraft machine guns here and there. It was rather obvious where the Cubans expected the main threat to come from. Johnson could only hope that they were right and that there really was such a threat.

Now that they were in the city there were more organized groups, shouting slogans and jeering at the troops. Some of them began throwing eggs and rotten fruit, which Johnson could see was being handed out from an official-looking van. There were several television crews filming the scene with their minicams, stopping to shoot for a few moments and then piling into a waiting car and driving farther on up the line of march.

Johnson smiled at the first film crew he saw pointing a camera his way, hoping that his mother might see this footage. Then a hunk of rotten papaya slapped into his face. He instinctively reached for his pistol, but stopped himself in time. From then on he merely stared at the back of the head of the man in front of him and counted the steps to the reckoning at the reviewing stand.

Chapter Twenty-nine

Featherstone walked slowly around the compound of the Soviet Embassy. He had his assignment for the afternoon, the rather modest one of helping to guide the escapees to the various areas of the compound set up to receive them. Meanwhile, everyone else seemed too busy to bother with him, as men rushed about within the compound buildings, and made strenuous efforts not to appear to be rushing when out in the yards.

Featherstone rather liked the compound. It occupied over four city blocks, fronting on the broad Avenida Calzada and extending back toward the sea. Behind the compound were two blocks of one- and two-story houses between it and the beach. These houses had been evacuated by the Cuban authorities since the start of the crisis, and Featherstone could see that there were troops occupying some of them. The entire compound was surrounded by an eight-foot wall facing streets that were at least two lanes wide on each side.

Inside the compound was the broad concrete structure of the embassy building itself, four stories high, with a broad parking area in front and an ornamental fountain in the center, surrounded by flowers. On top of the embassy Featherstone could see the remnants of a three-hundred-foot communications antenna that had formerly dominated the Havana skyline. The only real violation of either the Soviet Embassy or the American Interests Section had been that the Cubans had dismantled the array of antennae on both buildings, cutting off their normal satellite communications.

Behind the embassy building itself were two six-story apartment blocks where the bulk of the regular embassy staff normally lived. Between the two were a pool and gardens. Scattered between these apartment blocks and the outside wall on both sides and the back were a series of low buildings in which were housed the embassy motor pool and other maintenance facilities. The tunnels had been completed that connected both apartment blocks to each other and to the embassy itself.

In front of the embassy compound, across the divided six-lane Avenida Calzada, some six square blocks had earlier been cleared for the construction of a park and some government buildings. It was in this cleared area that the reviewing stand had been set up, leaving nearly two hundred meters of open ground between the stands and the avenue. It was in this area that the prisoners would be formed up.

At the front gate of the compound an iron gate some forty feet wide guarded the opening in the wall. By arrangement, this gate now stood wide open. Six young KGB men stood by the gate, openly carrying their AKSU-74 submachine guns, miniature versions of the AK-47, which the Cuban government had seen fit to permit them to retain. Rodriguez, Gunny Michaels, and two marines were also lounging near the gate. The marines carried Remington pump riot guns, also allowed by the Cubans. After all, what harm could they do to a country with twenty-four divisions in the field?

Featherstone could now hear the faint strains of music from the band marching with the prisoners. He walked closer to the gate and could see what appeared to be the head of the column approaching. He found himself rubbing his hands furiously. He had written a long letter to Anne. One copy was in his pocket, another in his overnight bag. Just in case, he had told himself.

He had just left Fleischmann in the lobby of the embassy, where he was crouching with some thirty armed men, waiting for the moment to dash to the gate area. Other men were lurking near the side and rear walls of the compound.

The music was getting louder now, and Featherstone moved still closer to the gate. The two young marines were dressed in fatigues and wearing their flak jackets.

Just outside the gate lounged some eight Cuban soldiers, most of them near a GAZ jeep with a machine gun mounted on the back. Over the past couple of days the KGB security guards had made a point of befriending the Cubans, offering them cold drinks in the afternoon and coffee at night. As the column of prisoners began to fill the open area in front of the reviewing stands the KGB guards moved closer to the gate and even ventured a few yards beyond it, the better to watch the spectacle, of course.

Chapter Thirty

HOMESTEAD AIR FORCE BASE, FLORIDA: 1130 HOURS,
1 FEBRUARY

Capt. Todd Spinelli, a rifle company commander in the 2d Marine Division, sat nervously inside the VN-22 Osprey tilt-rotor aircraft. The Osprey was still largely an experimental device as far as Spinelli was concerned. Its twin rotors were turned straight upwards as the craft sat on the ground, and it would take off like a helicopter. Once aloft, however, the rotors would swing forward like those of a conventional propellor-driven aircraft, and the machine would move out at three hundred knots. With this speed and a range of some twelve hundred nautical miles, yet with the ability to land and take off vertically from any flat spot, such as the deck of a ship or a small clearing, while carrying up to twenty-four combat-equipped troops, the Osprey far outperformed conventional aircraft or helicopters in the role of vertical assault.

It had long been under development for the Marine Corps, but cost overruns and design problems had pushed the program farther and farther down the list of Department of Defense priorities until it had almost been cancelled outright in 1989. Congress had finally approved the purchase of two twelve-plane squadrons, primarily as a testbed for tactics and to help work any further problems out of the system. Spinelli knew that when the crisis in Cuba had arisen General Weems had pulled every string possible to get the existing planes transferred immediately to the JCTF as the best available craft for getting troops into a hot area straight from a land base in Florida. Spinelli had only recently completed a tour at the Pentagon working on developing tactics for the employment of the VN-22, and he was intimately familiar with all of the congressional hassles regarding the program. He and his superiors, to say nothing of the lobbyists for the manufacturers of the plane's components, had fought desperate bureaucratic battles to keep the plane alive, and they had just barely won.

Now he was crammed with his headquarters platoon in the stuffy insides of the aircraft he had helped save, and a wide variety of interesting engineering problems came to his mind. Suppose the two tilt rotors were not exactly synchronized as they began their turn forward with the airplane several hundred feet off the ground? Suppose one turned and the other didn't? That would twist the aircraft into a pretzel, probably sending one spinning propellor ripping through the fuselage, where he was seated, and imparting to the entire structure the aerodynamics of an electric can opener. Spinelli had heard about similar problems with the Harrier jump jet during its early development, and he wondered if the engineers had really worked out that particular bug.

There was nothing for it now, however, as the vibrating aircraft began to rise slowly off the hot tarmac of the airfield. Assuming that the plane did not self-destruct en route, Spinelli mused, this was the best way to get into a bad situation. The ship could come in faster than a helicopter, low to the ground, then flare up and settle down on any convenient spot. He and his men would be out of the craft and it would be on its way in seconds, without the hassle of trying to round up scattered paratroopers in a built-up urban area. Helicopters could do the same, of course, but they didn't have the range without external fuel tanks, which were a hazard and cut load capacity. For that reason Spinelli did not really envy the 82d Airborne units being lifted in with UH-60 Blackhawks. More choppers in the air to deliver the same load meant more targets for the enemy to shoot at.

Through the small window of the Osprey Spinelli could see pairs of F-15s and F-16s rocketing skyward from another runway. Everything depended on the air force and navy fighters and their Soviet counterparts clearing the skies of the Cubans. Without total air superiority neither the choppers nor the Ospreys would be able to go in. Even the amphibious landing would be in doubt, as Cuban MiG-23s could stand off and pop their Kerry air-to-surface missiles at troop-laden ships, and the Cubans would also probably have shore-launched missiles, which the planes just had to knock out, either on the ground or in the air after they were fired.

The hardest part, however, was not being sure whether they would go in at all. Washington had approved the basic outline of General Freeman's plan for an action to secure the hostages, all of whom would be concentrated for a couple of hours in a tight area near the coast. However, the briefers had been very explicit that there would be no order to go in unless "something" happened that would give the rescuers the vital hour or so needed to get between the hostages and their guards. Failing that, the Cubans could massacre the bulk of the prisoners in the time it would take Spinelli and his men to land, dismount, and get into action, and it would all be for nothing. What the devil they expected to happen was beyond Spinelli's understanding. There had been plenty of scuttlebutt about a Delta Force raid or some kind of coup attempt inside Cuba that would keep the enemy occupied at the crucial moment, but none of it had sounded very promising. Spinelli just sat back as best he could in the cramped plane and checked the action on his M-16 once more, setting an example for his men to do the same. It was out of his hands now.

Chapter Thirty-one

Soviet Navy Lt. Igor Rokossovsky jerked back on the stick of his SU-27 Flanker B fighter and the aircraft rose quickly skyward. Rokossovsky had only recently qualified as a carrier pilot, but then the *Tblisi* was the first real aircraft carrier in the Soviet Navy. Unlike the earlier, smaller carriers, such as the *Kiev*, which was also with the fleet in the Caribbean, the *Tblisi* carried a complement of conventional fixed-wing aircraft, SU-27s and SU-25 Frogfoot attack aircraft, rather than merely helicopters or the YAK-36 jump jet, the Soviet equivalent of the Harrier. The *Tblisi* was substantially smaller than the massive American nuclear carriers, such as the *John F. Kennedy*, and had only about half as many aircraft on board, just one squadron each of SU-27Bs and SU-25s, plus a suite of antisubmarine helicopters. It also lacked the catapults typical of American carriers, relying instead on a ski-jump ramp to assist in takeoffs. Still it was the pride of the Soviet fleet as evidence of the true "blue water" status their navy had now achieved.

Rokossovsky had seen some action flying a MiG-23 in Afghanistan on a rotational assignment, but there the only threat was from mujahidin Stinger missiles, which did not really present much danger to high-performance aircraft at altitude. Here they would be up against truly integrated air defenses: MiG-23s and MiG-29s of the Cuban Air Force, SA-2, SA-5, and SA-8 surface-to-air missiles, anti-aircraft guns, the works. This month he would really have to earn his salary.

Rokossovsky had confidence in himself and in his aircraft. The SU-27B was similar in appearance and role to the F-15C air superiority fighter, a single-seat, twin-tail airplane capable of more than twice the speed of sound. His plane was loaded with a total of ten air-to-air missiles, both short- and long-range, infrared heat-seekers and semiactive radar-homers, in addition to the 30mm chain gun, in the operation of which Rokossovsky was particularly skillful. At least he had been on training missions and in the simulator.

Off to the west he could see two specks, which must be the pair of SU-27Bs that would remain to provide air cover for the fleet, along with the YAK-36s from the *Kiev*. Other aircraft were still lifting off from the *Tblisi* to form up to head for the holding area some hundred miles northwest of Havana. His mission was to provide cover for the SU-25 strike aircraft, which would hit the main Cuban air base at San Antonio de los Baños, about twenty-five miles southwest of Havana. All of Cuba's three dozen or so MiG-23s and their twenty MiG-29s were based there, along with two squadrons of MiG-21s. Three more squadrons of MiG-21s would be at Santa Clara in central Cuba, and probably as many at Holguín in the southeastern corner of the island, but those would either be out of the fight or would be dealt with by the Americans operating to the east.

Some thirty more SU-27s would be coming in from the base in Texas, along with another squadron of SU-25s that would be responsible for suppressing the antiaircraft missile batteries while the Frogfoot squadron from the *Tblisi* hit the airfield itself.

Since the Soviets had expended much in the way of resources helping the Cubans construct bombproof aircraft shelters, the main emphasis of the attack would be incapacitating the runways. Naturally, if any Cuban aircraft were unlucky enough to get caught out on the ground the twin-barrelled 30mm guns of the SU-25s would make short work of them, but the plan was to crater the runways to prevent the aircraft from taking off. To accomplish this each SU-25 would release hundreds of bomblets, criss-crossing all of the runways at the air base, turning the place into Swiss cheese and permanently keeping any aircraft still in the hangars out of the fight. Most of these craters could be repaired in relatively short order, a few hours perhaps with well-trained ground crews, but according to the briefing he and his colleagues had received aboard the *Tblisi*, *if* the order were given to go in, the entire operation wouldn't take more than a few hours. Also, if necessary, Rokossovsky and his comrades would be more than happy to pay a return visit. With missile batteries knocked out and enemy interceptors downed, the second attack would probably be even easier. He did not want to think about how attrition might affect the numbers of the attackers.

Rokossovsky checked his radars. There was nothing hostile as yet, but the sky was virtually aswarm with "friendlies," both American and Soviet. The SU-27s' Doppler pulse radar, with a lookdown, shoot-down capability that permitted the identification of low-flying aircraft or cruise missiles amid ground clutter, had a range of one hundred and thirty miles, and he was just over that distance from the Cuban coast now. His primary guidance would come, however, from a large Soviet Mainstay aircraft, the equivalent of the American AWACS. This aircraft's powerful radars would be able to pick up the takeoff of virtually any Cuban plane on the island and direct the interceptors to the best possible angle of attack. Rokossovsky did not even have to establish visual contact with the target to fire his longer-range missiles. He only regretted that the Soviet Union had seen fit to sell MiG-29s to the Cubans not long ago, since the MiG-29 had essentially the same capabilities as his own aircraft.

As he reached the assembly area with his wingman he put the aircraft into an easy racetrack pattern to await the order to attack or to go home. When he reached the easternmost tip of his pattern he could just make out what appeared to be a pair of robin's-egg blue F-15s. He held course a few seconds longer to get a closer look and thought he saw one of the American pilots wave to him as he banked back westward. Rokossovsky had trained and dreamed of meeting these aircraft in the sky for years, but he had never dreamed that it would be as allies, waiting to attack other fliers piloting aircraft he himself had once flown. Well, he thought, stranger things have happened, although he could not think of just when.

Chapter Thirty-two

WASHINGTON, D.C.: 1200 HOURS, 1 FEBRUARY

Wiznezhsky sat in the Oval Office, staring at a battery of television screens that had been erected. All of the screens carried different views of the same event, the victory parade in Havana. One was tuned to Cuban National Television, a second to the coverage being transmitted by Spanish television, and a third carried a black-and-white overhead picture being fed in by a satellite miles up in the sky over Cuba. The sound on the regular television programs had been muted, but since Wiznezhsky did not speak Spanish this was of little importance to him. He could still hear the rhythmic chanting of the crowd, a sort of sea noise, and as he watched the prisoners gradually filled up the rectangular area in front of the reviewing stand. The stand was crowded with important-looking men, some dressed in combat fatigues. In the center of the stage stood a broad-chested man with a full beard, his fists braced on his hips. Castro was enjoying the show very much.

Also present in the room were Generals Weems and Dolgoruki, Judge Webster, Secretary Baker, Ambassador Bogdanov, several staff aides, and the president. The president occupied a central chair and was staring immovably at the screens. He was slouched down, his jaw fixed and his hands dangling from the ends of the armrests.

Webster was stroking his chin repeatedly, also staring at the screens, and Wiznezhsky knew that both were expecting, hoping, to see Castro suddenly jerk backward and total pandemonium ensue, but so far all was very festive in Havana, and Castro was approaching the battery of microphones to speak.

The hostages had marched into the formation area normally, but on a signal communicated from one of the armored vehicles leading the parade all had placed their hands behind their necks. Actually, Wiznezhsky could see that not all of the men were doing this, and the occasional Cuban guard darted in from the wings of the column to administer a butt stroke with his rifle to force compliance, but even this did not convince everyone. When the last of the marchers had taken his position in a vast rectangle of humanity, all were permitted to drop their hands to their sides.

General Weems had seized the ends of the armrests on his chair with such force that Wiznezhsky had half expected him to rip them off. He could also plainly hear the gnashing of teeth coming from General Dolgoruki. Wiznezhsky also thought he saw the shine of tears beginning to form in the president's eyes, but the president rubbed the bridge of his nose with thumb and forefinger, and the tears disappeared, if they had been there at all.

No one spoke in the room. Everyone was waiting for something to happen, and no one knew exactly what.

Chapter Thirty-three

Ogarkov stared with his pale blue eyes directly at Castro as the latter began an impassioned speech. Ogarkov spoke excellent Spanish, but he did not focus on the words. He only wanted to smash the smug look of satisfaction off of that bearded face.

He looked about him. Thankfully, he noted that every group, at least the ones he could see in the front of the formation, had reached its appointed position. He glanced at his watch. The speech had just started: about nine minutes to go until the weapons came out. The ranks of the formation, despite some probably well-intentioned shouts of guidance from Cuban NCOs on the flanks, were a disgrace, just as he had hoped. Security guards and other troops were posted just as the KGB's source had said they would be. The bottom of the reviewing stand was shielded by a dark blue tarp with holes cut in it to let the wind pass through, and Ogarkov thought he could see an occasional eyeball peep through one of the holes. So that information had been accurate as well. Good.

Ogarkov was pouring sweat. It was warm, but that had little to do with his perspiration. He glanced at his watch again: about six minutes to go. He consciously avoided looking around him. Zhdanov was standing just in front of him, and he could see Zhdanov's shoulder muscles twitching nervously. Four minutes to go. Ogarkov started tapping his foot, rocking back and forth, any kind of movement to try to relieve the tension, but the hands on his watch seemed to be frozen still. It was all he could do not to stand there with his wrist poised directly in front of his face. Two minutes to go.

Inside the compound Osman was in his position by a window on the fourth floor of the embassy. From here he could see all the way to the reviewing stand. He could also see individual young men strolling casually toward the gate or the walls around the compound. The KGB gate guards were all outside the gate now, intermingled with their Cuban counterparts, seemingly enraptured by the spectacle and engrossed by the unintelligible speech, which crackled over the large public-address system outside. Osman clenched one hand into a fist so hard that his nails bit deep into his palm, while he kept a pair of field glasses pressed to his eyes with the other.

Ogarkov turned his head slightly. He had instructed the men to fidget and move about a good deal, another violation of normal military discipline. This would hopefully prevent the Cubans from noticing when the men began to assemble their weapons. He now saw the soldier who would handle the machine gun duck out of sight. The man carefully pulled the trigger housing group out from under the shirt of the man in front of him and dropped to his knees. The man on his right pulled the barrel from under the shirt of the man to his right and helped the machine-gunner assemble the gun. The man to his left produced a belt of ammunition and helped to load the weapon. Then the machine-gunner carefully crawled forward between the legs of the men in front of him.

All through the formation men were slipping magazines into their AKMs and pulling pistols and grenades from under their shirts. Ogarkov reached into his left-hand pocket and withdrew a long silver whistle. With his right hand he reached around the back of his belt and slowly drew his Makarov, first slipping off the safety and pulling back the hammer with his thumb. Then the droning of the speech was interrupted by a shrill whistle that was soon answered by a dozen others.

Castro looked around with a glare that asked who had the nerve to blow whistles during his speech and savored the imminence of their punishment. This look was almost immediately replaced with a wild-eyed expression of shock and terror. Ogarkov saw the flap under the reviewing stand flutter with movement, but then a snarling rip from the machine gun, which had been quietly placed on its bipod just behind where the first rank of prisoners had been standing, shredded the tarp from one end of the reviewing stand to the other. The Russian generals, who had formed a small body in front of the formation, had dived to their right like Olympic athletes to get out of the line of fire. Had the situation not been so deadly serious Ogarkov would have found their grace hilarious.

Four husky security guards with submachine guns had rushed to the front of the reviewing stand at the first hint of trouble, blocking Castro from view, but men with AKMs standing in the third row of prisoners brought them down with carefully aimed shots. The people in the bleachers set up well to the left and right of the formation area were screaming and pushing in a rush to escape, and the hundreds of unarmed prisoners had already begun to pour toward the Soviet compound.

Johnson was moving toward the reviewing stand the second the first whistle blast reached him. His pistol was in his hand, and he and the other marines were letting out a deep, "Oooo-Rah!" There had been Cuban guards lined up along the right side of the formation, about twenty yards away, but a quick glance told him that most of them were now sprawled on the ground, streaming blood, without even having been able to unsling their rifles. In any case, they were the responsibility of the flank men.

He raced toward the steps up to the platform and found two startled Cuban soldiers desperately trying to bring their AK-47s to bear. He didn't stop to aim as he should have, and quickly pumped two rounds at the chest of each one, but at this range that was good enough, and both men jerked to the side and fell. He took the stairs three at a time, with Captain Meese right behind him, his fist grasping Johnson by the back of his collar and shoving him up the stairs.

At the top the thirty-odd people there were in total panic. The half of the group on one side of the platform had first run toward the nearest stairway and, finding that under assault, had turned toward the other stairway, colliding in the middle with the other half of the group, which had performed the same maneuver on its side. One Cuban officer made a grab for Johnson as he reached the top of the stairs, but Johnson smashed his pistol into the side of the man's head and sent him to the floor. Johnson then continued straight back to the rear of the platform to cut off escape from that quarter.

As he reached the back of the stand he leaned over the railing and saw a large black sedan screeching away in a cloud of gravel. He raised his gun to fire at the car but was distracted by two security guards in civilian clothes, who opened fire on him with their submachine guns. He fired his remaining rounds at them, killing one and sending the other rolling for cover behind a jeep.

Meese and his squad had dived directly into the midst of the milling, shouting crowd, grabbing one officer after another, most of whom were unarmed, and clubbing them to the floor. Suddenly he ran into Major Zhdanov and his men, coming from the other side. Zhdanov was panting heavily, and Meese could see smoke coming from the barrel of his upraised pistol.

"Where's Castro?" both men said simultaneously as they grasped each other. They looked around. Their men were quickly tying up or handcuffing prisoners around the platform, but Castro was nowhere to be seen.

One of the Soviet soldiers shouted something in Russian, and both officers turned in his direction. The man was holding a smoking AKM in one hand, and his other hand grasped the long, greasy hair of a rather corpulent man in fatigues. The Cuban was dead, and he wasn't Castro, but his body was half-wedged into a small trap door in the floor of the platform where the Russian had shot him.

"Shit!" screamed Meese. Zhdanov said something rather longer in Russian, but Meese assumed that the general sentiment was the same.

Osman couldn't hear the whistles from his observation post, but he saw the vast mob of men in the formation suddenly surge in many directions, like a calm pool of water into which one had dropped a stone. He looked down at the gate. One Cuban guard was on the ground, his throat slit by the KGB man who had been standing next to him. Another KGB man sprayed the Cubans in the machine-gun jeep with automatic fire, tumbling them out of the vehicle, and the other gate guards had quickly raised their hands and surrendered to the Russians.

He saw the embassy vehicles racing toward the gate to form their barrier for the escapees as Rodriguez and the marines raced to seize possession of the machine gun in the Cuban jeep. Osman could see the men around the walls leaping to their firing positions and blazing away at Cuban soldiers stationed around the compound.

More men, Russian and American, were sprinting out of the gate, armed with AK-47s and Molotov cocktails. It was vital that the defenders of the compound clear the gate area before the rush of prisoners reached it, to prevent a hopeless traffic jam. Osman beat his fist against his leg as he swept his field glasses over the heaving mass of humanity in the square before him. The cars were in place now, armed men using them for cover as they fired at the few remaining Cuban guards who were not either already dead or in full flight, and hundreds of prisoners now tore through the gate into the compound.

Featherstone was at his post about twenty yards inside the gate when the shooting started. He saw the Cuban guards at the gate go down and then the embassy vehicles race past him to take up their blocking positions outside. A moment later the first of the prisoners came running through the opening. The men who had been armed by the Soviets had already been briefed as to the positions they were to take up inside the compound, but most of the others had not and needed to be guided. Featherstone's job was to direct the Americans who came into the compound with weapons to the rear wall of the compound, which had been designated the American portion of the perimeter for defense, and all other Americans to a double door at the right side of the embassy entrance, from which they would be directed to shelter. Other, Russian guides were also posted nearby to direct the Soviet escapees.

Featherstone was reminded of the rush for lawn seating at a popular rock concert by the crush of young men pelting through the gate. Then he began to see the wounded being helped along or carried by their comrades. It seemed that while most of the Cuban guards had been cut down by the initial surprise burst of fire, a number had survived and had let rip into the heart of the mob with automatic fire. With the dense concentration of men in the square, they could hardly help but find a mark with every round.

Some of the men who rushed in were exultant, others terrified. A fair number of the men were armed, and some even had two or three AK-47s slung over their backs, undoubtedly taken from felled Cubans. As one of these puffed past Featherstone, he thrust a rifle into his hands.

"Here you go, pal," said the man, a sailor evidently. "It's got at least half a mag left. Sorry, but I didn't get any more ammo." Then the man was gone in the rush toward the embassy building.

Featherstone did not know quite what to do with the weapon. He went on giving his directions mechanically, and the stream of men gradually began to thin out. He then started to move closer to the gate, unslinging the rifle from his shoulder but uncertain as to how he should use it.

He could still hear heavy firing coming from outside the walls and all around him. The men on the firing steps were blasting away at targets he could not see, and he now saw one of them pitch over backward, his forehead torn away by a bullet. The men on the barricade of cars were also firing steadily, and he made up his mind to join them.

A trickle of men was still coming through the gate, most of them now bringing wounded or even dead men with them. Featherstone could see that the square was almost deserted now, but littered with bodies. A large crowd of men still collected around the reviewing stand, over two hundred yards away across a four-lane divided avenue and the bare formation ground.

Featherstone crouched down and scuttled over to where Rodriguez and the American marines were positioned by the captured Cuban jeep. One of the marines was firing the machine gun mounted on a pedestal at the back of the jeep, and Rodriguez was directing his fire at a cluster of Cubans huddled behind a garden wall off to the left of the field, from which the Cubans were firing on the prisoners still in the open. Featherstone raised his rifle and pressed the trigger, but nothing happened. He searched for the safety switch, but he could not read the Russian characters and selected the next setting. He pressed the trigger again, and a burst of fire made the rifle kick and the barrel rise up in his hands. Must have been automatic, he thought as he moved the switch to the next setting and was able to squeeze off single shots after that.

Suddenly there was a whoosh, and a cloud of smoke appeared off to his right. He saw a small projectile shoot out from where a Russian had fired an RPG-7 at a vehicle—very much like an old American half-track from the World War II movies, except that this one had four rear wheels instead of tracks—that had just poked its nose around the corner of a building. The projectile struck the vehicle just at the passenger-side door, and the whole thing disappeared in a cloud of smoke and flame. Featherstone saw several men leap from the burning vehicle, one of them on fire, and bullets from the Russians on the barricade cut down the others.

Featherstone could see that the group of captured Cuban officers was now being herded across the open ground, but bullets were kicking up puffs of dirt all around them, and he thought to himself that they had a very long way to go.

Paco was dreaming of people chasing him, dead people. He could hear them screaming at him and shooting at him. He awoke with a gasp and found himself lying on the bed next to the dead woman. He leaped from the bed and flattened himself against the armoire, staring at the motionless form. His breath came in quick pants but he couldn't seem to get enough air.

Suddenly he realized that the sounds of screams and shooting had continued even after his dream had ended, and he ran into the kitchen to look out the window. He saw a huge mob of men racing toward the Soviet compound. Other men were firing weapons in all directions, out from the mob and into the mob. He saw an eight-wheeled armored car burning brightly not far from his building. What the devil was going on?

He looked quickly at the reviewing stand. The platform was crowded with men, many of them with their hands raised. He picked up his rifle and looked through the scope. There were Americans there, and Soviets, with guns! There were several dozen Cuban officers who had apparently been taken prisoner. Other Americans and Soviets were picking up guns from fallen Cuban guards and blazing away at anything that moved outside the square. The crazy bastards hadn't wanted to wait for him and had taken matters into their own hands! And a good thing too, he quickly corrected himself, as his head pounded and his stomach churned.

All thought of the night before immediately vanished from his mind. Here were his adopted countrymen fighting for their lives, and he had a rifle! He braced the weapon on the top of the low refrigerator and began to squeeze off rounds. Some Cubans were setting up a machine gun behind a low garden wall about two hundred yards from his position. While one held the tripod base, another lowered the gun onto it, and the third was opening boxes of ammunition. He took the ammunition man first. The man with the tripod looked up when his comrade keeled over, and Paco shot him in the face. The third grabbed the pistol grip of the gun and swung the barrel around in the direction from which the shots must be coming, but Paco put one through his chest before he could complete the maneuver.

Then he saw the crew of an antiaircraft gun frantically working the cranks of the twin-barrelled 23mm piece to bring it down from its almost perpendicular position to point it at the running men in the square. Paco was not sure which of the two men in the attached seats was the gunner, so he shot the one on the left first, then the one on the right. One of the remaining crewmen turned and ran, and Paco shot another who was carrying a box of ammunition. Two more had taken cover behind the gun and he could see them peeking out, trying to see the source of this fire. It would take them time to disentangle the dead gunners from their seats, so Paco searched for a new target.

A T-54 tank was just pulling out of a side street to the right rear of the reviewing stand area, over five hundred yards from where Paco was standing. Both the tank commander and loader were standing up through their hatches, and the commander was manning the 12.7mm machine gun mounted on top. Paco aimed carefully, allowing for the movement of the tank, and fired. The commander's head jerked back and he collapsed inside the tank. The loader didn't wait to investigate and dropped inside as well, pulling his hatch shut after him. The tank stopped and then backed slowly out of the square.

Then Paco ceased fire. He had no more clear shots from his position, and he was confident that in the confusion not even his immediate neighbors could have been aware that shooting had come from the apartment. He pulled the magazine out of the rifle and replaced it with a full one, reloading the partially empty one with loose rounds from his pocket.

Glover and his men had whipped out their weapons and shoved the intervening ranks of men to the ground, cutting down the half dozen startled Cuban guards in their path. Then they sprinted around the corner of the reviewing stand. Glover came face to face with a pair of security guards in civilian dress who had been lounging in the open doors of a sedan parked next to the stand. They attempted to draw their pistols, but Glover cut them down with a long burst from his AKM. He paused to peek through one of the small holes in the tarp around the base of the stand and could see the sprawled bodies of over a dozen security guards entangled in the scaffolding of the stands.

He continued around the next corner and saw the black sedan that had escaped Johnson disappearing in the distance. His men engaged in a hot firefight with several Cuban soldiers they found behind the stands, which left all of the Cubans and two of Glover's men dead. He then had his men spread out in a rough semicircle, using the scattered cars and jeeps left in the area as cover. He gave the thumbs-up signal to Captain Vlassov, whose team had secured the other side of the stands.

Glover and Vlassov saw the ZSU-23/2 antiaircraft gun at about the same time. They also saw its crew members begin to drop dead for no apparent reason. Vlassov's men, from their angle, made short work of the two crewmen who had taken cover from Paco's fire.

Glover shouted, "Lerner's section, follow me!" and took off toward the gun with half a dozen marines in tow. If they could get the gun's wheels in position and drag it to the compound the firepower of those twin 23mm guns would be a very welcome addition to the defense. Vlassov saw his intention and also raced for the gun with several of his men. The Russians were more familiar with the piece and its workings, but the Americans watched them and copied their actions, and within seconds the gun was on its four wheels and a team of Americans and Soviets was pulling it slowly toward the compound. Others in the group snatched up heavy boxes of ammunition and also began the long trek.

Meese and Zhdanov had shoved their prisoners down the reviewing stand steps and were herding them toward the embassy. By a quick count they had six army generals, two from the air force, an admiral from the navy, the minister of interior, several senior Communist Party officials, half a dozen colonels, and a couple of security guards who had thought discretion the better part of valor. They also had the ambassadors from Libya, China, and the PLO, most of the other diplomatic functionaries having been seated in a special section of the bleachers off to the right of the stands. The military prisoners were sullen and unruly, but the diplomats, except for the Chinese, who was positively stoic, ranted and protested like madmen.

Meese grabbed the PLO representative by the collar. The man was making a very creditable effort to compete for the Yasser Arafat Lookalike Award, scruffy beard, headdress, and all. He complained bitterly of this gross violation of diplomatic immunity. "Hey, Goldstein," Meese shouted to one of the marines, "here's one for you!"

A tall, stocky marine with curly black hair grabbed the PLO ambassador's arm in a viselike grip and placed the barrel of his Makarov at the base of his neck. "I never did plant a tree in Israel, but I'll plant you wherever you like, asshole." The Palestinian saw no further purpose in discussing his diplomatic credentials, and he joined the march toward the embassy.

Featherstone had long since expended his ammunition, but he stayed with Rodriguez on the barricade. He could see Meese and the prisoners nearing the barricade now. Behind them the screen formed by Glover's and Vlassov's men was also falling back, dragging their captured gun with them.

The heaviest firing was coming from behind Featherstone, in the direction the parade had come from the Plaza de la Revolución. There the hundreds of route guards had begun to come up in the direction of the sound of battle. While the first of these had been ambushed by fire from the compound walls, the others had moved through the buildings and gardens along the route and were now aiming a desultory fire into the other side of the barricade. Fortunately, Meese and his men kept their prisoners close, and these guards were afraid to fire in their direction for fear of hitting one of the hostages. At least two armored cars had also attempted to come up from this direction, but RPG-7 rounds had stopped both of them.

Finally Meese and the prisoners, then Glover and Vlassov, passed through the barricade and into the compound. Featherstone grabbed Meese's hand and shook it vigorously. Meese glanced at the AK-47 in the diplomat's hand and raised his eyebrow. "Been into some heavy negotiating, have we?"

Featherstone laughed. "I think we can say that we had a frank and open exchange of views." Then he looked back out across the open area to the reviewing stand. There were certainly more than a hundred Cuban dead scattered about, but there were also at least twenty or thirty dead Americans and Soviets lying out on the bare ground. Featherstone wondered where war ever got its reputation for glory.

Chapter Thirty-four

Wiznezhsky had just reached to pour himself a glass of water from the jug on the table next to him when he heard a shout of "Holy shit!" from General Weems. He looked around to see what had happened and then began to hear shouts and screams and explosions coming over the muted television sound systems. The cameras were being jostled. People were running back and forth. The Cuban National Television network picture immediately became jumbled.

He focussed on the overhead satellite picture and could see the tiny figures of men running in all directions. At this resolution he couldn't make out the actions of individuals, but he could see two separate groups moving quickly toward the reviewing stand while the bulk of the prisoners poured in the direction of the compound.

"They're breaking out!" shouted General Weems. He pointed toward the picture from Spanish television, which had steadied now. They could see several Soviet prisoners armed with rifles firing at the Cuban guards. "They have weapons!" A hand suddenly was capped over the lens of the Spanish television camera. They caught a glimpse of an angry Cuban in uniform and heard some shouted words just before that picture, too, went out.

Only the satellite coverage remained. The stream of prisoners was entering the compound now, and they could see the barricade of embassy vehicles that stretched across the avenue in front of the compound. They could also see several military vehicles burning.

"Look here!" shouted Wiznezhsky. "Look at the roof of the embassy."

Some metal panels had just been laid out on the flat roof of the building. Wiznezhsky couldn't read what appeared to be Russian, but the English message was clear enough. "COME IN NOW . . . HELP."

The president was half levitated out of his seat, his hands braced on the arms of the chair. "This is it! GO NOW, General!"

Hands reached for telephones around the room. General Weems had already raised the receiver of his even before the president spoke. "Freeman?" he shouted into the mouthpiece. "Weems here. Are you watching? Here are your orders: Code Green, repeat, Code Green! It looks like all of the hostages are in the Soviet compound area and that they have seized arms. Lay down a protective fire all around them and send in the standby force to secure the area. Order the MAB to move on Beach Red as soon as the MCM units have cleared a channel. Do you read me?"

General Dolgoruki grasped Weems's forearm. "Tell him to use the word '*Suvorov*' with the Soviet forces."

"Freeman," the general added, looking slyly at the Russian, "tell your Soviet counterparts '*Suvorov*.'" So the Soviets had subordinated their units to American command, Weems thought, but they had to have a code word to authorize actually taking hostile action. Not a bad precaution to take.

The president was on the red phone. His conversation was rather more stilted, having to pass through interpreters first. "Yes, Mr. Secretary, we're watching too. I've ordered our troops in. I don't think we'll ever get another chance like this, and I don't think this one will last very long. Yes, Mr. Secretary, good luck to all of us."

Wiznezhsky had unconsciously moved closer and closer to the television screen, and now his nose was practically pressed against the glass, although he did manage to stay out of everyone else's line of vision. He twisted his head one way and then the other, trying to make out what was happening in the grainy image. Suddenly he jumped back and pointed, "Look here! You saw those groups of men going toward the reviewing stands? Two small groups went up each side. Now they're coming down, but they're bringing everyone from the stands with them, and they're heading for the compound. *They're taking hostages!*"

"All right!" Baker yelled involuntarily. "What goes around comes around."

"You know," Webster observed, raising his index finger, "Castro was in those stands. Do you suppose they got him?" It had been impossible to tell from their first viewing of the various films whether the entire event might have been triggered by Castro himself being assassinated in front of the formation. Analysts even now, both in Washington and in Moscow, would be going back over the tape, second by second, to determine just this. It was Webster's gut feeling, however, that this had not been the case. The sudden explosion at all parts of the formation had been too simultaneous to have been prompted by some external act. Even if Castro had been shot, half of the men would have been standing about for some time saying, "What happened?" No, this looked like a premeditated plan. Where had those weapons come from? It was frustrating. It was like being in a dream, suspended helplessly above the action, seeing it all and not being able to influence events.

"Well," General Weems sighed, "if they didn't get Castro himself, they got just about everybody else in the Cuban military and government. If nothing else, that will screw up their chain of command and stymie their mobilization plans for awhile. In any case the wheels are in motion. We should have rounds on target in Cuba within fifteen minutes."

Chapter Thirty-five

The gates of the embassy compound had been pulled shut. They wouldn't be much of a barrier to tanks, but infantrymen would find their half-inch iron bars formidable enough. Teams of men were frantically digging firing positions and slit trenches all around the compound yard. Despite the eight-foot walls surrounding the compound, there were several fairly tall apartment blocks within five hundred yards of the place that afforded lines of sight into the yard. Once the Cubans placed machine guns and snipers on the roofs of these buildings survival outside the compound buildings would be possible only if the defenders could keep under cover.

At the gate two large positions were quickly dug out and reinforced with sandbags, one on either side of the opening just inside the wall, thus affording an interlocking field of fire on the approaches to the gate without exposing the defenders to fire from anywhere except directly in front of the opening. Since the front wall of the compound angled inward from the corners to the gate, the men in these positions were also able to sight along the outer edge of the wall to prevent the enemy from sneaking up along its base.

Firing positions on the roofs of the embassy buildings and at a few points along the wall had similarly been protected with sandbags and other barriers. Glover's antiaircraft weapon had been hauled up the steps of the embassy and emplaced directly in front of the entrance, and was now being surrounded by sandbags and heavy office furniture dragged from inside the building.

General Akamirov, who was now in overall command of the defense, expected that the men would not be able to hold the wall itself for long. He hoped only to force the Cubans to deploy to take the wall before falling back to the buildings. He knew that he couldn't hold the embassy indefinitely, if only because he had limited ammunition, but time was the key factor. If he could hold out for a few hours, that might be enough.

Featherstone and Osman stood together in the ambassador's office. Most of the rest of the building, especially the ground floor and the basement, was jammed with refugees. Meese, Ogarkov, Akamirov, and Fleischmann strode into the room, all of them armed, and they sat in chairs facing Osman's desk.

Osman took his own seat and said, "Well, General, what's the situation?"

"The compound is secure, Mr. Ambassador. We took just over thirty prisoners, including several common soldiers, seven flag-rank officers, one cabinet member, several members of the Politburo, and a handful of ambassadors of the PRB nations. At least two other army generals were killed during the assault when they resisted. The bad news is that Castro got away."

"I'm aware of that," Osman said unhappily. "I saw his car tearing off. I suppose we'll have to wait and see how much he values the lives of his generals. How is the defense coming along?"

"Our men picked up between eighty and one hundred AK-47s, a few pistols, a couple of machine guns, and even an antiaircraft gun. All together we have the equivalent of a good battalion of light infantry dug in here. It would take at least a regiment to root us out. Our major weakness is that we have only about fifty rounds of ammunition per rifle, a couple hundred for each machine gun, and almost nothing in the way of explosives. If the Cubans use artillery, it's all over. Even if they decide not to commit their general staff to the role of Martyrs of the Revolution, they can use armor to get through the outer wall and then follow up with infantry to assault the buildings. I estimate, based on the KGB reporting on enemy troop deployments, that it would take them at least an hour to mount even a hasty attack with the men on hand in Havana. Since we gutted at least one battalion in our breakout I think we can handle what's left if they try a quick assault. It will take at least a couple more hours to move the 101st Armored Division here from the Managua Barracks, but then they can take us whenever they get into position. Our only hope is that we can get enough pressure generated from outside to prevent them from concentrating against us and that our air power can interdict major troop movements on the roads. Then we stand a chance."

"My worry is how we can make sure that help is indeed on the way," Osman said. They could just hear the crackle of a bullhorn as Rodriguez announced in Spanish to anyone listening outside the walls that they held a number of Cuban general officers, listing them by name and rank, and stating that no harm would come to them at the hands of the defenders. Rodriguez also warned, however, that they could not guarantee the safety of the prisoners if heavy weapons were used against the compound and that the prisoners would have to face the same risks as the defenders.

Suddenly Featherstone raised a finger. "Here's an idea! Are the phones working?"

"Are you suggesting we just place a collect call to the White House?" General Akamirov asked.

"Only the domestic Cuban system is functional," Osman said. "We can't call off-island, if that's what you mean."

"Not exactly," Featherstone continued. "First, I think we should call over to the Army High Command and repeat our statements about the prisoners directly to the military, just in case. Next, I think we should start calling all over the island, to hotels, private homes, any number we can get our hands on outside of the Havana area, and just tell them our situation."

"What the devil for?" asked Osman.

"How are long distance telephone messages transmitted, even within Cuba?"

"By microwave, I suppose," said Osman, obviously getting a little bored with this line of discussion.

"And who listens to microwave transmissions, other than the intended recipient?"

"NSA!" shouted Meese, slapping his palm on his knee. "They must be live-monitoring everything coming out of Cuba these days."

"Exactly," said Featherstone. "If we can just get a few people to stay on the line long enough to get our message out, in Spanish, English, Russian, or whatever, someone's bound to pick it up. Then it will be a question of whether or not the wheels of the intelligence community can turn fast enough to get the information to where it's needed in time."

"It's worth a try," said Osman. He gestured to a staff aide who was seated by the door. "You heard him, Leonid, I want every telephone line occupied except my direct line, which we'll leave open in case the Cubans want to talk to us. You can have people call the resort hotels at the beaches in English or Russian, and have Spanish-speakers just call private homes anywhere outside of the immediate Havana area. There are phone books for the whole island down in the Commercial Section office." The aide jumped up and raced out of the room.

"Well," Akamirov said, "it looks like the ball is in the Cubans' court now."

Chapter Thirty-six

Castro was leaning over a large table with a detailed map of northern Havana spread out on it. He was screaming orders to the assorted colonels and majors who were present. Virtually all of the more senior officers had either been killed or captured at the reviewing stand. Estigarribia and a squad of TE men stood along one wall, their submachine guns prominently displayed, as Castro was convinced that the events of the last half hour were part of a vast conspiracy. Already Estigarribia and his men had marched General Ibarra of the DGCI out into the courtyard of the headquarters area and shot him against a brick wall.

"How many artillery pieces do we have within range of the Soviet Embassy?" Castro asked in a shrill voice.

"Well," stammered an army captain, "we have a battalion of twelve 155mm self-propelled guns here, and we could have them in firing position within half an hour. There is also a SCUD rocket battalion stationed with the 101st Armored Division at the Managua Barracks, about fifteen kilometers southeast of here. They could fire from where they are."

"Good," said Castro, "and what about air power?"

222

"We have the Hind gunships at Cienfuegos," chimed in an air force captain. They would be the most accurate for use in the middle of Havana—"

"Listen to me, Captain," Castro sneered. "Just be good enough to answer my simple questions, and leave out your stupid advice. I know where the target is, and I don't give a shit! We'll give the civilians around the embassy fifteen minutes to evacuate, and the soldiers can dig in where they are. Is that clear, or would you rather have a new posting as aide-de-camp to General Ibarra?"

"No, sir," stammered the captain. "Excuse me, sir. We also have the SU-24 light bombers at San Antonio de los Baños. It would take about an hour to ready the aircraft and have them over the target."

"That's better," said Castro. "I want the artillery and SCUDs to open fire exactly one hour from now. We'll communicate an ultimatum to the embassy that if they do not surrender by that time every living soul in the place will be killed and the buildings razed to the ground. We'll hold the aircraft in reserve to follow up if necessary."

"I don't think that would be wise, Jefe."

Castro turned furiously toward the source of this comment. General Murguia stood in the doorway of the room, cradling an AKM in his arms and flanked by fully armed infantrymen. Estigarribia could see that there were more infantrymen in the hallway behind Murguia, all wearing the shoulder patches of the 101st Armored Division.

"I'm sure no one has bothered to point out to you that the majority of our High Command were taken alive at the reviewing stand," Murguia continued calmly, "and that an artillery attack would almost certainly result in their deaths as well as those of the prisoners—that is, the former prisoners. The Soviets and Americans in the embassy have announced that they will not harm our officers. Of course it would be suicide for them to do so. But they will afford them no special protection if we choose to use heavy weapons either."

"I'm not here to debate things!" Castro screamed. "I have given an order. Are you going to carry it out or not?"

"It was an order based on misinformation," said Murguia. "No, I am not."

Castro raised his hand, and several of the TE men began to swing the barrels of their weapons around, but they were met by the far greater number of weapons in the hands of Murguia's men. "Jefe," said Murguia, "I have no wish to overstep my authority, but neither are the armed forces willing to permit the slaughter of their most senior officers. It would be well if you would permit the military to handle this matter."

Castro's eyes narrowed to slits, and he nodded with a look that told Estigarribia that he would settle the score with Murguia soon enough. "How lucky we are, Murguia," growled Castro, intentionally omitting Murguia's rank, "that you were not present at the ceremony, that you are now here to help us deal with these hooligans."

"As you are aware, Jefe," Murguia said, "a report has been filed with your office about the commando attack earlier this morning. I informed you that I would be placing the units of my command on full alert and would come to Havana when those measures were completed, and here I am. It is fortunate for you that I chose to bring the recon battalion and one mechanized infantry regiment from the 101st with me. If this action is the prelude to a major military inter-vention by the superpowers, as I suspect it to be, then the road from here to the Managua Barracks will soon be a death trap swarming with enemy fighter bombers. We beat the cutoff, as my troops are now entering the suburbs of Havana and will be available either to storm the embassy or to resist an invasion."

"What an incredible piece of luck!" Castro said. "Now what do you propose to do about this situation, since you apparently have appointed yourself commander-in-chief?"

"We have two options," Murguia said. "We can wait until my troops are assembled and ready for an attack, which should take about two hours. On the other hand, we can launch an immediate assault with the troops available right now and hope to hit the em-bassy before they can prepare proper defenses or before the Yankees get here in force. I tend to believe that if we hurry we can shoot our way in, and the ex-prisoners will not harm their hostages. I favor this latter option as, if we do this quickly, we might be able to forestall any major military effort the superpowers may have in the offing. If we fail in this assault, we can still go ahead with the set-piece attack with the troops of the 101st later just the same."

"And what troops are currently available?" Castro asked. Estigarribia suspected that Castro had decided to grant this round to Murguia in order to prevent his own immediate overthrow by coup d'état. Later, experience had proven, the vacillating nature of the Cuban generals would permit Castro to weed out the ones in sympathy with Murguia one by one, but he must not place his own position of authority in jeopardy just to make a point now.

"There was over a mechanized division's worth in the city before this assault, but these took most of the casualties from the surprise attack. Furthermore, I would want to keep the bulk of these troops in defensive positions to fend off any attack from the outside. Clearly the best-prepared troops for this job are the TE. I understand that there are about six hundred of them in Havana right now, apart from your own security detail."

Castro winced at the reference to his personal security, as his informants had advised him that the military frequently joked about his private army of bodyguards. "The TE also took heavy casualties in the assault on the Soviet mechanized brigade, but, yes, there are about six hundred available in the city."

"Precisely," continued Murguia. "Apart from being available, their high level of training makes them ideally suited for taking the embassy with the minimum risk to the hostages."

"Oh, yes," Castro said in a condescending tone, "and we wouldn't want to risk the lives of any generals now, would we?"

Murguia stared Castro in the eye with a look that would have frozen fire. "We have already had an exceptional piece of luck today in that you were able to escape unharmed from that deadly trap. We shouldn't take any more risks."

Castro just glared at Murguia. "Very well then," he shouted. "Go on and get the attack organized. I want troops over the wall within an hour." And Castro stormed out of the room, trailing his TE men behind him. As Estigarribia turned to leave he nodded discreetly at Murguia, who gave him a polite wink in return. So far, so good, thought Estigarribia.

Chapter Thirty-seven

Rokossovsky's radio crackled to life. "Condor Flight Leader, this is Center Six."

"Center Six, this is Condor Leader. Go ahead," Rokossovsky heard the flight leader answer.

"*Suvorov, Suvorov*," the voice said. "Execute Plan Number One as briefed."

"Roger, Center."

Rokossovsky could see the SU-25s below him peeling out of their racetrack pattern and heading south toward the Cuban coast. The plan called for the first wave of SU-25s to hit the Cuban anti-aircraft batteries with ARM missiles, which would home in on their radar emissions, and with bombs. The satellite and aerial photography had carefully identified most of the enemy emplacements, and the others would have to reveal themselves in order to engage the attackers. A second wave of SU-25s would then make for the Cuban air base at San Antonio de los Baños, about fifteen miles inland.

It would be the job of Rokossovsky and the other SU-27 pilots in his squadron to keep enemy fighters off the backs of the attack aircraft. From the reports they had been receiving from the Soviet Mainstay aircraft Rokossovsky knew that there were half a dozen

Cuban MiG-21s, a pair of MiG-23s, and a pair of MiG-29s airborne in the immediate vicinity of Havana. There were more MiG-21s patrolling farther to the east, but the Americans would probably take care of them. The only other question was how many additional Cuban aircraft could get off the ground before the bombers destroyed their runways.

He turned toward the coast along with the other aircraft in the squadron, maintaining thirty thousand feet of altitude and kicking the airspeed up past Mach 1. The Cubans were vectoring in on the first wave of SU-25s, which they had obviously been monitoring for some time, waiting for them to make a move. Another report came over the headset. Naval gunfire was already hitting those enemy antiaircraft missile batteries nearest the coast that had been identified. Rokossovsky could see puffs of smoke from regular antiaircraft guns appearing in the air ahead of the bombers, at their lower altitude.

Rokossovsky and his wingman were being directed by the Mainstay toward a pair of approaching MiG-21s. This was not much of a match-up. With the sophisticated avionics of the SU-27 and its up-to-date missiles Rokossovsky could go for a head-on engagement at considerable range, something the MiG-21s couldn't do. He selected an AA-10C semiactive radar-homing missile, waited for the proper tone in his headset, and pressed the "fire" button. The aircraft jerked slightly with the missile release, and he banked away to the left.

The sky around him was filled with the twisting, turning shapes of aircraft and missiles. A warning beep sounded in his ear, and he released a series of flares and banked wildly to avoid a heat-seeking missile. With one eye he also watched the progress of his own missile and noted the tiny flash on his radar screen as the missile impacted on its target. His wingman also called in that he had destroyed his target.

The Mainstay reported that at least four more MiG-21s and half a dozen MiG-23s had gotten off the ground. The bombers had already eliminated most of the antiaircraft sites and the second wave was fast approaching the airfield. Unless these new fighters were dealt with they could still cripple the strike before it closed the runway.

Rokossovsky had long since crossed the Cuban coast and recognized Lake Ariguanado, just north of the airfield, below him. He whipped his aircraft around in a tight turn, feeling the excitement of having a machine of this power and weight respond to his slightest gesture at the controls, and headed down after a darting speck that was trying to lose itself in the ground clutter.

It was a MiG-29. Rokossovsky dove after it, his wingman keeping station behind him and off to one side. The pilot of the MiG-29 was jinking violently, trying to keep Rokossovsky from being able to line up for a shot with his 30mm cannon, but Rokossovsky stayed with him, his finger caressing the trigger on his joystick. He watched the reticle in his heads-up display, waiting until it was aligned with the MiG-29. Then he fired. The plane shook with the force of the gun blast, and a stream of tracers tore across the sky, ripping into the wing of the MiG. The enemy pilot tried to turn away but Rokossovsky had anticipated the move, and the second burst of cannon fire literally sliced off the target's tail, sending it into a spin. The two planes were at only about four hundred feet of altitude now, twisting between the hills of northwestern Cuba, and the Cuban pilot had no room to try to regain control of the aircraft. It flipped into a wooded area, sending up a huge column of flame and smoke.

Rokossovsky pulled up and levelled off his flight path. To his left he could see the Cuban airfield. Smoke was coming from several of the hangars, and he could see craters dotting the main runway. Fingers of fire still criss-crossed the sky, as Cuban antiaircraft guns lashed back at the attackers, but the bombers had done their job. There would be no more MiGs taking off this afternoon.

Rokossovsky's squadron was called back to its station off the north coast. The few Cuban fighters that had survived had withdrawn to central Cuba. Another American air raid had also hit the Cuban air base at Holquín in the southern tip of Cuba, and further waves of fighter bombers would be coming in to deal with any antiaircraft batteries that had lain low during this attack, but the way now seemed clear for the troop transports to come in.

Back at his station Rokossovsky learned that one of the other fighters in his squadron had been hit by ground fire but had returned to the *Tblisi*. Another had been jumped by a MiG-29 and destroyed. Rokossovsky had been singing into his headset, elated at his first two kills. Now he realized that for the first time in his career he would return to a ready room to face the empty seats of his former comrades. The fact that his own seat might have been emptied just as easily did not occur to him, but it seemed out of place now to rejoice in his victory.

Chapter Thirty-eight

Featherstone crouched, peering out of a window on the fourth floor of the embassy building. He and Osman had been taking turns looking through the latter's field glasses for some ten minutes, watching truckloads of Cuban troops dismounting among the houses off to the left of the embassy, about two blocks away. Through the shattered windows they could also hear the high-pitched squeaking of tank treads from the same direction.

"It looks like they're going to attempt an assault after all," Osman said. American and Soviet planes had overflown the compound in the last few minutes at tremendous speed, and it looked as though an air battle was being fought farther out to the west. They could hear bombing and secondary explosions, and they could see the puffs of antiaircraft shells exploding in the air over the city.

An American A-10 had come streaking past the compound at barely one hundred feet of altitude. It was an ugly airplane, with short, stubby wings, a bulbous canopy well forward, and two oversized engines mounted externally near the tail. Featherstone could see why the air force pilots he had known had not considered it the ideal machine for an aspiring fighter jockey. They had seen a Cuban tank twisting frantically at the far end of the open area in front of the

230

embassy, past the reviewing stand, but the A-10 had fired a burst from its cannon and set the tank alight before banking away to the west. Then a Harrier had come in very low as well, but this time they had seen several small missiles dart up from the houses to the east of the embassy, possibly from the hand-held SA-7s. The pilot had corkscrewed wildly trying to shake the missiles, and had dropped a string of flares, but one of the missiles had stayed with him and disappeared into his engine exhaust. They didn't see the plane crash as it disappeared behind a taller block of apartments, but they heard the horrible explosion a split second later.

A loud crump drew their attention to the east wall of the embassy. A column of white smoke rose from the street outside. Another crump followed, and another, and another, and soon they could no longer see even the wall for all of the smoke. The rattle of small-arms fire grew in volume, as did the noise of tank engines and the clank of their treads on the pavement.

Fleischmann had climbed into a small firing position near the east wall. The backs of the defenders were protected by a barricade of sandbags, and several small slits had been punched through the perimeter wall to permit them to fire into the street. Fleischmann's eyes were watering from the smoke, but he and the men with him fired short bursts at the shadows that darted back and forth between the shifting walls of smoke. Suddenly the ground around them shook with a terrific explosion, and clouds of dust were added to the smoke.

"They've blasted the wall," shouted Fleischmann as he pushed over some of the sandbags to open up a field of fire for the men along the inside of the wall to their right. The smoke was beginning to clear in the brisk breeze that blew through the city at this time of day, and he saw the first dark figures leap over the rubble through a yard-wide gap in the perimeter wall about twenty meters away from where Fleischmann was standing. Fleischmann pulled a grenade from his belt, yanked out the pin, and heaved it in the direction of the breach. There was a flash and a thump, and he heard a scream of pain.

The other men in the firing position were blazing away into the thinning smoke, but there were Cubans in the yard now. The man next to Fleischmann took a round in the chest and collapsed back against the wall with a sigh. Another explosion behind Fleischmann now told him that another breach had been opened farther back in the wall, toward the sea. Fleischmann blew his whistle in short blasts, the signal to abandon the wall and fall back to the main buildings. He and his remaining men ran, half crouching, up a slit trench only a foot and a half deep that led toward a side door to the embassy. Another man stumbled, and when Fleischmann stopped to help him up he saw that the man's head was dangling by a thread. He had only two men with him when he leaped over the low sandbag barricade that housed a small firing position at the doorway, and he turned to help cover the retreat of the other wall defenders.

Suddenly a sound like tearing paper magnified a thousand times caused him to duck his head instinctively. When he looked up he saw a solid stream of tracer rounds lashing back and forth across the open front courtyard of the compound as Glover's twin-barrelled antiaircraft gun tore into the attackers. He saw a line of Cubans who had just begun to sprint toward the embassy steps literally cut in half by a long burst from the gun. A machine gun that the Cubans had set up in the first breach in the wall was also silenced in a blaze of 23mm bullets.

Bullets spattered in the ground and off the wall next to the defensive position located at one side of the main entry gate. Fleischmann could see the antennae of a tank bobbing in the air over the wall as the tank moved along the outside of the compound wall, heading for the gate. One of the men in the sandbagged pit fired an RPG-7 rocket, and Fleischmann saw the flash of the explosion, but the tank kept on moving, its frontal armor too strong for the small rocket to penetrate, and a burst of machine-gun fire cut down the RPG-7 man. Fleischmann dashed across the open courtyard, ducking low as if running against a strong wind, to the firing pit at the near side of the gate, the one the tank driver could not see because of the wall.

He dove head first into the pit and grabbed a Molotov cocktail, letting one of the other men light the wick. Another man there, an American sailor, did likewise. They waited until the sound of the tank was just on the other side of the wall, and both jumped onto the impromptu firing step formed by the backs of two other men who had braced themselves against the wall. Fleischmann could see the round turret of the tank just below him, and he heaved the large bottle down onto the rear engine grate, where it smashed and burst immediately into a cascade of flame. The American tossed his, hitting the top of the turret, and trickles of flame washed over the sides of the vehicle. Both men then dropped back down into the pit.

They could hear the tank continue to run, but clouds of black, oily smoke were now pouring over the wall. All at once the men in the opposite pit leaped to their feet and poured a murderous fire through the gate, cutting down the tank crewmen as they tried to escape from their burning coffin. The tank continued to roll slowly forward until it wedged itself into the gate opening at an angle, pushing aside the iron grillwork as if it weren't there, but sticking fast.

Fleischmann shouted an order, and all of the men from both pits ran for the embassy as the cannon shells inside the tank's turret began to cook off and explode. The men took up new positions near Glover's gun at the embassy entrance and Fleischmann went inside to report.

He found General Akamirov, his face blackened with smoke and grease, in an interior office on the ground floor of the building. "We seem to have stopped their first assault," Akamirov said to the officers, American and Soviet, assembled in the room after he had heard the individual reports of each. "There are about fifty enemy dead within the compound, and we estimate at least as many more outside. We've also knocked out two T-54 tanks and several BTR-60P armored cars. It's worth noting that except for the tank crews and a few odd policemen almost all of the men involved in the assault have been TE. I take that to mean that they don't have any regular troops to spare, because Castro wouldn't commit his pets if he had another choice. We've lost at least twenty dead and more than twice as many wounded, but the big problem is that we've expended more than half of our ammunition, even taking into consideration the little bit we've managed to salvage from the enemy dead. We've also been pushed back from the outer wall positions all around the compound. That was to be expected, but it gives us that much less maneuver room nonetheless.

"As far as good news goes," he said, brightening, "I expect you've all seen the American and Soviet planes overhead. We've seen them hitting the bridges over the Rio Almendares, which will help slow the arrival of reinforcements for the Cubans from the east. It also looks as if they've hit the air base at San Antonio de los Baños, so we probably won't be seeing any Cuban aircraft for awhile, at least. Some American A-10s have been trying to give us close support, but with no direct communications between us and them they're limited in what they can do. We can say, however, that there's no doubt now that the outside world is aware of our situation and that they're doing what they can to help."

The other men in the room were grinning broadly, many of them still panting heavily from their exertions in the defense. "Now," Akamirov continued, "I want you all to make your rounds. Make sure that ammunition is redistributed to those who need it, and try to get lookouts back out to the wall if you can, so we can have some advance warning of the next attack. That is all."

Fleischmann and the others filed quickly from the room, and they could hear the sound of increasing small-arms fire coming from outside. The men responsible for the area from which the shooting seemed to come started to run in that direction, but Fleischmann stopped a moment to light a cigarette. Another man came up and patted him on the shoulder. It was Gunny Michaels.

"Saw what you did to that T-54, Major," the sergeant grinned. "You'd have made a fair marine if you weren't a fucking commie." The sergeant laughed at his own humor.

Fleischmann was not accustomed to this level of familiarity from enlisted men, but he had to smile too. "I haven't seen the papers this morning, Sergeant, but I think we're Social Democrats now."

"Ah well, that explains it then."

The TE colonel who had supervised the assault on the embassy compound stood before General Murguia. The colonel's uniform was still neat and pressed, although he carried an AKSU-74 slung over one shoulder as a martial accessory.

"So," Murguia said, without looking up from his desk and the maps and papers that littered it, "I suppose you've come to report that you've taken the embassy."

The colonel shifted his feet. "No, sir. We breached the wall in half a dozen places and penetrated the courtyard, but my men have lost nearly a third of their number in killed and wounded. They can't go on against these odds."

"'These odds'?" said Murguia, now looking up at the colonel. "You had six hundred elite troops backed up with a platoon of tanks and one of armored cars against a couple hundred escaped prisoners armed with a few captured rifles and Molotov cocktails. Those odds aren't favorable enough for you? I think perhaps you TE men have gotten too used to the good life. High pay, benefits, and the only enemy you fight is the occasional political dissident taken in the middle of the night in his pajamas. I've seen your kind in Nicaragua, playing at advisor and letting the others do the real killing and dying."

"But General," the colonel protested, "this isn't the kind of role my troops were trained for at all. This is a job for regular infantry."

"I know what kind of role your troops are trained for. Castro keeps you here in Havana, fat and pampered, hoping you'll save him if the army wants to launch a coup d'état. But let me tell you something. If I wanted to take Havana away from you with my veterans from Angola they'd go through your men like a hot knife through butter. Now I want your men to make another assault within the hour, and I want you to take the embassy or I want someone else to come back here and tell me how you died trying. Is that clear?"

"Yes, General." The colonel saluted, trembling, and turned and left the room.

The commander of the mechanized regiment of the 101st, his battalion commanders, and the commander of the divisional reconnaissance battalion had been seated around the room in silence. Now they stopped trying to control themselves and burst out laughing.

Finally the regimental commander, Colonel Garcia, spoke up.

"As much as I enjoyed seeing that pompous ass put in his place, the embassy might well be a harder nut to crack than it appears."

"I know that," said Murguia, smiling. "The fact is, we don't know where the hell they got their weapons in the first place, much less how many of them they have. I've been watching the fighting very closely, including tapes of the original breakout, and you'll see the Soviets and Americans risking their lives to recover one magazine of ammunition. That must be their weak point. Our men won't be ready for at least another hour. In the meanwhile I'd rather that the defenders of the embassy put their remaining rounds into the TE's bodies than into ours. Then we can just walk in and clean things up later."

"But what about the Yankees and Soviets coming in from the outside? It looks like our air force has thrown in the towel."

"The navy too," observed Murguia. "While the enemy aircraft were pounding our flyers the battleships *New Jersey* and *Iowa* were blasting the naval bases at Cabañas and Havana harbor. Their sixteen-inch shells sank the Koni-class frigate at Havana and half a dozen Zhuk patrol boats, and they destroyed all ten of the Osa guided-missile boats at Cabañas. I think the Osas got off only one or two Styx missiles, and it looks like both of those were shot down by American fighters before they reached their targets. There are plans for several Osas to sortie out of Nicaro, but that's way down the coast, and I seriously doubt that they'll make it up here in one piece.

"I expect that the enemy will be coming in both vertically, by helicopter, and by sea, over the beach behind the compound. I've spread out an entire infantry regiment there with every surviving antiaircraft unit, and that's not many. I've also issued every hand-held SA-7 in the city. When the TE have expended themselves I'll feed the survivors in there too. Hopefully, that curtain of fire will cut down their choppers and hold off their amphibious units until it's too late.

"What I want you to do is concentrate the recon battalion among the houses on the east side of the embassy to make a diversionary assault. The mechanized regiment, less one battalion, will make the main assault on the west side. Use your mortars to provide smoke cover, and don't be afraid to drop smoke rounds right inside the compound. Have your sappers blow wide breaches in the walls and drive your personnel carriers right inside, but have dismounted infantry up with them to keep the enemy at a respectful distance. Drive right through the doors of the embassy, if you can. I've got two Mi-8 helicopters stashed in the woods near here; we'll put three squads in each one and try a vertical assault on the roof of the embassy. I'll have the pilots swing around and come in from the sea side, and maybe the defenders will think they're being rescued. We'll have to give the word to all antiaircraft units to hold fire for about five minutes when we do that. Then we'll work our way through the buildings simultaneously, floor by floor and from top to bottom, looking for our men."

"What about my other battalion?" the regimental commander asked.

"We'll hold that in reserve here, along with your headquarters support elements," Murguia said, but the other officers in the room knew that Murguia was hedging his bets against an effort by Castro to wreak his vengeance on the general. That was all right with them. "So get your men into position and report back to me when you're ready to roll."

Paco could see that policemen were beginning to go from house to house, evacuating the civilians from this area. He would have to get out.

He folded the stock on his rifle and placed it back in his bag, throwing some assorted clothes on top of it. Then he replaced the pistol in the side pocket of the bag and slung the bag over his right shoulder. He took one more look back toward the bedroom. The mission was over. It was a failure, but now he could do something that might help save the lives of the men who had taken refuge inside the embassy. That was something.

He let himself out the service door of the apartment and locked it after him. It sounded as though people were already leaving the building, but they were using the front stairs. Once he was out of the immediate area of the apartment no one would be able to say that he didn't belong there.

At the entrance to the building a small crowd of people had gathered, everyone carrying suitcases, boxes, or shopping bags filled with as much of their poor possessions as they could gather. Paco fit right in with this group, and followed them out to the street. There were a number of policemen on the street, directing the growing crowd of civilians in a generally easterly direction, away from the embassy. Paco joined them until he reached an area of particularly heavy shrubbery and then just melted out of sight.

He made his way through the backyards and gardens of the houses and apartment buildings of the area in the direction of the beach behind the embassy. He had watched the abortive attack by the TE troops and had picked off a few officers from the apartment, and he had seen that they were massing for another attack. If he could get in with them he could shoot them up with relative impunity, and he might be in a position to get to the American lines if a rescue attempt were launched over the beach, as he expected would be the case.

He had managed to dart across one street, but when he attempted to cross the next a harsh voice called out to him to halt. He found himself facing a TE lieutenant and two men, all of whom kept their automatic rifles pointed in his direction.

"You're going the wrong way, comrade," the lieutenant told him. "Civilians are supposed to be evacuated from this area, not entering it. Don't you know that there's a war on?"

Paco suddenly had an idea. "I'm not looking for evacuation," he said. "I have important information for the officer in charge."

"You can give me any information you have, comrade," the lieutenant said in a disbelieving tone. "I'll see that it gets to the right people, but the colonel can't be bothered with every crackpot who thinks he's seen George Bush hiding in his backyard."

"I'm not a crackpot," Paco protested. "I'm a construction worker. Here are my papers," and he handed over his false identity papers to the lieutenant with his left hand. "I was working on a sewer connection in this neighborhood less than a year ago, and I think I can show you how to get into the compound underground. I've been watching the fighting, and I can see that you're in trouble." He gestured with his free hand toward the body of a TE soldier which still lay in the street. With his other hand he toyed with the flap over the pocket of his bag where his pistol was hidden. "I was in Angola. I know infantry fighting, and I can get you inside there without all of these casualties."

The lieutenant looked up with decided interest. "Come with me," he said, keeping Paco's papers despite the latter's outstretched hand.

Paco followed the lieutenant and the two soldiers fell in behind, still covering him with their weapons. They walked about one block closer to the embassy and entered the garage of a house, which the colonel had turned into his command post. The lieutenant entered and saluted the colonel, while Paco and guards waited outside.

"I've found a man who says that he can get us into the compound underground, sir," Paco heard the lieutenant say.

"Bring him in here, quickly." The colonel turned to another officer. "Get ahold of Vasquez. Tell him to hold off the attack until I give the order. We may have something here." Paco smiled. If nothing else, he might have bought the defenders a few minutes.

Paco presented himself to the colonel, who was examining his documents carefully. "So you claim that there's a way into the compound through the sewers or something?" the colonel asked.

"Yes sir," Paco answered, rendering a proper salute. "If you can show me a diagram of the sewer system I can show you how you can come up right next to the embassy building. I did it myself by accident and got in a hell of a lot of trouble."

"That will take too long, my friend. We have a plan of the embassy itself here. You just show us on that."

"Sorry, sir," Paco said, "but the sewers are like a maze down there, and I was only there once. I'm sure I can show you the route from the diagram, but if you send men down there without it you'll never find them again."

"Damn!" the colonel said. "Sergeant, get over to the Water and Power Office right now and get the sewer diagrams for this sector. If anybody gives you any lip, shoot them!"

"Yes, sir." The sergeant jumped into a GAZ jeep and raced off. Good, thought Paco, a few more minutes.

While the Soviet and American air force and navy jets still tangled in the dull blue sky over Havana two CH-53 Super Stallion helicopters raced toward the coast from the U.S. Navy assault ship *Tarawa*. One carried twenty U.S. Green Berets, the other an equal number of Soviet Spetsnaz commandos. The helicopters hung low to the water, their powerful rotors kicking up spray from the waves. A pair of American F-16 fighter bombers flew cover over them, but otherwise they went in without protection and in the face of antiaircraft defenses that were still far from suppressed. The Green Beret colonel and his Soviet counterpart were counting on the confusion of the air attack to mask their approach and permit them to land in the soccer field at the back of the embassy compound.

The coast was in sight, and one of the F-16s fired an ARM missile at a Cuban SA-8 Gecko mobile antiaircraft missile unit that had just activated its radar. The pilot of the leading CH-53 saw a flash and a plume of smoke arising from beyond the line of palms behind the beach, indicating that the missile had generated a secondary explosion. They were racing toward the shore at over 150 knots, and then they were crossing the beach.

Suddenly a puff of white smoke off to the right of the lead aircraft showed the launch of an SA-7 hand-held missile. The pilot released a string of flares designed to decoy the heat-seeking missile, and he felt the jolt as the missile exploded behind him. Tracer rounds criss-crossed in front of and all around the chopper, and the pilot could hear the pang of those that struck the fuselage. He had throttled back now and was skirting the last few houses before the compound wall when a heavier thump shook the aircraft and the controls went slack in his hands. He turned around and saw the compartment behind him filling with smoke. The helicopter was dropping fast. The last thing the pilot saw was a crowd of Cuban soldiers blazing away at his cockpit with their rifles. Then the chopper smashed headlong into the compound wall.

The second chopper, carrying the Soviet contingent, had the advantage that the several SA-7 teams in position to fire had all fired at the lead chopper, and the two or three seconds' lapse between the passage of the first and the second did not permit them to reload. This helicopter, too, had to pass through a hail of small-arms fire, which riddled the body of the craft, wounding some of the passengers and cutting several hydraulic lines, but it crossed the wall and landed heavily at the far end of the soccer field, just short of one of the embassy apartment blocks.

There was smoke coming from the helicopter's engine compartment and the pilot knew that he could not take off again, so he, his copilot, and the crew chief, all U.S. marines, piled out along with their passengers and sprinted toward the building. Bullets from Cuban snipers in the tall buildings nearby kicked up clods of earth around them, but a squad of Soviet infantrymen charged out of one of the doors of the building and lay down covering fire, and the entire group made it into the interior of the building, albeit dragging three badly wounded men with them.

Fleischmann was waiting just inside the door. He immediately recognized the leader of the group. "Yuri!" he shouted. "What a nice surprise. You should have called first."

"Gregor!" the Spetsnaz captain replied. "We were just on our way to the beach and thought we'd drop in. Let me introduce you to our driver, Major Williams." Yuri brought the panting marine pilot by the arm from where he had slouched against the wall.

"I'm very sorry about the other helicopter, Major," Fleischmann said. "How many men were on board?"

"Twenty plus the crew," he answered. "All Americans. But they were the only reason we were able to make it in at all."

"Yes," said Fleischmann. "I can see that your helicopter will need some work, but we're glad you made it. Now, what did you bring me?" he asked, turning to Yuri.

"Well, we figured you'd be needing pretty much everything, so we brought ten AT-4 antitank missile systems with a few reloads, half a dozen PKM machine guns, a couple of 40mm grenade launchers, and as much ammunition as we could carry, about ten thousand rounds. Not much, but the best we could do. What's more important is that I've got most of the details on what's coming in behind us. Let's get to your commanders ASAP."

Featherstone had seen the crash landing of the second helicopter from the window of the office, where he had been on the phone almost constantly for nearly an hour. The twenty phone lines of the embassy had been in regular use by a team of officials calling all over the island, generally to total strangers, explaining the situation of the embassy in English, Russian, and Spanish, regardless of whether the listener understood or not. It was a long shot that NSA would not only pick up these conversations but would process the information fast enough for it to be of use in Washington.

General Akamirov, Osman, Meese, and Featherstone had agreed on the basic text of the message. That some ten thousand or more former hostages had taken refuge inside the embassy compound and were defending themselves with captured weapons. That they had some thirty Cuban prisoners, including most of the High Command, and that they were holding out until help arrived. They reiterated their position that while they would not harm the Cuban hostages themselves they would not take special steps to protect them if the Cubans attempted to use artillery or rockets to reduce the defenses.

About one recipient in five had hung up the phone in horror as soon as it became apparent that the caller was a foreigner, and this is the response that Featherstone had actually expected from most of the people. About as many had listened without comment to the message and then hung up, probably thinking the thing some kind of bad joke, another reaction that Featherstone had expected. However, at least half of the people entered into animated dialogue with him, asking about the circumstances of Raul Castro's death, the nature of superpower plans, and mainly, whether the Americans and Soviets planned to come in to rescue their countrymen. Featherstone assumed that this had to do with a natural curiosity as to whether the country was about to be plunged into total war, and he had taken the opportunity to assure the people of his nation's innocence of any wrongdoing, the likelihood that Fidel had had his own brother killed, and the certainty that a rescue force was on the way, adding that this would pose no threat to the average Cuban citizen. Featherstone found that the other American and Soviet officials involved in the telephone campaign had had similar experiences. While some of their calls had gone to the far corners of the island they had concentrated their efforts on the telephone zones just outside of Havana, since the calls tended to go through faster.

It was over an hour before the embassy phone lines were cut. Featherstone suspected that with the other things going on, monitoring of the embassy's telephone calls had taken a severe drop in priority, and it had taken time to get someone of authority interested in the matter. During this period he estimated that they had made over two hundred individual calls. If the NSA was listening, that should do it.

Chapter Thirty-nine

NSC members, cabinet officials, military officers, and aides had been coming and going frantically at the Oval Office for the past two hours. Wiznezhsky still cast frequent glances at the satellite image of the embassy grounds, but not much could be made out through the thick pall of smoke that hung over that part of Havana. They had watched part of the Cuban attack on the compound, but it was apparent that it had been beaten off. Someone in the control room had been occasionally switching back and forth between the current close-up, in which the compound and the area within one city block of it filled the screen, and a wider view that covered much of western Havana. Wiznezhsky thought he had seen the shape of a jet fighter flash across the screen once or twice, but the image had passed so quickly that he could not be sure. He could see the still, black spots all around the compound that were almost certainly dead bodies, and that robbed him of the boyish excitement he had originally felt at the scene.

Everyone else seemed to have a telephone of his own, communicating with his own empire in the bureaucracy. As the president's national security advisor Wiznezhsky had an office, of course, but he didn't really have an organization at his beck and call, and he felt rather left out. Webster had just gotten off the phone with the NSA and had reported the gist of the messages from the Soviet Embassy telephone calls around Cuba, but this had merely confirmed what they had largely surmised before. Weems was on the phone to the JCTF and was reporting the progress of the air battle over Cuba. Baker had been on to the American UN mission and to various embassies around Washington, advising them of the military intervention. The president had spoken personally with Gorbachev, then with Prime Minister Thatcher, President Mitterrand, Chancellor Kohl, and a number of other European, Asian, and Latin American leaders.

Finally the president hung up his phone and called out, "Where exactly are the missiles at this moment?"

Weems cupped his hand over the mouthpiece of his phone and answered. "The missile carriers are still nearly twenty-four hours out of Cuba, and still under escort by the Argentine carrier 25 de Mayo and some Brazilian and Venezuelan ships. We have naval air and submarine units tracking them, but they have orders not to interfere with their progress."

"Should we consider hitting the Cuban ports to prevent the offloading of the missiles?" the president asked, jotting notes down on a yellow legal pad as he thought.

"Taking into consideration the size of the missiles, their transporters, erectors, and other equipment, there are only a couple of ports in Cuba with the gear necessary to unload them. If we hit Cienfuegos and Manzanillo, the ports they're undoubtedly headed for, that would certainly throw a monkey wrench into their plans, but we would have to hit Havana harbor again with that in mind, plus several others to make certain. We can do it, if we commit additional air units from Stateside, but we will have to take into consideration the additional casualties among the air crews, since most of the antiair defenses in these other places haven't been touched yet. I would recommend postponing a decision on additional raids for another twelve hours or so. We'll have a better idea then how the hostage rescue mission is coming, we won't have to divert any assets from the embassy fight, and we'll still have time to do something about the ports if we want to."

Wiznezhsky was ever more impressed with Weems. Perhaps he was one of those people who worked best under pressure, of which there certainly were plenty to go around. He had had him pegged as a knee-jerk warmonger, but it was now apparent that while Weems did not recoil from the possibility of armed action, neither did he rashly court it.

"It might be worth the effort," Wiznezhsky chimed in, "to keep up the impression that our only concern at this time is the freeing of the hostages. That will help keep the rest of the Third World off our backs somewhat. We should also be making very public the fact that the debt relief plan, ours that is, is not dependent upon the outcome of the fighting in Cuba." Baker, who was still listening to someone on the phone, nodded emphatically and gave a thumbs-up signal.

"My next question is," said the president, "when will the troops be landing?"

Weems had now hung up his phone. "We just sent in two Special Forces choppers, one of ours and one with Soviets aboard. Only one made it." The president grimaced, and Wiznezhsky saw his knuckles turn white as he grasped his pen harder. "They went in before the antiaircraft defenses were fully suppressed, but we will have to figure on fairly heavy casualties among the helicopters from the small, man-portable missiles. There's a strip of housing between the compound and the beach, only about two hundred yards wide, and the place is crawling with enemy troops equipped with SA-7s. It's too close to the compound for a full-scale bombardment, although we will have the destroyers hit the area with their five-inch guns just before the Ospreys and Blackhawks come through. If we wait for the marines to hit the beach with their amphibious craft, that will take at least another two hours, probably more, and we can't be certain that the embassy will be able to hold out."

"Why is it taking the marines so long?" asked Baker, who had also finished his phone call.

"It isn't taking long at all," contested Weems. "Considering the problem of getting the men into the landing craft and all, the only thing that's letting us do it this quickly was the order to have the men in the boats, cruising just outside the twelve-mile limit. And, fortunately, the sea is quite calm now. But we have to let the mine-sweepers clear away any mines, which they are doing at this moment, and then the landing craft make only about ten knots, so that makes over an hour just to cover the distance to shore. We have found a number of mines, by the way, and the minesweepers have been coming under sporadic artillery fire from the shore." He added gravely. "One has been sunk by a shore-based cruise missile."

"If I understand you correctly, General," the president said, "we will have to go in with the helicopter-borne troops fairly soon, even though it will mean heavy casualties."

"We just can't guarantee that the Cubans won't overrun the compound if we wait for the amphibious troops. I'm surprised that they haven't tried a new assault yet, and we have to assume from the messages NSA picked up from the telephone conversations that the defenders don't have much ammunition, although they could be faking that part of it for the Cubans' benefit."

"I'll give the order then," said the president, rubbing his forehead with the tips of his fingers. "Give the helicopters as much cover as you can, but go in as soon as you can. We can't afford to let the Cubans seize the hostages again. Those men put their lives on the line and even took prisoners of their own. We just can't let them down." Wiznezhsky noted that the president called our people hostages and the Cubans prisoners, a little of the politician leaking through, but Wiznezhsky thought that he was perfectly right, dammit! They started it, and now we'd see how they liked it.

Weems was already on the phone again, talking in quiet tones to someone in Florida.

Chapter Forty

Murguia was raging when he climbed out of his GAZ jeep at the command post of the TE colonel. He had given an order to attack and these TE cowards were still milling around. Most of the antiaircraft defenses in the Havana area had been smashed, and there was almost nothing standing in the way of a vertical assault on the compound. What were they waiting for?

Murguia and his now-customary escort of a platoon of heavily armed infantrymen brushed past the guards in front of the command post garage and found the colonel poring over some detailed blueprints with a man in civilian clothes, some kind of workman with a bag over his shoulder. The colonel straightened up suddenly when the general entered, sensing the purpose of his visit.

"General," the colonel began, "this man says he knows a way into the compound underground."

"Then why the fuck aren't you inside the compound already?" the general screamed. Several of the TE junior officers apparently remembered urgent business elsewhere and slipped quietly out of the garage by the side door.

"Well, sir," the colonel stammered, "we had to get copies of the sewer plans, and now we're trying to find the route into the compound."

248

"Give the order now, you fucking coward," Murguia raged. "Either you lead your men over the wall or through the sewers right now, or I'll have you shot in the garden. Which is it to be?"

"WELL?" the colonel said shrilly to Paco, the whites showing all the way around his tiny eyes.

Paco had delayed as long as he could. The mission was over. "Wait a minute," he said brightly, "I made a little diagram of my own from memory that should help us. I have it right here."

He reached into the side pocket of the bag with his right hand. In the garage with him were the colonel, two TE captains, this newly arrived general, and half a dozen soldiers, all armed. He had only six rounds in his pistol, but if he could create enough confusion he might be able to get out his rifle as well. The colonel's eyes bugged out farther as the soft-nosed bullet tore into his chest, and the nearest captain also crumpled to the floor without a sound as Paco silently shot him. Paco's body blocked any view of what was happening from the general and his men, but when Paco swung around the others could see the spreading bloodstains on the victims' shirts.

Paco fired twice more quickly, hitting one of the soldiers, and then threw himself over backwards behind the table, but it was no good. Four other soldiers, who had been on alert for some kind of trouble from the TE, had their AK-47s on full automatic and blasted right through the thin plywood sheets of the table. Paco was dead before he hit the floor.

"Shit!" Murguia exclaimed. "A fucking spy!" Murguia had generally been under the assumption that most spies were created by the imagination of men like Castro as pretexts to kill off their political rivals. It was just as well that this stupid colonel had paid for his mistake with his life. Murguia would have obliged him himself a few minutes later in any case. There was no more time to waste.

"Captain!" he shouted at the remaining TE officer, who was still trembling with shock. "Get all of the TE troops into position between the compound and the beach. They will be placed under the command of the infantry regiment in that sector." Murguia looked at the shaken man with little pity. "And you might want to change your pants, too, when you get a chance."

Murguia called out to his command vehicle. "Lieutenant!"

"Yes, sir," answered a young man, sticking his head out the back door of the armored personnel carrier, the roof of which was festooned with radio antennae.

"Get Garcia and tell him to get ready to go. There'll be no preliminary attack. The helicopters will hit the embassy roof at precisely—" he stopped to check his watch, "—1500 hours. He should launch his attack at 1455. Then get on to the commander of the infantry regiment behind the compound and tell him that from 1455 to 1505 friendly helicopters will be coming over and that he is not, I repeat, NOT to open fire."

"Yes, sir," the man answered and ducked back out of sight.

Murguia looked around the wreckage of the command post. Now the ball was in his court. He had taken a macho stand with Castro and with the TE. Now he had to deliver the embassy or it would be all up with him too.

Akamirov had seen that the ammunition and the special weapons brought by the Spetsnaz troops had been distributed around the defensive perimeter. The ammunition would provide only another twenty or so rounds per rifle, but that was better than nothing. The real benefit was the bunch of AT-4 Spigot antitank missiles. The only drawback to these was that they had a minimum range that the missile required to arm itself. The Spigot required less than most, only about seventy meters, but this would still limit the areas in which it could be deployed within the confines of the compound. Akamirov had posted several of them to the upper floors of the embassy, balancing the risk of fire from their back blast against the broader fields of fire there and the ability of the crews to fire down on the weaker top armor of any tanks that might accompany an attack.

The Spetsnaz troops had also brought the welcome word that amphibious troops were on the way and that a path was being cleared through the Cuban minefields to the beach. A helicopter assault was also expected, but the experience of the two Special Forces helicopters did not make Akamirov particularly sanguine about the chances of this approach. The air force simply could not suppress the fire of the SA-7s, which the Cubans had in abundance and which they had apparently emplaced in the strip between the compound and the sea. Something else would have to be done.

Captain Yuri Grechkov, leader of the Spetsnaz detachment, Rodriguez, and Fleischmann entered the office where Akamirov sat waiting. "Gentlemen," Akamirov began after they had traded salutes, "I have a very special request to make of you. I don't need to tell you of the danger that the presence of the enemy antiaircraft missiles presents to the paratroopers and marines who will be coming in by helicopter in a very short while. I also don't have to tell you that the proximity of the Cuban troops to our own positions will prevent naval gunfire and air strikes from having much effect on them. The only thing I can conceive of that might improve the chances of a successful insertion would be a simultaneous ground attack, a sortie from within the compound. Even if we don't take any ground, we might be able to keep the Cubans' heads down long enough to let the choppers get through."

The three younger officers looked back and forth at each other. "I thought we were doing pretty well just holding on by our teeth," Rodriguez commented. "How large-scale an attack did you have in mind?"

"Not very," said Akamirov. "I thought that two groups of maybe twenty men each would serve the purpose without weakening the defenses too much."

"Well, I'm sure I won't have trouble coming up with twenty volunteers from among the marines," Rodriguez said, "and things have been getting awfully dull around here for the last five or six minutes."

"When do we go?" asked Grechkov.

"The choppers could come through as early as 1500 hours, so you should take off within the next fifteen minutes. Can you do it?"

"Let's go," said Grechkov, and the three men raced out of the office.

Ten minutes later Rodriguez was crouched at the back door to one of the apartment blocks, peering out across the compound recreational area toward the wall. There was a breach that the Cubans had blown in the wall about eighty yards away, and another that had been created by the crash of the CH-53, but the wreckage was still smoldering and effectively blocked that route.

Sergeant Glover knelt at Rodriguez's side. "The signal to go will be a barrage of 40mm grenades into the first row of houses beyond the wall. They've already sent out the men with grenade launchers through the shrubbery to get them closer to the wall. They'll also let go the first smoke grenades to try to cover our rush," Rodriguez said. "We'll make our first goal the hedges next to the wall. From there we'll toss smoke and frag grenades into the street beyond and bull our way across. If we can fight our way through that first block and hold one house we'll take under fire anything we can see from there, and the Russians will do the same on their side, to the left. Then we'll just hole up there and wait for rescue from either the para-troopers or from the sea. There's no point in our trying to fight our way back here."

Johnson spoke up from behind them. "I don't suppose the pa-perwork for my transfer to Finance has come through yet, huh, Sarge?"

"Okay," said Rodriguez, sighing, "I'll admit that about the only thing that this plan has going for it is that the Cubans would never think anybody'd be crazy enough to try it, but we don't have a choice. If the choppers get a reception like those first two got we're going to be up to our armpits in dead paratroopers. If there's anything we can do to improve their odds, we've got to try."

There was a general chorus of "Let's just do it!" from the tight group of marines waiting in the dark hallway, followed by assorted "Ooo-rahs" and grunting noises.

Suddenly the popping noises of grenade launchers brought si-lence to the group of marines. Rodriguez could see the smoke puffs of the grenades' impact among the houses and the growing clouds of white smoke from the smoke grenades.

"Let's go!" he shouted, and the twenty men raced out the door, crouching low. The marines manning the firing position in front of the door began firing at the suspected positions of enemy snipers and yelled encouragement to their comrades. Rodriguez carried an AKM, but was only concentrating on running as fast as his legs would carry him. He heard a cry of pain from behind him and heard something heavy hit the ground, but he didn't look back. A grenadier was hiding behind a bush to his front and jumped up to join the rush, but he quickly flipped over on his back, his mouth shot away by a sniper's bullet. Rodriguez scooped up the grenade launcher in one hand and kept running for the wall.

Then the louder crump of heavy mortar shells landing could be heard. Rodriguez could see a solid wall of white smoke building on both flanks of the embassy compound. Damn! he thought. The Cubans are trying something of their own. On the one hand the smoke cover was welcome, but he was more than a little concerned about running headlong into an assault by a tank battalion. After what seemed like an eternity, he threw himself down at the base of the wall just to the side of the breach and tried to catch his breath.

One after another the marines crashed to the ground all around him. He looked around and counted. Fourteen, fifteen, sixteen, plus two grenade-launcher men. That was all. No time to wait. He grabbed his grenade launcher as a signal to the others and fired his one grenade toward the window of a house across the street. The others fired too, and the remaining marines heaved smoke grenades randomly into the street.

Rodriguez waited a moment for the smoke to thicken and then leaped over the rubble of the wall and charged across the street, firing short bursts from his rifle. He could see Cuban soldiers firing from some of the windows of the neighboring houses and he could hear a machine gun, set up in the breach by a marine, firing to suppress them. He jumped the low wrought-iron fence of the garden of the first house and hurled himself through the door, sprawling flat on the floor inside. He spun around in time to see a Cuban soldier rushing out of a back room. Rodriguez fired and the Cuban fell. Two more Cubans had been firing through the front living room window, but Johnson cut them down with a burst from his AK-47.

"Ammo. Get their ammo," Rodriguez gasped as he scrambled to his feet and staggered through the other rooms of the house. Two more Cubans were found and killed in the other rooms, and

Rodriguez paused to count up. Only twelve men left, and three of those were wounded. He put a fresh magazine into his rifle and braced himself by the back door of the house. They would have to cross the small yard, scale a six-foot wooden fence, and fight their way into the house behind. That would be their objective.

"Three, two, one, GO!" he shouted, and two marines posted at the rear windows of the house let loose a long burst of fire through the thin planks of the fence. The one remaining grenadier popped a 40mm grenade in the direction of the back door of the target house, and Rodriguez again rushed out the door. He was across the yard in four long steps, placed one foot on an upturned garbage can, and vaulted over the fence. He had the sling from his rifle over one shoulder and his right hand on the pistol grip, to permit him to fire with one hand. Two Cubans were kneeling in the yard of the other house, working with a bazookalike device and several long missiles that were laid out nearby. An SA-7 team. That's what we're here for, Rodriguez thought as he blazed away at the men. The next marine over raced past Rodriguez and charged into the house. Rodriguez could hear a flurry of firing as other marines followed him in, and Rodriguez stopped to snatch up the SA-7 before running on into the house.

Inside the house he found four more dead Cubans and two dead marines. He looked around. Only nine men left in his group, including Glover and Johnson, who were both slightly wounded. He wondered if the Soviets had done any better, but at least his group was where they had wanted to be. He quickly posted men throughout the house, and one immediately opened fire on another Cuban SA-7 team in the next yard, killing them.

The ground around them now began to shake. Naval gunfire, thought Rodriguez, and he and his men had just risked their lives to fight their way into the target area. Great! But the shells were falling mainly along the beach and well to the east and west of the compound. It looked as though Rodriguez and his men were still close enough to the compound to be immune to artillery fire. Then the whop-whop sound of helicopter blades could be heard.

"Watch out for SA-7 teams. If they're going to break cover, now's the time," he shouted to his men. But while bullets periodically tore through the walls and windows of the house from the nearby Cuban positions, they could see neither antiaircraft missile teams nor the smoke trails of their missiles being fired. That's odd, he thought.

Gunnery Sgt. Frank Michaels was peeking over the sandbags in the first-floor strongpoint at the embassy. All he could see through the shifting smoke of the screen was an occasional glimpse of the wall. Then a puff of green smoke mingled with the white. It was the signal from his lookout that there were enemy troops just on the other side of the wall. Michaels and several of his men poked the barrels of their Soviet grenade launchers, mounted under standard AK-47 rifles, over the top sandbags and fired at the prearranged setting and elevation. They pulled the short, thick tubes forward, fed in the next grenades, clamped them shut, and fired again. They repeated this two or three more times and ceased fire. With their high-angle trajectories, the rounds should have dropped just beyond the wall in the street, showering anyone there with shrapnel.

They had certainly hit some of the attackers, but not all. A few seconds later there was a series of massive explosions and large sections of the wall disappeared in a cloud of shattered concrete and debris. A puff of red smoke told Michaels that not all of his lookouts had been killed in the blast, and that enemy troops were crossing the wall. A machine gun began spraying the area of the wall. The gunner didn't need to see his target, as he had sighted his gun in and could lay a stream of fire at about knee height all through the courtyard of the embassy even with his eyes closed. Michaels also saw the smoke trails of two or three antitank missiles streak out from the upper floors of the embassy and saw the flare of burning fuel and munitions as they found their mark somewhere in the smoke.

Suddenly the dark shape of an approaching BMP armored personnel carrier loomed through the smoke. It was raking the building with machine-gun fire, although the 73mm cannon it carried in its turret was silent. They're playing by the rules, thought Michaels, but the machine-gunning was bad enough, and he saw a man farther down the line buckle and fall to the floor. Michaels reached for one of the few remaining RPG-7s. The BMP was too close now for the antitank missiles, but it was moving off to Michaels's left, leaving him a shot at the thinner flank armor. He popped up the flip sight, aimed at the driver's compartment, and fired.

The whoosh of the rocket rolled him back on his heels as it slammed into the side of the vehicle, bringing it to a halt. Just then a flaming Molotov cocktail arced down from an upper floor, striking the BMP just behind the turret and spraying burning liquid in all directions. The back door of the BMP opened and several infantry-men leaped out, only to be cut down by the riflemen in the building.

Then Michaels began to detect a dull roar over the rattle of small-arms fire and the squealing of APC tracks. It grew in volume steadily until it sounded as if the entire building were shaking with the noise. The smoke was beginning to thin now, and he thought he saw a sil-very shape in the sky in the direction of the sea. Suddenly there was a terrific flash and the sound of tearing metal as an A-10 roared by, sweeping the street beyond the wall clean with its 30mm cannon fire. He saw explosion after explosion flare up beyond the wall as the A-10 tore up the vehicles waiting on the other side. Another A-10 made a sweep, firing rockets into the houses on the other side of the street. He could see more and more planes swooping in, dropping bombs farther away and then peeling off for another run. In the distance he could also hear the dull thump of naval gunfire, although the crash of the landing shells was indistinguishable from the general hell around him.

Captain Meese came running by, out of breath. "It looks like the air force has broken the back of another attack. There was a weaker probe over on the other side of the building, on the east, but they plastered that too, just as it was kicking off. We can see the Cubans pulling back from the upper floors. It looks like we won another one."

Michaels looked around him. Ten American and Soviet service-men lay dead along this stretch of wall, and at least twice as many wounded had dragged themselves downstairs to the aid station. He looked at the still-smoldering carcass of the BMP, which had rolled to a halt less than five meters from the row of windows through which Michaels and his men had been firing. "One more victory like that and I think we've had it, Captain," Michaels said.

"With any luck we won't have time to prove that," Meese shouted, clapping a hand on Michaels's back. "We've got choppers and transports coming in from the sea."

Capt. Todd Spinelli could just see through the passageway into the cockpit of the Osprey from where he was sitting. Through the windscreen he could see columns of smoke rising from beyond the beach. He had heard the A-10s rocket past a few moments earlier. Now the Ospreys were racing toward the beach at over 250 knots, nearly twice the speed of a helicopter, and close enough to the water to stir up the waves with the prop wash. He could hear the pilots talking on their radio.

"Badger One, this is Tumbler Three," the pilot was saying. "Whose choppers are those up ahead? Over."

"This is Badger One. Say again Tumbler Three. Over," the voice crackled over the headset that Spinelli was wearing.

"I say again. This is Tumbler Three. We have three choppers about two clicks ahead of us. Whose are they? Over."

"Aren't they yours? Over," came the bewildered reply.

"Negative, negative. All of the choppers in our group are well behind us. Could they belong to the cousins? Over." Spinelli was always amused by the efforts of military radio operators to doubletalk around things for which there was no accepted code or for which they had forgotten the code word.

"We have no information on that. We have a pair of Fours on call, should we have them engage?" the voice asked.

"That's not my call," the pilot said. "Besides, they're over the compound by now. Let's just hope they're friendlies."

The Ospreys raced over the strip of white beach and the houses beyond. The lead ship roared low over the compound wall, slowing its speed and rotating its engines skyward. The pilot had dropped a string of flares behind him, but there were no missiles to decoy. The ship landed heavily in a grassy area near one of the apartment blocks. A second and third landed on the soccer field. The others raced past the compound and landed in the open area in front of the compound, protected by the repeated strafing runs of the A-10s and Harriers. The cargo doors opened and the two dozen marines in each one poured out, hauling heavy ammunition crates along with their personal weapons.

In less than a minute all twenty-four aircraft had landed and un- loaded. They then gunned their engines, which had never stopped running, and took off, straight up. A stream of machine-gun bullets from a house near the reviewing stands ripped through the cockpit of one, sending it spinning, cartwheeling against the stands and bursting into flames. Another was caught by an SA-7 as it rose, as the missile man had evidently realized that the Cubans had nothing like it. Its starboard engine exploded, flipping the plane over on its back and into the ground. But the others gained altitude and speed, shifting their engines forward again and racing seaward, and they were gone.

While Spinelli and his command group ran into the nearest building sixty of the men who landed within the compound, under one of the company commanders of the battalion, immediately stormed back over the compound wall to start to clear the houses between the compound and the beach. Their purpose was to do what Rodriguez and Grechkov had started, to eliminate the antiair threat to the second wave of heliborne troops. Similar groups fanned out from the front of the embassy to attempt to secure the houses ringing the square where the formation had taken place so shortly before.

One Cuban Mi-8 helicopter had landed on each of the apartment blocks within the compound and one on the embassy itself. They had had their Cuban markings painted out and Soviet ones quickly painted over them. The men stationed on the roofs had waved as they touched down and several had moved, bending low under the turning blades, to welcome the reinforcements. They died before they realized their mistake. Each helicopter disgorged twenty-eight infantrymen, and they quickly swept the roofs clear of the surprised defenders.

Word had not gotten through to the helicopter crews that the ground attack had been broken off, and as the choppers lifted off again the men continued with their instructions and began to work their way down into the buildings.

In the first apartment block luck was not with the Cubans. They entered the stairwell just as a squad of Soviet infantrymen were climbing it to relieve the men on duty there. The leading Soviet had squeezed the trigger on his AKM almost as a reflex as he heard the Spanish and saw the Cuban uniforms appear in front of him, killing the first three Cubans through the door. His alert sergeant had then pitched a grenade through the open door to the roof, killing more of the Cubans who were bunched around the entry. The alarm was raised throughout the building, and the Soviets quickly mopped up the remaining Cubans after a vicious firefight.

In the second apartment block the Cubans had begun to clear the top floor, but they had found nearly fifty marines stationed there with nothing much else on their minds since the ground attack had been stopped. After an initial surprise encounter these Cubans, too, were rounded up and eliminated.

The lieutenant leading the group that landed on top of the embassy building, however, saw his primary mission as sowing as much confusion as possible within the enemy defenses, not attempting to clear the whole building by himself. He therefore had his men descend the staircase as quietly as possible, slipping a seven-man squad onto each floor before remounting the stairs to lead the squad on the top floor himself.

He could hear confused firing from down the staircase as he let himself into the first corridor. A surprised embassy official in civilian clothes came out of an office and was immediately stabbed to death with a bayonet. The men then spaced themselves down the corridor and simultaneously kicked in several doors, spraying the rooms with automatic fire. One of the Cubans was shot by a KGB security man, but the others went from office to office, with one man guarding each of the two stairwells against the arrival of enemy reinforcements.

Osman was sitting in his office congratulating himself. He could see the American marines shooting their way into houses around the square, and the first of the Blackhawk helicopters was now landing, unloading still more American paratroopers. No, the Cubans would not be retaking the embassy. Nor would they be returning him, a humiliated man, to the Soviet Union for disgrace, discharge, or worse. He would go home a hero. Osman, the Fighting Ambassador! That had a nice ring to it. With the growing popularity of real elections in the USSR, maybe he would even run for office. Yes, that would be a nice cap to his illustrious career.

He heard the door of his office open behind him, and he prepared to greet the commander of the American marines. The blast of the AK-47 threw him backward through the one remaining unbroken window in the office and down the four floors to the pavement below.

It took Fleischmann and a platoon of Soviet infantrymen nearly half an hour to root out the last of the Cubans in the embassy. It wasn't until a search for the ambassador had turned up nothing that someone noticed his mangled body, lying with the others in the courtyard of the embassy compound.

Chapter Forty-one

The president could hardly hear Featherstone's voice on the telephone over the loud talking, laughing, and occasional cheering in the Oval Office. He stuck one finger in his free ear and tried turning toward the window, away from the crowd of men in dark suits and uniforms that filled the room. He could have quieted them down, he supposed, but they deserved to let off some steam. A few minutes later a Filipino steward in a white coat would be bringing in the champagne he had ordered served.

"Yes, Mr. Featherstone," the president was saying, "we just got the official word of the ceasefire. There will be no interference with the removal of all our people as long as the Cuban officers are turned over to the Cuban Army on the beach. They'll even deliver the several American and Soviet fliers who were captured during the fighting at the same time. It's a great moment. I speak for everyone in the country in saying that we thank God for your safe return and we thank you and the men with you for your courage and for keeping the faith." He listened for a moment and then went on. "Yes, I've just spoken with your wife. Anne, isn't it? Yes, she's waiting for you in Miami. And listen, Bill, take a couple of weeks off, on me. If anyone bothers you about a debriefing or after-action report or anything like

261

that, you just refer them to me. I'll be looking forward to speaking with you, say, Sunday morning around sevenish, but other than that you're free as a bird. I'm passing that on directly to Secretary Baker. Goodbye."

Judge Webster was sitting by himself, happily drinking a cup of coffee. The recent lack of sleep could still be seen on his face, but the fire was back in his eyes as he raised his cup in mute toast to Wiznezhsky across the room. He was watching the satellite picture, which showed the rows of AAV-7 amphibious vehicles drawn up on the beach near the embassy. The dark forms of helicopters dotted the landscape all around, as the rest of the Soviets and Americans were ferried out to the waiting carriers and amphibious command ships lying off the coast.

Finally Webster got up and walked over to the president, taking General Weems by the elbow and drawing him along. The three men stood close together behind the president's desk.

"There's still the question of the missiles," Webster said, beckoning Wiznezhsky to come over. "They might not have the hostages anymore, but the missile carriers are still protected by the other Latin American navies."

"We could hit them after they unload but before they're operational," Weems suggested. "That's supposing the Latin Americans don't stick some of their personnel on the ground, too, to act as a sort of human shield."

"I really wonder now," said Wiznezhsky, "whether the Latin Americans will push this issue now that they've got their debt relief and the hostages have been freed. I would recommend that we hold off for a few hours at least and consult with the Latin American heads of state."

"That's not so very simple, Jacob," the president said with a sigh. "At least I think we're agreed that we *can't* do anything until after the Latin American navies get out of the way. Then we can deal with the question of whether to take the missiles out as they're being installed. That will give us a couple of days to see how things shake out."

"There's something funny going on in Cuba, speaking of that," Webster said. "Our analysts don't know quite what to make of it, but for the last several hours the telephone lines all across Cuba have been absolutely flooded with calls. We don't have the readings yet on what they're talking about, just a computer run showing the overall volume. It's unprecedented."

"Well, time will tell," the president said, returning to the festivities.

Chapter Forty-two

Castro stood in the large conference room, flanked by half a dozen swarthy security men, part of a detachment of Libyans who had been flown in secretly to serve as his personal bodyguards. There was also a strong unit of TE troops scattered in the room and throughout the building. General Murguia entered the room followed by his own escort of infantrymen. The two men stared at each other grimly for a moment, and then Castro spoke.

"So, General," he said, making the rank sound like an insult, "after all of your tough talk and boasting, you failed after all. You criticized my Special Troops, wasted elite forces in assaulting a fortified position, and then your own men turned and ran at the sight of the first American warplane. Very impressive."

"I'm not going to trade insults with you about the combat value of the Special Troops, who opted out of the battle altogether, wasting precious time. In fact, I think we should wait until everyone is here before we discuss anything of substance," Murguia said coolly.

"Really," sneered Castro, "and who else is coming?"

"We're here now!" said a booming voice, as a dozen flag officers of all three services filed into the room, including all of those captured in the embassy. "We've just been discussing tactics with General Murguia. Perhaps you'd care to summarize your own suggestions for the taking of the embassy. I believe it had something to do with artillery and air strikes," one of the army generals commented.

Castro's face went white. "I don't have to answer to you! I made you!" he screamed. "Every one of you signed your names to Ochoa's death warrant. Every one of you. Which one of you is so fucking important that your life is worth risking the Revolution? You send your soldiers off to die, but you're too important to be at risk yourselves? I have half a mind to have you all shot for counterrevolutionary activity right now." Several of the Libyans began to step forward, but Murguia's men raised their weapons in answer.

Castro looked to Captain Estigarribia and his TE detachment. Estigarribia smiled, first at Castro, then at Murguia. He walked over in Castro's direction, quickly drew his pistol, and blew out the brains of the nearest Libyan. The other TE men whipped their submachine guns out to join Murguia's men in covering the others. The Libyans carefully laid their weapons on the ground and raised their hands.

"You'll find that we've taken the precaution of disarming your other foreign mercenaries outside, Jefe," Murguia said. "The ones who are still alive, that is."

Castro began to tremble with rage. "It's over, Fidel," Murguia said. "You've run this country into the ground for thirty years. The only thing we've learned to build in that time has been soldiers and you sold us to the Soviets. Then you wouldn't even let us bring our dead home with us. Well, now you've got a real army, and it's fucking mad. You were going to risk burning this whole country to the ground so you could continue to play the bigshot and pull the superpowers' tails. Well, we have a little surprise for you."

Later that evening, as the last of the American and Soviet marines were being loaded back into their landing craft and helicopters, a Cuban GAZ jeep drove up. The TE captain in it got out with two small cardboard boxes. Under the escort of two American marines he approached Spinelli and Grechkov, who were drinking Cokes while they supervised the loading.

"General Murguia sent me with these presents for your two governments, as a sort of peace token," the captain said.

Spinelli looked at one of the marines.

"We've checked them out. They're not exactly bombs, if that's what you're worried about, sir," the marine said.

The captain handed the larger package to Grechkov. The latter opened it and grimaced in horror. He showed it to Spinelli. The box contained the severed head of Fidel Castro, a cigar still stuck between its teeth.

"I'm afraid to think what this one is," Spinelli said.

"Oh, it's just his hands," said the captain. "We always heard that the CIA director has Che Guevara's hands stashed in the back of his safe. We thought these would make a nice set."

"Gee, thanks," said Spinelli.

"General Murguia is heading the new Government of National Reconciliation. I suspect your governments will find him much easier to deal with than the former management." Estigarribia smiled and climbed back into his jeep. "When do you all expect to be out of here? Not to rush you or anything."

"It will take until tomorrow, about 0800," hours Grechkov replied.

"Fine. Well, come again," Estigarribia laughed and drove off.

Chapter Forty-three

Featherstone had his arm firmly around Anne's shoulders as he sat chatting with Ogarkov, Meese, Rodriguez, and Akamirov in the anteroom of the Oval Office. The others were all busy regaling Anne with stories of Featherstone's wisdom and courage when the door to the office suddenly opened. Featherstone had expected to see an aide or a secretary, but it was the president himself who waved them in, smiling broadly.

"Come in please, Anne, gentlemen," the president beamed. "I have something amazing to tell you."

As they walked in they saw the several television monitors still displayed around the room. One of them showed a black-and-white overhead image of Havana, centered on the embassy compound. Featherstone studied it. He recognized the compound easily enough, but the streets all around the city were choked with a black, swirling mass that he could not identify.

The president began. "I asked you here to chat informally over breakfast and to hear your news from Cuba, but it looks like I have some news to impart to you." The president pointed to the screen, putting his finger on one of the streets. "You see all this black stuff?" The guests nodded. "It's people. Hundreds of thousands of people. As near as we can figure, those phone calls you made from the embassy, Bill, sparked something that had been simmering just below the surface in Cuba for a long time. Thousands of people called their friends all over the island and headed for Havana. It seems that the original idea of most of them was simply to hitch a ride back to the States on one of our transports, since we were in the neighborhood. Then the news of Castro's execution got out, and of his murder of his own brother, and everything just fell apart. The crowds turned on the Communist Party offices and the troops joined in. It's Eastern Europe in late 1989 all over again.

"We figure this General Murguia had in mind setting himself up as a typical Latin American military dictator, like Pinochet, but things went too far too fast. His own troops couldn't be trusted, so, being the sharp cookie he apparently is, he quickly got on the bandwagon and announced elections for six months hence, freedom of the press, elimination of the internal security apparatus, amnesty for all political prisoners, the works. He even 'gratefully' declined the offer of the Chinese missiles, but that was a moot point anyway. It looks like the Chinese got wind of the demonstrations even before we did, and their ships turned around on the high seas an hour ago, maybe fifty miles outside of Cuban waters."

At that moment a Filipino steward came in with trays of coffee and pastries. General Akamirov picked up a cup. "This is not really the stuff for a toast, but I think we should drink to the memory of our many friends, from both our great countries, who have died in the past few days on that island. Like most soldiers, they didn't know what they were fighting for half of the time, but they fought for themselves, for their families, and for their comrades-in-arms. I, for one, am glad to have lived to see the day that that could be said for Soviets and Americans. I think it will be a cold day in hell before any man who was on that island lifts a finger against one of his comrades from 'the other side.'"

Everyone lifted a cup in silent accord. Anne was crying. Featherstone was crying. Akamirov was draped over Rodriguez's shoulders, and both were sobbing. Featherstone was thinking, maybe he could put in for one more tour, maybe in the Soviet Union. He had lots of friends there now.